STARS
MA~

VOICE OF
MARS

BOOK THREE
OF THE STARSHIP'S MAGE SERIES

This edition published in 2018 by:
Faolan's Pen Publishing Inc.
22 King St. S, Suite 300
Waterloo, Ontario
N2J 1N8 Canada

ISBN-13: 978-1-988035-60-4 (print)
A record of this book is available from Library and Archives Canada.
Printed in the United States of America
1 2 3 4 5 6 7 8 9 10

Second edition
First printing: September 2018

Illustration © 2016 Jack Giesen

Faolan's Pen Publishing logo is a trademark of Faolan's Pen Publishing Inc.

Read more books from Glynn Stewart at faolanspen.com

STARSHIP'S
MAGE

VOICE OF
MARS

BOOK THREE
OF THE STARSHIP'S MAGE SERIES

GLYNN STEWART

**FAOLAN'S PEN
PUBLISHING**
faolanspen.com

CHAPTER 1

THE YOUNG MAN in the black suit set the shuttle down gently on the concrete pad. Heavy winds buffeted the spacecraft as the mountains around the massive hydroelectric dam channeled air down and over the immense man-made cliff.

As the flames of the engines died away, he eyed the warning light on the console that informed him at least two surface-to-air missiles were locked onto the craft. He could see one of the launchers through the transparent steel window in front of him, a crudely hacked-together cradle mounted on a truck—but holding a *very* modern looking sensor suite and attack missile.

Unbuckling himself from his seat, he made certain that the gold medallion at his throat that marked him as a Mage was secure. Tucking a second golden amulet in the shape of a closed fist into the breast pocket of his suit jacket, he picked up a pair of long black leather gloves, drawing them up his arms to cover the swirling silver runes engraved into his flesh.

There was no one else in the shuttle. The terrorists that had seized the Christopher Holder Hydroelectric Plant had demanded he come alone, and he had agreed to that request.

Stepping out of the spacecraft onto cooling cement, he wrapped magic around himself to protect himself from the heat and approached the entrance to the plant. Armed men, clad in retro-medieval black frock coats, emerged from the building.

As they approached, he activated a command on the computer wrapped around his wrist. The engines on the shuttle suddenly rotated, their motion providing enough warning for the Neo-Puritans to curse and retreat before the thrusters flared to life.

New heat hammered against his shield from behind, and he smiled confidently as he approached the armed men waiting for him.

His name was Damien Montgomery, Hand of the Mage-King of Mars, and he was here to pass judgment.

"Stop right there!" one of the armed Neo-Puritans snapped. "Keep your hands where we can see them."

Damien stopped, eyeing the four terrorists calmly. They approached him carefully, their gaze resting on the medallion at the base of his neck for a long moment.

"You were supposed to come alone," the same man, clearly the leader of this little squad, said. "Who's flying the shuttle?"

"The computers," Damien told him quietly. "Autopilots are wonderful things."

And if they thought that he'd used the autopilot to land as well as takeoff, that was their mistake, not his.

"Check him for weapons," the leader ordered.

Damien stepped back as the others moved forward.

"I am unarmed," he said. "But I will not submit to a search. That was not part of the deal."

"And what exactly are you going to do?" the Neo-Puritan demanded. "We have the power here."

"You have the hostages and the guns," Damien allowed. "But we have the orbitals. Sooner or later, we'll give up on getting the hostages out."

It was an open question whether the Neo-Puritan Liberation Front had enough information to be aware of just what kind of ship Damien had arrived on. They knew a Hand was here, but it was possible they didn't know there was a *battlecruiser* in orbit.

"I will speak to John Oliver," the Hand continued. "No one else. Now, take me to him."

The Neo-Puritan didn't look happy, but he had no choice. Not taking the man empowered to negotiate with John Oliver to the NPLF's leader wouldn't end well for the trooper.

With a grunt, he gestured for Damien to follow him. The black-coated men fell in around the young Hand as he obeyed. They crossed the smooth top of the immense concrete dam in silence, allowing Damien to appreciate the view to his left.

The first colony on Panterra had been founded almost two hundred years before in the George Fox Valley. The dam had been installed around the same time, a massive project funded directly by the Mage-King of Mars to provide power to the fledgling Quaker colony.

Even now, a full quarter of Panterra's population lived in the valley, and a patchwork of neat, old-fashioned farms stretched for thousands of hectares along the river until they reached the edges of Friends City, almost twenty kilometers away.

Friends City lacked the towering skyscrapers and arcologies of cities on other worlds, but glistened in the morning sun rising over the sea. Most of the groups who had settled Panterra had sought 'a simple life', but 'simple' did not mean 'primitive'.

"Here," the lead terrorist snapped as they reached the supporting tower in the center of the dam. He swung open a door, tiny against the immensity of the man-made cliff around it, and gestured for Damien to go in front of him.

Damien obeyed, stepping into the starkly bare utility corridor and following it. He was all too aware of the four armed men behind him. Their weapons were vastly more modern than their dress, and he was going to have some serious questions when this was over about how the NPLF had acquired modern weaponry.

Panterra's *government* didn't have modern weaponry. The system's minimal spaceborne infrastructure left it poor by Protectorate standards, if still able to provide almost any desire of its citizens. The Panterran Planetary Defense Force was armed with century-old Martian

7

surplus—but the weapons herding him deeper into the concrete tower were brand new.

Finally, they reached an elevator. Designed for freight, Damien and his escort fit easily into the car and it lurched upward.

He resisted the urge to check the time. It would take as long as it took, and if his escorts had any idea just what a Hand's personal computer could do to the network surrounding him they would, correctly, regard the device as a weapon.

The elevator eventually opened onto an observation deck, even higher above the valley below than the top of the dam itself. A fenced balcony opened out over the artificial cliff beneath them and an even more breathtaking view of George Fox Valley.

Another half-dozen frock-coated Neo-Puritans stood around the deck. They'd set up a temporary command center, with high-powered computer consoles tucked into corners and linked into their crude surface-to-air missiles across the dam.

One of those computers was linked to explosives along the base of the dam that would destroy the facility and unleash millions of tons of water on the innocent citizens of the Valley. Another was probably linked to similar explosives set up to kill the Neo-Puritans' hostages.

"I see you finally arrived," the tallest of the black-coated men—there were no women in the room at all, Damien noted—said loudly. "You should have come faster. Your prevarication has cost three lives."

John Oliver gestured towards a spot on the balcony railing. Blood smeared across the concrete marked where three hostages had been executed and their bodies thrown over the side of the dam. One an hour since Oliver had made his demand.

Damien's ship had still been *two hours* out of orbit at that point. There had never been any way for the Hand to have arrived before Oliver had killed three innocents. He might have meant the threat to force the local government to negotiate without the Hand to back them up.

"You made your choice, Mister Oliver," Damien told him quietly, feeling very, very, tired. "'*Whoever sheds man's blood, By man his blood shall be shed, For in the image of God He made man','* he quoted. "No one bears guilt for the blood shed by your hand but you."

Oliver spun to face Damien, his face clouded with anger.

"How *dare* you quote the word of God to me?" he snarled. "*I* am his chosen champion, his Elect. I know his will for this world and my people!"

"You walk your own path," the Hand said, his voice still quiet. "I am here to speak for Mars. Will you listen?"

"You are authorized to speak for the Hand and negotiate for the Mage-King's Protectorate?" Oliver demanded.

With a small smile, Damien removed the amulet he'd tucked into his suit pocket and allowed the golden fist to slip between his fingers and dangle in the air, catching the light of the rising sun.

"I *am* Hand Montgomery," he said flatly. "I speak for Mars. Will you listen?"

The leader of the Neo-Puritan Liberation Front gawked at the golden hand for a long moment, the tall man with the sandy hair and piercing eyes completely taken aback.

"You know our demands," he said finally. "There will be no negotiating. Every hour until they are met, one of the hostages will die."

A small portion of the NPLF's demands made sense, Damien reflected. The Neo-Puritans had been one of the last groups to settle Panterra. They'd been forced to settle in a less fertile area, far from the rest of the colony, out of reach of the power supply from the Christopher Holder Dam or even easy reach of the colony's higher education institutions. Given the available land, that had been an entirely petty decision of the Panterran government, starting a policy of treating the Neo-Puritans as second-class citizens that they'd never really halted.

Demands for increased access to higher education, more funding for local education, and the reversal of legislation specifically crafted to exclude Neo-Puritans were items Damien could sympathize with. Demands for pardons, money, and actions blatantly harmful to the *rest* of the planet were a different story.

"You do not understand," Damien said finally. "I am here to speak for Mars. I have the *power* to negotiate, but I no longer have the *ability*."

"What?" Oliver demanded, clearly not following.

"Any ability I had to negotiate with the Neo-Puritan Liberation Front ended three hours and thirty-four minutes ago," the Hand said flatly. "The Protectorate does not negotiate with terrorists. We can be flexible on the *definition*, but murdering hostages is self-evident.

"My terms are this: you and your men will release your remaining hostages and lay down your arms. You will face trial for murder and conspiracy to commit mass murder.

"In exchange, I will guarantee your lives, and order the formation of a Mars-backed Commission to review the status of the Neo-Puritans on Panterra."

John Oliver was a tall man and Damien was a small one. The Hand had to bend his neck back to meet Oliver's gaze, but his anger sung in him as he met the bigger man's eyes.

"There will be no negotiating," he repeated back at Oliver. "You will surrender or you will be destroyed."

The observation deck at the top of the dam was silent for a long moment, and Damien took advantage of the fact that everyone except Oliver was staring at the Neo-Puritan leader to tap a pre-programmed command on his wrist computer.

Oliver continued to stare at him in shock, then burst out laughing.

"You seem to forget who is holding the power here," he finally replied. "Adding yourself to our hostage collection gains you no leverage, Mister Montgomery. My terms stand, and unless you concede them in the next twenty minutes, I will have no choice but to add another dead hostage onto your hands."

"Blood is only ever on the hands that shed it," Damien told Oliver, his voice gentle. "You always have a choice. My offer is the only step back from the precipice."

He didn't expect the other man to accept. He never had. From the moment the first hostage—the dam's night shift manager—had fallen lifelessly down the dam, Damien had known how this was going to end. Nonetheless, he found himself hoping that Oliver would see reason.

"Take him away," Oliver ordered, shaking his head. "Put him with the other hostages—apparently Mars sends fools and madmen instead of negotiators. They'll learn."

Silently, Damien allowed the frock-coated terrorists to grab his arms. He was a small man in more than just height, and they lifted him completely off the ground. They roughly cuffed his hands behind him, carefully securing the cuffs over his gloves. Someone in the Neo-Puritan movement had at least *some* idea of how to deal with Mages.

Two of the Neo-Puritans dragged him back to the elevator, dropping him on the floor while they rode it down deep into the bowels of the dam. A rumbling noise began about halfway down the shaft, and when the doors opened he was unsurprised to see a massive open space containing the rows of turbines providing power to the Valley.

He was also sadly unsurprised to see the dark-gray blocks of explosives placed on each of the turbines close enough for him to make them out. The Neo-Puritans seemed determined to kill a whole lot of people if their demands weren't met.

Huddled against the front of the vast chamber, under guard by another half dozen frock-coated terrorists with disturbingly modern weapons, were the hostages. Even the night shift of a facility the size of the Holder Dam was over sixty people. Technicians, janitors, engineers—people who had *nothing* to do with the political state the NPLF objected to.

People they were planning to murder one by one unless their demands were met.

Even as he was being carried over to the hostages, Damien was counting. Sixty-four men and women. According to the report he'd been sent before he'd landed, there should have been sixty-eight on the staff—with three murdered, one was missing.

Hopefully that one had been the inside agent who'd got the NPLF past the security that was *supposed* to drop a team of SWAT on the dam if someone so much as sneezed aggressively in its direction. It was, after all, the main source of water and power for twenty million people, and positioned to kill about a quarter of those twenty million people if it were to, say, be blown open.

The terrorists in the room were dressed and armed almost identically to those elsewhere in the dam—which was mildly creepy. Either the Neo-Puritans in general went for a disturbingly limited wardrobe, or the NPLF had taken the time to put together a uniform for its foot troopers.

Now that he was closer to the weapons, he could tell they were Legatan battle carbines. That raised unfortunate questions as Legatus was a perennial problem child for the Protectorate—and weapons from the planet kept being found in the hands of people like this.

His 'escort' tossed Damien to the ground next to the other hostages.

"Boss says to add this one to the pile," one of them—the same lieutenant as on top of the dam—told the guards. "Some high muck from Mars, probably the best token we've got so far."

Damien struggled to his feet, gratefully nodding to one of the hostages who helped him rise, and turned back to face the terrorists.

"You realize you're all doomed, right?" he asked conversationally. "We can't negotiate now, not once you've started killing hostages. So unless your boss has a sudden change of heart, it's only a question of how long until the Valley is evacuated. Then the Governor calls in fire from heaven, and you all *die*."

"He won't write off the Valley," the lieutenant told him. "We hold all the cards."

"Except, apparently, the one telling you about the cruiser in orbit," Damien told them. "Do you know how I know that we will bring down orbital fire before we let you go? Because I gave that order before I left.

"Surrender and you will live."

For a weapon Damien *knew* had a barrel barely seven millimeters across, the carbine suddenly pointed in his face appeared to be a gaping maw into hell.

"Why don't you just shut it?" the Neo-Puritan lieutenant snapped. "You are a mouthy one, aren't you?"

Damien smiled, stretching his hands against the cuffs behind his back.

"I am," he agreed. "Last chance."

The other man lifted the gun and rested its barrel against Damien's forehead.

"Before what?"

CHAPTER 2

DAMIEN'S ANSWER to the terrorist's question was two-fold.

First, he slammed a shield into place around the hostages—a layer of air suddenly rendered as dense and strong as steel plate, easily able to withstand the small arms the Neo-Puritans were carrying. Now, so long as *he* survived, the hostages were safe.

Second, he threw out a wave of pure force at the men surrounding him. With his hands bound, it was difficult for him to direct energy accurately, but throwing half a dozen soldiers to the ground didn't *need* precise direction.

The lieutenant was closest, his gun leveled at Damien's head, and was thrown furthest. His gun went flying and the man slammed into the back concrete wall, sliding to the ground in a disturbingly boneless lump.

Before any of the surviving soldiers had time to regain their feet, Damien's hands lit up with a bright white flame. His gloves—and the lower arms of his suit—vanished as energy poured from the runes wrapped around his forearms and carved into his palms.

The handcuffs lasted a moment longer, steel puddling then running like water. The molten liquid hit the shield protecting his skin from the actinic fire and sloughed off, hitting the concrete with a sizzling hiss as Damien brought his now bare hands in front of him.

He couldn't fault the terrorist's courage. Their leader wasn't getting back up—only time would tell if he was dead or just unconscious—and they faced the deadliest nightmare of any enemy of the Protectorate, but they grabbed their weapons and rose regardless.

Oliver had clearly chosen only his best and most dedicated to guard the hostages as three of them opened fire on them. Their bullets slammed into the barrier of solid air Damien had conjured and ricocheted away.

The rest opened fire on Damien. Gunfire echoed in the massive chamber for a few seconds, bullets slamming into his personal shield of hardened air. Damien winced as the impacts transmitted through to him as a bone-rattling vibration, and then retaliated.

Lightning flashed through the air, the energy *directed* now. The men firing on the hostages went down first, spasming as electricity blasted through their bodies. Those firing at him didn't last much longer, and less than twenty seconds after putting a gun to the forehead of a Hand, every Neo-Puritan terrorist in the room was on the ground.

Most would probably live. Damien dropped the shield around the hostages and checked them over with a glance. They all appeared to be physically okay, if shaken.

"Tie them up," he ordered the hostages, gesturing at the Neo-Puritans.

Checking his wrist computer, he confirmed that he had remote access to the NPLF's computer setup. With a single keystroke, he shut the whole system down.

"Mage-Captain Jakab," he said calmly as he opened up a link to the battlecruiser *Duke of Magnificence* in orbit. "The bombs have been disabled. You may deploy your Marines."

"Understood, my lord," Kole Jakab responded. "Shuttles are en route, ETA ten minutes. Can you hold?"

There was probably a manual backup for the explosives—but it would be down here with the bombs. Anyone who wanted to blow up the dam or kill the hostages now was going to have to go through Damien Montgomery.

He smiled.

"I can hold."

"You are go to deploy," Mage-Captain Jakab's voice crackled over the speakers in the shuttle's cockpit. "Special Agent Amiri has tactical command. Good luck."

"*Finally*," Julia Amiri snapped. "Get us moving," she ordered the pilot. The tall, heavily muscled, ex-bounty hunter-turned special agent was *not* impressed with her charge today.

"We are breaking clear, as are the other shuttles," the young woman in the pilot's seat replied. She wore the insignia of a Royal Martian Navy Lieutenant and seemed unperturbed with the large, aggressive, woman in her copilot's seat. "How do you want to handle this, Agent?"

Technically, this was a Marine drop. The four assault shuttles carried eighty Royal Martian Marines in full exosuit battle armor. In practice, since the whole operation was taking place under the auspices of a Hand, the Secret Service Special Agent tasked with keeping said Hand *alive* ended up in charge.

"According to Damien's shuttle, there are a dozen SAM launchers along the dam," she pointed out. "Even if he's knocked out their computer network, those can almost certainly be operated in local control. Plus, if his *idiotness* manages to get himself killed before we get down there, none of us will have jobs tomorrow. What do you think?"

"Fast and hard it is, ma'am," the Lieutenant said cheerfully. "I suggest you hold on."

Julia watched with poorly concealed impatience as the four shuttle craft drifted away from their multi-megaton mothership, then was slammed back into her seat as they rotated and lit up their main engines.

"I make it six minutes to the dam," the pilot said into the shuttle's PA. "We'll be hitting the SAMs on the way down and kicking y'all out the hatch at fifty meters and three hundred kilometers an hour. Thanks for flying Royal Navy!"

The young officer turned to Julia with a brilliant grin.

"I suggest you go back and get into your armor, ma'am. This is not going to be a ride for the squishy."

"What do you need us to do?"

The speaker was probably the youngest of the dam's staff, a young and quite attractive brunette in a prim black suit. The holographic badge on her lapel identified her as one of the handful of engineers on the night shift.

Damien smiled at her, hopefully reassuringly. Most of the hostages were still looking panicked and unsure, and he was keeping his eyes on the elevator. There was only so much he *could* do at this point.

"I need you all to get behind cover," he told her, pitching his voice loudly enough so that they could all hear him. "The turbines should do—I've jammed their ability to remote detonate the bombs, so they have to come down here to set them all off."

"That would kill..." the engineer trailed off, then nodded firmly. He could see the realization of what the Neo-Puritan Liberation Front meant to do finally fully sinking in. The threat to her had probably been so immediate she hadn't followed through the purpose of the bombs across the turbine chamber.

She turned away from Damien and started chivvying her coworkers into cover. The older, more senior, or just more aware among them joined in. By the time the elevator reported its return, both the former hostages and their ex-guards had been tucked away out of sight.

When the elevator doors opened again, the only person in the path of the fusillade of bullets the terrorists unleashed was Damien. Oliver had apparently taken the time to set up a pair of heavy machine guns in the elevator before sending it back down, and the deadly weapons unleashed a hail of death.

The heavy slugs slammed into Damien's barrier of solidified air, the impacts managing to drive him back a step and make the runes wrapped around his arms and torso heat up with the energy he was exerting.

Hoping to short-stop the attack before it became dangerous even to him, he threw a fireball back into the elevator. The bolt of energy froze and shattered before reaching the terrorists, and Damien realized he was facing another Mage.

He slammed his barrier forward, blocking the entrance to the elevator completely just as the *other* heavy weapons the NPLF had brought down fired. The heavy armor piercing rockets slammed into the wall of solidified air with ground-shaking force.

Unprepared for *that* level of force, Damien's barrier failed to stop the rockets' shaped charges from penetrating the shield. Jets of fire and molten metal blasted a dozen feet past his barrier towards him, and the heat sent him reeling backwards.

None of the jets reached him, and the back-blast from their impacts turned the interior of the elevator into the depths of hell. The sound of machine gun ammunition cooking off was almost an afterthought, the heavy bullets shredding anyone still left standing.

Even as the fireball was fading, John Oliver walked out. The Neo-Puritan leader was wrapped in a shield of magically chilled air, deflecting away the heat of his people's destruction, and his face was twisted in wrath.

Oliver raised his hands, and Damien easily identified the 'projector' rune of a trained Combat Mage on the other man's palm. *That* was a piece of intelligence no one had managed to pass on to him before he'd agreed to meet the man.

"*I am the Elect of God*," the terrorist thundered. "I will not be denied." He raised his hand and lightning hammered out from the rune, energy flashing across the void of the turbine chamber with vicious power.

Damien had the same projector rune carved into his left palm, above the interface rune used for Jumping starships present on both of his palms. Unlike the other man, he also had Runes of Power carved into his forearms, shoulders, and upper chest. Each Rune doubled the power of a Mage who, other than his ability to read the flow of power well enough to *create* them, had been of mediocre power at best.

With five, Damien had no equals but the Mage-King himself. He knocked Oliver's lightning bolt aside, carefully directing it *away* from the explosives scattered around the room, and followed up with lightning of his own.

The force of the Hand's strike drove Oliver to his knees, his defense barely holding against the impact.

"Surrender," Damien told him. "It's over—you've already lost."

Even as he spoke, he heard a thumping impact above him that was almost certainly his inbound assault shuttles taking out the SAM launchers.

"I. Am. The. Elect. Of. GOD!" Oliver repeated in a bellow, somehow rising to his feet again. He charged Damien, fire flaring from his hands as he tried to reach the Hand.

He made it halfway before Damien met him with a blade of pure force that sliced through his defenses as if they weren't even there—and cut the terrorist leader in half.

Julia left the shuttle in the middle of the pack, flanked by a pair of Marines who had been told in no uncertain terms by their platoon leader that the Special Agent was coming back intact.

She didn't have the heart to tell the adorable pup of a Lieutenant that she had more hours in the two-meter-tall exosuits than any three of his Marines combined. The two 'bodyguards', at least, had at least got the hint when she'd slotted into the massive battle armor and booted up in under thirty seconds.

They flanked her on her way out of the shuttle, but made no attempt to guide her down. The chute mounted in the back of the suit blasted out as soon as they were clear of the shuttle—there was *no* time in a high speed, low altitude drop like this.

The chute had only moments to slow her descent, aided by one-shot rockets strapped to the suit's legs and arms. She was still going over a hundred kilometers an hour when she hit the ground, an impact even the exosuit's powerful shock absorbers couldn't make gentle.

"Hoorah!" one of the Marines with her exclaimed. "Can we do that again?"

That left Julia smiling, even as the bullets started to fly in their direction. The SAM launchers were smoldering wrecks, but it looked like the NPLF still had people on top of the dam.

The entire twenty-man platoon that had dropped from her shuttle, however, followed her as she identified a blinking icon on her display and charged towards it. With eighty Marines dropped onto the dam, she could leave the terrorists on the top of the concrete cliff to the *other* three exosuit platoons.

She followed the icon showing her Montgomery's location to the central buttressing tower. The door might technically have been a secured entrance, but it failed to even slow the battle armored Marines down.

"Elevator is at the bottom and stuck," the point man reported over the platoon link. "No response to regular or override commands."

"Out of the way," Julia ordered brusquely. She brushed past the soldier, ripped the elevator door off its hinges, and stepped off into the shaft.

With neither a chute nor the one-shot rockets to slow her, it was a short trip. She crashed into the burnt out wreckage of the elevator car moments later, wincing as the suit's shock absorbers took *most* of the impact.

A loud crashing noise heralded the arrival of her two personal Marine puppies, followed shortly by a small groan.

"I take it back," the previous speaking Marine whispered on the radio. "Let's *not* do that again."

Smirking, Julia smashed her way through the debris and into the main turbine chamber. The humming sound of the turbines filled the air as she scanned the open void, her rifle sweeping for potential targets.

Scorch marks splayed out from the wrecked elevator door, ending just short of a ripped apart body. The only living person visible was Damien Montgomery. The Hand looked... exhausted.

"Am I late?" she asked dryly.

"No," he replied quietly. "Just later than Mister Oliver." He gestured to the body. "I think we're done here, Agent Amiri. We'll need pickup for the hostages."

"You saved them all?" Julia *knew* the hostages were why the Hand had gone in first. She still hadn't quite expected him to succeed.

"Everyone who was still alive," Montgomery confirmed. "If we can get a Marine demo team in here as well, I'm sure a *lot* of people will be happier once these explosives are disarmed."

CHAPTER 3

DUKE OF MAGNIFICENCE was a twelve million ton *Honorific*-class battlecruiser, one of the most powerful warships constructed by the Royal Martian Navy. An immense stark-white pyramid driven by anti-matter engines and containing the most advanced technology known to man, she would still have been bound to the star system of her construction without the silver runes carved throughout her hull and linking to a tiny simulacrum of the ship at her heart.

With that rune matrix, a Jump Mage like Damien Montgomery himself could teleport the vessel vast distances in a moment. With the jump matrix and the Protectorate's carefully maintained caste of Mages, the Mage-King of Mars held together a loose collection of almost a hundred star systems.

When the mighty warship had been assigned to Damien as his personal transport, he'd argued. Most of the Hands had made do with destroyers or even personal yachts for years. Desmond Michael Alexander, Mage-King of Mars, was, however, as implacable as a falling mountain when his mind was set.

So a day after rescuing the hostages on the surface of Panterra found Damien, in a brand new suit, in his 'office'—the smallest of the *Duke*'s observation decks—staring out the window at the blue and green planet below.

"I have the document you requested, Lord Montgomery," a voice announced behind him.

Damien smiled.

"'Hello, Damien.' 'How are you, Doctor Christoffsen?' 'I'm fine, Damien, how are you?'" he mock-quoted back at his political aide, a man almost twice his age who wouldn't have looked out of place in tweed. "Does any of this sound familiar, Robert?" he asked.

"I reserve the niceties for when I think we have time for them, my lord," Doctor Robert Christoffsen, holder of three Ph. Ds that Damien was aware of and former elected Governor of the Tara System, replied. "Governor Rose's shuttle is on her way. If you have any changes you wish made to this, we have limited time."

Damien turned away from the view through the magically transparent steel window and gestured for his aide to hand him the parchment.

"I never get tired of seeing worlds like this," he murmured to Christoffsen as he skimmed the parchment. "It helps remind me what it's all about."

"Sixty-three million souls," the ex-Governor replied. "At last census, five point eight million of them are either Neo-Puritan by religion or descended from Neo-Puritan colonists."

"How close is your report to being ready?"

"I'm only synthesizing what our observers already reported," Christoffsen told him. "The key points are there," he pointed to the parchment, "but the full report will be ready by tomorrow."

"Thank you, Robert," Damien said quietly. "I'm not sure I could do this part of the job without you."

"His Majesty taught you well," his aide told him. "While I would hardly diminish my contributions, I suspect you'd do fine. Ardennes is shaping up well, after all."

The younger man winced. Ardennes had been his first mission for the Mage-King, almost six months ago now. He'd ended up overthrowing a hopelessly corrupt local government and imposing temporary direct Martian rule. The last he'd heard, things were progressing well and the interim Governor was expecting to hold elections for the new parliament a full year ahead of schedule.

"I can't take all the credit for that," he pointed out. "I was there less than three weeks, after all."

"You gave them a foundation," Christoffsen replied. "That's all we need to do here. Do you have any changes to the proclamation, my lord?"

The Hand finished skimming the document, then folded it up. Crossing to the desk tucked against one side of the observation window, he removed an archaic-looking physical seal and pressed it down on the fold. The seal automatically applied its own wax, closing the document and then stamping the image of a single closed fist on the seal.

"No," Damien answered, looking down at the formal parchment. "Governor Rose's shuttle is here," he noted, gesturing out the window at the bright light of the decelerating spacecraft.

"Are you planning on meeting her, or are we playing games today?" Christoffsen asked.

"She's happy with me now, and she'll be angry with me later," the Hand replied with a smile. "Let's soften her up some more. We'll meet her in the landing bay."

Mage-Captain Jakab's people had done Damien proud. By the time Governor Rose exited her shuttle, a double file of Marines had formed a ruler-straight honor guard leading her towards the Mage-Captain and Damien himself.

The Governor was a short, somewhat dumpy woman, with silvering blond hair and a seemingly perpetual smile on her face. A trio of men in plain suits so identical as to be a uniform followed, each of them with a shoulder-mounted camera tracking every aspect of the scene.

Jakab stepped forward as the Governor approached and bowed slightly. The tall and pale officer's gaze flicked to the cameras before focusing on the leader of the planet beneath them.

"Governor Rose, welcome aboard the *Duke of Magnificence*," he greeted her warmly. "We are honored to have you aboard."

As his ship's captain was speaking, Damien noted the trio following the Governor and sighed. The Hand had yet to meet a camera whose footage didn't make him look *far* younger than his actual age. Nonetheless, as the cameras rotated to focus on him, he pasted a smile on his face and stepped forward to meet the Governor.

"Hand Montgomery," she greeted him brightly. "Allow me to offer the thanks of my entire world for your timely intervention! Without your actions..." she shuddered. "Oliver was insane."

"Insanity would be an excuse, madam Governor," Damien replied. "His actions were evil, and he paid the price for them. Mars would provide a poor Protectorate if we failed to protect, wouldn't we?"

"Of course, my lord," she agreed instantly. "Nonetheless, thousands rest in safety today thanks to you."

Damien bowed his head, accepting the praise carefully.

"We have matters to discuss, Governor," he said softly. Glancing at the cameras, he added: "In private."

As Damien and Rose entered his office, he watched as Amiri effortlessly and implacably cut off the camera crew. While the Governor appeared to understand his meaning, the crew had the same assumption of rectitude that reporters and camera crews had always had.

His ex-bounty hunter bodyguard simply stepped into the gap between Rose and her crew and *looked* at them. It helped that Amiri, over a foot taller than Damien's own diminutive height, towered over all three members of the crew.

The door slid shut behind them and Governor Rose crossed to the massive window looking out on her world with a gasp.

"I... forgot how beautiful it is," she admitted, looking out across the planet. "My ancestors were determined to keep life on Panterra simple. No space stations, no ships. I have seen my world from shuttles from time to time, but this is... magnificent."

"Panterra is only the fourth world I've seen through that window," Damien noted. "Mars, Earth, Tellemar, and now Panterra. Even on Earth or Mars, you can't see their scars from orbit."

Rose nodded slowly, taking a deep breath and turning back to him.

"I meant every word I said for the cameras, Hand Montgomery," she told him quietly. "We were trying to evacuate, but that same desire for a simple life, well... we don't have the capability to move millions of people on a few hours' notice. Millions would have died without you, my lord. And bringing Oliver and his scum to justice? We are infinitely in your debt."

"I serve Mars, Governor," Damien reminded her. "But you must remember that I cannot solve all your problems for you."

"With the intelligence retrieved from Oliver's people's computers and the aid of your Mage-Captain Jakab's Marines, the Neo-Puritan Liberation Front will shortly be no more," Rose replied in satisfaction. "You've certainly solved our largest problem."

"Killing terrorists buys time, Governor," the Hand said gently. "It's not really a solution." He picked up the parchment Christoffsen had handed him earlier, studying the seal while carefully not looking at the Governor.

"I call the destruction of the NPLF a pretty good solution, myself. What's your point, my lord?" she asked.

With a sigh, Damien handed her the parchment. Rose looked at it in confusion, then back up at him.

"What is this?"

"*That*, Governor, is the formal notification that the Government of Panterra has been found in violation of the Charter of the Protectorate," he explained. "The status of the descendants of the Neo-Puritan colonists as second-class citizens does not meet the standards required of member governments on a number of criteria. My staff will have a formal report with detailed recommendations to you by tomorrow.

"In any case, a Commission will be impaneled by the Protectorate within thirty days," he continued. "We dispatched a courier to the nearest Runic Transceiver Array last night. The lead members of that commission should be on their way from Mars—or wherever his Majesty decides to pull them from—within a few days."

Governor Rose tore the seal open, reading the stark formal words of the notification.

"I did not expect this," she said bluntly. "I thought you were to *help* us."

"Governor Rose, it is not my job to uphold your government or maintain your society," Damien said bluntly. "It is my job to serve the Protectorate.

"Killing terrorists is necessary. As I said, it buys you time. *True* solutions require the removal of the underlying issues. I do not pretend that this is easy, or quick, or that we, as outsiders, have all of the solutions. The purpose of the Commission is not to tell your world how to exist.

"The purpose of the Commission is to help your people find a better way."

CHAPTER 4

"SHE LOOKS UPSET," Amiri noted, stepping into Damien's observation deck office. "Is she going to be a problem?"

"No," Damien told her. "She'll come around quickly, she's just *very* angry at the NPLF right now."

His bodyguard walked across the excessively large room, her footsteps echoing on the metal floor. "How can you be so sure?" she asked, joining him in looking out the window.

"Because the wheels that turned to create the Commission started about twelve years ago with the doctoral thesis of one Maria Rose," he replied. "She's angry right now, but *she* was the one who drew the Protectorate's attention to the problem and predicted that, without a solution to the political and economic ghetto the Neo-Puritans were stuck in, we'd see an armed insurrection or terrorist movement inside of twenty years.

"She'll come around," he repeated. "Governor Rose understands she rules the *entire* planet, not just the fifty-eight percent that voted for her."

"Is that based on one meeting with her?"

"We were provided extensive briefing materials by the local Protectorate office," Damien pointed out gently. "They covered her career in some depth."

"My focus was on the parts of the briefing about the people who were going to be *shooting* at you," Amiri told him. "Speaking of which, what part of the briefing said that *actually* going alone when the terrorists ask you to come alone was a good idea?"

"The part where I was pretty sure said terrorists could tell if I was alone in the shuttle, and had explosives set up to kill ten million people," he said gently. "You know I'm not *suicidal*, Julia."

"I've watched you in action, my lord," she replied. "There are days I have my doubts."

Damien turned to look at his bodyguard, shaking his head with a tired smile. 'Tired' seemed to sum up how he felt most of the time these days.

"Did you look into their weapons?" he asked.

"I did," she confirmed, sighing. "It's not as blatant as it might have been. The missiles were Tau Ceti manufacture. The rocket launchers and machine guns came from Amber. Hell, the body armor was *Martian*."

"But?"

"But the guns were top-line, latest-issue Legatan manufacture," Amiri continued. "The sensors you mentioned? Top-line, Legatan manufacture. The handful of machine guns we recovered intact had been updated with the latest optics and electronics—some Amber, some Legatan.

"If I wasn't *looking* for a common point, I don't think I'd have been suspicious," she pointed out. "But, since I *was*, there's enough. The biggest point I noticed? The gear the NPLF had varied in age and quality—but where they had top-line, brand new equipment it was Legatan."

"I figured," Damien sighed.

Legatus was one of the Protectorate's Core Worlds, the earliest colonies mankind had established after the Mage-King had built the jump-ships and trained Jump Mages to take humanity to the stars.

Unlike the other Core Worlds, when the Legatan colonists had arrived, they'd ordered their Mages to get back on the ships and go home. Legatus was the first, and still the most important, UnArcana World. Magic was banned on those worlds. Mages identified in their population were shipped off-world to be taken in and trained by Mage families on other worlds.

Legatus and the other UnArcana Worlds worked with the Protectorate and the Mage Guild—they had to, or no cargo would ever travel to their systems—but their laws on magic were *very* strict. They accepted the Charter of the Protectorate... but not the Compact between Mundane and Mage.

It made them problem children for the Mage-King—and Legatus was the largest problem child of all. Damien's involvement in the rebellion on Ardennes had brought him into contact with a Legatan agent, and he'd learned that the secretive Legatus Military Intelligence Directorate had funneled weapons and supplies to that rebellion.

Now, they could see the same ploy in action on another Protectorate world.

"What do you think they're up to, Julia?" he asked Amiri.

"Trouble," was the only answer she could provide, and he grunted agreement.

His brooding over the rebels' equipment was interrupted by a ping on his wrist computer. The *Duke*'s bridge crew was contacting him.

"Montgomery," he answered calmly.

"My lord Hand, we have a jump flare in the outer system," one of the junior officers reported. "A courier ship has jumped in. They are requesting your authorization codes to release an encrypted packet."

"A response from our courier to Tau Ceti?" Damien asked. "That was fast."

"No, sir," the officer told him. "They apparently are here directly from Mars."

"Get me a channel," Damien ordered. "I'll transmit my codes."

A courier that had come directly from Mars looking for him was definitely important—and almost certainly bad news.

The courier ship was a tiny little thing barely big enough to contain quarters for the five Mages and ten regular crew who ran it. It was small enough that maintaining the runes necessary to provide magical gravity was a minor task for her crew—and too small for any type of artificial gravity but magical.

Courier ships like this one also had some of the most secure computer storage available to the Protectorate, and it turned out that Damien not only needed his regular security codes but actually had to remote link his Hand itself into the courier's computer.

The tiny gold icon that served as the symbol of his rank as a Hand of the Mage-King of Mars, authorized to speak with Desmond Michael Alexander's Voice and wield the Mage-King's authority outside Sol, also functioned as an override chip for most computers built in the Protectorate.

Finally, once the courier's computers accepted that he was who he said he was, they disgorged a single digital file that downloaded itself to his computer and then wiped itself from the courier.

Damien had never seen security like it before, so he was unsurprised when the desk console chimed and part of the window facing out over Panterra turned into a wallscreen showing the familiar gray-haired face of the Mage-King himself.

"Damien, I hope the situation on Panterra has been resolved," the King said crisply. "This courier was dispatched less than a day after you left Tellemar. Since I had all the information here and the courier would only be a day later than one from Tellemar, I'm sending it directly from Mars.

"If the situation on Panterra is not resolved to your satisfaction, I leave how long you must stay to your discretion. But we have a major situation in the MidWorlds, and you are both my closest Hand, and have relationships I hope can help to cool things down."

"The Mínglìàng System has laid a formal complaint against your home system Sherwood and their new Interstellar Patrol," Alexander continued. "They have accused Sherwood of piracy, murder, and effectively waging an undeclared war against them.

"Tucked in the details of their complaint is a reference to the Antonius System and what Governor Wong calls 'claim-jumping' there by Sherwood miners. Regardless of what is actually going on, I suspect the Antonius System is a key factor."

Damien paused the video and quickly checked his wrist computer. Antonius was roughly halfway between Mínglìàng and Sherwood, an uninhabited and uninhabitable system that was nevertheless extremely rich in easily accessed resources. Neither Míngliàng nor his home system had large asteroid belts to fuel their industries, but Antonius, eight light years from both, had had at least five planets reduced to asteroids by some cataclysmic event in the past.

There were enough resources in Antonius to fuel both systems' industry for ten thousand years, but the records he'd downloaded from Mars before leaving showed a trail of complaint and counter-complaint going back five years. Sighing, he unpaused the recording.

"The courier has all of the information we have on all three systems," Alexander stated. "We are obligated under the Charter to investigate Governor Wong's complaint. Almost more importantly, Míngliàng has a fleet of sixteen Tau Ceti-built *Lancer*-class destroyers. If Wong decides to take unilateral action, Sherwood's Patrol may or may not be able to handle them, but we *would* face the first inter-system civil war of the Protectorate's history."

The Mage-King of Mars paused, shaking his head at the camera.

"That would be a disaster, Damien," he said. "If Sherwood *is* engaging in piracy on a national scale, we are facing one of the worst crises of the last century. If they're *not*, the potential for civil war is a worst case scenario all on its own.

"I considered sending someone else," Alexander admitted. "It is your home system being accused, after all. But you're the closest by far. Even if you take a day or two to wrap up everything on Panterra, you'll be there a week before anyone else I could send.

"More, whatever the hell is going on, the McLaughlin is more likely to *listen* to you than anyone else I have."

Damien was surprised. Unless something had changed in the last four years, there was only one person who would be called *the* McLaughlin: the head of the system's most powerful Mage family. Apparently Miles James McLaughlin had been elected again.

"I've forwarded all of the information we have," Alexander repeated. "The courier commander has been ordered to accompany you to Míngliàng and remain at your disposal while you deal with the situation.

Neither system has completed a Runic Transceiver Array yet, so you'll be limited to communication by starship courier.

"Don't go without the *Duke of Magnificence*," the Mage-King ordered. "Beyond that, I leave the resolution to your discretion. You have authority to commandeer whatever force you need to secure the situation once you know what's going on.

"I have faith that you can keep it from coming to that," he concluded, "but I trust your judgment. Stop this mess before Wong or McLaughlin can drag their people into a goddamn war.

"Good luck."

CHAPTER 5

"THAT... IS going to be a giant headache," Mage-Captain Kole Jakab said calmly. The *Duke of Magnificence*'s commanding officer was a tall man, with the pale skin of a lifelong spacer for all he'd been born on the mother world itself.

Damien had called Jakab, Christoffsen and Amiri together to view the Mage-King's missive. While arguably for his eyes only, his chief three subordinates would be called upon to help him take on the task. He preferred them to be fully briefed.

"I intend to head directly to Míngliàng," he told them, feeling drained. "There, I will speak with Governor Wong and see what we can sort out. I've reviewed the evidence provided by Governor Wong and, well, none of it is decisive."

"That seems odd," Christoffsen replied. The ex-Governor had already started pulling up information on his wrist computer. He had the rare talent, often found in academics, of being able to read and carry on a conversation. "He's leveled a formal complaint and asked for Protectorate intervention. That's not something a Governor would do lightly."

"They've had a lot of attacks, Robert," Damien noted. "Eighteen, at last count. Fifteen of them were on ships traveling to or from the Antonius System, a system Míngliàng and Sherwood technically share possession of... and they aren't being particularly polite about the sharing. There have been no survivors, which means over a thousand of

Governor Wong's citizens are dead, and Sherwood appears to be the most likely suspect."

"That's your homeworld," Amiri said softly. "What do *you* think?"

"Governor McLaughlin spent his military career *fighting* pirates," he replied. "I find it difficult to believe he'd turn his brand new *anti*-piracy patrol into pirates. Regardless of whether or not *Sherwood* is responsible, however, someone has killed over a thousand people. We have no choice but to intervene."

Jakab had been checking something on his wrist computer, and he now threw an image up onto the wallscreen layered over the observation deck window. The image was a swept back shape with smooth lines, looking like it belonged underwater instead of in deep space.

"This is a Sherwood *Hunter*-class frigate," the Navy officer explained. "She's six megatons—over five times as large as one of our modern destroyers, almost exactly six times as large as the export destroyers Mínglìàng has. Our last reports say that Sherwood has *six* of them, with another six nearing completion.

"There's your reason for the formal complaint, Professor," he told Christoffsen. "Governor Wong is terrified that Sherwood will shortly have enough jump-capable warships to attack his system directly. Hell, if the McLaughlin flies four or five of those into Antonius and declares he's taking complete ownership of the system, there is nothing Mínglìàng's fleet can do."

"If Wong knows that, he has to be doing something about it," Amiri said. "Even if he's sent a complaint to us, if he and Sherwood are in competition, there's no way he can allow the McLaughlin to build that much bigger a fleet than Mínglìàng."

"An arms race," Damien agreed with a nod. "When I left Sherwood, no one really cared about Mínglìàng. A few of the business people were grouchy about the deal over Antonius, but... the man in the street wouldn't have been willing to embrace war."

"My main concern, my lord," Jakab said calmly, "is that the *Duke of Magnificence* is not capable of engaging either system fleet. Either sixteen *Lancers* or six *Hunters* would be an even match at best for my ship."

"I have no intention of single-handedly waging war against an entire planetary government, Mage-Captain," Damien told him dryly.

"This time," his bodyguard muttered, and he turned a tired, but amused, glare on her.

"I had a battleship last time," he pointed out. "No, Captain, if it appears that it may become necessary for us to fight, I will call for re-inforcements. That is a large part of why His Majesty has assigned Mage-Commander Renzetti's courier ship to us.

"We are going to Míngliàng to stop a war. I have no intentions of actually *fighting* one."

Dismissing his subordinates to begin preparations for their departure, Damien took a few minutes to ground himself. He hadn't been back to Sherwood since he'd left over four years ago aboard the jump freighter *Blue Jay*. When he'd left, the Sherwood Interstellar Patrol hadn't *existed*, and he'd paid so little attention to his home system since leaving that he hadn't even known it had been created.

He didn't have much attachment to Sherwood these days. His parents had died when he was a preteen, living long enough to know they were among the very few non-Mage families who could apparently produce Mages but not long enough to see him become an adult.

His teen and young adult romances and friendships had been with other Mages attempting to become Jump Mages. His one-time off-again, on-again, girlfriend, Grace McLaughlin—granddaughter of *that* McLaughlin, he'd discovered too late to run away screaming—had left on a jump ship shortly before he had, and his other friends had followed the same path.

He was more likely to run into people he knew on starship transit stations than back 'home'. While he found it hard to believe Governor McLaughlin would do what he was accused of, he felt no desire to defend the man against the evidence being assembled.

Damien nodded firmly. His job required him to be impartial and fair. If he'd thought for even a moment he *wasn't* able to do so with his home system, he would have had to inform Desmond Alexander that another Hand needed to be sent.

Certain he could do the job, he checked the status of *Duke of Magnificence*'s systems. It would be some time before the warship was ready to move. The courier FN-2187 was still decelerating into orbit in any case, so they would leave once Mage-Commander Renzetti's ship was in position to accompany them.

He tapped a few commands on his wrist computer, which relayed them to the more powerful desk console that ran his office's systems. The transparent wallscreen over the window faded into visibility. An image of a golden sheaf of wheat—Panterra's planetary seal—appeared on the screen.

After a moment, it faded into the image of a young man with straw-blond hair.

"I need to speak with the Governor," Damien told him. "Immediately."

"Of course, my lord Hand," the receptionist replied. "Please hold one moment."

There weren't many in the galaxy who would keep a Hand waiting; although there were excuses Damien was perfectly willing to accept. What little time he'd spent with Alaura Stealey before her death had made one thing clear: one of the main reasons the Hands' authority was respected and honored was that they didn't abuse it.

Governor Maria Rose appeared on his screen after roughly two minutes' wait, by which time Damien had refreshed his coffee and was studying the jeweled necklace of simple satellites that provided Panterra's weather forecasting.

"Hand Montgomery," she greeted him. "How may I assist you?"

"This is a courtesy call, Governor," he replied. "A courier from Mars has arrived in-system."

"Do you have news of the commission?" Rose asked.

"No," Damien shook his head. "I'm afraid I'm being called away to another crisis. The nature of the galaxy does not permit His Majesty to have idle Hands."

"I see. You will not be participating in the commission you have called, then?"

"I was never intending to," the Hand admitted. "My purpose here was to neutralize the NPLF. We have specialists with skills far more useful to such an endeavor, and they are on their way."

"As you say, my lord Hand, the galaxy does not wait on our wishes or our desires," the Governor allowed. "Your arrival was timely and your intervention a literal lifesaver." She sighed and shook her head.

"I will await the arrival of your Commissioners," she promised. "You are not wrong about my world. I'm not sure an outside perspective is what we need to fix things, but I will grasp at any straws to avoid further bloodshed."

"I can't speak to the solutions required, Governor Rose," Damien told her. "I am a Hand. It's my job to bandage wounds, not perform surgery. I wish you and Panterra luck."

"You've given us *time*, my lord Hand. That may be more important than luck."

"I hope so," he replied. "Now, Governor, I must join my officers in preparing for our departure. I can't speak to where we must go, but another shadow falls."

"And the King's Hand must lift it," she replied. "Good luck, Damien Montgomery."

At the heart of every starship was the simulacrum chamber, where all of the thousands upon thousands of silver runes carved on and throughout the hull of the ship converged onto a single point, containing a silver model of the ship. That model magically changed to match any damage or modification to the ship, and was, in a strange but absolutely true sense, the ship.

On a civilian ship, the jump matrix converged on a simulacrum chamber with walls covered in runes and screens, showing the world around the vessel. It was a quiet, calm, place rarely entered by anyone except the Ship's Mage.

The *Duke of Magnificence*'s simulacrum chamber was also her bridge. As Damien joined Mage-Captain Jakab for the first jump away from Panterra, it was a hive of activity. While the spherical chamber had the same all-encompassing screens showing the world outside, and the same not-quite-liquid silver simulacrum as the civilian version, it also had no less than four circular tiers in the middle of the sphere.

Mage-Captain Jakab stood on the center tier next to the simulacrum. Around him were all the paraphernalia of a warship command. Each tier had consoles, chairs, and the systems needed to manage the massive ship.

For all of the firepower at Jakab's command, however, the simulacrum itself was the *Duke*'s deadliest weapon. Where a civilian jump matrix could only augment the teleportation spell, allowing a Mage to move the vessel a full light year through space in a moment, the military *amplifier* matrix could augment any spell.

From the simulacrum chamber and bridge of a warship, a Mage could teleport the same light year as aboard a civilian jump ship. They could also turn regular self-defense spells into ship-killing weapons, defend their ship from incoming missiles, and in general wield magic a thousand times more powerful than their normal spells.

Put *Damien* in Jakab's chair, and link his Runes of Power into the amplifier, and he could perform outright miracles. Access to the amplifier in Olympus Mons had allowed the first Mage-King to complete the terraforming of Mars in days and throw entire fleets around the Sol System like toys.

Of course, the *Duke*'s amplifier was a pale shadow of the one in Olympus Mons. No one was quite sure how the silver dust simulacrum of the entire solar system in the heart of the mountain had been built. The Eugenicists who had built it had used the amplifier to identify the tiniest scraps of magical talent in their test subjects and breed magic back into humanity.

The fact that they'd killed some ten thousand children who *hadn't* shown magical talent along the way helped explain why no one who'd known where the Olympus Mons amplifier had come from had lived long enough to answer questions.

"We have confirmed we are clear of Panterra and the star's gravity well," the navigator reported. "Panterra Control wishes us a pleasant trip and informs us we are clear to jump."

"Give Panterra Control my regards," Jakab replied calmly. The Mage-Captain took the last half-step up to the simulacrum and removed the skin-tight gloves almost every Mage wore. Panterra's star was still large enough in the surrounding screens that its light glittered off the silver runes inlaid into the man's palms.

"All hands, prepare for jump," he continued as he laid his hands on the simulacrum.

Damien's sight—the talent that marked him as a Rune Wright and almost unique even among Mages—tracked the energy flow out from Jakab's hands and back from the ship. The energy of the ship reached out for the Mage-Captain, encasing him and surrounding him in a way only Damien could see.

To his gaze, Mage, simulacrum, and starship were all one.

And then Jakab *jumped*, and the flare of energy forced Damien to close his eyes.

When he opened them again, the *Duke of Magnificence* was in deep space—on her way to Mínglìàng.

CHAPTER 6

MÍNGLIÀNG WAS a gorgeous planet from space. From their emergence point, hundreds of thousands of kilometers away, it was a blue marble heavily reminiscent of humanity's home world. It lacked the reddish tinge of terraformed Mars, the purple tinge of Ardennes, or the lavender tinge of Sherwood. The blue was almost the same hue, the white almost the same white, as Earth.

With a quick command on his PC, Damien overlaid sensor data and the ship's tactical display over the view from his window. The *Duke's* computers happily flagged the destroyers and corvettes of the Mínglìàng Security Flotilla. Eight of the destroyers held equidistant patrol orbits around their home. A pair of two-ship patrols swanned around the rest of the system.

The remaining four ships were probably either in the Antonius System or sweeping the usual jump points one light year out from the system. The system also flagged thirty corvettes, home-built ships in the quarter-million ton range. Tapping one of the icons, Damien brought up the ship's information on the vessels: fleet-footed ships with heavy laser armaments but no jump matrices.

The MSF was very capable of defending its home system and, unlike many system militias, could also project firepower outside its system. It wasn't an investment many of the second-wave colonies—the MidWorlds—would have made, but it was one Mínglìàng could afford.

As the world grew closer, its differences from Earth became clearer. Earth had distinct landmasses, continents making up almost a third of its surface. Míngliàng did not. It was a world of islands and archipelagos. Fishing and tourism had fueled its economy in the beginning—the white beaches of Míngliàng were famed throughout the Protectorate.

The revenues had been well-invested. Later, immense tidal power stations had provided near-infinite amounts of power to fuel massive, carefully maintained, floating industrial platforms.

Those platforms, in turn, had provided the muscle to build one of the few space elevators not on Earth itself. That immensely tough bean-stalk rose from another floating platform into orbit, providing the anchor point of an orbital industry that put Panterra, founded alongside the Core Worlds, to shame.

Most MidWorlds had a single large space station. Míngliàng's orbital stations were far smaller, but more plentiful. Fourteen stations, each one kilometer in length, were spaced equidistantly along the geostationary orbit. A fifteenth, twice the size of the others, hung at the counterweight point of the space elevator.

The small stations were efficient for production and docking, but weren't big enough for the large construction slips needed for million-ton-plus interstellar freighters or warships.

Their civilian shipping resembled their corvettes—small ships, mostly without jump matrices. A construction site drifting in one of the Lagrange points showed the beginnings of a larger yard to change that.

Míngliàng was one of the four most industrialized, most powerful MidWorlds. Between their wealth and their ability to take matters into their own hands, their accusations had to be answered by one of the Mage-King's Hands, to make sure things didn't get out of control.

What worried Damien, as his ship gently set its course for one of the geostationary stations, was that the system they were laying their complaints against was Sherwood. Not only was Sherwood his home, Sherwood was the *second* most industrialized MidWorld.

Míngliàng's fight was easily in their 'weight class'; which meant that any war would be a bloody, drawn-out affair.

Exactly the sort of thing the Protectorate existed to stop.

Special Agent Julia Amiri had access to all of the resources of a fully modern battlecruiser, including a full twelve hundred strong regiment of the Royal Martian Marine Corps, hundreds of suits of exosuit battle armor and dozens of assault shuttles, to keep her charge safe.

Montgomery, on the other hand, hated being a passenger and hated pomp and ceremony. It was part of his charm, to be sure, to an ex-criminal bounty hunter turned bodyguard-slash-enforcer for one of the most powerful men alive, but also a giant headache.

This time, she'd at least convinced him to bring along Marines as an honor guard—and Amiri would have *words* with the Major if their dress uniforms were less than perfect—and let someone else—someone like, say, one of the Navy pilots trained in evasion and combat landings—fly the shuttle.

As twelve dress uniformed Marines led the way onto the shuttle, she could hear Damien chuckling to himself.

"My job is to keep you alive," she told him. "You don't make it easy."

"Julia, I appreciate all you do for me," he murmured. "But we both know I don't actually need a bodyguard."

"It's not always about keeping you safe, Damien," she replied. "If you want to stop these people from starting a war, you need to make an *impression*. They need to remember who you are and what you represent."

The Hand was silent as they stepped onto the shuttle, but as she took her seat she saw he was smiling. It was at her expense, but it was still worth it. It was getting rarer and rarer to see the younger man smile.

"What?" she asked.

"Julia, if I didn't agree with you about making an impression, do you really think you'd have won the argument?"

The shuttle dropping away from the *Duke* robbed her of any response but a sharp glare.

Damien waited patiently for the shuttle's sensors to declare the landing pad outside cool enough to walk on. The Marine Mage-Lieutenant heading the bodyguard Amiri had picked out was the only other person on the shuttle who could protect themselves against the heat, and ceremony dictated the Marines went first.

Finally, the Marines began to troop out of the shuttle onto the concrete. He watched on the shuttle's screens as they formed a neat double file, linking up with the local Míngliàng Planetary Security troops to form a corridor of armed and uniformed men and women.

With the preparations complete, Damien finally exited the shuttle, Amiri one step behind and to his right, where she could more easily draw a weapon to cover him, and Christoffsen one step behind and to his left. Both of his aides had sub-vocal microphones linked to Damien's concealed earpiece.

The skies over the landing pad were a bright shining blue, and the smell of sea salt mixed with the normal burnt concrete smell of a landing site. The pad was on a hill overlooking one of Míngliàng's famous beaches, and he could see the sun reflecting off the waves behind the welcoming committee.

The welcoming committee itself consisted of two men and a woman. The woman and the taller man were in military uniforms, the woman in the black and blue of the Míngliàng Security Flotilla the man in the black and red of Míngliàng Planetary Security.

The short, dark-skinned man with the pronounced epicanthic folds around his eyes in between the two officers wore a neat business suit. He stepped forward as Damien approached and offered his hand to Damien.

"Good morning, my lord Hand," he said softly. "I am Wong Ken, Minister for Trade and First Husband of Míngliàng. My husband sends his regrets, but he was pulled into an emergency meeting as we were about to leave. He should have the immediate crisis resolved by the time we reach Government House."

Damien shook the man's hand and nodded to the military officers.

"The duties of Governor Wong's position are often onerous," Damien allowed. "I look forward to meeting with him."

"Of course, my lord," Wong Ken agreed. He gestured to the two military officers with him. "If I may present General Matija Avery, the commander of Mínglìàng Planetary Security, and Commodore Ratree Metharom, second in command of the Mínglìàng Security Flotilla."

Avery gave Damien a firm nod. The man responsible for keeping Mínglìàng itself secure was almost entirely uninvolved in the current crisis. Commodore Metharom smiled and half-bowed.

"Admiral Yen Phan sends her regrets as well," she told him. "She arrived in the system shortly after you did and remains aboard the destroyer *Light of Peace*. She is in conference with the Governor as we speak, and looks forward to meeting with you once she makes planetfall."

"It sounds, gentlemen, Commodore, that there are matters in play that should not be discussed in even a semi-public setting," Damien said quietly. The pad was behind several layers of security, and he could see several armed vehicles on the perimeter, but it was also on the edge of the main spaceport. Outside, all of the security in the world could be foiled by a skilled journalist with a half-decent shotgun microphone.

"We have vehicles ready to take everyone to Government House," Wong Ken confirmed. "I assume your Marines will accompany us as well?"

"If you have sufficient transport."

"I've read at least the public reports of your trip to Ardennes, my lord Hand," the First Husband explained. "I presumed you would be more comfortable with a full escort."

"I appreciate the thought, Mister Wong."

Government House on Mínglìàng was a sprawling complex of low-slung buildings built along the top of a sharp cliff. Their convoy passed the Planetary Assembly building, a baroque three-story structure based on the original parliament building in London, on their way into the complex.

The complex appeared undefended, and the pair of armored vehicles escorting Damien's convoy looked distinctly out of place. Appearances were deceiving, however, and Amiri maintained quiet commentary as they traveled, pointing out the green hillocks that concealed surface-to-space missile launchers and similar defenses.

Finally, they pulled up in front of the Governor's residence, a surprisingly small building built of the local stark-white stone.

"Follow me," Wong Ken told Damien. "Our people will take care of your Marines—you're welcome to bring a couple if you'd like, but there's not a lot of space in the House's secured facility."

"Amiri, Lieutenant Nguyen, pick two of your troops," Damien instructed. The traditional almost wordless communication of soldiers followed, and he soon had a small party of four trailing him as he followed the Governor's husband into the house.

Wong led them through a white marble lobby that seemed subdued for a planetary governor's residence to an apparently plain wall underneath one of the curved staircases. He placed his hand against a whorl in the stone Damien would have thought was perfectly natural otherwise. A moment later, a six foot wide section of stone recessed into the wall and slid aside to reveal an elevator.

"After me, please," Wong repeated and stepped into the elevator.

The elevator dropped like a stone, rapidly releasing them into an underground corridor carved directly from the stark white stone of the native cliff. The floor had been laid with a decorative, hard-wearing, carpet—but the walls and roof had simply been smoothed and polished.

The effect was more impressive than any decoration that could have been done. Damien estimated the bunker was a hundred meters beneath the surface, but it was in many ways more attractive than the surface buildings.

Security at this point was less concealed. A security barrier, staffed by two uniformed soldiers and backed by a ten-centimeter-thick blast door, blocked the way further into the bunker.

The two soldiers quickly checked the IDs of the three Míngliàng officials, despite likely seeing the same three every day, and then asked for Damien's. Wordlessly, he dropped the golden fist icon of his office onto their reader, which promptly beeped cheerfully and declared him cleared with no further confirmation.

"Sir, we need some form of visual identification," one of them ventured carefully.

"Soldier, the Hand is only active if it's been exposed to the correct DNA in the last thirty or so seconds," Damien told him quietly. "Believe me when I tell you that it's more certain of my identity than your scanner ever could be."

"I know who they all are, son," General Avery told his soldier cheerfully. "I'm not sure they even have ID other than that Hand our systems would recognize. Clear them through—the Governor's expecting us all."

"I have to log this as a protocol exemption," the soldier said stubbornly, and Damien stepped up to the man. For all that the guard was easily ten inches taller than Damien's own five foot height, he looked nervous as the Hand gestured for him to lean in.

"My people have Protectorate government ID," he murmured. "Your system should read it just fine. We *are* in a hurry, though, so faster is better."

Damien couldn't help pausing in the door of the conference room Wong Ken had led them to. Either whoever had designed Mínglìàng's Emergency Command Center had also designed Ardennes's Emergency Command Center or had stolen from the same inspirations.

The room was *identical* to the space in which, bare months before, Damien had gambled for fifty million lives. He'd *won*, and Ardennes was dramatically improving as they cleaned up after years under their corrupt Governor, but it was still a shock to see an almost-identical place.

It was only a moment, though, and as he walked further into the room he could see the differences. Where Ardennes had used immense screens, Mínglìàng's Center had several giant holographic displays. Where Ardennes's Center had been abandoned moments before he'd entered it, here half a dozen technicians and officers busied themselves reviewing the status of every spaceborne object in the system.

Right now, the central holo-tank was showing the image of a woman in the black and blue of the Míngliàng Security Flotilla with pitch-black skin and hair and a pair of gold stars on either side of her collar.

"Ah, I see Hand Montgomery and his people have arrived," the man in a black business suit talking to Admiral Yen Phan announced. He was a pale-skinned man with slanted eyes and a shaven head, and his gaze and smile were mostly for Wong Ken as he approached the newcomers.

Wong Lee, elected Governor of the planet and star system of Míngliàng, kissed his husband swiftly but determinedly, and then turned his attention to Damien.

"I hope you are here to answer our complaint, my lord Hand," he said bluntly. "The situation has degraded since we sent our missive to Mars."

"For the moment, I am here to listen," Damien replied. "I am here to review evidence and study the situation. What action will be taken depends on what I judge to be required."

Wong Lee grunted and gestured towards the tank with his chin. "Follow me, then, Lord Montgomery. You need to hear what Phan has to say."

Damien inclined his head to the Admiral in the holo-tank. Unlike the ship's Captain standing next to her, Phan did not wear the gold medallion marking her as a Mage. Given that only Mages could jump the starships, a non-Mage officer in command of an interstellar deployment was rare. Phan's command of the MSF spoke to either competence or connections.

Either way, she was not to be taken lightly.

"Admiral Phan," he greeted her. "I understand you have just returned to Míngliàng."

"Indeed," she replied. "As Governor Wong states, you need to understand what has happened. We have exchanged fire with Sherwood warships."

Slowly, carefully, Damien reached the tank and looked up to meet Phan's eyes. He'd been afraid of that. Not much else would have dragged the Governor away from meeting a Hand of the Mage-King of Mars.

"Explain," he ordered. "Start at the beginning."

CHAPTER 7

ADMIRAL YEN PHAN brought up a three-dimensional star map next to her in the holo-tank. Two stars flashed green—Damien recognized them as Mínglìàng and Antonius. A broad orange ribbon connected the two stars and Phan tapped it.

"Given the incidents over the last year, we've provided our freighters with a specific series of jump points to use for the transit between Antonius and Mínglìàng," she explained crisply. "This has allowed us to maintain patrols that are in reasonable sensor range of where the ships will be."

She paused, then shook her head.

"This would be more successful if the pirates didn't seem to know exactly what our patrol schedules were," she admitted. "We've had four attacks since implementing the patrols, and we'd never had a destroyer close enough to see anything until today."

The map zoomed in on a specific point on the orange ribbon, three jumps out from Mínglìàng and five from Antonius.

"This last run was a two-ship patrol I arbitrarily decided to launch without notice or warning to anybody," Phan noted. "We arrived at Jump Three roughly two and a half days before the next scheduled sweep of the point and found the freighter *Dreamer* under close attack by a Sherwood frigate."

"Show me," Damien ordered, stepping closer to the hologram.

The star map and orange ribbon faded away to a tactical display. Four icons blinked on it—the two Mínglìàng Security Flotilla ships, the

Dreamer, and one unknown flashing red. Sensor codes, the standard ones from the Protectorate Navy, appeared on the hologram, denoting weapons fire.

"We detected six-gigawatt laser fire," the MSF Admiral said calmly. "Prior to our arrival, they may have been trying to take the ship intact. Once they detected us, however..."

The tactical display icons told the story. The *Dreamer* had been a *Venice*-class freighter, similar to the one Damien had left Sherwood on years ago. It wasn't capable of surviving sustained battle laser fire and the icon flashed and disappeared as he watched.

"They sustained fire on the *Dreamer* for approximately twenty-six seconds," Phan continued, her voice oddly flat. "At those power levels, that barely leaves *debris*, Lord Hand."

"I know," Damien said quietly. "I've seen it. What did you do?"

"They were in the act of piracy and murder," Admiral Yen Phan told him coldly. "I ordered my ships to open fire. We were at extended missile range, but given my ships likely couldn't sustain a close engagement with a frigate, it seemed safest."

As she spoke, the icons flashed onto the display. Phan's ships fired forty-eight missiles, and the Sherwood vessel replied with sixty. It was a heavy salvo for a vessel of the frigate's size, but Damien's information on the ships noted their extremely heavy missile armament. The frigates were designed to kill ships with heavy laser armaments from well outside laser range.

That also made them quite effective against ships trying to use an amplifier matrix as a weapon like, say, the warship of the Royal Martian Navy.

"You survived, I presume," he noted dryly.

"They withdrew after a single salvo," Phan reported. "Our missiles didn't even reach them before they jumped, and I decided to do the same. We *might* have been able to weather the salvo, but with the complete destruction of the *Dreamer*, there was no point in hanging around."

Damien nodded slowly, watching the ships vanish off the plot.

"Did you get visual confirmation on the ship?" he asked.

"What?" Phan demanded.

"You have military-grade long-range optics aboard your vessels," Damien pointed out. "Did you get visual confirmation that you were engaging a Sherwood frigate? Energy signatures and armaments can be faked, after all."

"I did not. Sherwood has been destroying our ships for months, and you want me to *prove* it was them?"

"Admiral," the Hand said coldly, "all I have seen before today is supposition and conjecture, not proof. I will not—I *can* not—condemn star systems based on that. The involvement of a Sherwood frigate in the destruction of the *Dreamer* is damning indeed—but I need incontrovertible proof, beyond not just reasonable but *any* doubt, before I take the responses this action requires."

"So our people are just to keep *dying* until you have your proof?" the Governor demanded. "This is not the response I expected from Mars!"

"I did not say that," Damien pointed out. He stared at the holo-tank which had just shown the death of a ship very like the one he'd once served on, then turned to hold the Governor's gaze. "I will not bring the Navy in and force the Patrol to disband on this evidence," he continued, "which if I had incontrovertible evidence *would* be the response."

Wong Lee returned Damien's glare but, finally, nodded.

"You have other options then, I presume?" he demanded.

"I do," Damien confirmed. "First, I will want *all* of the information you have on all of the attacks forwarded to the *Duke of Magnificence*. My staff and I will need to review it before I decide on my next steps.

"Understand me," he said calmly, "I am not questioning if your ships are being attacked. I am concerned that we may be leaping to conclusions as to the perpetrator—and I am not allowed to leap to conclusions."

"I understand, my lord Hand," Admiral Phan allowed, her voice cold. "I suspect that once you have reviewed our data, *you* will understand why the Sherwood Interstellar Patrol is the only possible suspect."

Damien had taken over an empty office in the above-ground portion of Government House and begun the process of reviewing the data Mingliàng had provided. A team of Mage-Captain Jakab's people on the *Duke* were reviewing it from a military perspective, but Damien wanted his own eyes on it.

Except for the attack the previous day, there was no smoking gun in the data. A total of twenty-one attacks now, each completely destroying a merchant ship. Some ships were larger, others smaller, but all told almost two thousand people—forty-five of them Mages—had died.

There were common threads. All the destroyed ships had been on the Antonius-Mingliàng route. All were based on Mingliàng—where other systems' ships carried cargo from Antonius they went unmolested.

When the attacks had started, four ships a day had arrived in Mingliàng from the mining outposts. Now, two or three days passed between ships. In the aftermath of the *Dreamer*'s destruction, Admiral Phan was ordering the establishment of a convoy system—it would now be almost a week between shipments, but the ships would fly under escort.

Unfortunately, as the *Dreamer*'s fate had demonstrated, the Mingliàng Security Flotilla's destroyers couldn't engage Sherwood's frigates. If the attackers were Sherwood privateers, those convoy escorts would need to be fully *half* the MSF's strength to be able to stand off one frigate.

Other than that the ships were Mingliàng vessels traveling from Antonius, Damien didn't see a clear pattern. Some of the ships had been mostly intact when found, their crews murdered and their cargoes stolen—but their black boxes and sensor records removed. Others, like *Dreamer*, had simply ceased to exist.

The damage, where ships were found, was inconsistent with the attack that Admiral Phan had witnessed—six-gigawatt battle lasers didn't leave wreckage. The damage did, however, match up with the *half*-gigawatt weapons that both the MSF and the SIP's ships used for missile defense.

None of the material evidence prior to Phan witnessing the last attack unequivocally pointed to Sherwood. A lot of systems had a handful of destroyers, usually built in either Tau Ceti or Sol, and any of those ships could have carried out the attacks. Damien wasn't even prepared to exclude the possibility of one of those 'export' destroyers ending up in pirate hands, though most pirates flew modified civilian ships.

The last attack though. They had the MSF's military-grade sensor data on the attacker. Sadly, the high-powered optics that would have provided visual confirmation were a secondary system that a human had to activate. One no one had thought of at the time.

The scan data was as solid as it was likely to be. The emissions scans were fragmentary, but the energy signatures, performance parameters, and weapons used all fit the profile for a *Hunter*-class frigate.

But... many of the scans were fragmentary, broken, diffused, or confused. The ship had been running its electronic warfare suite at full power—hardly necessary for dealing with one small freighter. Everything fit the profile for a Sherwood frigate, but with that level of ECM it could have been another vessel specifically *trying* to look like one.

Or... or the Hand born on Sherwood was grasping at straws to avoid condemning his home world. Damien stepped up to the window, looking out at the light of Mínglià ng's two small moons reflecting off of the water in the dark.

He had all of the data. He just wasn't liking his answers.

"Did he leave at any point?" Julia asked the Marine, a Corporal Ashley Williams, standing guard outside Montgomery's coopted office.

"Bathroom break during Corporal Anders's shift," the young blonde woman replied promptly. "Not since I took over three hours ago though, Agent."

Julia shook her head. That wasn't what she meant, though the detail suggested that the Marines were keeping as careful an eye on her Hand as she was.

"Any trouble from the locals?"

"Not a peep," the Marine said. "They gave us full access to the House's security feeds, too. One of Sergeant Tomlin's people is in their main security center. They're being perfectly cooperative so far as we can tell."

"It's like they want something," the ex-bounty hunter muttered, then shook her head at the Marine's questioning look. "I'll let you know if we need anything," she told the younger woman.

"Should I have food sent up?"

Julia laughed, considering the young man on the other side of the door.

"Good idea. Food and coffee," she agreed.

Giving the Corporal a thankful nod, Julia stepped into the office. The first thing she noticed was the view—the office was on the corner of the top floor of Government House facing the ocean. Mínglíàng the star was slowly rising over the horizon of Mínglíàng the planet, lighting up the oceans in a glittering array of blue and gold. The office was comfortably, if plainly, appointed and had an incredible view—she doubted it had 'just happened' to be free for the Hand's use.

Julia was not at all surprised to see Damien Montgomery face-first in his hands on that comfortable desk. A glass of water, mostly empty, sat just beyond his reach, and the desk's holo-display was paused at the end of a replay of the encounter at Mínglíàng-Antonius Jump Three.

Asleep over his desk, the Hand looked far younger than his roughly thirty years. The slight twitch to his eyes that rippled through his muscles added to that impact—Julia knew how old and tired the gaze in those eyes was these days.

Montgomery jerked suddenly, falling out of his chair and flinging it away from the desk as something in his dreams startled him. Julia was fast enough to grab him before he hit the floor, but not fast enough to grab the chair—which promptly crashed into an empty bookcase in a clatter of falling shelves.

"Wait, what?"

"Wake up, Damien," Julia told him, helping one of the most powerful men alive to his feet. "Nightmare?"

Montgomery's lips twisted.

"Yeah."

To her knowledge, Julia was the only person aware of Hand

Montgomery's nightmares. She hadn't been *supposed* to have been aware of Hand Stealey's nightmares when she'd worked for her, but she had been. The Special Agent figured they were part of the job.

"Find anything useful?" she gestured towards the display.

"Yes," he admitted. "Just not anything I like. I'll wait for Jakab's people for the final call, but I'd say it was almost certainly one of Sherwood's frigates. The whole situation doesn't make sense to me, but Wong has clear grounds for his petition."

"Food and coffee are on the way," Julia told her boss, grabbing his chair. "Want me to grab Christoffsen?"

"Not yet," the Hand replied, running his hands over his face. "Food is good. Coffee's better. Need to think."

Corporal Williams knocked at that moment, opening the door to allow one of Government House's staff to enter with a steaming tray of food and—bless the Marine's heart—*two* cups of coffee.

Julia snagged one off the tray as it passed her, then waited as Damien took a somewhat paltry stab at the food. Bodyguarding a Hand sometimes seemed to involve making sure the somewhat excessively dedicated man she worked for *ate* as much as stopping assassins.

"So, where do we go from here, boss?"

"I'll need to set up a meeting with Jakab, you and Christoffsen back aboard the *Duke*," Montgomery answered after chugging half the cup of coffee. "Go over everything, see what your opinions are."

"Last time I checked, you were the Hand," she pointed out. "So where do we go from here?"

She recognized the signs of Damien dancing around a decision he'd already made.

"The only place that makes sense, Julia," he admitted. "From here, we go to Sherwood and present Wong's complaint. What happens after that... depends on the McLaughlin."

CHAPTER 8

MAGE-CAPTAIN JAKAB'S steward made fantastic coffee. This was more important than usual, as Damien wasn't entirely sure how much sleep he'd got after falling asleep on that desk, but it hadn't been nearly enough.

Most of the time, he could follow presentations like the one the *Duke's* tactical officer had just put on, but today he'd got lost sometime between 'antimatter drive emissions spectrum' and 'phased laser wavelength'.

Despite that, he was reasonably sure Commander Rhine had gone on for long enough that he probably *should* have come to a conclusion, and from the expressions of the other people in the conference room aboard the *Duke* he hadn't yet.

"Commander Rhine," he interrupted. The dark-haired officer stopped short, looking confused. "The Mage-Captain and I can follow you. Special Agent Amiri can probably follow you. Professor Christoffsen has no background in spacecraft and the poor man's eyes just glazed over. Can you summarize, please?"

From the grateful expression his aide shot him, Damien hadn't been too far off the mark there.

"Apologies, Professor, my lord," Rhine recovered quickly. If he hadn't been at least *somewhat* quick on his feet, the man wouldn't have been tactical officer on a battlecruiser. "It's rare to have to delve this deeply to try and identify a ship, I'm afraid I may have been a little enthusiastic."

"That's fine, Commander. Summarize, please?" Damien repeated.

"Of course." With several taps on his wrist computer, Rhine brought up the main holo-tank in the middle of the conference table. A zoomed in view of the data provided by the Flotilla appeared.

"In short, the weapons used are consistent with a Sherwood frigate," he noted. "All energy signatures detected are also within parameters for a *Hunter*-class frigate given the level of interference. The only item keeping me from being certain this was a *Hunter* is the level of electronic warfare in play—not only did it render a confirmation on the energy signatures impossible, but it is also a higher power ECM suite than our data says the ships possess."

"So Sherwood has upgraded their ships since our last update?" Damien asked.

"That is the most likely scenario, yes," Rhine agreed. "While I cannot be certain, I would say it is about seventy to seventy-five percent likely that this was a *Hunter* out of Sherwood. No one else has built an equivalent ship to date."

That was what Damien had concluded as well, though he couldn't have put a percentage on his opinion.

"Mage-Captain Jakab," he turned to the *Duke's* commander. "As of our last update, what was the strength of the Sherwood Interstellar Patrol?"

"Sherwood created the Interstellar Patrol after the *Blue Jay* incident," Jakab said. "I believe you were involved in that, my lord?"

"Yes," the Hand confirmed. "Two pirate attacks on the same ship. It didn't end well for the pirates, but it made Sherwood look unprotected."

"And the Patrol was the result," Jakab agreed. "They purchased three Sol-built destroyers six months after that, while laying the yards and creating the design for the *Hunter*. The first set of six ships was commissioned a year ago after eighteen months construction."

"The yards are still present, though?" Damien asked.

"Yes," the Captain confirmed. "A second set of frigates was laid down once the first was complete—they should still be six months from completion."

Damien took over control of the holo-tank from his wrist computer and brought up a star map.

"Gentlemen, the nearest Navy base to here is the Corinthian System," he noted. "Unfortunately for our needs, the base there is small. Mage-Commodore Teller has six destroyers and no cruisers—an insufficient force to change the balance of power in this region.

"The nearest Runic Transceiver Array is in Amber," he continued. "Both Míngliàng and Sherwood have Arrays under construction, but neither is less than a year from completion."

Magic could teleport a starship a full light year, but instantaneous communication between systems had to cross vast distances using one spell. The solution was the Runic Transceiver Array, a massive construction of runes and magic that could project a Mage's voice—and *only* a Mage's voice, despite hundreds of thousands of person-hours of experiments—to another RTA in another system. Complex and huge, the Arrays took years to construct and were hugely expensive.

There were only six in the MidWorlds to date, four of which had been funded by the Protectorate for security reasons.

"Since we will need to call in forces via the RTAs regardless, I see no reason to detach Mage-Commander Renzetti and the Twenty One Eighty Seven just yet," Damien told his staff, nodding to the courier's commander. "What is our ETA to the Sherwood System?"

"We are twelve light years from Sherwood. Since, unlike Commander Renzetti, I only have four Mages aboard including myself, that's a full day's travel," Jakab told him. Meeting the Captain's somewhat surprised gaze, Damien gestured towards Christoffsen with his chin. He, Amiri, and the officers all knew the limitations of Jump Mages and the number aboard the *Duke*. The ex-Governor did not.

"Coordinate with Míngliàng Orbital Control," Damien ordered. "Make sure both ships are fully replenished on all consumables. The sooner we're on our way, the better."

"Sir, this ship cannot engage the entire Sherwood Patrol on its own," Jakab pointed out. "I hope you have a plan."

"My plan, Captain, is to order the Patrol to stand down and provide all of their sensor data for our review," Damien said quietly. "Even if the McLaughlin has decided to stoop to piracy and murder, it's a long way from picking a fight with Míngliàng to picking a fight with Mars."

"So, you agree with us now?" Governor Wong Lee demanded. He and his husband had come aboard the *Duke of Magnificence* to discuss Damien's conclusions. They'd come without the military officers this time.

"I never disbelieved you," Damien pointed out, pouring the two men coffee. "Understand that there are still limits to what I am willing to do, but I will be moving to Sherwood to inform them of your complaints."

"I hope you plan to do more than that," Wong Ken growled. "We are losing people, my lord Hand."

"I will be ordering the Patrol to stand down while I investigate further," Damien replied. "If they do not comply, the situation becomes rather more straightforward."

"It seems straightforward enough to me," the Governor's husband snapped.

"I cannot disagree. But I still hope that my intervention can end this crisis without further conflict. Despite evidence to the contrary, I do *not* enjoy bringing the Navy down on our member systems," the Hand observed. "I have a number of options short of that. Professor?"

Christoffsen leaned forward.

"In the best case, Sherwood will capitulate upon arrival," the political advisor told them. "More likely, we will find ourselves in an extended stalemate, where Sherwood is not in a position to argue with the Hand, but is not prepared to concede.

"Our first task is to end the violence," he continued. "Once that is complete, it will be necessary for us to bring you and the McLaughlin together to try to sort out just why this all started."

"They want us out of Antonius," Governor Wong said flatly.

"Complaints of claim-jumping by Sherwood crews have increased three-fold over the last two years. I will *not* concede our claim to that system, my lord Hand. The deal we negotiated with Sherwood was more than equitable."

"That is a discussion for once the violence is over, Wong Lee," Damien told him. "For now, I promise that the violence *will* end."

"If there's anything Mínigliàng can do to assist, let us know," the Governor replied. "All of my resources are at your disposal."

"For now, as soon as we've refueled, we'll be on our way. I have many questions for Governor McLaughlin. We shall see how I like his answers."

CHAPTER 9

"JUMP COMPLETE."

"Verify location," Mage-Captain Kole Jakab ordered. He trusted every one of the Mages on his ship completely, but the extra time to verify was a small cost.

Mage-Lieutenant Jessica Philips bowed her head to him slightly from where she grasped the simulacrum. He smiled and shook his head at the youngest Mage on his ship.

"Go get some rest, Jessica," he ordered.

"Clean jump," Lieutenant Patrick Carver announced. "We are dead on the center of Mínglìàng-Sherwood Jump Nine."

Philips had waited for the confirmation before releasing the simulacrum, but once assured she'd done her job she saluted Kole and swiftly left the bridge—hopefully headed for a nap, but the black-haired woman was *very* young.

Kole smiled to himself. She was even younger than the Hand the ship was ferrying around, and that was a warning not to underestimate her if nothing else was. Other Navy Captains had occasionally mocked him for becoming a taxi driver after the *Duke* had been assigned as Montgomery's personal transport. The *Duke*'s Captain ignored them.

They hadn't been the one approaching a planet, praying for Montgomery to succeed so they wouldn't have to nuke one city in the probably vain hope of saving five more. Mage-Captain Kole Jakab had.

He'd understood why the order had been given—and why Montgomery had made it non-discretionary.

If Montgomery had failed, he would have followed those orders, and then resigned his commission. Instead, Damien Montgomery had stopped a madman and saved fifty million lives and Kole Jakab's conscience.

Kole could live with being a glorified taxi driver.

"Sir, we have a contact on the sensors," Carver told him. "No jump flare, they've been here all along."

"How did we miss them on our initial scan?" Kole asked.

"They showed up as soon as we did a radar sweep," his junior officer replied. "They're running cold so we didn't pick them up on passives. Wait... they must have seen us, they've lit up their transponder."

Kole leaned forward, studying the screens around him. "What do we have?" he said softly, studying the icon.

"*Santiago*-class freighter—pretty standard rotator-type, four ribs, six megatons cargo capacity," Carver reeled off. 'Rotator-type' freighters had a central keel cargo pods were attached to and curved 'ribs' that rotated around that core to provide pseudo-gravity.

"Transponder downloaded complete," Carver concluded a moment later. "Sherwood-registry, sir—the *Tidal Wave.*"

Sherwood registry on its own wasn't suspicious. Combined with lying low until pinged though, the *Tidal Wave* was making Kole's back itch.

"Sir, we're receiving a low-band transmission from them," another junior officer—twenty-four hours into the trip, Jakab had his C-shift on duty—reported. "They're..."

"They're what, Lieutenant Rain?"

"They're requesting to move into our weapons envelope for protection," the shaven-headed junior coms officer reported. "They advise that they believe they detected a pirate vessel in the area on arrival."

"Did we pick up anything?" the Captain asked, glancing at Carver.

"Emissions trails, nothing that really stood out," the redheaded young man replied. He glanced over his data. "Wait... there's a relatively recent *antimatter* trail in here," he announced. "That seems... odd."

"Yes," Kole agreed slowly. He looked over at Rain. "Lieutenant Rain, inform the *Tidal Wave* they can close to five light seconds. Ask Mage-Commander Renzetti's people to close to one hundred kilometers."

"Sir?" Carver looked at him questioningly. It looked like Rain wasn't sure of his intentions either, but she was busy sending the requested orders.

"I don't trust the *Tidal Wave*," the Mage-Captain admitted. Training junior officers was, after all, why the Captain was on duty with C-shift. "I want them close enough we can protect them, but far enough out that they can't hurt us by surprise. FN-2187, on the other hand, is our only truly vulnerable asset in the area so I want them well inside our defensive zone to prevent anyone getting ideas."

His junior officers nodded their understanding. He also noted that they were being careful to watch their consoles as well as pay attention to him pontificating. That little bit of multi-tasking was one of the best skills a junior officer could learn.

It was one he'd mastered a long time ago, and he'd been watching the main screens while *he* was pontificating. He saw the two jump flares before Carver announced them.

They'd appeared practically *on top* of the *Tidal Wave*.

Kole Jakab was a thirty-year veteran of the Royal Martian Navy who'd worked his way up to command a capital ship in a peacetime Navy. There hadn't been *many* actions in his career, outside the Battle of Ardennes itself, but he knew an attack jump when he saw one.

"Take us to General Quarters," he ordered. "Pursuit vector on those ships *now*. Prep missiles for long-range defensive fire—cover the *Tidal Wave*."

C-shift or not, his officers leapt into action with admirable speed. Everything they saw was ten seconds old, light suffering its ancient delay reaching them.

Nonetheless, he felt his ship *lurch* as she went from drifting in preparation for a jump to her full ten gravity acceleration. Missiles blasted out from her forward tubes, covering the distance at over twelve thousand gravities.

"Laser capacitors charging," Carver reported. "Sixty seconds to full charge."

Kole laid his hands on the silver simulacrum of his ship, linking into the amplifier matrix and reaching out with his senses. Nothing, not even a Mage's sense of spells being worked, traveled faster than light. Seconds ticked by.

"What am I looking at, Carver?" he demanded.

"I'm reading a pair of destroyers," the Lieutenant told him in a surprised voice. "One million kilometers clear of the *Tidal Wave*, but closing at eight gravities. I'm not reading any missiles, but..."

"They don't need them at this range."

"I have laser fire!" Carver snapped. "Looks like a warning shot, no impact."

"And now they see *us*," Kole murmured, watching the timer. The warning shot had been fired thirty seconds after emergence. Without the *Duke of Magnificence* bringing her engines up, the attackers probably hadn't seen her—but they'd been fully active thirty seconds after seeing the jump flares.

"*Shit!*"

In theory, the *Duke*'s Captain should have reprimanded whichever of the officers had sworn. In truth, his own reaction was barely muffled as the two destroyers both opened up with a dozen three-gigawatt lasers.

The *Tidal Wave* came apart in a blast of vaporized metal.

"How many," Kole coughed, swallowed, and then tried again. "How many crew are aboard a *Santiago*?"

"One hundred ten minimum," Carver said softly.

"Time to missile impact?"

"Three minutes, twelve seconds."

"Tell me I have lasers," he snapped.

"First phase capacitors charged in ten," the junior tactical officer replied crisply. "We'll only have ten beams, thirty seconds more to having the rest of the beams online."

Duke's sensors were still resolving the data on the destroyers, but the power of their beams said everything. The weapons that had killed *Tidal Wave* were three-gigawatt beams. The *Duke of Magnificence*'s heavy battle lasers were *twelve*-gigawatt beams.

"Five beams per target," Kole ordered. "Dispersion pattern Kappa-Five. Fire when ready."

"Firing!" Carver announced.

"We have incoming!" Rain snapped from her console. The shaven-headed com officer had taken over sensors when Carver had needed his tactical console to engage an enemy. "First beam set have missed, missile ETA is three minutes, forty seconds. Forty birds."

"Too late you bastards," Kole murmured. Carver had kept up his gunnery practice—he nailed the K-5 attack pattern perfectly—and Kole had guessed right. One of the destroyers was untouched, but the other took a twelve-gigawatt ultraviolet laser directly to the tip of the hundred meter pyramid.

The ensuing explosion of energy ripped the destroyer open, but warships were built tough. Despite the damage, he watched in surprise as the half-crippled destroyer rotated and kept firing. More lasers flashed out, several landing glancing blows on the *Duke of Magnificence*.

The cruiser shuddered, brushing aside the impacts on her armor for now.

"Secondary capacitors spun up," his junior tactical officer announced. "Switching to dispersion Lambda-Nine, going to sweep on all beams."

As Kole held onto the simulacrum, he noted Commander Rhine charging onto the bridge. His often stuffy tactical officer half-ran across the room to his station... and promptly dropped into the *junior's* seat, leaving Carver in charge of the battle the junior had already started.

"I have the missiles, focus on the beams," the Captain heard Rhine whisper, and his own screens noted Rhine taking control of the two salvos of missiles Carver had already put into space.

"Add more spin to the course, Lieutenant Rain," Kole ordered, wondering where his Navigator was. "Let's keep them from landing too many hits."

"Lieutenant Carver, Commander Rhine—let's *not* let these bastards get away, shall we?"

Even as he finished speaking, the sweeping cuts of dispersion pattern Lambda-Nine caught up with Bandit Two's half-crippled attempts to dodge. At least two twelve-gigawatt beams lanced down the hole opened by the earlier salvo—deep into the heavily armored heart of the ship where the simulacrum chamber and antimatter storage were concealed.

The stark white light of a matter-antimatter reaction flared into a tiny new sun marking Bandit Two's grave.

"Missiles on autonomous terminal mode," Rhine announced. "Say what prayers you've got, I'm targeting our inbounds."

A twenty second communication loop didn't allow much fine control on the final approach, but a Phoenix VIII was a *smart* missile. Kole had ordered the missiles launched hoping to defend the *Tidal Wave*, but his reflex served them well as eighty missiles swarmed in on Bandit One.

No destroyer built had the defenses to withstand that, and with Carver's lasers boxing in any attempt by Bandit One to dodge, she never stood a chance. Twenty-two one-gigaton weapons penetrated every defense the *Tidal Wave*'s murderers threw up—and an even brighter stark-white sun marked Bandit One's annihilation.

"Their missiles, Rhine?" Kole asked. The inbound weapons were Phoenix VIIs—a *lot* more advanced than any pirate should have, but still slower weapons than the *Duke*'s and launched later.

"Hold on a second," the Commander replied, then tapped a final command on his screen. *Duke of Magnificence* shivered as a hundred one-gigawatt defensive turrets slewed about, selected their targets, and fired.

Two seconds later, the second lasing crystal on each turret cycled into play. The beams fired again, focusing on even fewer missiles.

Rhine didn't need a third volley.

Damien was woken up by the General Quarters alert. He had his bedroom wallscreen showing him the tactical display before he was even dressed—just in time to watch the *Tidal Wave* be vaporized.

He could read the icons himself, if not as well as some of the experienced officers aboard. The pair of destroyers were completely outclassed by the *Duke of Magnificence*, and he knew better than to jog the elbows of the ship's crew in a fight.

He carefully dressed, watching the battle unfold on the screen. Once the missile salvo had been destroyed, he tapped the command to link to the bridge. An image of Kole Jakab appeared on his screen, the pale-skinned officer standing at the command console next to the silver simulacrum of the *Duke*.

"Mage-Captain," he said calmly. "Our status?"

"We are undamaged," Jakab replied. "I can't say the same for the freighter who was hoping for our protection."

"I saw the jump sequence, Captain," Damien told him quietly. "Those ships already knew where she was. Unless you'd *jumped* to her the moment you saw her, there was nothing you could do to save that ship, Kole."

"I know," Jakab ground out. "I still don't like it."

"Move us in and search for survivors, Mage-Captain," the Hand ordered. "We can hold position at this jump until we're damned sure no one escaped. Even the pirates. Who were they?"

"Still analyzing," the Captain replied. "Not Sherwood, I can tell you that much—the Patrol doesn't *have* destroyers anymore."

"Too many players in this game," Damien muttered. Míngliàng and Sherwood—and now unaffiliated pirates? Pirates with *destroyers*? It was possible—while the companies that built them were careful about who they were sold to, the regional militias were often less careful when *they* decommissioned them.

And for that matter, no one was entirely sure how the Blue Star Syndicate had acquired the *Navy* cruiser they'd tried to kill Damien with before he was a Hand. Similar shadowy channels could have shuffled a few destroyers into the hands of pirates.

"Agreed, my lord," his ship's Captain said grimly. "This is getting messier all the time. The *Tidal Wave* asked us for protection—they were worried about pirates at the jump, which means this has already been happening."

"They might have been going off the attacks on Míngliàng shipping," the Hand pointed out. "Trust me, Captain, unless someone specifically warns them that the attacks are focused, merchant shippers are just going to put the whole lot in the 'pirate attacks threaten me' category."

"Fair," Jakab shook his head, muttering a curse Damien didn't quite catch. "My lord, we're *supposed* to stop things like this. What the hell is going on in this sector?"

"Um, sir, my lord," Commander Rhine stepped into the view of the camera. "I'm going to have to run some more detailed analysis to confirm, but the computers just churned through the first analysis. They were faking their emission spectrum—some electronic warfare, some specific heat projectors. Would have worked on most militia sensors, but ours saw through it."

"And?" Damien demanded. Rhine was going into more detail than he needed again, but he was assuming there was a point.

"Sir, under the fake spectrum... like I said, I need to run confirmation, but the system gives me a seventy percent probability the pirates we just killed were Míngliàng Security Flotilla destroyers."

CHAPTER 10

SEVENTEEN.

That was how many people had survived in the one rotating rib of the *Tidal Wave* that had blasted free when the freighter was vaporized. They'd confirmed that there had been one hundred and fourteen people aboard the ship.

Damien already knew he wasn't particularly good at focusing on the survivors. It turned out that Mage-Captain Kole Jakab wasn't any better, which at least had the benefit of forcing the Hand to look past his own frustration to attempt to curb his subordinates.

He'd basically dragged the Captain down to the landing bay when the shuttle returned with the survivors. He found the fact he could realize the *Captain* needed to see their success more easily than he could find solutions to his own concerns ironically amusing.

They'd sent out five search and rescue shuttles, but only one was returning. The other four continued to sweep the debris of the two destroyers, looking for any clues to confirm or deny Rhine's analysis. There wasn't much chance of retrieving anything useful from Bandit One—twenty-plus gigaton explosions didn't leave much for analysis. Bandit Two had been destroyed by its own fuel cells going up, so there was a chance something useful had been blasted free.

Corporal Williams was the first off the shuttle, opening the door and waving the waiting medical team forward. The blonde Marine stepped aside as the medics charged forward, then spotted Damien and Jakab.

Approaching them, she saluted crisply.

"My lord, sir. All the survivors are stable," she reported. "Five had major vacuum exposure and three were injured by shrapnel; they need immediate medical attention." Behind her, the first stretchers began to leave the shuttle, the worst cases already secured by the Marines in preparation for transport to the *Duke*'s shipboard hospital.

"The others have various minor injuries, mostly frostbite and minor vacuum exposure," she continued. "They'll all need medical attention, but they can walk themselves to the doctors."

"Thank you, Corporal," Damien murmured, watching as the eight stretchers hurtled their way deeper into the ship. Few hospitals anywhere in the galaxy could rival the facilities aboard a Royal Martian Navy cruiser—having made it aboard the *Duke*, those men and women's survival was now guaranteed.

"Wait, *Damien?*"

The voice was familiar, but it took Damien a moment to even locate the speaker. A gaunt, dark-skinned man of his own age had paused halfway out of the shuttle. His golden medallion marked him as a Jump Mage, though his rough flannel pajamas didn't exactly carry rank insignia to say if he was a senior or junior Ship's Mage.

His name was Charles MacLeod, a scion of Sherwood's second oldest and second most powerful Mage family. He and Damien had gone to school together—they'd been romantic rivals for a time before Grace McLaughlin had made it clear that she was only interested in Damien. MacLeod had taken that with relative poise, though he and Damien had never been close.

"Charles?" he asked. "You were on the *Tidal Wave?*"

Shakily, his old classmate stepped down from the shuttle and nodded. "Ship's Mage and Executive Officer. God... Did Riley make it? The Captain?"

"The only survivors were in Rib Two," Jakab said. "I'm sorry, Mage?"

"MacLeod. Charles MacLeod. Why are you here, Damien?"

"You know the Hand?" the Mage-Captain asked, and MacLeod froze. His gaze met Damien's, then slowly traveled down, to the gold medallion at his throat, and then to the golden fist icon of his office hanging on his chest.

"Hand?" he whispered. "Grace said something, but I didn't realize... damn."

"What happened, Charles?" Damien asked. "We had no reason to expect piracy near Sherwood—I understand that to be the whole point of the Patrol."

"I don't know much, just what Grace told me when she asked me to come home," MacLeod admitted. "Said they were over-stretched, needed Mages willing to put on the uniform and help protect people. Came through Mínglìàng, which has its own problems... is this entire sector coming *apart?*"

"That's what I'm here to find out," Damien told him softly. "When you're feeling up to it, my people will want to interview you."

"My god, *your* people?" MacLeod looked around the landing deck. Even with four SAR shuttles out, there were still rows of spacecraft lined up in neat rows. The closest row was assault shuttles, menacing looking craft with visible weaponry.

"I'm on a goddamn Navy cruiser, and it's Damien fucking Montgomery's personal transport?"

"Yes," Jakab said shortly. "Now, Mage MacLeod, we really do need to get you and the other survivors to our doctors. The Hand will interview you later."

Twenty-four hours of searching had sadly found exactly what they'd expected to find of two ships destroyed by antimatter explosions: nothing.

Damien had insisted they make certain, and the shuttles had carried out alternating sweeps across a large portion of the surrounding space, in case something had been blasted clear before the antimatter missiles and fuel tanks had gone up.

A full day after the short battle found his senior subordinates once more gathered in the meeting room next to the *Duke's* bridge, and Commander Rhine once more preparing to present his findings.

GLYNN STEWART

"Well, Commander Rhine?" Damien asked. The tactical officer looked more nervous this time than when he'd presented the data from Admiral Phan. That was, Damien reflected, probably at least partially his fault.

"My staff and I have completed our analysis of all of our sensor data on the two destroyers," Rhine said slowly. "Without going into too much detail, a number of measures had been taken to conceal the emissions signature and other identifying factors. The measures would have been sufficient against civilian sensors and the sensors available to most regional militias." He tapped a command, and holograms of two identical vessels appeared above the table. Sections of the ships were fuzzy where the *Duke* hadn't seen them as clearly, but most of the ships were clear.

"These measures were not sufficient against the sensor and computer capability of a Navy battlecruiser," Rhine concluded, his voice very satisfied. "While we didn't get complete emission signatures, I am reasonably confident we got *accurate* signatures."

"You said before that they were Mingliàng ships," Damien pointed out. "Have we managed to confirm or deny that yet?"

"We do not have a detailed emissions profile list for the Mingliàng Security Flotilla," the tactical officer admitted. "The regional militias prefer to keep that kind of data to themselves, and we didn't request it before we left. Without those profiles, I cannot confirm with one hundred percent certainty that the ships were MSF vessels."

"I'm hearing a 'but'," Jakab interjected. "What *can* you confirm, Commander?"

"Both ships were constructed by Tau Ceti Nova Industries," Rhine told them. "TCNI builds their vessels in eight ship batches, and each batch is slightly but noticeably different from those before and after. They also provide the RMN a lot more information on those batches than I suspect the militias buying the ships realize."

A third ship appeared on the hologram. Sections of it were highlighted in blue—with matching sections highlighted on both of the ships they'd destroyed.

"I can state with a ninety-two percent confidence that both ships were part of TCNI Batch Twenty-Four-Fifty-D. According to the records I have here, the entirety of that batch was purchased by the Míngl
iàng Security Flotilla."

"So Governor Wong is *fucking* with us," Damien said calmly. He was angrier than he could let his people see. He'd trusted Wong—the man hadn't felt like he was lying to the people who were his only apparent hope for saving his people. "Was the data the MSF provided faked?"

"The thought crossed Lieutenant Carver's mind as well," Rhine replied. "We triple-checked—the data Admiral Phan provided was unaltered. My confidence that *that* vessel belonged to Sherwood is unchanged."

"Would the conclusion that these two governments are already waging a shadow war against each other seem justified?" Professor Christoffsen asked mildly. "We already know that Míngl)iàng's interstellar forces are not capable of destroying the SIP. Commerce warfare on the MSF's part would seem a logical response if they didn't trust us to resolve the situation."

"That seems to be the case, yes," the Hand agreed. "Certainly there is no question that Governor Wong's people have engaged in a level of duplicity I do *not* find acceptable. Commander Renzetti!"

That worthy was attending by a holo-projection at one end of the table, but the young Mage-Commander—only three years older than Damien himself!—came to attention and saluted crisply.

"Yes, my lord?"

"I need you to transit to Amber and pay whatever fees they require for use of their RTA for classified transmissions," Damien ordered. The Amber System's government was intentionally a joke, a series of cooperatives set up by a libertarian colony program to provide the minimum services the Protectorate required. Nothing in that system, including access to the RTA that Mars had built to keep an eye on said system, was free.

"I need you to contact Tau Ceti Nova Industries and find out when they're expecting to make delivery of Mínglòiàng's warship order."

The room was silent for a long moment.

"Son of a *bitch*," Amiri snarled. "You think he's using us to buy time?"

"I know he's using us to buy time," Damien corrected mildly. "What I'm wondering is whether he's allowing for the possibility of success on our part and acquiring warships as a backup plan, or if he is *only* using me to buy time to prepare for an outright attack on either Sherwood or Antonius."

Apparently neither his military nor political advisors were *quite* that paranoid. There was more reason than one that he was the Hand.

A Navy warship didn't have much in stock for civilian clothing, so someone had set MacLeod up with an officer's undress uniform without insignia. Certainly, the tall and gaunt Mage couldn't have borrowed *Damien's* clothes—they shared a build, but MacLeod had easily ten inches on the Hand.

Amiri showed the Sherwood Mage into Damien's observation deck office. She hesitated for a moment, watching the steward laying the food on the table, and Damien arched an eyebrow at her.

"There are three places at the table for a reason, Julia," he pointed out dryly. "There are twelve hundred Marines on this ship, two of them standing outside that door. Bodyguarding me here is a little redundant."

For once, she didn't argue with him, taking a seat at the round table the stewards had set up earlier in the day.

"Please, Charles, have a seat," Damien told his old classmate. "The *Duke's* kitchen staff put on quite a spread when I let them."

"And quite a fit the first time you told them to, what was it? 'Throw some food from the buffet on a plate and send it up, just make sure it's a balanced meal'?" Julia noted.

Damien winced, but MacLeod's hesitant smile was what he was aiming for. It had to be a shock to find that one of your classmates from five years ago was now a Hand of the Mage-King.

"That is about right," he admitted. "I'm no gourmand, so they may as well send me the same food as the crew. My *coffee*, on the other hand…"

"Gets forgotten and left to go cold far too often for something that costs what you spend on it," Amiri pointed out.

"Charles, this is Protectorate Secret Service Special Agent Julia Amiri—my bodyguard and general busybody," Damien introduced them as Amiri finally took her seat.

"Is there anyone around you without a mouthful of titles?" MacLeod asked, eyeing the plate in front of him carefully. Damien wasn't sure, but he *thought* that they'd served up a poached pacific salmon. It had probably come from the actual Pacific Ocean on Earth.

"Christoffsen?" Damien glanced at Amiri in question.

"You mean His Excellency Doctor Robert Christoffsen, Ph. D, Ph. D, Ph. D, Governor-Emeritus?" his bodyguard replied sweetly.

"Right," the Hand said slowly. Glancing over at MacLeod, who was looking somewhat stunned, he shrugged. "The Professor is here because the Mage-King knows that I have limited real-world political experience and called in a favor. He is my political advisor in the same way Mage-Captain Jakab is my military advisor. And despite Julia's official role, she acts more as my trouble-shooter than my bodyguard."

And this time, she even held her peace on why. It might have been because she was eating. Following her example, Damien finally tried the food the warship's head chef had prepared for him.

It was good enough that the next few minutes passed in the silence of contented consumption until the food disappeared. Then Damien broke open the bottle of wine the chef had provided and poured it out— to choking noises from Amiri.

"What?"

"That's a twenty-four-forty Gray Monk," she pointed out. "It's eighteen years old, and a bottle goes for over five hundred—give it *some* respect, boss."

Damien checked the bottle a bit more carefully. His bodyguard was right. The wine was apparently a Canadian Riesling, bottled in two thousand, four hundred and forty. Of course, he had no idea what any of that *meant*, but he could at least respect the age.

MacLeod took his glass, sniffing at it delicately, and leaned back in his chair.

"I've answered a bunch of questions about what happened here," he said bluntly, "but I'm guessing you have more questions."

"More about Sherwood than here," Damien told him. "I trust my Navy people to know the questions to ask about a pirate attack better than I do."

"I didn't leave Sherwood long after you did," MacLeod warned him. "With the two pirate attacks on the *Blue Jay*, your departure made more of an impact than you might realize. The responses and legislation that birthed the Patrol were born out of that mess. They hadn't started on the warship yards when I left, but it was only a few months later."

"You haven't been back?"

"No," MacLeod laughed. "I know it must seem strange to you, but my family was *overwhelming*. Love them all, but a few dozen light years between us was the perfect distance in my mind."

MacLeod was a Mage by Blood, born into a family of Mages. Tested and confirmed at an early age, he'd always had a family to support him and understood every step of his path. Damien, on the other hand, was a Mage by Right—the first Mage born in his family, identified by the testing every adolescent underwent, then orphaned by an accident shortly after.

"If you hadn't been back, why were you going back?" Damien asked slowly.

The other Mage sighed, looking down at his wineglass—and at his left hand.

"Riley—Riley Damokosh, the Captain of the *Tidal Wave*—was... my wife," he admitted. "We separated a few months back, paperwork for the divorce is registered on Corinthian. Grace's message arrived at the perfect time, and Riley agreed to give me a lift home. We found a cargo and set out and... well, this happened."

"I'm sorry," Damien told him. His relationships tended to end with people heading to opposite ends of the galaxy. Losing someone the way MacLeod had was completely outside his experience. "You said Grace sent you a message—Grace McLaughlin?"

"Yeah," MacLeod said shortly, taking a couple of deep breaths and large gulp of the expensive wine. "Not knowing what you've been up to," he gestured around the ship and the window to space next to them, "I figured you'd have got the same message. She was reaching out to all her old classmates, looking for Mages to come home and join the Patrol.

"She said she couldn't guarantee me a ship, but they'd have XO slots opening up soon and she could promise one of them if nothing else," MacLeod continued. "I could probably find an XO slot on a freighter at this point, but after everything came apart, I kind of did want to get smothered by family and feel wanted again."

"You were joining the Patrol?" Damien asked. "Did she say why they needed more Mages?"

"She didn't say much," his old classmate replied. "That kind of 'spread until we find you' message is pretty insecure. I got the impression they were expanding the Patrol as fast as they could—her grandfather thinks someone's threatening the system. I can't say I disbelieve that now," he finished with another drink.

"Grace could promise you an XO slot? That seems a lot to lean on her grandfather for," Damien said.

"She wouldn't need to lean on him for anything," MacLeod said in confusion. "Didn't you know?"

"Know what?"

"*Commodore* Grace McLaughlin *runs* the damn Patrol."

CHAPTER 11

COMMODORE GRACE MCLAUGHLIN never tired of the view from her office. Buried under the upper curve of the Sherwood Interstellar Patrol frigate *Robin Hood*, the designers had included a transparent 'sky-light' to allow the ship's Captain—who was also, in the *Robin Hood*'s case, the Commodore of the entire Patrol—an unrivaled view of space.

That skylight covered her roof and a good chunk of one wall and right now was allowing her an unrivaled view of Sherwood below. The oceans glittered in a slightly iridescent blue, and the vast pale-lavender forests of Sherwood Oak that dominated the main landmasses shaded the surface purpler than many worlds.

The petite redhead in the dark blue uniform loved her world. At her grandfather's request, she'd come back sooner than most who'd signed onto interstellar freighters and had been one of the first Ship's Mages of the Patrol.

She'd seen it from the beginning, with all of its warts. Over the six months since she'd taken command, she'd started excising as many of those as she could, but it remained a work in progress.

The admittance chime to her office sounded, reminding her of the visit she'd been expecting. It wasn't scheduled, the man was just predictable as clockwork.

"Enter."

The man who entered wore the same dark blue uniform as she did, but his had two gold circles on his collar where her rank tab was a single crystal oak leaf. He was taller than her, though that wasn't saying much, with a paunch that would have been unacceptable in the Martian Navy and the beginnings of a bald spot for all that he was her own age.

"Commodore McLaughlin," he greeted her, with the same slight emphasis on her family name he always used.

"Commander Grayson," she said to her executive officer. "How may I help you?"

"I just saw the posting of the command staffs for the Phase Three frigates," he replied. "I couldn't help but notice that every surviving executive officer is moving to command a frigate... except me."

"Yes, that is correct."

"That's *correct?*" he demanded. "Surely you must be joking!"

"Rodrick," Grace said patiently, "you've been a Commander in the Patrol for fourteen months. Your commission was granted as a favor to your father the Senator. You were still expected to attempt to *do* your job."

Grayson started to splutter, but she raised her hand to shut him up and met his gaze calmly.

"In those fourteen months, you have not, to my extensive knowledge, so much as attempted to learn what your job *requires*," she continued calmly. "Despite repeated warnings on my part and questioning from your juniors, you have continued to act as if your role on this ship was 'Chief Party Organizer.' This is not a goddamn cruise ship, Commander Grayson. Despite being the Commodore of the Patrol, I have spent much of my time dealing with the minutiae of *one* vessel because my executive officer cannot do his job."

She smiled.

"So no, Rodrick, you are not getting a command." She slid two datapads across the table to him. "In fact, I've been waiting for you—and so have these."

"After a year of service, *this* is the thanks I get?" Grayson demanded. "What, did you expect me to spend my time slaving over a console like some merchant ship wage-slave?"

"You were the only officer commissioned directly at Commander who had not previously served on a merchant ship," Grace pointed out softly, tapping between the datapads with one finger. "That was a mistake. A mistake I am going to rectify."

"Oh really? *I'm* a mistake? I'm not granddaddy's bloody princess stuck in command!"

The tapping finger turned into a palm slapping the desk, hard.

"Commander Grayson!" He stopped and she smiled again. "One of these documents requires your signature and mine. I've already countersigned it—it is your resignation from the Patrol.

"The other only requires mine. It's your discharge for cause. It isn't authorized... yet."

"I am not going to resign!" Grayson snapped. "You have no grounds to humiliate me like this!"

"Rodrick Grayson," Grace replied, her voice soft and sweet, "I have the grounds and evidence to charge you with multiple counts of theft of Patrol property. Even the discharge is a compromise. Sign the letter. Either way, you're leaving this ship."

"I will *not* be treated like this!" he bellowed.

Grace shook her head and pressed her thumb to the second datapad. As Grayson started to splutter, she tapped a key on her desk.

"Sergeant Gibbons?" she said crisply. "Please come in."

The towering red-head who led her personal guard detachment stepped into the room.

"Yes, ma'am?"

"Mister Grayson has been formally discharged from the Patrol," she told Gibbons calmly. She slid the datapad to the gaping Grayson. "Please escort him to his quarters. He can have fifteen minutes to pack—but I want him off my ship in thirty."

Gibbons saluted crisply, a wide grin ruining his professional demeanor. "Yes, ma'am!"

Six hours later, Grace was watching the terminator line sweep over the rotating linked rings of Sherwood Orbital in its geostationary orbit over Sherwood City. *Robin Hood* was in a high orbit, playing guard dog to the planet's main civilian station. Her sister ship *Maid Marian*—Grace was not a fan of the naming scheme, but it had been set before she was Commodore—hung in a similar orbit over the new Sherwood Defender Yards where the frigates had been built on the opposite side of the planet.

The space station had just finished vanishing into the dark when her console chimed, informing her she had the communications request she'd been waiting for since she'd kicked Grayson off her ship. Without even looking at the screen, she accepted the communication.

"Hello Governor," she said quietly.

"Hello yourself, Commodore Granddaughter," Governor Miles James McLaughlin, now a full year into his eighth—and he insisted, final—term as Governor of Sherwood greeted her. "I feel anticipated somehow."

"Not so much you as Senator Grayson," she told him. "To be honest, I expected to hear from you over an hour ago."

"I heard from the Senator two hours ago," the Governor replied dryly. "As much havoc as he was raising, however, I then entered a briefing on the most recent information we have on the attacks and had other priorities. How's my eldest granddaughter?"

"Being reminded of a man named Hercules and a certain set of stables. At least they took the source of the bullshit *out* of the stables for him."

"And he had one night to do it in," the McLaughlin said dryly. "Senator Grayson, as I'm sure you're surprised to hear, intends to level a formal complaint against the Patrol for the 'cavalier, high-handed and unjust' way his son's case was handled. He feels there should have been some form of tribunal and process before such an action."

"There *is* a process," Grace pointed out. "Multiple verbal warnings and two written warnings. I can provide the files to the good Senator if he wants."

"Grace," her grandfather said softly, and she finally turned to face the screen. Miles James McLaughlin looked *old*—far older than his seventy-eight Terran years justified. Almost thirty years of running a planetary government did that, she supposed.

"Senator Grayson runs a significant and powerful bloc in our Senate," he pointed out gently. "One that has helped support the creation and funding of the Patrol. While I trust that you did have reasons, flippancy doesn't help."

She sighed and nodded.

"You can inform Senator Grayson," she said flatly, "that if he wishes to reopen discussion of his son's file, I will have to pass said file on to the Patrol's legal department. At that point, the Patrol will have no choice but to level charges of corruption, theft and abuse of power against Rodrick Grayson.

"Discharging him *was* a compromise, Grandfather. If his father wasn't who he is, the younger Grayson would be heading for a jail cell."

"I see," the Governor acknowledged. A moment later, he started chuckling. "I will make certain to pass the message on," he told her. "I will probably need to forward you the video of his reaction."

"Patrick Grayson knows damn well what his son is," Grace told him. "He bought the man's commission to stop him being a drain on his own purse—but that turned him into a drain on the Patrol's, and the Patrol can't *afford* that."

"I agree," he replied. "I'll make sure Patrick understands as well. I am, as always, convinced I made the right call in making you Commodore. Can you afford to lose one of your Commanders at this point though?"

"I have enough calls out to Mages and merchant officers from Sherwood to fill the holes," she told him. "I've got enough new trainees and junior officers to spread out my experienced people across the new ships. The *Nottingham* and *Lionheart* already have crews aboard in final work-up. The other four Phase Three ships should have crews as they commission."

"Will eleven be enough for what we need?"

Grace turned back to the window, looking out over her world. She'd become intimately familiar with the destructive capability of even her 'regional militia' warships. Planets, orbital stations... everything was so very, very vulnerable. The loss of the frigate *Wil Scarlet* to 'pirates' several weeks ago had only driven that home.

"I don't know, Grandfather," she admitted softly. "There's a reason I pushed for Phase Four."

"With the attacks and the loss of the *Wil Scarlet*, the vote won't even be close," he assured her. "Even if Grayson decides to be a twit, I'll have the votes to fund those six frigates."

"Thank you," she told him. A light started flashing on her console. "Sorry, Governor, my bridge is paging me."

"Do your job, Commodore. I have faith."

Grace inclined her head to her family patriarch and then cut the signal to bring up her bridge crew.

"McLaughlin, what is it?" she asked.

"Ma'am, we just had a big jump flare," her new executive officer told her. "The sensor net is still resolving details, but we're pretty sure it's a Martian cruiser."

CHAPTER 12

DAMIEN JOINED Jakab and his crew on the bridge for the emergence into Sherwood. For his first look at his home system in over four years, he didn't really want to be reliant on his own eyes. All he'd be able to see from here was the star and the planet.

"We are on course, twenty-one hours out from Sherwood orbit," the navigator reported. "We've already sent in our request for an orbital slot, should hear back in about twenty minutes."

"Thank you, Lieutenant," Jakab said.

Damien stood at the back of the bridge, watching the activity as the crew efficiently processed data from the *Duke of Magnificence*'s vast array of sensors and scopes into a coherent view of the star system. The surrounding walls showed the empty space of a star system, but were being rapidly filled in with icons of a system that was even busier now than when he had left.

Looking for things he recognized, he spotted the multi-kilometer length of Sherwood Prime, the orbital station he'd left from. Touching a screen next to him, he zoomed in on the station. Nothing seemed to have changed about the platform, a single massive cylinder with twelve rotating habitation rings wrapped around it.

Of course, zooming back out, he spotted two smaller stations built on similar designs, with only eight rings each. Further out, he saw that what had been the beginnings of a freighter shipyard in one LaGrange point when he had left was now a busy industrial complex. As he looked at the yard, an analysis program swept through and identified fifteen individual jump-freighters in various stages of construction. The two Royal Martian Navy destroyers present in the system hung just outside the civilian yard, sheepdogs guarding the flock of defenseless transports.

"That's odd," Jakab murmured, just loud enough for Damien to hear him. "My lord, check out the Defender Yards."

He'd been briefed on the existence of the new military shipyard that was producing the Patrol's frigates, but it took him a minute to find it. Unlike the civilian yard at the LaGrange point, the Sherwood Defender Yard was in geostationary orbit, much closer to the planet. The *Duke* was approaching from high enough above the ecliptic to see all four of the geostationary stations.

"What am I looking at, Mage-Captain?" Damien asked as the icons popped up in his screen. The station itself was surprisingly unimpressive, a collection of glorified gantries wrapped around empty space and armored hulls. The cruiser's computers and techs had labeled four icons as frigates under construction.

"The Defender Yards are rated for six ships at once, my lord," Jakab murmured. "Two of the bays are empty—not even keels. And the other four..."

"They're further along than I'd expect," Damien replied quietly, looking at the complete hulls in the zoomed in optics. "Are the other pair complete?"

"I'm reading four frigates in the system, sir," Lieutenant Carver reported. "Two in high orbits keeping an eye on the orbitals, and two moving in company in the outer system... I'd say the latter pair are on commissioning trials."

"Wait," Rhine added to his junior's report. "One of the ships in orbit has changed course. She's headed our way—I read the transponder as the frigate *Maid Marian*. The other ship in orbit is..." the dark-haired man checked something, "the *Robin Hood*, the Patrol's flagship."

"Hail both ships," Damien ordered. "Inform them of my presence, and advise both the Patrol and the Governor that I expect to meet with

Governor and Commodore McLaughlin immediately upon our arrival in orbit." He paused.

"For now, let them choose the location," he finished. Let the McLaughlin think he was in control. It might buy him some goodwill when things got complicated later.

It would be interesting to see what stories Grace spun when faced with proof her people were attacking civilian ships.

"*Who* did you say?" Grace asked her communications officer, staring in shock at the young woman.

"Hand Damien Montgomery has requested that you and the Governor meet with him upon his arrival," Lieutenant Amber repeated. "He's asked us to suggest a location—I'm guessing we leave that to the Governor's office?"

"Yes, let my grandfather's people handle that," Grace agreed distractedly, her thoughts a whirl. She'd heard about Damien's elevation—running a regional militia meant she was *very* up to date on the news and had what she thought was a near-complete version of the events on Ardennes—but she hadn't expected to ever *see* him again.

If he'd followed a different path, he'd have been first on her list to ask to come home and join the Patrol. Instead, she'd assumed his path would forever keep him away from Sherwood—yes, the petition they'd sent to Mars had been likely to bring a Hand, but she'd assumed they wouldn't send Damien.

She shook her head swiftly and focused back on Lieutenant Amber.

"Please confirm the location with the Governor's Office," she told the junior officer. "Have my shuttle prepped as well. We won't be meeting aboard the *Hood*."

"So, Commodore Grace McLaughlin?" Amiri said questioningly as they settled into the shuttle for the trip to Sherwood Prime. "Is this the Grace McLaughlin I think it is?"

"Would you believe me if I said it was a common name?" Damien asked, glancing at his companions and wishing he'd been able to fly the shuttle himself.

"Wait, am I missing something?" Christoffsen interjected. "I checked Miss McLaughlin's file—she's roughly your age, but..."

"We went through our Practical Thaumaturgy and Jump Mage programs together," Damien admitted with a sigh. "And before Julia decides to reveal *all* of my secrets, yes, we were... together. On and off for about three years."

"And then you got on ships heading to opposite ends of the galaxy, considering the usual fate of lovers in Jump Mage programs?" the Professor asked. "And then you..."

"Became a Hand, and she came home and became the head of a military force we now suspect of waging a vicious pirate campaign against another star system," Damien agreed. "I haven't heard from her since I left Sherwood—I have no idea what she's up to, or even really who she is anymore."

"I hate to ask this, my lord Hand, but is your relationship going to compromise your judgment?" Christoffsen murmured.

"No more than the fact that my home system is involved in this god-awful disaster will," Damien answered grimly. "I don't think so—but I also trust both of you to *tell* me if you think it has. You follow me?"

"I'm frankly honored that you trust my judgment so far," the Professor replied. "I will let you know if I have any concerns."

"And you know damn well I'll tell you when you're being an idiot," Amiri finished. "I don't expect you to *listen* to me, but I'll tell you."

"In this case, I probably will," he told them both. "This whole mess is making me twitchy. I don't think any of us are in direct danger, but watch your backs—and mine, if you please."

"Watching your back is my job," Amiri pointed out. "I'll keep an eye on the Professor too—so long as he returns the favor."

Christoffsen snorted at them.

"You two do realize that I am the least dangerous person on this shuttle, *including* the pilot, by an order of magnitude or so?"

In his time traveling through Sherwood Prime for school, and later living on the station as he tried to find a Ship's Mage position, Damien had never actually seen the VIP docking zones at the 'north' end of the station.

Unlike the portions of the central hub he'd visited, the VIP zones had the silver-inlaid runes on the floor that provided artificial gravity on the warships of navies with enough Mages. The runes had to be regularly refreshed by a Mage, making them an expensive luxury almost anywhere in the galaxy.

Murals and frescoes of Earth and Sherwood forests covered the walls of the main lobby where he and his staff exited their shuttle. A greeting party, escorted by four burly young men in dark blue uniforms, waited for them.

Damien's mental processing of his surroundings and the greeters stuttered to a complete halt at the sight of the woman in the center of the group.

Grace McLaughlin looked nothing like he remembered, and he would have recognized her instantly anywhere in the Protectorate. Her hair, worn long when they were younger, was now cropped short, barely past her ears, but still glowed with the deep red of the morning sun. She was still a petite woman, a bare few inches over Damien's own unimposing height. The years had filled out her figure, but also added new lines around her eyes and a strange weariness in her eyes.

He knew that weariness. He saw it in the mirror every morning.

It took Damien a moment to recover from the unexpected impact of seeing her again. His only consolation was that she seemed just as taken aback, and he wasn't sure anyone other than the two of them had noticed.

"Hand Montgomery," she finally greeted him. "Welcome back to

Sherwood. May I introduce my executive officer, Commander Liam Arrington, and the head of my security detachment, Sergeant James Gibbons."

She gestured to a tall fair-haired man on her left first, and then to an imposingly bulky redhead on her right second.

Damien nodded to the two men, swallowed to make sure he could control his voice, and stepped forward to offer Grace his hand.

"Commodore McLaughlin," he said quietly. "I appreciate the welcome. This is my bodyguard, Special Agent Julia Amiri, and my political aide, Doctor Robert Christoffsen. We are meeting with Governor McLaughlin I presume?"

"He arrived shortly before you did and was called into a remote meeting," the Commodore told him. "He asked to pass on his apologies, and he will meet us in the conference room on Ring One his staff have arranged."

"Of course," Damien allowed. "Lead the way."

With a smile that brought back fond memories the Hand immediately tried to repress, McLaughlin gestured for everyone to fall in around her. Damien ended up beside her as they followed the path marked out by the gravity runes through the hub.

"I have to admit," she told him, "we weren't expecting a response to our petition nearly this quickly. Our ship would only have reached Mars a few days ago."

For a moment, Damien considered trying to pretend he knew what she was talking about, then remembered that the woman had always had a special ability to see right through him.

"What petition was that?" he asked softly. "I have to admit, Commodore, I am not here in response to any petition from Sherwood."

Most people wouldn't have noticed her half-missing a step. Grace had always had a certain... grace to her movements. She recovered from the stumble with enough poise that only years of intimate exposure allowed Damien to realize she'd been surprised.

"If you're not..." she paused, and swallowed. "We sent a petition to Mars twenty-three days ago after we confirmed the destruction of the Sherwood Patrol frigate *Wil Scarlet*. We believed, and believe, that she—as well as a number of civilian ships—was destroyed by warships of the Mínglìàng Security Flotilla."

That was a whole new mess. Attacks on freighters were a large enough problem, but if one of the sides had started taking out vulnerable warships, this was escalating even faster than he'd been afraid of.

"When you have a moment, have your people forward the petition and all available information to my ship," he told her. "Since I'm already here, after all."

"If you're not here in response to our petition," Commodore Grace McLaughlin said softly, "why *are* you here?"

"I think I should wait until we have the Governor present to discuss matters in detail," Damien told her, "but I am here in response to a petition laid by Mínglìàng's Governor."

CHAPTER 13

THE CONFERENCE ROOM in Sherwood Prime Ring One was clearly set aside for the use of the planet's Governor. Massive, hand-carved, wooden versions of the planet's eagle and bagpipes held pride of place on two walls, and tapestries of each of the twelve major clans' tartan covered the remainder of those walls, with the McLaughlin and MacLeod tartans flanking the wall screen that covered the rest of a third wall.

All the chairs had been upholstered in the McLaughlin tartan at some point in the last twenty-odd years, and the massive black Sherwood Oak table—a luxury item everywhere else in the Protectorate that remained the planet's main export—had the eagle and bagpipes seal set into it in gold.

Another Sherwood Interstellar Patrol Captain and Commander, presumably the CO and XO of the other frigate in orbit, occupied one side of the table. Commodore McLaughlin and her XO joined them, a small hand gesture sending the guards to stand outside the door.

A single man and two women, all middle-aged and dressed in prim black suits with subtle tartan shoulder patches, sat along another side of the square table.

Damien gestured his companions to the side of the table closest to the screen, nodded genteelly to the officers and government officials, and crossed to the lectern tucked to the side of the wall screen. It momentarily argued with his wrist computer's attempt to take control of the display system, but rolled over at the application of a Hand override code.

"Do we know when His Excellency will be joining us?" he asked softly, facing the table.

"He left his remote meeting four minutes ago," the older of the suited women stated calmly. "He should be arriving about now."

As if summoned by the aide's words, the door to the conference room opened, and two young men in crisp black suits and sunglasses—with *very* obvious shoulder holsters—stepped through. They swept the room with concealed gazes and then stepped back out to join the Commodore's guards.

In what was likely a hugely practiced movement, Miles James McLaughlin slipped between the two bodyguards as they exited the room, surveying the room with calm eyes as he stepped up to the table.

It had been over five years since Damien had seen the McLaughlin in person, at a family party he hadn't been warned would include his planet's ruler, and the years had not been kind to him. He looked worse in person than in any of the official imagery and videos, haggard and tired with deep lines carved into his face under his pure-white hair.

For all that, he still had the iron-backed posture of the Navy officer he'd been for a quarter-century, and his eyes were calm as he laid his hands on the table and leaned forward, effortlessly dominating the entire room.

"Damien Montgomery," he said fiercely. "After you defied my orders to sign onto the *Blue Jay*, I never expected to see you again. Welcome home."

"Thank you, Governor McLaughlin. The Hands of Mars go where they must."

"Indeed. I appreciate the speed of your response to our petition, my lord," McLaughlin replied.

Damien winced and slightly inclined his head.

"I apologize, Governor, but there has been a failure of communication," he admitted. "Your petition has not yet reached my vessel. I am here in response to a *different* petition, one *against* your system."

"I am afraid I do not know what you mean."

"Sit down, Governor McLaughlin," Damien ordered softly. "I am here because Governor Wong of the Míngliàng System has accused the

Sherwood Interstellar Patrol of piracy and mass murder. When I left Mínglìàng, they had confirmed twenty-one attacks, with a total of over two thousand dead. The vast majority of these attacks were on vessels in transit to or from the Antonius System that they share jurisdiction over with you.

"During the course of one of these attacks, a pair of Mínglìàng Security Flotilla destroyers arrived at the jump zone, interrupting an attack. In response, the attacker destroyed the ship they were attempting to capture and engaged the MSF vessels."

Damien tapped a command on his wrist computer, snapping up the most detailed imagery of the pirate vessel the MSF had fought.

"While the engagement was inconclusive, they did acquire significant sensor data of the pirate vessel," he concluded. "While the data is insufficient to identify a specific vessel, its armament, acceleration, energy signatures, and mass are all consistent with a frigate of the Sherwood Interstellar Patrol."

He met Miles James McLaughlin's gaze levelly as the Governor's face grew colder and colder.

"Your frigates are custom-built vessels," he said gently, refusing to meet Grace's gaze. "There are almost no other warships in the *Protectorate* that match them in size. I do not have a conclusive match against an individual vessel of the Patrol, but we have a high certainty that this vessel *was* a Patrol ship."

"No Patrol ship has done any such thing!" Grace snapped, and Damien finally allowed himself to look at her. His ex-girlfriend was still sitting, but she'd leaned forward and her eyes were flashing with anger. "We have full data on where every Patrol ship goes, what every Patrol ship does. The black boxes record *all* of that, and we have no record of any vessel engaging the MSF!"

"You should let me finish, Commodore," Damien told her gently. "I will admit, ladies, gentlemen, I set out from Mínglìàng to Sherwood with the intention of impounding the Patrol until I could find the truth. Other events, not least the discovery of your own petition, have impacted that plan."

He looked around the table. The Patrol officers looked horrified, the civilians angry. Grace McLaughlin was furious, and Miles McLaughlin was a frozen statue.

"I still see no choice, given the evidence I have received, but to restrict the operations of the Patrol," he said bluntly. "A three light year radius of the Sherwood System should suffice to carry out your anti-piracy duties."

"What about Antonius?" the second Captain, who hadn't been introduced before Damien started dropping bomb-shells, asked.

"I am officially declaring Antonius under the protection of the Royal Martian Navy," the Hand said flatly. "I will be redeploying the destroyers assigned to Sherwood to Antonius as an initial measure, and barring *all* regional militia ships from the system until the situation is resolved."

"And what situation, exactly, is that?" the McLaughlin demanded.

"Mínglìàng believes you are attacking them, and has evidence to that effect," Damien told him. "I will want those black box downloads Commodore McLaughlin has mentioned, and I will want full emissions profiles on all of your ships... *including* the *Wil Scarlet*."

"The *Wil Scarlet* was destroyed—*by* Mínglìàng ships," Grace snapped. "Did they mention *that*?"

"They did not," Damien agreed. "Like you, they did not say anything about their vessels being engaged in a shadow commerce war. However, vessels we have near-conclusively identified as Mínglìàng Security Flotilla ships attacked the *Duke of Magnificence* en route to this system. Combined with your petition and the destruction of the *Wil Scarlet*, I am suspicious of *everyone*.

"But I want the *Scarlet*'s emissions, Commodore, to compare to Mínglìàng's data. Because if the *Scarlet* is the vessel in their scans, an entirely new possibility arises."

Damien sighed, looking at the scans of the ship that had attacked the MSF behind him.

"I will answer your petition," he said quietly. "I will also answer Mínglìàng's petition. As the first step to both, I will be restricting the MSF to a three light year radius of their system as well. Bluntly, I have grounds to be suspicious of you both."

"And we are simply to acquiesce to these accusations and lies?" the older woman, presumably McLaughlin's aide, demanded.

"Ma'am, I am the Hand of the Mage-King of Mars," Damien said flatly. "I speak with his Voice, I act in his name. The information I am requesting could well prove you innocent. It could well condemn you. *Refusal* to provide it *will* condemn you."

"We will provide all of the information you need, and restrict our operations as so requested," Grace said bluntly. "As soon as the RMN takes over security of Antonius."

"You don't have the auth..."

"Yes. She does," Governor McLaughlin overrode his aide. "Even if I disagreed with her, Commodore McLaughlin can adjust the operations of the Patrol as she sees fit."

Governor and Commodore met gazes across the table, and McLaughlin nodded once, firmly, and turned his attention back to Damien.

"I allow this under protest," he noted aloud. "And only because I understand that a presumption of innocence cannot apply on this scale. Understand, my lord Hand, that this will not pass without consequence."

"I speak for Mars," the Hand said very, very, softly as he met the McLaughlin's gaze. "I will not permit a war to be fought under my watch, Governor. Let the consequences fall as they will. I speak for Mars," he repeated. "Will you listen?"

"Aye, my lord Hand," the Governor ground out. "We will listen."

Grace had never thought she would ever see Damien so... cold. Not just to her, she'd caught a glimpse of personal warmth when they'd spoken in the corridor, but in general. The Hand had been harsh, if not necessarily unfair, and almost statue-like. Her grandfather had walked in, owning the room the way he always did... and then Damien had run over him like a rogue freight shuttle.

The Hand did not own a space the way her grandfather did. He had no more physical presence now than when he'd been a youth. He just didn't *care* who owned a space, certain in his reasoning and his authority.

Damien was first out of the room, followed by the elderly man he'd introduced as his political aide, and the imposingly attractive woman he'd called his bodyguard. Grace was behind them, though she kept herself to the slow pace decorum required.

She felt more than saw her bodyguards fall in behind her as she followed Damien into the hallway and didn't, *quite*, shout after him.

"Lord Montgomery."

He stopped, fast enough that his bodyguard almost walked into him. She had a sudden flash of memory, of the first time she'd stopped him in the university hall to ask him out. The same sudden, jerky halt, as if he hadn't expected to hear the voice speaking to him. A tiny hint of the awkward youth, sneaking through the terrifyingly self-assured man.

"Yes, Commodore McLaughlin?"

The words were formal, the voice cold, but there was something in his eyes as he met her gaze. Something reminiscent of the hope in his eyes that first time he'd stopped like that for her. Something that made the heart of the woman in charge of a star system navy unexpectedly flutter.

"I will have all of the requested data ready this evening," she told him, resolving that she'd make *very* sure her people had it together. "If you would like to go over it with me, I believe I can break my evening open."

Everything she said was true, and there was real value to having the opportunity to present her people's data to Montgomery in a quieter setting. Part of her also very much wanted to just... *talk* to Damien. Away from the crisis, away from the titles and the uniforms.

"I will need to meet with the skippers of the *Last Stand at Alamo* and the *Dreams of Liberty* before I make further plans," he told her calmly. He coughed sharply, and some of the ice flowed out of his expression.

Unless she was *severely* mistaken, the bodyguard had just subtly elbowed him.

"That should only take a few hours," he continued after a pause. "I suspect it would be valuable to go through the data with a native guide. I will have my staff contact yours."

"Of course, Lord Montgomery."

CHAPTER 14

"SO, JULIA, are you *trying* to cause trouble?" Damien asked sardonically as the shuttle cleared the docking bay, headed back to *Duke of Magnificence*. "Given our history, I'm not certain that putting Commodore McLaughlin and I alone in a room together is going to look good."

"Why does that matter?" Christoffsen replied before Amiri could answer. "Your reputation is not going to be a factor here. No one is questioning your authority."

"Yet," the Hand pointed out. "I'm not sure the McLaughlin has quite separated the boy he knew who defied him from the Hand who can command him. If he thinks I'm sleeping with his granddaughter that lack of separation could cause us problems."

"Damien, boss," Amiri interjected, "we really don't know what's going on here yet. Your connections with the McLaughlins may be our only chance to find out the truth of what's going on in Sherwood."

"I haven't so much as traded holiday cards with Grace in four and a half years," Damien pointed out. "Exactly what connection am I supposed to be playing on here?"

"You went to school with her, trained with her, and *dated* her, for years," Christoffsen replied. "Most people still consider that a connection some *decades* later, let alone four years."

"Besides," Amiri continued with a grin that Damien *knew* was trouble, "did you *see* her come out after you? Doing her best not to give the impression of a star-struck schoolgirl and failing miserably?"

"I am... reasonably certain you're exaggerating," the Hand replied. "Mostly because I know you were following me, not watching the door behind us."

"*Touché*," his bodyguard admitted. "Seriously, though, what she's offering is actually valuable, and her knowledge of this system and its politics could save us a lot of trouble. Not to mention, on a completely unrelated note, the both of you clearly *want* to sit down and catch up, and this is a justifiable excuse."

Damien looked at Amiri flatly.

"I'm pretty sure you're not supposed to be micro-managing my social life," he pointed out.

"She's not," Christoffsen assured him, looking *far* too amused. "She's just pointing out that it's clearly your duty to throw yourself on that un-exploded redhead for Mage-King and Protectorate."

By the time Damien returned to the *Duke of Magnificence*, the captains of the two Martian destroyers that had been assigned to provide security in Sherwood had reported aboard. Jakab's people had slotted them into the conference room near Damien's observatory office, and they were waiting—surprisingly patiently for people used to being the master after God of their vessels—when he and Jakab arrived.

"Thank you for your patience," he told them as he took a seat at the head of the table. "I wasn't expecting you to arrive so promptly."

"We've got two million tons of warship to provide security for a system with *forty*-two million tons of their own ships," Mage-Captain Ann Bonaventure, commander of the *Last Stand at Alamo* replied. "John and myself are hardly, ah, busy."

Captain, not Mage-Captain, John Arrow agreed with a sharp nod. He was a bulky man of average height, almost plump. He was also the first Royal Martian Navy ship commander Damien had ever seen who wasn't a Mage, capable of jumping his ship and fighting her amplifier himself. It said volumes about his competence.

"We're decorative," he said crisply. "More of an embassy than a real patrol posting."

"I don't necessarily agree with your assessment," Damien pointed out. If nothing else, the destroyers carried four Mages each to the Sherwood Patrol ships' three. In an emergency, they could bring help faster than anyone else. "Nonetheless, you're right that your mission here can be abandoned without great risk. I have tasks for both of you."

Bonaventure and Arrow came as close to attention as they could while sitting, both officers utterly focused.

Damien brought up a star map of the sector.

"I have officially declared the Antonius System," he highlighted the star, eight light years from both Míngliàng and Sherwood—and twenty from the next closest system, "under Martian protection and ordered the regional militias to withdraw from that system. Captain Arrow."

"Yes, my lord?"

"You will take the *Dreams of Liberty* to Antonius, where you will take over security for the system," Damien ordered. "You will also carry a message from me to the Míngliàng Flotilla force in the system—they are to withdraw to a three light year radius of Míngliàng. The same restriction," he noted as he saw Arrow's concerned expression, "has been imposed on the Patrol. I want to avoid further incidents until I have established the truth of events."

"I understand, sir," Arrow said calmly. "What are my duties in the system itself?"

"Once you have seen to the withdrawal of any and all militia ships in the system, you will be fully in charge of system security and peacekeeping until we can get you reinforcements," Damien told him. The stout Captain swallowed hard, but nodded.

"I don't plan on leaving you hanging for long," the Hand assured him. "Captain Bonaventure."

"My lord?" the *Last Stand at Alamo*'s commander replied.

"I'm sending you first to the base at Corinthian and then onto Nia Kriti. You're to commandeer warships, under my authority, from both commands," Damien instructed. "We still have yards under construction at Corinthian, so I don't think we can take more than half of their destroyers—but that's still four more ships to back up Captain Arrow until you can pull the cruisers from Nia Kriti."

"All of them, sir?" she asked. "That's a lot of firepower."

There were, according to Damien's update, twenty-four destroyers and eight cruisers at the Nia Kriti Navy Base, with responsibility for almost a third of the Fringe.

"Admiral Medici will understand," Damien promised. "He once saved my life. I'm sure he'd love to add to the ledger."

"Yes, my lord," Bonaventure said calmly. "But..."

"Captains, understand this—right now, I have grounds to believe that both Mínglìàng and Sherwood are engaged in a shadow conflict attacking each other's civilian shipping," the Hand said grimly. "I want enough firepower in place to be able to defeat *both* their fleets. Combined, if necessary."

"Nia Kriti is also a long way, sir," she pointed out. "It will be three weeks before I can return with Admiral Medici."

"I know," Damien admitted. "But it's closer than any of the Core Worlds, and not all of them have a full cruiser squadron. Ardennes would have been better before Commodore Cor's mutiny, but that station no longer has any more ships than Sherwood. Admiral Medici is our best option."

"Then I'll get him for you, sir," Bonaventure promised.

"I'm more concerned about you, Captain Arrow," Damien told the other commander. "Do *not* hesitate to commandeer transports to send as couriers. I will either be here, in Antonius, or in Mínglìàng until this situation is resolved. We should be able to reinforce you inside forty-eight hours from either system, depending on the speed of the freighter you send.

"If we're evicting the regional militias, then responsibility for the system falls on us," he reminded his three Captains. "And what point is His Majesty's Protectorate if we fail to protect his people?"

"Status report," Kole Jakab requested as he returned to the command chair on his bridge. The Mage-Captain *hated* the meetings he got dragged to along with the Hand. When Damien wanted or needed his advice, he'd give it, but he was no fan of the politicians and local jokers-in-uniform the Hand tended to meet.

"We have a fifth frigate on the scopes, the *Alan-a-dale*," his XO, Mage-Commander Larry Bruce, reported. "Just back in from a patrol to Antonius, they're reporting no issues or incidents. The pair of frigates on trials are doing live fire laser testing, which is always entertaining to watch, and Sherwood Orbital Three is having traffic congestion."

"And that last is important why exactly, Commander Bruce?" Kole asked dryly.

"Because it's the most exciting thing happening in this system, skipper," Bruce replied. "If these people are plotting a war, boss, they're being damned subtle about it."

"Wouldn't you be, with a Hand in the system?" the Mage-Captain asked. "The Commodore's people were supposed to reach out to schedule a meeting with Lord Montgomery. Any word yet?"

"Rain?" Bruce asked, glancing over at the bald young woman running coms. "I got the summary, but give the skipper the details."

She nodded, turning away from her console to face her senior officers.

"I spoke to Commander Arrington," Lieutenant Rain reported crisply. "They'll be forwarding the black box data from the *Maid Marian* and *Robin Hood* in about an hour. He figured it would take them another couple of hours to pull together the data for the *Wil Scarlet* and the two ships out of system, and an hour to get a full update from the *Alan-a-dale* once she docks.

"He thinks they'll have everything together by about twenty hundred hours Olympus Mons Time and suggested the Hand and Commodore meet for a late supper on Sherwood Orbital. The Commodore apparently has an apartment and office on Ring One."

"The Hand's schedule is fully open," Kole noted. No one on his staff needed to know any of the undercurrents being discussed amongst

Damien's personal subordinates. "We're here until Commander Renzetti returns, so if a late supper works for the Commodore and her data analysts, book it in."

"Yes, sir," Rain confirmed, turning back to her console.

Kole turned to Bruce. "Larry, notify the Deck Officer to have a shuttle prepped to take the Hand over for a twenty hundred hour meeting. Probably just him and Special Agent Amiri, but check with Agent Amiri on the level of protection she thinks is necessary."

Bruce shook his head.

"You realize that the Hand is more dangerous than any bodyguard we can send with him, right?"

"He's still only got one set of eyes, Larry," Kole said. "Hand or not, he'll still die if someone shoots him in the back—and I am *not* going to be the one explaining *that* to Desmond Michael Alexander!"

CHAPTER 15

GRACE ALARIE MCLAUGHLIN was the Commodore of the Sherwood Interstellar Patrol. The uniformed commander of an entire planet's spaceborne defenses, answerable only to the Governor. She was meeting with a senior representative of the interstellar government that included her world, to face harsh and dangerous accusations against the military force she commanded.

She was also, at this moment, utterly convinced that she was an idiot. Despite the weight of the meeting she was supposed to be having with Hand Montgomery, she found herself nervously waiting for his shuttle to arrive like a teenager on a first date.

Fortunately, if Sergeant Gibbons could tell, the big Patrol non-com was pretending otherwise. Grace very carefully did not turn around to see if her bodyguard was smirking. She'd learned the gradations of the soft-spoken man's smirks over the last year and didn't care to see which one was on display tonight.

Finally, Montgomery's shuttle locked to the docking collar and promptly disgorged Damien—accompanied by a pair of women, one the tall brunette from the meeting and the other a lanky blond whose Marine uniform seemed inappropriately tightly cut to Grace's eyes.

"Lord Montgomery," she greeted him, stepping forward and offering her hand. Shaking his, she noticed the long black gloves he wore. Most Jump Mages wore gloves of some kind, as did any formally trained Combat Mage—both professions came with necessary runes being carved into your palm—but she'd never met anyone who wore gloves that went up to their elbows.

"Commodore McLaughlin," he replied with a slight nod of his head. "I do appreciate your willingness to assist in this matter."

"If you'll come this way, I have all of the files prepared in my office," she told him. She met his gaze and he smiled, the lines stretching all the way up into his eyes with a spark that brought back warm memories.

"Of course, Grace," he said softly. "Lead the way."

They made it through the station with small talk about nothing in particular. Their professional discussions couldn't be held in public, and if there was a personal discussion to have... well, that was even more private.

Reaching her office—which Grace was suddenly very aware was connected to her station-side apartment—she turned to face Damien again. The gravity was ever-so-slightly noticeably heavier here at the outside of the rotating ring, which had to be the reason for her fast-beating heart.

"I've had my steward prepare dinner," she told him, glancing towards the bodyguards. "I'm sure we can make more for Agent Amiri and...?"

The Special Agent smiled and *winked* at Grace.

"Corporal Williams and I will join Sergeant Gibbons, I think," Amiri told them. "Between the three of us, I think we can manage to scare up some food and keep anyone from interrupting your meeting."

Gibbons's smirk expanded and Grace tried not to glare at her bodyguard.

"That seems reasonable to me, ma'am," he agreed. "You don't want to have to explain the difference between hydrogen and antimatter to us security types. We'll keep things under control out here while you two sort through the files."

"Of course," Montgomery allowed, though there was... something to his voice suggesting this was a surprise to him, too. "After you, Commodore?"

Hoping the assorted subordinates couldn't see her nervousness, Grace opened up the door and walked into her office. Her steward had set up a small table with two chairs and covered trays of food, in a spot where both of them could see the wallscreen, exactly as she'd instructed.

The door hissed shut behind her and Grace inhaled sharply at the realization that, for the first time in over four years, she was alone with Damien Montgomery.

Damien took one of the seats at the table, trying to conceal his own awkwardness. The last time he'd been alone with Grace McLaughlin, it had been the last night before she left Sherwood on a jump ship—and they'd spent it in bed together.

There was enough hesitance to her taking her own seat for him to suspect she was feeling a similar awkwardness. With everything going on, with the fate of two star systems on the line, it was bitterly amusing to him that their own personal history was clearly high in both their minds.

"You wanted to walk me through these files," he finally said. "Was there anything specific you wanted to show me?"

"A few things," she confirmed. "We should eat, the trays will only keep food warm so long."

He was willing to let her set the tone of the evening for now. He doubted Grace was planning on *outright* lying to him, so the clues, if any, would be in what she didn't show him as much as what she did.

Laying aside his gloves and removing the tray, he stopped as the smell of mint marinated lamb chops and asparagus wafted up—the same meal they'd eaten on their first date almost eight years ago now. He arched an eyebrow at Grace and was gratified to see a hint of a blush wash over her cheeks.

"I did *not* specify a menu, if you're wondering," she said quickly as she laid aside her own tray cover. She *saw* the runes on the backs of his hands and wrists—runes no other Mage would have—but clearly chose to focus on the mundane. "Kyle is a fantastic cook, though. It looks delicious."

A few bites in and Damien could not argue. Grace took several bites of her own food and a sip of her wine, then tapped a few commands. The wallscreen lit up with the new seal of the Sherwood Interstellar Patrol—the encircled bagpipes and eagle of Sherwood split by crossed swords, with a trio of stars on either side of the blades.

"I was glad to see the *Alan-a-dale* return," she told him. "Captain Wayne is one of my best officers—he brought over most of his crew from his old merchant ship, and they're one of, if not *the*, best drilled crews I have.

"But, most importantly, *Alan-a-dale* was the ship that discovered the *Wil Scarlet*'s fate," she continued, "and while we keep backup copies of all of the black box data, I figured you'd be more comfortable with a direct, complete, download of the *Alan-a-dale*'s box back to commissioning."

"It'll make Mage-Captain's Jakab's analysts happy," Damien agreed. "The cleaner the data the harder it is to hide anything."

"We're not hiding anything," McLaughlin snapped, and sighed. "We really aren't, Damien. I know you can't believe that, but..."

Damien looked away from her, focusing on the data on the screen as it filled with the image of the *Alan-a-dale*. Sherwood's frigates were odd ships to his eyes, a long uneven curve on top with a flat bottom and stern, where the Protectorate used even-sided pyramids. That curve mounted a lot more weapons than any given side of a Protectorate ship, but a frigate was vulnerable if approached from 'beneath'—though in space, they'd presumably see an attack coming in plenty of time to rotate the ship.

"Wait," he said aloud as he reviewed the numbers the screen was showing. "This says the *Alan-a-dale* returned missing two full salvoes of missiles?" He checked the dates. The patrol was just the right timing for them to have clashed with Admiral Yen Phan three jumps out from Mínglìàng.

"They're authorized to expend missiles on live fire exercises," Grace pointed out. "Like the Royal Martian Navy, I subscribe to the theory that the best training for a crew in firing their weapons is for them to fire their weapons. You'll note she came back with a full stockpile of anti-matter *warheads*."

"I doubt I need to tell you that the warhead is almost incidental on a full velocity Phoenix missile," Damien said quietly. "Can you be *certain* Captain Wayne did test-fire those missiles?"

"I trust Michael completely," she replied. "But, if you give me a moment..."

She tapped away on her wrist computer for a moment, and then the screen resolved into the black of space. It split into multiple different windows, several showing visuals of the space outside *Alan-a-dale*, others showing her sensor data, her location and her status according to her internal sensors.

Seconds after the screen changed, missiles blasted away, shooting into empty space. A second salvo followed half a minute later.

"See?" she asked triumphantly. "I have full records of every live fire test, every jump, everywhere my ships have been and what they've done. I *know* my people haven't been attacking anyone's shipping."

"Show me the *Wil Scarlet*," Damien said after a long moment's thought. "What happened to her?"

"I had that one as a canned routine," the woman at the table told him with a smile as she hit a button. Once again, the screen showed the *Alan-a-dale*, but now the space it showed wasn't empty.

There wasn't much in it. Antimatter explosions didn't leave a lot of debris. Damien studied both the visual and the sensors with a practiced eye. Everything looked right, but...

"You said they retrieved the black box?" he asked. "There's not a lot of intact debris, I'm surprised it survived."

"Captain Vlahovic apparently ejected the box when he realized the battle was lost," Grace said after a long moment. "We don't actually have the ship's destruction on record, though it's pretty obvious," she gestured at the screen.

"Show me," Damien ordered.

With a sigh, she nodded and hit another command. The *Alan-a-dale* vanished, replaced with the same data and screens for another ship—the *Wil Scarlet*. The feed was paused, showing the situation in the frigate's final moments.

Eight ships, all one megaton destroyers, had the frigate surrounded. Missile salvos were sweeping in from six different angles and the weakness of the *Hunter*'s design was clear. Against a single enemy or formation of enemies, a *Hunter* could orient herself to face them. Surrounded, ambushed by a prepared enemy, there was no way the *Wil Scarlet* could maneuver to defend herself.

McLaughlin entered more commands and a new screen appeared—one showing the bridge of the frigate. Captain Vlahovic was a tall man with black hair down to his shoulders, surprisingly obese for his height and role.

The video started playing, and Vlahovic was speaking.

"Unidentified vessels, this is the *Wil Scarlet*," he snapped, his voice desperate. "We surrender. I repeat, *we surrender*."

"No response, sir."

"Damn." Vlahovic's voice was very quiet, empty of all hope. "Stand by all point defenses. Eject the secondary black box—let's hope that *someone* finds out what happens to us."

"Ejecting... now."

The image froze again.

"Debris and radiation patterns suggest the detonation of in excess of forty antimatter warheads," Grace noted softly. "If he'd ejected the box any later, we would have had no data at all. *Our* analysis says those are Tau Ceti-built ships, and the only people for fifty light years in any direction with enough of those to spare eight for *any* mission are the Mínglìàng Security Flotilla."

She glared at him across the table.

"My people are *dead*, Damien," she snapped. "Spacers under my command. Merchants under my protection. For God's sake, Damien— *Kyle* is dead."

They were both silent after that. Damien hadn't known. Kyle McLaughlin was technically Grace's uncle, but he'd been the same age as Damien and Grace—he'd shipped out on the same freighter as Grace had.

"I didn't know," he admitted.

"Never seen anyone else take to the merchant life so well," she said softly. "Left the *Gentle Rains* after eighteen months—about when I came home—to be XO on another ship. Had his own ship two years ago. Was on a run home six months ago. Never made it." She shook her head. "Too many dead, Damien. And you tell me you don't trust *us*?"

"Mínglìàng has as many dead and more," he reminded her, his voice very soft. "Grace, I have *unaltered* footage that unquestionably shows a Sherwood frigate killing innocent spacers. I *want* to trust you," he continued, his voice so fierce it surprised even him.

"I want to believe you," he told her, and it was so true it *hurt*. "But I have *evidence* that says that at least one of your Captains is murdering people."

"Then give me a copy," she snapped. "You can run it against emissions profiles and black box data for years, but if they've done a good enough job, you'll never nail down the ship. My analysts have *months* of data—from ship sensors, from builder scans, from the system defense net. Give me what you have—I've as good a chance to identify the ship as you do—if not better."

Suddenly she was holding his hands, *pleading*.

"Please, Damien," she said softly. "If one of my people is doing this, let me help find them—and if I do, I will by God *hand-deliver* Governor Wong's invitation to their hanging."

She was right. Even if he *couldn't* trust her—and despite all logic and reason, everything told him he could—giving her the data couldn't hurt.

"Okay," he said quietly. "I'll make sure you get a copy. I will find the perpetrators, Grace—whether they're rogue factions, criminals, or system government, I *will* find those who killed Kyle and everyone else. I promise you that."

Somehow they'd stepped away from the table, but their hands were still together. She'd also taken her gloves off to eat, he noticed, and her skin was warm against his. She was very, very close—well within arm's reach.

She was short, but he was even shorter. He found himself leaning his head upwards and both of them started to move towards each other...

Then the floor exploded outwards—and Damien realized that Grace's office was right at the outer hull.

CHAPTER 16

EVERYTHING SEEMED to move in slow motion, with Damien's brain registering *everything*. First, the explosion was too neat, too perfect to be an accident. Someone had run a line of foam explosive around the exact outline of the office from the outside of the hull and detonated it one blast.

The entire floor of the office dropped into space, flung free by the centripetal force of the spinning ring. The furniture, the *air*, and Damien and Grace followed it. He could feel the air escaping, scattering into the surrounding void.

There was a time to be circumspect, to conceal power so your enemies underestimated you—and there was a time to *act*.

The Runes of Power inlaid into his flesh warmed against his flesh as he channeled energy. He didn't care about the furniture or the floor. He cared about Grace—and he cared about *oxygen*.

A ball of force slammed into place around them, rapidly contracting to catch the fleeing air and freezing as a sphere perhaps four meters across, half the size of the office itself. He pulsed energy gently against his shield, confirming that it would hold, and then brought up a tester on his computer.

"Point seven atmospheres," he said aloud. "We'll live."

A second command activated his emergency beacon as he looked out into the void around them. There wasn't much he could do about their momentum, and their explosive ejection from Ring One had flung them into space with the full force of the station's rotation.

"How did you...?" McLaughlin trailed off, her eyes wide as she looked at him. "We should be dead, Damien."

"Or shortly, if not yet," he agreed. There was no gravity. He could provide some, but the air bubble was a strain to maintain on its own. These days, his limit was more how *long* he could sustain a flow of magic, not how much he could channel.

"How?"

"Bubble of force, holding the air in."

"That's imp..." she started.

"Not easy," he corrected sharply. He could feel his breath growing shorter too, and his computer happily informed him they were already starting to run low on oxygen. "I don't have much energy to spare if I'm to sustain this for long," he continued. "But we are burning our oxygen fast. Can you scrub?"

Damien *saw* her magic flare, a sight only the handful of Rune Wrights in the galaxy could ever share, as she answered by doing. The carbon scrub spell was a simple one, taught to almost every Mage alive just in case they ended up in an enclosed space or on a spaceship where the filters broke.

A few moments after her energy began to mingle with his, the oxygen counter on his computer started ticking back up into safe zones.

"Thank you," he said softly.

"I was not anticipating this when I asked you to meet with me," Grace said frankly. "Someone just tried to kill us. Explosive decompression..." she shivered. "I guess it's a reliable way to kill a Mage. I would have thought it was a reliable way to kill a Hand. Damn it, Damien—you're a *weaker* Mage than me. How?"

"I *was* a weaker Mage," Damien told her gently. "Now I am a Hand." He hesitated and then sighed. "And that is all I am permitted to tell you."

The very existence of the Rune Wrights, the Mages who could read the true flow of magic instead of the crude script humanity had created to chain it, was classified. He was the only one who wasn't a direct descendant of the first Mage-King of Mars. Careful genetic engineering had kept the Gift active in that line, but the geneticists responsible for that engineering had practically salivated over the samples they'd got from Damien while he'd been at Olympus Mons.

"All you are *permitted* to tell me?" she repeated.

"Are you truly surprised that the Hands are privy to secrets we cannot share?" Damien asked. "We stand at the side of the Mage-King of Mars, Grace. I have seen things both wondrous and terrible that I cannot speak of."

"Fine," she said shortly. "So what happens now?"

"I can't move us without spending air I'd like to breathe," he said dryly. "So we wait. My emergency beacon is active, Julia will find us."

"SAR is my people's responsibility, not hers."

"Amiri is a Secret Service Agent responsible for the security of a Hand in danger," Damien replied. "Your people don't have jurisdiction."

"She's very dedicated," Grace said neutrally. "Are you and she...?"

It took Damien a long moment to realize just what his ex was asking.

"No," he finally replied with a laugh. "She's dating a politician on Ardennes—the man we're currently grooming to be the next Governor, though the election could theoretically go against him."

"Oh," Grace replied, suddenly seeming more relaxed. "Nobody, then?"

"Not since the *Blue Jay*," Damien admitted. He remembered having to say goodbye to Kelly far too vividly to risk anything else.

"Damn... wait, blonde named Kelly? Green eyes, legs out to *here*?" The gesture proved to be ill-advised without gravity and it took Grace a moment to arrest her spin.

"Yeah, why?"

"I almost took service on Captain Rice's new ship before Grandfather called me home," she told him. "We were in Tau Ceti as he was about to leave in the *Peregrine* and he was recruiting multiple Mages. I went home instead in the end, but not until after I'd met the officers. Kelly was asking questions about Sherwood, guess she must have been trying to find out if I knew you."

The thought of Kelly and Grace having extended discussions about him was... more nerve-wracking than it should have been to one of the Mage-King's top enforcers.

"Guess so," he admitted. "Been a while. You have anyone?"

The question came out before he could stop himself. He wasn't entirely sure, but he thought she'd been about to kiss him before the floor had exploded.

"Captain Wayne and I were, um, almost an item," she admitted softly. "Then I got promoted to Commodore. He still doesn't seem to get that the head of the Patrol can't be with a ship CO. It's been... enough of an issue for me to be glad nothing happened. Otherwise, nothing in years."

Damien nodded. The conversation helped to distract him from the fact that they were stranded, floating in the void with his magic their only protection.

He'd had better days.

Julia barged into the on-station command center without paying much attention to the pair of Patrol guards outside. Their protests died off as they spotted Gibbons following in her wake, and she stormed across the floor to the central command dais.

"What the *hell* is going on?" she snapped at the trio of Patrol officers standing there. "Where are the SAR shuttles? Why is everyone still just *sitting* here?"

"Who is this?" a sandy-blond man in a Captain's uniform demanded. "This is a secure facility."

"I am Special Agent Julia Amiri," Julia told him. "Now, are you going to tell me why no one is out looking for the Hand and the Commodore, or are you taking a rapid trip to the *Duke's* brig?"

"I am Captain Michael Wayne, and with the Commodore out of the picture, I am the acting commander of the Patrol," he replied. "Now that we've beaten our chests, why don't you get out of the way and let the professionals do their job? This is a murder investigation at this point, Agent. Attempting to retrieve the bodies risks running into traps laid by the attacker. We *will* retrieve them, but for now securing the safety of this station is more important than recovering my friend's body." His voice twisted with the last few words and he glared at Julia.

"You are making two incorrect assumptions here, Captain," Julia told him, *trying* to be polite as the Captain appeared more than a little upset. "Firstly, you are assuming that the assassination attempt *succeeded.*"

"The entire contents of Commodore McLaughlin's office and apartment were blasted into space, Agent," Wayne said gently. "No one, not even a Mage, could survive that."

"Damien Montgomery is no mere Mage," she snapped. "He is a *Hand*, Captain Wayne—underestimate him at your peril.

"Perhaps even more importantly, his emergency beacon was *manually* activated forty-eight seconds after the breach," she pointed out. "My Hand is alive, Captain Wayne. Which means that Commodore McLaughlin is almost certainly alive. Every second you waste risks that changing."

"I see," he said slowly, exhaling a deep breath. "I'll need to see that beacon, Agent," he said bluntly. "I want to believe you, but you're asking me to put people's lives at risk."

"I'm not asking, Captain, because your second assumption is that you are in charge here," Julia snapped, gesturing for Williams to join her. The Marine had quite sensibly refused to be disarmed, which Gibbons appeared to have backed her on as no one was injured.

"As a Protectorate Secret Service Agent whose principal is in danger, I am assuming full jurisdiction of this investigation and rescue effort," she said formally. "Check the Charter for my authority if you'd like, Captain, but first get me a shuttle."

He blinked at her, but the woman standing next to him, clad in a different dark blue uniform, shrugged at him.

"She's right, sir," the older woman replied. "With a Hand in danger, this is Protectorate jurisdiction."

"Then get her the damn shuttle," Wayne snapped at her, striding away to review some other aspect.

"I'll need your station sensors," Julia told the woman, realizing she finally had someone she could work with. "I have *no* idea how

Montgomery will have survived, and I'm losing the beacon *fast*. I'll feed your computers the code and frequency."

"Right here," the other woman told her, leading Julia to a computer console. "I'm Mirella Harrison, Section Chief of the Sherwood Security Service aboard Sherwood Orbital. If you've got a beacon for Montgomery, let's find him."

Once Wayne was out of the way and Harrison was on-side, it took less than ten minutes to have Julia in a shuttle with a pilot, Gibbons and Williams in tow. The big Patrol bodyguard had attached himself to her without a word, and had tagged along without allowing any discussion.

He'd done anything she asked instantly, but Julia suspected that *not* bringing the Sergeant along would require violence. In his place, well... she had just ripped one of the Patrol's Captains a new one for *trying* to put her in a similar place.

"We've got the beacon signal being relayed from Sherwood Prime and your cruiser," the pilot reported. "They are well away and gone, I don't know how they're still alive."

"Because people always underestimate Hands," Julia told him softly. "Take us out after them."

The pilot threw the beacon up on the screen as a flashing gold icon. The shuttle's computers happily filled in data—the beacon was moving at a little under a hundred meters per second, and after almost twenty minutes was over a hundred kilometers away from Sherwood Prime and heading for deep space.

"Captain Wayne's comments are making me twitchy, Agent," the pilot, a graying older man with red-flushed cheeks, admitted. "Are you rated on this weapon suite?"

The copilot's seat Julia had claimed also controlled the weapons. Julia tapped a few commands, bringing up the weapons listing. A single fifty millimeter high velocity railgun and a quartet of short-ranged chemical rockets. Not much of a suite, but she could make it work.

"I've used similar before," she replied.

"I requalified on our Mark Four six weeks ago," Gibbons rumbled. "You didn't even bring up the RFLAM. Let me do it."

A side-click revealed that, yes, the shuttle *did* have a Rapid Firing Laser Anti-Missile system. A sad little six barrelled hundred-megawatt system, but still a more potent defense than anything else the shuttle possessed.

Julia carefully pulled herself out of the seat against the shuttle's very gentle acceleration, gesturing for the big Patrol Sergeant to take her place.

"I know when I'm beat, Sergeant. Keep us alive."

"Wilco," he said crisply and belted himself in.

"All right," the pilot announced, "since we're on an unknown time limit, I'm going to close the gap as fast as I can and then slow down. Any idea what I'm looking for visually?"

"Not a clue," Julia replied cheerfully. "What I can tell you? The beacon hasn't changed, so he's still breathing."

"A living Dutchman without a suit," the pilot muttered. "That's just creepy, ma'am."

She let that go without comment, watching the distance and speed measures shift as the pilot swept them in towards the tiny radio beacon. Somehow, some way, her charge was still alive. She didn't know how long he would stay that way.

"Something on radar," Gibbons rumbled. "Looks like the hull came off in one big chunk."

"I see it," the pilot replied. "We're within five kays, slowing us down to take a look around."

"Don't stop!" the Patrol Sergeant snapped. "I have missiles on the scope!" He hit a command on the com channel as Julia desperately looked around. "*Duke of Magnificence,* this is Sherwood Prime Shuttle Seven. Vampire, vampire, vampire—we have incoming!"

The conversation had eventually died off. Even four years of missed history was hard to catch up on when you were floating in space, surrounded only by empty void. Damien could *see* Sherwood Prime—the station was a dozen kilometers long, it was hard to miss even at this distance—but that wasn't helping much.

Closer to them, Damien was watching the floating chunk of metal that *had* been the floor. It had been blasted clear of them by the explosives, but the added momentum from the blast was minimal compared to the angular velocity of a ring that provided a full gravity of centrifugal acceleration on a seven hundred meter radius.

The chunk of metal was large enough and close enough to be visible. It had been a piece of the outer hull as well, which meant it could well have useful supplies on the exterior of the fragment. He was studying it, trying to judge if he could safely bring it over to them, when the missiles launched.

The fragment of outer hull had apparently been booby-trapped with six single shot missile launchers. Damien had no way to judge what they were shooting at, or even what kind of missile they *were*, but he could guess why they were firing.

Someone was coming for him.

Splitting his attention was *hard*. He could feel the splitting headache he would have later start as he concentrated on holding the air bubble keeping them alive together—and *reached* out with his magic.

Lightning flashed in space as he struck out. Missile after missile exploded as electricity arced from one to the next. Circuits fired, explosives detonated, and five deadly weapons were rendered fragments and debris in seconds.

The sixth flew just far enough, just fast enough, to elude his attack. He could reach further than most Mages, but even relatively slow missiles were *fast*.

He watched it fly, praying... and then cheered aloud when it intersected a laser beam and exploded.

Moments later, cutting through the debris cloud, a shuttle emerged.

"Here they come," he told Grace. She'd been silent from the moment of the missile launch, and now was looking at him strangely. "What is it?" he asked.

"I'm still getting used to my college boyfriend being kind of scary," she admitted. "You saved my life. Thank you."

"Part of the job now," he told her. "Save everyone I can."

"Now *that* sounds like my Damien," Grace told him with a smile. With a tiny burst of magic, she was suddenly *very* close to him.

He kissed her before she could. For a moment, they hung in space and clung to each other, shocked just to have survived.

As the shuttle came closer, they slowly separated, and he returned her smile.

"Back to work," he murmured.

"When this is over, you *are* coming back to Sherwood," Grace ordered. "For now," she sighed. "You're right. Game faces on, my lord."

"No one saw that," Gibbons rumbled.

"No one else is close enough to have our level of mag," the pilot agreed swiftly. "Nobody else saw anything."

"You didn't follow the Sergeant," Julia said calmly, watching the couple on the cameras separate—shortly followed by the big Patrol noncom erasing the footage from the missile explosions to now. "*No one* saw that. Understand?"

The pilot's cheeks flushed even redder, but he smiled and nodded.

"Saw what, ma'am?" he asked, returning to his controls. "I've never made rendezvous with a force bubble in space before. What, exactly, should I do?"

"We're close enough for me to link to Damien directly now," Julia replied. Thousands of kilometers outside the satellite network that normally supplied the planetary data-net, and dozens away from the station with its repeaters, she'd had no way to do anything except track the emergency beacon for a while.

Tapping her wrist comp, she trained the shuttle's transmitters on the beacon and turned them on.

"Hand Montgomery, this is Agent Amiri, do you copy?"

A moment of silence, and she was afraid they still weren't close enough, and then the speakers crackled.

"This is Montgomery," her boss's voice announced. He sounded younger than usual, which could probably be chalked up to near-death and a missile attack followed up with what looked like a *very* thorough kiss. "I have Commodore McLaughlin with me. We are alive and unharmed. I'm guessing you're in the shuttle that ticked off those missiles?"

"We are. Thanks for the assist," she told him. "My pilot is wondering how the hell we're getting you out of that bubble."

"All he has to do is get close," Montgomery replied. "If he's within a hundred meters or so and near a velocity match we can jump right onboard."

"You got that?" she asked the pilot.

"Can do," he replied. "Sixty seconds, give or take." The older man shook his head. "This is going to be a story for the kids. Not that they'll believe me! Bubbles in space?"

Julia watched the distance to the beacon shrink. Five hundred meters. Three hundred meters. One hundred. Eighty.

Suddenly, the distance disappeared. The shuttle was *insisting* that Montgomery was aboard... and the bubble had just *vanished*, its contained atmosphere rapidly dissipating into the surrounding vacuum.

Gibbons and the pilot both gaped at the measure, wondering just what had happened.

Julia turned in her chair, glancing back into the main cargo compartment behind them. The Hand and the Commodore were floating in the middle of the compartment, already grabbing for straps.

"Take us back in, pilot," she ordered.

"But what?" the man turned and saw Montgomery flash him a thumbs up as the man grabbed a headset for the internal network. "How?"

"It amazes me," the Hand noted on the network, "how many people forget that Jump Mages are trained in personal teleportation long before we ever touch a ship. Jumping even a few kilometers back onto Sherwood Prime while moving would be a problem. Jumping a hundred meters into a shuttle with no relative velocity? Easy."

"Good to see you, my lord," Julia told him, shaking her head. "And you Commodore."

"Details will have to wait until we're back on the station," McLaughlin said, "but I formally offer the apologies of the Patrol for this. This attack should not have happened."

"A lot fewer people died than the last time someone tried to assassinate me," Montgomery noted, his voice grim. "I'd rather you caught the bastards than apologized."

"Believe me, my lord Hand, I intend to."

CHAPTER 17

A GOOD NIGHT'S SLEEP aboard her flagship had restored Grace's energy, if not necessarily her calm or equanimity. Montgomery appeared to have taken someone trying to kill him and most of an hour floating in deep space with enough calm to make her wonder about his new job, but both of those were new and unpleasant for her.

"What do we have on the bomb?" she demanded, looking around the meeting room. Captain Wayne and Section Chief Harrison were attending by viewscreen, as was her grandfather and the Sherwood System Security investigator who'd been coopted and shoved on a shuttle to orbit late last night.

"Not much yet," Inspector Javier Accord responded. "We are reviewing all access and exits through the station's airlocks over the last week, but while it is possible someone snuck the explosives through the station, there are only a handful of airlocks large enough to accommodate the missile pod used to trap the debris. The security records show no such device, so I suspect our search of the lock footage will be fruitless."

"Do we have *anything* helpful?" Grace demanded.

"I can't say yet," Accord replied. "We're investigating all maintenance flights, but..." he shrugged, and the screen showing him in his borrowed hotel conference room office split, a second image filling the other half.

Grace leaned in, studying the image. She recognized the exterior hull of one of Sherwood Prime's rings and looking closer she saw a strange box. A missile pod—of a type usually mounted to armored vehicles as an anti-aircraft weapon.

"Study of the image I'm showing you also shows the foam explosive to be in place," Accord noted. "This image is from an SSS cutter that happened to be sweeping the area with their optics. It's the most recent detailed image of that section of the hull we have." The Inspector shook his head grimly.

"It's forty-three days old," he finished simply. "The next most recent image we have is from the annual exterior maintenance review—three months ago. Since Sherwood Prime's maintenance staff aren't *idiots*, I'm unsurprised that image is clean."

Grace stared at the image, a chill settling over her. Someone had set up an assassination attempt on her over a *month* ago. The trigger had almost certainly been pulled to try to take out Montgomery, but the weapon had been put in place to kill *her*.

"That gives us a fifty day window in which the device could have been placed. I will continue to review the flights and investigate any that appear suspicious. I *do*," he stressed, "expect to find some answers with this route. However, some guesses or clarity as to motivation might help us narrow it down."

The Commodore sighed.

"Arrington, everyone, if you could please drop off the channel," she ordered. "I'll bring you back in a moment, but I think I need to discuss this with just Governor McLaughlin and Inspector Accord."

Her XO gave her a crisp salute and slipped silently out of the room. Section Chief Harrison looked... irritated, but cut the channel. Captain Wayne started to open his mouth but Grace cut him off with a hand gesture.

"We'll talk later, Michael," she promised him. "Be patient."

With a noncommittal grunt, Wayne cut the channel, leaving her with just her grandfather and the Inspector.

"Understand, Inspector, that I am classifying what I am about to tell you and my grandfather as Top Secret," she said grimly. "I am also, in effect, derailing your investigation. The matter is related, but you will tell *no one* of the new focus. Do you understand me, Inspector Accord?"

Both of the men on the viewscreen were staring at her, but Accord nodded firmly.

"Depending on what you need me to do, Commodore, I may need to inform my staff," he noted.

"Only as absolutely necessary, Inspector," she told him. "If this is leaked, we may lose the chance to stop an interstellar war."

Now she had their complete attention.

"Grandfather, Inspector Accord, I have the data records from the Mínglìàng Security Flotilla vessels that engaged what they believed to be one of our frigates," she said calmly. "I've only taken the most precursor of looks for obvious reasons, but... so far, I have no basis to disagree with Hand Montgomery's people's analysis.

"It's our ship," she said bluntly. "I'll forward you the footage and as much information on our vessels as I can, Inspector, but you can understand why I want an outside figure involved."

"You want me to investigate the possibility that one of our ships has gone rogue?" the Inspector asked. His tone was clarifying, not incredulous.

"I'm afraid that it may not be merely a possibility," she admitted. "It would explain a lot. Tying back to the assassination, I want you to focus on ships that," she sighed, "have some connection to the Patrol."

"Are you sure about this, Commodore?" her grandfather asked. "We both know you've attracted political opposition as well."

"The timeline doesn't work, Governor," Grace told him. "I've only been dismissing the strongly connected officers—like Grayson—in the last month or so. That device was in place for *two* months."

"I'd hoped we'd done better in selecting our commanders," her grandfather admitted. "But... I place my faith in your judgment, Grace. As I have done since I gave you that oak leaf."

"Thank you," she replied. "Do you have any immediate questions, Inspector Accord?"

"Not yet," he replied. "I will need to examine the data you've promised and fit this possibility into my mental matrices. I will be in touch," he promised.

"Thank you, Inspector."

"Captain Wayne," Grace greeted her senior subordinate as she reopened the channel to his ship. Accord was now busily devouring the data she'd sent and her grandfather had been consumed by the many demands of his job. It was probably better she have this conversation without them, anyway.

"Grace. It's good to see that you're all right," he replied, his eyes soft in a way that would normally make her uncomfortable. Today... today she was just pissed.

"No thanks to you, as it turns out," she told him bluntly. "So you're aware, Section Chief Harrison will be filing a formal complaint about your behavior—not, to be clear, your refusal to assist Agent Amiri, but in your seizure of command aboard the station on specious grounds."

"For all we knew, the entire station was at risk," he replied. "I had to act quickly!"

"No. Section Chief Harrison had to act quickly," Grace pointed out. "You interrupted their safety procedures and assumed command authority on a basis that Chief Harrison couldn't validate or deny at the time— but that *you* bloody well knew was bullshit."

"I thought you were *dead*," he whispered, turning his face away from the camera. "There was *no* way you could have survived that. I... dammit, Grace, you know how I feel about you! I couldn't leave finding your killers to anyone else!"

"So you let your emotions compromise your judgment—*and* the safety and search efforts of those responsible for securing the station?" she snapped. "Then you stonewalled a *Protectorate Secret Service Agent* until she had to pull rank because you wouldn't cooperate?"

"So far as I knew, you were dead," Wayne repeated. "And it seemed likely that if it was an attack, there would be booby traps—like the one they *did* trigger. We needed to secure the station and *cautiously* go looking for you—so that we weren't risking lives to find bodies."

He looked up, meeting her gaze at last, and his eyes were red.

"I fucked up, Grace," he admitted. "I'll take the hammering for it— Chief Harrison and Agent Amiri are right to lodge complaints. I should have recognized that my emotions were in the way... but dammit, I've been burying them for months. You can't keep *doing* this to me."

"*I* am not doing anything, *Captain* Wayne," she said shortly. "You've continued to push the boundaries of what is acceptable as a subordinate for months, and now your feelings are interfering with your ability to do your job.

"So tell me, Captain, should I be considering relieving you? The Defender Yards could use someone who's held command of a *Hunter* as they design the *Valiant*-class for Phase Three. It would be a role that does not require interaction with me, which seems to be a problem for you."

He broke away from her gaze, staring down at the desk of his office, and then took a deep breath and looked back up.

"I take your point, Commodore," he said slowly, granting her the title in private for the first time in a while. "You will not need to relieve me. I will do my job."

"Good," she said gently. "But realize, Captain, that this is the final warning I can offer. Those complaints *will* go in your record, and if you try to presume on our *friendship* or allow yourself to be emotionally compromised by your 'feelings', you *will* be riding a desk so fast you'll be looking for the plate of the freight truck that ran you over.

"You follow me, Captain?"

"Yes, ma'am."

CHAPTER 18

IT WAS VERY QUIET in Damien's office as he watched Sherwood Prime. The rings rotated fast enough that even if he'd been close enough he wouldn't have been able to see the hole in Ring One, but he knew it was there.

"You know, my job would be a lot easier if people tried to attack you directly," Amiri observed behind him. The ex-bounty hunter still moved quietly enough to sneak up on him, to the point he was almost used to it.

Almost wasn't enough to prevent him from jumping as she spoke, and he turned to face her.

"Instead of freely engaging in collateral damage?" he asked softly. "Yesterday could easily have killed dozens—if the SAR shuttle that had found those missiles had been unarmed, what would have happened?"

"The door to the Commodore's office had a properly working emergency seal," Amiri pointed out. "No one outside that office was at risk. You're right about the missiles, though," she winced. "I commandeered a Security vehicle—we'd *probably* have been fine without your intervention. A civilian ship... would have died."

"I'm getting very, very tired of people dying around me while I do this job," he told her. "Feels like my showing up paints a target on everyone."

"Yes, because the assassination device that has apparently been in place for over a month is somehow your fault," Amiri pointed out. They'd been briefed on that tidbit earlier. "And the pirates, obviously, have somehow stepped up their attacks because you're here. Goddamnit Damien, you are not responsible for *everything*."

He gave her half a smile. She wasn't wrong, though it didn't feel like it every day.

"Almost five thousand people dead, Julia," he half-whispered. "*Dozens of freighters destroyed, at least three warships*—two of which we killed *ourselves*. This whole region is going to hell in a handbasket, and I feel like the straws I'm grasping at are lighting themselves on fire as I touch them."

He needed to get back to Mínglìàng—but he also needed to know what Renzetti had found out from Tau Ceti. Without that data, he could be walking into a nest of vipers.

Of course, he wasn't sure he wasn't *already* in a nest of vipers in Sherwood. He was reasonably sure he could trust Grace and probably even her grandfather, but that raised the possibility that they were not as in control as they thought they were.

"My job is just to keep you alive," Amiri pointed out. She grabbed a chair and pulled it up next to him, looking out the window. "Of course, that's easier if you *don't* have a death wish."

"I do *not* have a death wish," Damien argued. "The death rate *around* me, though..."

"Is a function of your job," she interrupted. "His Majesty doesn't send Hands into minor conflicts or personal arguments. He sends Hands when entire worlds are at risk. So the odds of you being somewhere where people aren't dying, sick, or desperately in need are pretty damn low unless you're on vacation."

He started to object, but she drove right over him.

"You can't save *everyone* Damien," she reminded him. "But you *can* stop the violence. Which means you need to stop beating yourself up over what *has* happened and start looking at what you can *make* happen."

Damien raised one hand in the ancient touché symbol.

"I'm keeping my eyes open," he promised her. "For now, I'm waiting on Renzetti. He should be here inside of two days, hopefully that will give me a crack I can wedge open."

"What will you do if Wong really has bought warships?"

"It depends on what he's doing with them," he replied. Further discussion was interrupted by an alarm triggering on his wrist computer. "This is Montgomery," he answered crisply.

"My lord, we need you on the bridge immediately."

Damien emerged onto the bridge of the *Duke of Magnificence* with Julia a few steps behind him. The often hectic beating heart of the ship was quiet... anticipatory. There was no chaos, but he could see and feel every eye in the room on him as he crossed to the center platform where the Simulacrum hung and Captain Jakab waited for him.

"Mage-Captain," he greeted Jakab. "What's so urgent?"

"Not urgent, perhaps, my lord," he said calmly, "but important." He gestured and one of the many icons on the screens showing the star system outside the *Duke*'s hull highlighted and zoomed in. It turned out to be a container ship, a three-megaton four-rotator-type—a *Venice*-class identical to the one Damien had left the system in.

"This is the jump freighter *Tsunami Dawn*," Jakab explained. "She just arrived from the Antonius System. Like a lot of bulk ships, she's only got one Mage aboard so the trip took her almost three days."

"I'm not seeing the urgency, Captain," Damien noted, studying the ship.

"The issue, my lord, is that the jump freighter *Mistletoe Solstice* left Antonius twenty-four hours before she did, with two Mages aboard," the Mage-Captain explained. "She has not arrived, and the *Tsunami Dawn* saw no sign of her in transit."

Damien studied the ship, remembering the level of sensors the *Blue Jay* had years before. It was unlikely *Tsunami Dawn* had a better suite, which meant she could miss quite a bit... but not an operating freighter or an emergency beacon.

"Overdue, missing, presumed lost," he murmured.

"Exactly, my lord. What do you want us to do?"

"What is the Patrol's normal response?" he asked.

"They'd sent a frigate back along the route looking for the lost ship," Jakab explained. "We'd do the same, with a destroyer to be fair, if we were running system security. Of course, with the restrictions we've imposed..."

"They can't finish the route," Damien agreed. "How long would it take us to sweep to Antonius and back?"

"Sixteen hours there, sixteen hours back," the *Duke*'s Captain replied instantly. Damien did the math in his head himself and nodded. Eight hours between jumps per Mage and four Mages allowed them to move twelve light years a day, compared to the Patrol ships that only carried two Mages and could only travel six.

"Get me Commodore McLaughlin," he ordered. A com tech leapt to obey, and he waited calmly until the channel opened.

"Montgomery," she greeted him crisply, no trace of the kiss they'd shared in deep space marring her voice or expression. A part of him—a *silly* part of him—resented that. But... that was how it had to be.

"Commodore," he replied. "My crew just updated me on the *Mistletoe Solstice*'s status."

"We will need to send a ship to investigate," she told him. "I formally request permission for one vessel to exceed the three light year limit."

"I understand." Damien said as he considered the time. Renzetti wasn't due for at least forty hours, which meant the *Duke* could make the run to Antonius and back well before the courier returned—presuming their far more powerful sensors couldn't find the missing ship.

"Given the tensions, and the continued issues, I have to deny your request," he told Grace. Her eyes flashed, and he raised his hand to cut off her speech before it began. "I *will*, however, take the *Duke of Magnificence* out myself. Someone has to investigate, and we're in the best position to do so."

He saw Grace swallow her words and consider the situation.

"I suppose that makes sense," she said slowly. Tapping a command, she brought up some sort of screen that she studied for a long moment, then turned back to Damien.

"I would request that you take one of our frigates with you out to the three light year line," she finally asked. "I'm aware that will slow you down, but I would be abdicating my responsibility were I to leave this entirely to you."

"Very well," Damien allowed after a quick glance at Mage-Captain Jakab. "We will be leaving shortly. Will your vessel be prepared in time?"

"I will confer with Captain Wayne immediately," she promised. "Both the *Maid Marian* and the *Robin Hood* are permanently assigned to Sherwood orbit. The *Alan-a-dale* should be replenished and ready to go."

"Have Captain Wayne talk to Captain Jakab once he knows how long he'll need," Damien told her. "We'll find your people, Commodore McLaughlin—one way or another."

The screen Grace was looking at was the replenishment status of the *Alan-a-dale*. She was currently orbiting just behind Sherwood Prime, being serviced by shuttles. She tapped a command, raising her dockmaster.

"Commander Law, I need you to accelerate the replenishment of the *Alan-a-dale*," she ordered.

"Yes, ma'am. How long?"

"I want her to ready to fly in an hour," she replied, watching the older man on her screen swallow, then nod.

"I can make it happen, sir," he confirmed. "Add it to the list of my miracles for review when my performance evaluation comes up."

"I suspect your eval will be fine, Commander," she told him. "Thank you."

With a textbook-perfect salute, the dockmaster signed off. With a sigh, she steeled herself for what was coming next and told her system to connect to Wayne.

"Grace!" he greeted her cheerfully, as if the earlier conversation hadn't happened. Her flat look in response depressed his cheer. He swallowed, hard, then corrected himself. "Commodore McLaughlin. How can I assist?"

"I'm assuming you got the brief on the *Mistletoe Solstice?*"

"Yes, Commodore," he said slowly. "I presume the *Maid Marian* will be checking it out?"

"No, Captain Wayne," she told him. "The *Duke of Magnificence* will be. We are, in case you weren't paying attention, restricted to a three light year operating radius."

"That's bullshit!" he snapped. "We have to do our jobs!"

"And our job technically doesn't exist in the Charter, which means the Hand gets to write the rules however he wants," Grace pointed out. "The Protectorate's founders didn't envision organizations like the Patrol, Captain. We weren't supposed to be necessary."

"Well, we are, and putting stupid restrictions on us won't help!"

"I hope you can control your opinions better when dealing directly with Hand Montgomery, Captain," the Commodore replied coldly. "I'm assigning the *Alan-a-dale* to accompany the *Duke of Magnificence* to the three light year limit. If you find something inside the three light year limit, you will assist Hand Montgomery's people in their investigation, and have one of your officers return to Sherwood aboard the *Duke* to hand-deliver your assessment of the situation."

"And what will I be doing while this courier is coming home?" Wayne asked.

"Regardless of whether you find the *Mistletoe Solstice* inside the three light year limit, you will then proceed to patrol *all* Sherwood Jump Three zones," she ordered. "I want to be certain no other vessel is in danger."

"That will take... days," he replied.

"It seems to me, Captain Wayne, that you need some time away from Sherwood to cool down," Grace told him sweetly. "Accompany Hand Montgomery on his investigation as long as he'll let you, then sweep our outer perimeter. In all honesty, Captain, I am worried that our enemy seems to know our shipping patterns far too well. I want you looking for spy platforms and similar threats. We owe the people coming to Sherwood that much peace of mind."

Wayne looked mutinous but slowly nodded.

"Very well, Commodore," he accepted. "I'll take my dose of medicine. I know I earned it. I'll coordinate with Law and Jakab, and we should be on our way shortly."

CHAPTER 19

MAGE-CAPTAIN KOLE JAKAB watched the stars around the *Duke of Magnificence* in silence, waiting for the response he was expecting from his crew. After two hours in the void of Antonius-Sherwood Jump Seven, his practiced eye had caught none of the signs he would have expected from a destroyed ship, and his crews hadn't said anything at all to suggest their scanners had found anything either.

"Jump Seven is clear," Commander Rhine finally said from behind him. "There's no engine trail or anything to suggest the *Mistletoe Solstice* even made it this far. The only signature in the last three days is consistent with the *Tsunami Dawn*."

"Understood," Kole replied. "And our Sherwood friend?"

"*Alan-a-dale* is sticking right with us, ten thousand kilometers off our starboard flank," his tactical officer replied instantly. "Given everything going on, having a Patrol ship that close to us is making my shoulder-blades itch."

"Sherwood or Mínglìang, I feel like both are measuring us for a target," Kole admitted. "No update to their jump schedule?"

"Nothing," Rhine confirmed. "We jump again in one hour, fifty-three minutes."

"All right. Keep an eye on our friend over there," he ordered. "If he does anything funny, I want to know about it before Captain Wayne does."

"Yes, sir."

The void of space looked much the same everywhere.

If Damien wanted, his computer could easily highlight specific stars and constellations and show him how Antonius-Sherwood Jump Seven differed from the hundreds of other jump zones he'd seen over the years, but that wouldn't change what the human eye saw.

Or what the human mind knew.

He'd never visited this specific jump zone before, but his first ship, the *Blue Jay*, had entered Sherwood via Antonius. Here, one light year short of their destination, they'd been jumped by pirates and nearly killed.

Here, Governor Miles James McLaughlin had lost his youngest son saving that ship from those pirates—pirates one Damien Montgomery had later killed.

There was no way, looking at the void of space around him, to know exactly where the *Blue Jay* had been. Any energy signatures of that years-ago attack were, well, light years away. It seemed... oddly right that the man trying to stop the Sherwood Interstellar Patrol from going to war would visit the location of the events that had created the Patrol.

"Sir, the *Alan-a-dale* reports ready to jump," Commander Rhine reported from the bridge. "Your orders?"

"There's nothing for us here, Commander," Damien replied. "You may jump when ready."

"We've got something," Commander Rhine reported.

Kole crossed to the tactical console. Jump Six had been as empty as Jump Seven, but he'd wondered if Jump Five would be more productive. It raised interesting questions, though, if the attack had taken place *exactly* as far away as Hand Montgomery's orders had restricted the Patrol.

"What do you have?" he asked.

"Look here, and here," the dark-haired tactical officer pointed out. He was highlighting curved sections of space, the outer segments of a dissipating sphere. "That's titanium mist. Thousands of tiny droplets, in a pattern consistent with vaporized titanium solidifying in a vacuum."

"So the *Mistletoe Solstice* was destroyed?" Kole said softly, eyeing the innocuous looking spectrometer results.

"Possible, but I can't be sure," his subordinate admitted. "It's hard to get a vector on a cloud like this, but the odds are we have a complete sphere or close to. My team is hunting for more sections of it, but after several days the zone could be huge."

"Sir, we've got something," Lieutenant Carver interrupted. "Two more mist clouds, one looks like the main debris plume."

"Show me," Kole ordered.

The young redhead flipped what he was looking at onto the screen Rhine and Kole were looking at. Instantly, the Mage-Captain could see Carver's point. One of the mist clouds was a little smaller than the first two—they'd been lucky to pick it up at all—and matched the curve set by those two.

The last was in the middle of the clouds and was larger than the other three by an order of magnitude. Studying the patterns, Kole could see that the other three clouds had spread away from the main plume.

"The main plume is also showing oxygen, hydrogen, carbon..." Carver shrugged. "I'd say we're looking at a major, *major*, breach—possibly the destruction of the ship's entire engine section—but not the destruction of the vessel."

"The numbers agree with him," Rhine confirmed his subordinate's hunch immediately. "If what we've detected is as much of the mass as I would expect... we're looking at a high energy laser straight into their engine section."

"So the *Solstice* is probably still out there?"

"There's no telling what happened to her *after* she lost her engines," the tactical officer pointed out. "But we should be able to back track these clouds and get a zone for closer inspection."

"Do it," Kole ordered. "As soon as you've got a sweep zone, pass it on to the *Alan-a-dale* and get us underway."

Rhine corralled his analysts with a gesture and starting setting to work, while Kole returned to the center podium, eyeing the empty void around his ship.

Somehow, knowing this nondescript section of space was where the *Mistletoe Solstice* had died made it feel that much more threatening.

"We've found her, my lord."

Jakab's quiet words interrupted Damien's review of the data Sherwood had provided on the Antonius System's recent issues with claim-jumping. About the only conclusion he'd reached so far was that the Sherwood data was completely one-sided, and that he needed Mínglìàng's data of claim-jumping by *Sherwood* miners for comparison.

"The *Mistletoe Solstice*?" he asked. It was unlikely they'd found any-thing *else*, but details could be important.

"Yes," Jakab confirmed. "The *Alan-a-dale* found her, actually," he ad-mitted. "We tracked the debris plume to the impact site, but she'd clearly been underway when she was damaged." The Mage-Captain shook his head on the video screen.

"She's been shot up bad," he continued, throwing an image of the freighter on Damien's screen. "All of her cargo pods are missing, and she'd been set on a vector that would take her a *long* way away from the jump zone."

"Any life signs?" Damien asked quietly.

"None. We don't think she even has atmosphere, and there are no power or electrical signatures either," Jakab said softly. "She's completely dead."

Damien studied the ship. The freighter had been a big ship, an eight-megaton, five-rotator design almost two kilometers long. The en-gines were gone. In fact, the entire rear section of the ship where the rotators would have converged on them was missing. All the rotating ribs showed the torque and blast damage inevitable from that hit.

A command to his computer brought up a bit more information, and he sighed.

"Sherwood registry. Two hundred and fourteen crew," he said aloud. "Are we able to tow her home?"

"We should be," the Mage-Captain confirmed. "I'll want to send a team over to make sure she's safe before we get too close."

"Of course," Damien agreed. "As I understand, you have a full forensics team aboard, correct?"

"From the PSS, yes. I take it you want to send them over as well?"

"I need to know what killed that ship, Mage-Captain. I'll talk to Agent Amiri. Get your boarding team prepped, and her people will come along for the ride."

"Yes, my lord."

The Mage-Captain's video screen closed, and Damien looked past it to the empty stars around the ship. His window, linked to the ship's computers, was automatically highlighting the one tiny light that was all he could see of the ten thousand kilometer distant *Alan-a-dale*, but otherwise all he saw was empty sky.

He hit a command, linking to Amiri's private com.

"Julia, can you come in please?"

The door to his office slid open almost instantly, and he shook his head at his bodyguard as she entered the observation deck and crossed over to him.

"This ship has hundreds of Marines, even if we ignore the entire detail of Secret Service agents you brought with you," he said mildly. "Why are you standing outside my door?"

"I do my best thinking standing," Amiri replied. "May as well stand someplace that helps me keep an eye on you. What do you need?"

"Jakab found the *Mistletoe Solstice*," he told her. "She's dead in the water, badly damaged. No survivors, no life signs, no energy signatures. He's taking a team over, and I want him to borrow the forensics people the PSS assigned you."

"That's what that team is for," she agreed. "I'll have them suit up and we'll join Jakab's team in fifteen."

"'We', Agent?" Damien asked with an arched eyebrow. "If this is a trap, Julia, I don't want you caught in it."

"If this is a trap, my lord, I don't want my *people* caught in it," she replied. "I'm better at spotting and evading traps than Jakab's Marines, let alone a bunch of tech and bio geeks I barely trust to put a space-suit on right!

"And," she continued with a familiar grin, "you did just point out that I'm redundant guarding your door."

"I could use direct eyes on the scene," Damien conceded, recognizing that he wasn't going to win the fight without pulling rank hard. "Fine, Julia. But be careful—I want you, your geeks, and Jakab's Marines back in the same number of pieces you leave in."

"Please, Damien—bringing people back alive used to be my *specialty*."

"Yes, but then you were allowed to tie them up," he pointed out. "Just... be careful."

CHAPTER 20

THE SERGEANT in charge of the Marine squad assembling in the *Duke of Magnificence*'s shuttle bay wasn't familiar to Julia. She gave him a wave that *almost* approximated a salute as she and her four forensics techs entered the cavernous space.

He, in turn, snapped a parade ground-perfect salute, marred only slightly by the fact that he was wearing the bottom half of an exosuit. His squad were already mostly in their gear, locking on helmets and picking up the over-sized weapons they would carry in this kind of boarding action.

The Marines *dwarfed* Amiri and the other Secret Service agents, who were clad in skin-tight regular space-suits. Of course, the Secret Service version of those suits was as well armored as any un-powered armor the Marine Corps issued.

"Sergeant Mark Garroway," he introduced himself. "Hunter Squad. We're your tour guides on this lovely safari the Protectorate is sending us on today."

As he spoke he continued to settle the bulky pieces of his armor around himself and latch them into place. When he finished, he picked up the big helmet and locked it on over his head.

"Check gear," he ordered his men. The faceless helmet rotated to-wards Julia. "Your crew need any help?"

"The Secret Service trains them well," she replied. "And I checked them all before I let them come anywhere near your boys. This 'safari' is almost certainly going to be morgue detail, you know."

"I know," he agreed, and she started as she realized he'd switched to a direct com link between their helmets. "And your agents know. And my Marines know. And they'll deal with it when we face it, but Horned One knows, I'm not inclined to rub their faces in it."

"I can respect that," she agreed. "Got a shuttle picked out for us?" she asked aloud.

"Delta-Two," he confirmed, gesturing to the nearest of the *Duke*'s assault shuttles. The deadly looking spacecraft could easily carry the seventeen people in Garroway's squad and her team, and packed enough firepower to make a big enough hole to extract them if needed. "The Navy has even promised a ride *back* this time."

"Then let's get going," Julia suggested. "We wouldn't want them to change their minds."

The faceless helmet couldn't nod, but she got the impression of the gesture anyway as Garroway turned away from her and started corralling his twelve man squad aboard the shuttle. The exosuits were, hopefully, overkill.

But if they ended up needing them, she'd be glad to have them!

"On final approach to *Mistletoe Solstice*," the shuttle pilot reported. "Main docking bay is just plain *gone*, folks, I'm going to bring you in as close to the wreckage of the keel as possible and extend a tube, but you may still need to jump."

"Understood," Garroway replied crisply. "Squad, you heard the man, be ready to rock-and-roll!"

Focusing on her own team, Julia gave their suits a quick visual checkover. For all that her four Agents were trained with the mini-rocket carbines they were carrying, this team were mostly forensics and computer techs—and most of their load was the technical gear for that trade.

"Watch your suits when we make the transfer," she instructed them. "The wreckage is going to be a mess and cutting your suit open twenty thousand kay from the *Duke* will suck. Your armor *should* protect you, but I need you finding out what happened here, not stuck in an emergency bubble needing to be towed home."

That got chuckles, but also serious double checking of the straps securing gear and weapons. Only one of the four was on their first boarding ever, though she didn't think any of them had seen anything as bad as what she was expecting.

"All right people," the pilot announced. "We are locked in place twenty meters back from what's left of the keel. I can't get any closer without risking the bird. Give me a second to run the tube out and..." He paused. A moment later, he spoke again, with triumph in his voice.

"All right, we got the tube almost all the way in. Just a meter or so gap, but mind the sharp and pointy bits."

"Marines first, ma'am," Garroway promptly told Julia, gesturing his squad forward.

"Semper fi!" the first exosuited soldier bellowed on the group channel and launched off. The shuttle had no gravity; everyone had been held into their seats with straps. A 'gentle' push from the powered suit of armor sent the man cannonballing out the inflated tube.

For all the apparent idiocy of the movement, the Marine was also using his exosuit's jets to control and direct his movement, and was inside the freighter in moments. The rest of his squad was only moments behind him.

Julia, for her part, waited for the giant metal men and women to lead the way into the wreck, then followed at a more sedate pace. Her suit had similar maneuverability to theirs, but it lacked the centimeter-thick armor.

A sigh echoed over her private channel with Garroway as she cleared the shuttle and started down the tube. "Your boys are going to need to break out DNA kits," he told her. "Looks like we weren't the first to come in this way."

Drifting into the main corridor running down the keel, Julia immediately saw what he meant. A massive containment door had cut off the back half of the ship when it had been blasted off, and anyone outside that door had been dead either when it closed or moments later.

GLYNN STEWART

Now, there was a hole blasted clean through that door, and suited bodies visibly floated in the microgravity of the dead ship, catching the lights of the Marine's helmets.

"Check it out," she ordered her team, assessing the situation as she jetted herself closer to where the Marines were cutting the door open to allow space for their suits. Someone had tried to make a stand here; all of the space-suited figures held weapons of some kind.

The walls were pockmarked with bullet holes where the defenders and attackers had traded fire, but if any of the attackers had gone down they'd taken the bodies with them.

"Tagging the bodies for retrieval," her bio tech told her. "I've got DNA samples so we can run IDs on *Duke*. If you," the tech gestured to the Marines, "want to *gently* get them against the wall, it'll make everyone's job easier."

Exosuits were massive layers of armor, machinery and powered motors laid over a human body, as much piloted as worn. They had the power to rip through walls and break men in half.

They also had the precision and care to allow the Marines to carefully and respectfully move the dead crewmembers of the *Mistletoe Solstice* against one of the walls, out of the way but easily retrievable by the morgue detail.

"Let's get to the bridge," Julia ordered. "Most likely our answers—and any traps—are there."

The journey down the length of the ship was a tortuous affair as the containment doors located every fifty meters had all slammed shut. Each had a hole blasted into it to enable the boarders to continue, though only a handful of holes were large enough for the Marine exosuits.

Once they'd passed the first door, they didn't encounter any sign of anyone for easily half the ship. The only light in the shadowy hall was from their hand and helmet lights, and the lack of air suppressed any sound.

Halfway through the ship, they found the first sign of a fight since the initial entryway. At the middle of the keel was the spherical simulacrum chamber where the two Ship's Mages would have jumped the starship—and at least one Mage had made her stand in the corridors outside it.

The containment door just short of the simulacrum chamber had been exploded outwards, and Julia winced as she envisaged the debris that would have gone scything through the boarding party when the explosives involved had triggered.

Scorch and blast marks covered the walls, the distinctive signs to her eyes of a Mage going all out with nothing to lose. Again, any of the attacker's bodies had been removed, but the Secret Service Agent could guess that easily dozens of men had died here.

It hadn't saved anyone. The Marines jetted forward, securing the section and sweeping it with their more powerful lights, and her bio techs checked over the bodies. It was hard to say which had been the Mage... for that matter, it was hard to say how *many* bodies there were.

The attackers had gone for overkill, and from the state of the bodies had brought up multiple fully automatic grenade launchers. Whoever they were, they hadn't been trying to take prisoners. The defenders had to have been in suits to be alive, but the mess of parts made it impossible to tell.

"Tag the pile and leave them," she ordered her people, swallowing hard. "We can identify the dead later, I need to know what happened here now."

Even through space-suits, she could see her people's urge to rebel and disobey, but after a moment she got sharp nods.

"Take us forward, Garroway," she instructed.

The *Mistletoe Solstice*'s crew had made a final stand in front of the bridge. There hadn't been many of them left, with most of the crew trapped or killed on the rotators and in engineering, but they'd done the best they could.

The attackers had kept the grenade launchers they'd used against the Mage mid-ships, and the results had been no prettier here. It would take Julia's techs hours to sort through the debris, identifying bodies.

Someone had been in a rush by the time the boarding had reached here and the vicious slaughter showed it. The crude barricades the crew had assembled had been shoved aside, the bodies callously crushed beneath debris as the attackers had proceeded to use explosives to blast open the bridge security door.

The bridge, a separate section from the simulacrum chamber on a civilian ship like this, hadn't survived the explosives or the following attack well. Several of the consoles had been shattered by debris, and gunfire had ruined more. The captain's chair was a wreck, riddled with bullets and targeted by at least one grenade.

The captain, however, had apparently survived the attack. A figure, clad in a space-suit of slightly but noticeably higher quality than the rest of the crew, floated in the middle of the bridge. His hands had been tied together, and the cable then attached to the remnants of his chair.

At some point, presumably *after* tying him up, someone had cut a series of slashes in the suit. The suit was of high enough quality to independently seal sections, which had kept the captain alive as sections of his body were exposed to vacuum.

Julia jetted over to him, examining him. The figure turned in the microgravity as she touched it, rotating to show her the shattered ruin of the face of an older black man. A single bullet had been fired through the faceplate and his forehead at point blank range.

"Whatever they wanted from him, I don't think they got it," she said softly.

"What makes you say that?" Garroway asked, the Marine carefully locking himself to the deck next to her. "Looks like they tortured him for info and then shot him in the head."

"Simple—he was *grinning*," Julia replied, gesturing to the permanently frozen expression on the freighter captain's face. "Who was he?" she snapped to her staff.

"Captain Tendai Afolayan," one of the bio techs replied, tagging the captain's body and taking a blood sample. "Sherwood native, owner-operator of the *Mistletoe Solstice* for ten years. Two of the ship's officers were his kids, and one of the Mages was his granddaughter, a Mage by Right."

"Damn, he must have been happy when she tested for the Gift," Julia said softly. A family of merchant officers and a family ship—a Mage in the family must have seemed a godsend.

"He paid for her to study on Mars," the tech confirmed, skimming through the data on her faceplate projection. "She only joined the ship six months ago, was the junior Ship's Mage."

"And we found *her* at the Simulacrum chamber," the senior agent concluded grimly, glancing over at the faceless suit of the Marine squad leader. Exosuits didn't transmit much body language, but they did a surprisingly good job with homicidal rage.

"Thoughts, Sergeant?" she asked on their private channel, hoping to bring him back to ground.

"This doesn't look like pirates," he ground out. "Afolayan's people fought like demons. The bastards took their dead with them, but I'd be surprised if they didn't lose fifty or sixty guys getting this far. Pirates wouldn't take those losses—once the ship was disabled they could detach the cargo and leave. Why didn't they?"

"Do we know what she was carrying?" Julia asked, glancing back at the same tech. She was still examining Afolayan, while the other bio tech was checking on the other bodies in the room and the two computer techs poked at the consoles to see if anything was intact enough to try to pull data from.

"Just ore from Antonius," she reported. "Platinum, titanium, gold, uranium... hundred million or so in high content rock. All of which is gone, but..."

"Nothing in that which would require them to board the ship at all," she concluded. "If they just wanted to be sure everybody died, a few more blasts with the laser that vaporized the back of the ship would do it. Why board it at all?"

GLYNN STEWART

"Ma'am, the black box is gone," the senior of her computer techs interrupted to report. He was floating at the rear of the bridge, inspecting an access panel. "Someone physically ripped it out and took it with them."

"So, they disabled the ship instead of killing her completely," Julia noted. "They stole her cargo, and then they boarded her to remove the black box. It's... like they *wanted* us to find her, and to have no idea who killed her."

"We're being taunted," Garroway growled. "Someone is trying to provoke a reaction... quite possibly, a *Protectorate* reaction."

"Agreed. But why torture Captain Afolayan?"

"I... think I may know the answer to that, ma'am," the Secret Service Agent checking over the black box container told her. "If you can come take a look?"

Activating her suit jets, Julia softly drifted over to him. A moment later, even more carefully, Sergeant Garroway followed.

"What is it, Banes?" she asked.

He tapped the loose wires in the compartment.

"These connectors here," he touched a set along the 'top' of the empty space, "are pretty standard. They're feeding from the ship's sensors, cameras, you name it. It's a high quality box, most wouldn't be including the ship's internal sensors, but this guy did. Expensive, unusual, paranoid."

"With my kids and grand-kids, I'd be paranoid too," Julia told him. "Doesn't help us."

"No, but, speaking of paranoid, this might," Banes replied, and grabbed a second set of wires. "*This* is a high-density data transfer cable—an *outgoing* data transfer cable. Captain Afolayan had a *backup* of his black box."

"Any idea where?"

"No," the agent replied, and glanced over at the captain's body. "And unless I miss my guess, Captain Afolayan *died* rather than tell his attackers where he kept it, so they couldn't find it either."

"All right," Julia said, clasping her hands together and looking at her team of Marines and Secret Service forensics techs. "I guess that means it's scavenger hunt time, doesn't it?"

158

CHAPTER 21

"SO THAT'S about it," Amiri told Damien over the radio. "There's a backup black box somewhere on this ship, and the folks boarding it were determined enough to destroy the evidence that they tortured the captain for its location."

"Isn't it likely they found it, then?" he asked. The Hand was back on the bridge, standing next to Mage-Captain Jakab as they reviewed the data feeds from the Marines and Secret Service agents. The mess in the middle of the ship gave him shivers—though it seemed to hit Jakab harder. Unlike his ship's captain, Damien had seen worse.

"We can't be sure," the Agent admitted. "My comp techs are going over what they can extract of the ship's files, and it looks like we *may* be able to retrieve some of the sensor and camera data, but if we can find the backup box it could save us days."

"You'll need more people to search the entire ship," Jakab noted. "I can have my Bosun pull together sweep teams from our engineering crews. We can probably sweep what's left of that hulk in a day, combine it with the morgue detail."

Damien considered it for a moment. If there was data aboard the *Mistletoe Solstice* about her killers, they needed it. On the other hand...

"Do we have any idea why they *didn't* just destroy her?" he asked. "If they wanted to be sure she couldn't identify her attackers, why not just blast her to pieces?"

"The black box is designed to survive that," the *Duke*'s captain noted. "Physically removing it and setting the hulk on a course away from the main zone could easily make it harder to identify it. And if his backup is a true copy of the box..."

"They might have figured it would be harder to detect its beacon when it was buried in the hulk," Amiri pointed out. "They'd have had to vaporize every last piece of her—doable, but time-consuming and more noticeable to anyone passing by."

"It still feels like someone is playing with us," Damien replied. "All right, Mage-Captain, send your people over to support Agent Amiri. I want some of your computer people backing up her techs—whether we find that box or not, I want whatever sensor and camera data we can extract from the systems."

"Yes, sir," Jakab replied, turning to start giving orders.

Damien kept his attention on the communicator.

"Julia?" he asked softly.

"My lord?"

"Be very careful. I don't trust this."

"No shit, my lord."

With that, his bodyguard cut the active voice channel, though the video feed from her helmet was still showing on the screen with everyone else's.

"Kole," Damien gestured the *Duke*'s captain to him. "I want everyone going over there either in or escorted by assault shuttles," he ordered. "I don't like this, and I want everyone watching for traps."

"I hear you, my lord," Jakab agreed. "I'm moving us closer, keeping the hulk inside our point defense envelope. Just... in case."

"Carry on, Captain," Damien told him, realizing Jakab had everything in hand.

"Sir, the *Alan-a-dale* is hailing us," Lieutenant Rain reported. "Captain Wayne wants to know if he can assist."

"The politicking is your job, my lord," Jakab told him with a small bow.

"And the boarding and sweep of the ship is now yours," Damien agreed with a sigh. "If I can borrow your break-out room to speak to Wayne?"

Jakab gave him a 'go-ahead' gesture and Damien stepped out of the bridge, with its all-encompassing view of the space outside, into the corridor leading into the rest of the ship. Jakab's breakout room was a small meeting room attached to his office, less than five meters away from the bridge.

"This is Montgomery," he said calmly as he opened the channel.

"Hand Montgomery," Captain Wayne greeted him with a calm nod. "I understand that your people have found evidence of a backup data storage for the cameras and such? Do you need help searching for it? My crew used to serve on very similar merchant ships and may have a better idea of where the captain may have hidden such a device."

For a moment, Damien was even tempted. He trusted Mage-Captain Jakab's people completely, but Wayne had just touched on his largest concern: Jakab's people were *Navy* personnel. The only time they spent aboard merchant ships was looking for contraband.

Of course, he would have to *trust* Captain Wayne and his people not to, say, 'accidentally' break the box when they found it. Even disregarding the fact that Michael Wayne rubbed Damien the wrong way, how much he could trust either of the regional militias involved in this mess was very much an open question.

"While that could be of value," he said slowly, choosing his words carefully, "I think I need to lock the *Mistletoe Solstice* down as a Protectorate-level crime scene, under my personal jurisdiction. Your offer is appreciated, but not necessary."

The Patrol Captain looked like he'd eaten something sour, but he nodded.

"I understand, I suppose," he admitted. "Is there any assistance we *can* provide, my lord?"

"No," Damien told him. "We have the area secure. If my understanding of your orders is correct, you may continue on your patrol."

"The Commodore wanted me to provide an observer and have one of my officers courier our observations directly to her," Wayne said. "Would this be acceptable?"

"Of course," Damien allowed. One Patrol officer, kept... suitably separate from the investigation, shouldn't be an issue. It wasn't really a question of paranoia, but of who one could trust the most.

That thought hit him like a thrown brick. Who one could trust the most. If you were the captain of a ship with your family aboard, trying to keep them safe... who could you trust the most?

"Send your officer over as soon as you're able, Captain Wayne," Damien told the Sherwood man. "We're going to be a bit busy with the *Mistletoe* for a while."

With a calm smile, he cut the connection and opened a shipboard link to Jakab as he started for the shuttle bay.

"Captain, get a shuttle ready for me to fly over to the *Mistletoe Solstice*," he ordered.

"Really, sir?" the Navy officer asked, charging blithely across the line marked insubordination.

"I think I know what they did with the box, Kole," Damien told him. "And it's not something anyone else is going to be able to see. Have the shuttle ready."

"You're the Hand, my lord."

Damien found Amiri waiting for him when he arrived aboard the *Mistletoe Solstice*, his bodyguard managing to get thoroughly unimpressed body language through a space-suit. Drifting out of the safety tunnel keeping the boarders away from the shattered wreck where the engines had been destroyed, he gestured for her to follow him and locked himself to the ground, looking around.

"We haven't even *started* cleaning up or really sweeping for traps," she told him over a private, gesturing to where a number of bodies had been pushed against the wall for later retrieval. "Why exactly are you here?"

"Julia, how many people aboard the *Duke* could identify and break a gene-locked illusion spell?" he asked gently.

"Damn, that's *possible?*" she replied, thinking. "Yeah, I think Afolayan would have done something like that."

"It's possible," he confirmed. "Difficult, and only really covered in Rune Scribe training. Which Nuru Afolayan had completed the first tiers of before leaving Mars to work on her grandfather's ship."

"Is that even breakable?" she asked, following him as he began to jet his way down the corridor, checking for magic with a trained eye.

"Normally, no. They're a *fantastic* security measure... assuming the Mage can renew them every month or so," he explained. "They do, like all runes, eventually fade. They're only so accurate on the genetic comparison, too. If Afolayan used one, any of her family would be able to pass it. She wouldn't be able to pick and choose members."

"So... we're looking for something magical, *hidden* with magic," she noted. "Since you're the only one who can even *see* this, am I going to have to escort you through the entire ship?"

"If necessary, but I hope not," he told her with a sad smile. "I was once a Ship's Mage, after all. I know where *I* would have put it, and that's a relatively short list."

Reaching the simulacrum chamber, he slowed unconsciously as they ran into a section of the vacuum inside the ship with visible floating blood globules in it. Even days later, the feel of magic remained in the metal and the void.

Reading the flow of magic through runes and people, the main gift of a Rune Wright, was easy enough to explain. The *feel* of magic after the fact was harder. Usually, Damien would describe it as a smell, but the lack of any air here robbed that explanation of any heft.

"One of the Ship's Mages made their stand here," Amiri noted. "Anyone they killed was removed, but..." she shrugged, gesturing towards where her bio tech was carefully going through the ruined body with two of the *Duke's* crew, "we're working on identifying the bodies."

Damien sighed, touching the torn metal to get the feel of the magic that had ripped it apart. A young woman, anywhere between twenty and twenty-five. There was only so much he could tell—there was only so much *to* tell, and it got harder as time passed.

"It was Nuru," he said quietly and certainly. "No idea where the senior Ship's Mage was, but this was her. Everything she could do to protect her ship and her family."

He shivered. Only the aftermath, years ago now, of an unarmored boarding team running into an exosuited soldier with a machine gun on the *Blue Jay* exceeded the horror of this dark and empty ship with its crew of corpses.

"This way," he told Amiri, glancing around to find the door he was looking for. He wasn't surprised, on pushing it open, to find that the room beyond had gravity. Gently controlling his own motion with magic, he stepped onto the runes the Ship's Mages had maintained in their own private workshop.

The workshop was bigger than the one he'd had aboard the *Blue Jay*, but the *Mistletoe* was a bigger ship. It had the same computer setup for jump calculations, with a chair surrounded by three massive screens for the view of the stars. It had two desks with regular screens, designed to link to a user's personal wrist computer. A massive, two-person, rune-working bench covered one wall.

"Right in her sanctum, I suppose." He felt more than heard Amiri land behind him.

The combination of the simulacrum chamber and workshop was often referred to as the 'Mage's Sanctum' on merchant ships, though the arrangement was obviously very different on a Royal Martian Navy warship, where the simulacrum chamber controlled the ship's most powerful weapon—the amplifier—as well as its ability to jump between the stars.

Damien didn't respond to Amiri immediately, studying the flows of magic around him. The gravity runes gave off their own slight glow to his eyes, which made it somewhat harder to see if anything was mounted on the walls. He ended up slowly walking the perimeter of the room until he reached the workbench itself.

There was nothing *visible*, even to his eyes, but... he pushed on a corner of the bench and it silently folded away, leaving what *looked* like a blank piece of wall—except to his Sight.

He studied the magic, the weave of power wound through the silver inlay that concealed itself behind its own power. Without genetics close to the creator's, even he couldn't see what was behind the spell. Unlike anyone else, however, he could see the magic itself. How it flowed, how it linked and meshed with reality to *change* reality.

"Found something?"

"Stand back," he ordered. "There will be an energy release."

First, he *carefully* wove a shield behind the panel—they couldn't afford to lose the box if it was there. Then, with an exhalation of breath, he ran a tiny blade of fire down the middle of the panel, slashing apart rune after rune until the spell finally collapsed and released its power.

Without air to carry the energy, there was no sound, but the flash heated the front of his suit to a dangerous level. Warning lights started flashing on the control panel at the bottom of his vision, and he shielded himself from the continued burn.

After a few moments, the danger passed, and the energy dissipated into the vacuum and the hull. A good chunk of the workbench had been melted, but the panel itself was mostly intact where his magic had protected it.

It was a relatively ordinary looking maintenance access panel, and he popped it open with practiced ease.

Inside, its status lights still glowing to show its internal power source had not yet failed, was the perfectly standard orange shape of a jump ship black box.

"Call in your techs, Julia," he ordered. "Someone *far* more experienced with computers needs to grab this."

CHAPTER 22

ONCE AGAIN, Damien and his staff gathered in the main briefing room of the *Duke of Magnificence,* just down the corridor from the bridge, while Commander Rhine prepared to present what his analysts had pulled together.

Damien was impressed by how quickly the *Duke's* tactical team had opened up and reviewed the data from the *Mistletoe Solstice's* black box. Less than twelve hours had passed since he'd broken through the spell the freighter's crew had used to hide the backup device, but Rhine said his people now had a solid enough idea of what had happened to share.

The odd man out in the room, sitting separated from the *Duke's* officer and Damien and his aides, was Lieutenant Kenneth Mac Duibhshíthe, the Patrol officer the *Alan-a-dale* had left behind. Mac Duibhshíthe was a gaunt youth with shockingly bright red hair and sunken, exhausted-looking, eyes who hadn't said more than a dozen words to anyone since coming aboard.

Rhine stepped up to the front of the room, tapping a command on his wrist PC which brought up an image of Antonius-Sherwood Jump Five, with the *Mistletoe Solstice* sitting in the middle of it.

"Some of what I am about to show you is a simulation put together by our computers based on the *Mistletoe Solstice's* data," the *Duke's* tactical officer explained. "We were able to resolve more from the data saved on the black box than the *Solstice's* computers would have been capable of, but we are working from a civilian ship's sensors. We are starting roughly ninety-six minutes after the *Solstice* arrived at Antonius-Sherwood Jump Five."

A moment later, the image on the screen started moving. Two jump flares appeared on the screen, slowly resolving into a pair of pyramid shapes that sent a ripple of shocked inhalations around the room.

Damien watched the destroyers close on the *Mistletoe Solstice* in grim silence. He wasn't surprised to see actual warships attack the freighter. He'd been expecting it. A note on the screen showed that time was being accelerated significantly as the ships closed the distance.

A missile blasted into space, a warning shot that lanced past the front of the *Mistletoe Solstice* and off into deep space. The freighter continued to run, pushing its engines to a level Damien knew to be *punishing* to the crew.

Unfortunately, the warships were equipped with gravity runes and could accelerate faster. They swooped down on the much larger freighter, and multiple three-gigawatt lasers flashed in the void. The engines and rear connectors vanished in a blast of vaporizing titanium, and sections of the screen grew much fuzzier.

Rhine paused it.

"At this point, the *Solstice* lost most of her sensors, especially those at the rear of the ship that would have got the best scan of the warships," he told his audience. "The destroyers' approach to the breach they'd opened was only visible on her omnidirectional infrared scanners. Nonetheless, they approached close enough before taking out her sensors to enable *our* computers to resolve a great many details of the vessels."

The wall screen zoomed in on the destroyers, splitting them out and highlighting specific sections.

"Both Bandit Alpha and Bandit Bravo are Tau Ceti-built *Lancer*-class destroyers," Rhine pointed out. "While we probably don't have enough data to identify individual ships we can, again, identify Tau Ceti Nova Industries batch numbers. Bandit Alpha," he sighed, then repeated himself. "Bandit Alpha was from TCNI Batch Twenty-Four-Fifty-D. As most of you may remember, that batch of destroyers was purchased in its entirety by the Mínglìàng Security Flotilla."

"*Bastards*," Mac Duibhshíthe hissed.

"I'm sorry, Lieutenant," Rhine said. "It doesn't get any better from here. Bandit Bravo was from TCNI Batch Twenty-Four-Fifty-One-F. Four of those units were bought into service by the Tau Ceti System Fleet. The other four were also purchased by the MSF.

"I would caution against taking this as definite proof," he continued. "Our identification certainties on this are only about seventy-five percent. However..."

"Commander?" Damien asked.

"We are quite certain that the Míngliàng Security Flotilla carried out this attack," Rhine said bluntly. "You'll see why as we go to the interior cameras."

The wall screen shifted to showing the central access way along the *Mistletoe Solstice's* keel. The big containment doors lacked the sequential breaches Damien had seen them with, and the interior lighting was still working.

Space-suited crew members were positioning themselves on the walls to absorb recoil and preparing to fight when the center of the big door blew in.

The defenders had clearly expected this, and none of them were in the blast path. They opened fire, spraying the breach with bullets and mini-rockets. More bullets answered them, and a pair of riot blast shields emerged in the middle of the hole.

The shields absorbed most of the defenders fire as the attackers pushed their way in, and grenades shot over the shields, the lack of gravity carrying them on deadly-straight trajectories before they exploded.

It was over in under a minute. One of the blast shields was shattered, the man behind it killed by repeated gunshots. Three more of the attackers were sprawled at the foot of the breach, and a man in a uniformed space-suit jetted through the hole, giving instructions with sharp hand gestures.

As the smoke and debris began to clear, Damien got a solid look at the officer in the space-suit. He recognized the pattern and insignia immediately, and as the invaders progressed down the hall he got a good look at the rest.

All of them were in the black and blue colors and insignia of the Míngl1àng Security Flotilla.

Rhine's team had put together a clean progression of events, switching from camera to camera as the MSF troopers advanced through the ship. Nuru Afolayan's stand at the simulacrum chamber was even more effective than Damien had thought from the debris, almost annihilating the entire first boarding party.

A second team, unfortunately, hadn't been far behind. They brought up heavy weapons, and the young Ship's Mage fell to grenades launched from halfway down the ship. From there, the augmented boarding team took no chances. Each breach opened in a containment door was followed by a salvo of grenades. The stand at the bridge door lasted moments—but still claimed several boarders as the bridge defenders had the only heavy weapons aboard the ship.

Storming the bridge ended in a fury of fire that left only Captain Afolayan alive—and clearly only because the boarders were aiming to keep him alive. The captain's wounds weren't even bound before he was cuffed and tied to his chair.

The same uniformed officer who had led the first boarding party now started interrogating the captain. He cut sections of Afolayan's suit with a large knife, slowly working his way up as he clearly didn't get what he wanted.

Behind them, suited MSF troopers were ransacking the offices and opening up the black box containment compartment. One of them jetted out from the captain's office carrying a mid-sized navy blue carrying case triumphantly.

Just as the trooper was presenting the case to his officer, the video froze.

"The backup black box was a direct copy of the main black box," Commander Rhine explained. "As soon as the main box was removed, its records stopped. According to its records, life support was still functional and there were still twenty-five crewmembers alive on the rotator ribs.

"At some point *after* the black box was removed, the computer systems were used to purge all atmosphere from the ship, and were then destroyed. Anyone left aboard only had whatever emergency oxygen was available to them, which ran out long before we arrived."

"What's that case?" Damien asked, gesturing towards the carrying case held by the trooper frozen on the screen. "By this point they'd already detached a cargo worth tens of millions."

Mac Duibhshíthe coughed.

"I can answer that question," the young Patrol Lieutenant told him, coughing again to clear his throat as he tried not to look at the screen with the scattered bodies. "We don't publicize it much, but the upper atmosphere of Antonius's gas giant has the perfect conditions to create naturally occurring silicon-carbon nano-filaments—the kind normally synthesized for use in high-powered computer cores."

Damien caught Jakab whistling and glanced over at the Mage-Captain.

"Those filaments are insanely difficult to produce," Jakab told him. "The *Duke*'s core uses just over a kilometer's worth of them to run at a level few civilian ships need or want. That kilometer of filaments costs as much as one of her *engines*."

"A case that size probably held three or four five hundred meter spools," Mac Duibhshíthe admitted. "It would have represented as much as ten percent of the value of the *Mistletoe Solstice*'s cargo, and only somem one involved in either the Antonius mining operations or security from Mínglìàng or Sherwood would know to look for it.

"Mínglìàng troops, Mínglìàng ships, Mínglìàng knowledge," he continued, his voice harsh. "But Sherwood deaths and innocent blood. This is an act of *war*."

"And unfortunately," Damien said quietly, "I have no choice but to bring it back to Governor McLaughlin."

"Unfortunately?!" Mac Duibhshíthe demanded. "Sherwood has a *right* to know about this!"

"I agree," the Hand said calmly. "But you do not have a right to go to war. It is the *Protectorate's* job to resolve this. *My* job. Which means that I would *rather* bring all of this to Governor Wong and demand answers and justice from him.

"But we have an obligation to inform the families, and I need to know what Commander Renzetti has learned," he continued. "So yes, we will be returning to Sherwood and you will have your chance to pass all of this on to the Governor. But realize, Lieutenant, that I will *not* permit a war."

He turned away from the rebellious looking Sherwood officer to Jakab.

"Mage-Captain, how long until we can be back in Sherwood?"

"We should have all of the bodies off of *Mistletoe Solstice* in a couple of hours," the captain replied. "All of my Mages are rested and we're only three jumps from Sherwood. I can have us back inside of an hour once we're on our way. Say four hours?"

"Should still be before Renzetti returns," Damien agreed. "Make it so, Captain."

He turned to his own staff.

"Amiri, Christoffsen, meet me in my office in twenty minutes," he ordered. "We'll need to go over this and make some plans."

Not least among them how to stop Sherwood from launching a war he was worried might well be justified.

They were close enough to the hulk of the *Mistletoe Solstice* that Damien could see it through the transparent titanium of his office's massive window. The ship was illuminated by the lights of the shuttles hovering around it, or it would have been invisible against the void with no lights and no nearby star to reflect off the hull.

Dead spaceships had a certain eerie finality to them. Only the presence of humans and a supply of power gave the metal and machinery life, and in the absence of either only metal remained. His practiced eye could pick out where along the keel the simulacrum chamber where

Nuru Afolayan had died trying to save her ship was, and he shivered as he remembered a few days of his own that could have ended just as permanently.

"My lord," Christoffsen greeted him.

He turned to find that both of his subordinates had snuck in while he was distracted, but Amiri had simply grabbed a chair and waited for him to stop staring at the dead.

"We failed them," he said simply. "The entire purpose of the Protectorate is so that people like Captain Afolayan don't get killed doing their goddamn jobs."

"There was nothing *you* could have done," Amiri pointed out. "We got involved as soon as we knew there was a problem. Unless we'd swamped every jump zone between Sherwood and Míngliàng with Navy warships, there's nothing more we *could* have done."

"And it should be pointed out that these pirates took on a Sherwood *frigate*, one of the most powerful warships in the possession of a regional militia, as I understand," Christoffsen added. "Had we, say, stationed a destroyer at every jump zone, all we might have accomplished would have been to add Navy dead to the tally."

"The timing to all of this is suspicious as hell," Damien pointed out. "We arrive in Míngliàng, and Admiral Phan shows up the next day having dueled with a Sherwood frigate? We head to Sherwood, and *we* get jumped by Míngliàng destroyers? While we're *in* Sherwood, there's an attack that allows us to definitely identify the MSF?

"It's all too neat, and I don't trust it," the Hand told his aide, finally putting the itchy feeling between his shoulder blades into words. "I am half-convinced that someone is *fucking* with us."

That silenced the other two for a long moment, but then Amiri started shaking her head.

"I can see why, but the timing is impossible," she replied. "If they had a fleet of cloaked couriers—which would require *dozens* of Mages as I understand hiding a ship is not-quite-impossible—and had a frigate standing by to jump Phan on command, *and* were prepared to sacrifice two destroyers to bait the trap... maybe. But that's a lot of stretching, Damien."

"I know," he admitted. "I feel paranoid, but the sheer amount of co-incidence, the degree to which something starts to aggravate the situation for one side or another as soon as we show up... I feel like there's a target painted on my back."

"Other than the bomber on Sherwood, no one is coming after us directly," Christoffsen told him. "If anything... no, that makes no sense."

"What is it, Professor?" Damien asked.

The ex-Governor sighed, shaking his head.

"I defer to Julia on how possible the level of communication is," he noted. "But if someone was playing a game here, we'd be irrelevant. Their only concern with us would be keeping us checking down rabbit holes while they get ready to kick over the whole mountain."

"It makes no sense," the Hand admitted. "Who benefits from a civil war between Sherwood and Míngliàng? There's no one else even in position to mine in Antonius. It's not even like we'd permit a war to last very long. They'd get a bunch of people killed, and then we'd bring in a cruiser squadron and maybe a battleship or two and force a ceasefire."

"It would tie up Protectorate resources, both political and military, for years," Christoffsen replied. "That might be the goal, but... I agree. I don't see anyone making money or gaining resources or power by kicking off this war."

"Even if there is no third party, I think there is at least one rogue faction involved," Damien told his people. "The attempt on Commodore McLaughlin's life suggests that she's not involved to me, and I don't see the Governor doing an end run around her.

"However, I *also* do not honestly see Governor Wong engaging in this scale of murder and piracy," he continued. "It's entirely possible I've misread everyone involved and they're *all* lying to me.

"Regardless, I think we've let this situation degrade enough. It's time for Alaura's first step."

Both of his aides had worked with Hand Alaura Stealey—Christoffsen on several specific missions, and Amiri as a forward agent. They knew her 'three step' process to dealing with issues: stop the fighting, resolve the dispute, and punish the guilty.

"I intend to restrict the Patrol to Sherwood," Damien continued. "That... is going to be one hell of an argument, but I believe I can make it stick without having to babysit them. I then intend to do the same with the MSF, and we are going to *sit* on Admiral Phan and her people.

"I'm also going to order all shipments into and out of Antonius held until Admiral Medici gets here with enough hulls for us to start running convoys under Protectorate authority.

"We're going to lock the players I know about down, and if there's a third party out there, let's starve them of targets—and then see if they want to dance with the goddamn Martian Navy!"

CHAPTER 23

"I'M AFRAID I don't have much for you, Commodore," Inspector Accord told Grace as he took the seat in front of her desk. Her steward had laid steaming cups of coffee out for her and her guest and then slipped out of her flagship office.

Thankfully, she'd mostly lived aboard the *Robin Hood* and hadn't lost too much of value in the destruction of her apartment on Sherwood Prime. A few small things that hurt—including, ironically, the only physical photo she had of herself and Damien Montgomery—but otherwise nothing she couldn't replace.

"Tell me what you have then, Inspector," she told Accord, leaning back in her chair and watching the spare, graying man across from her. "Because right now, I don't have *anything* other than 'someone tried to murder me'."

The Inspector nodded and tried the coffee. He took a larger, appreciative swallow after the first sip, then put it back down and looked her in the eye.

"All I've done so far is eliminate possibilities," he told her. "I can tell you this: the explosives on your apartment were *not* placed by a Patrol spacecraft. I've reviewed camera footage, weight records, and every other piece of data your people could provide me of every Patrol flight that came close enough. None of them dropped off the missiles or got close enough to lay the explosive."

Accord sighed.

"Unfortunately, I can *also* confirm that the missile pod was Patrol," he continued. "It originally belonged to Sherwood System Security and was shipped to the Patrol along with the heavy weapons for the Patrol's boarding squads. It was noted by the Patrol as an error, and on Patrol records was shipped back. SSS got the note about the error, but never received the return."

Grace nodded slowly.

"With the training scheme for the Phase Two ships, it could have gone astray anytime in the last six months," she observed. That gave them far too large a period to try and track a single box coming in or out of the Defender Yards.

Accord coughed. "Sorry, I should have been clearer. The pod was shipped with the weapons and armor for the *Robin Hood*'s boarding teams. Two years ago."

If she hadn't been sitting Grace would have had to sit down. Two *years* ago? The trap someone had used as part of an assassination attempt on her had been stolen before she'd been Commodore—back when she'd been the senior Ship's Mage on one of their initial destroyers.

"It wasn't stolen to kill me, then," she murmured.

"No. I suspect, and I have people running the analysis to be certain, that we'll find more equipment and weaponry that went missing in similar ways," Accord admitted. "Someone used your resources to assemble an arsenal of tools to make the Patrol look responsible for their crimes. Which makes me *very* concerned about the other task you've set me."

Grace nodded, quietly checking the security on her office. Her wrist computer had a few toys most of them didn't come with, and happily confirmed it detected no bugs or cameras.

"And have you found anything on that?" she asked.

"The only detailed imagery we have is of the engagement with Admiral Phan," he noted. "The vessel in that imagery is running a *lot* of ECM and is at long missile range. I," Accord sighed again, "am forced to agree with the assessment of Montgomery's people—it is most likely one of our ships, but I couldn't say which one."

"*How*, Inspector?" she replied. "We have full records of where our ships have been and what they've done. I can buy that they could hide missile expenditures in their authorized live fire training, but these attacks are light years away from where they're supposed to be."

"I am not aware of whether it's technically possible," the Inspector replied, "but I ran an analysis. If we assume that our black box records are compromised, we can only trust reports of our ships' locations from third parties. May I?" he gestured to the console on her desk.

She gave him a 'go ahead' gesture and he slotted a data chip into the reader. The wall screen lit up, and he started manipulating it from the console.

A star chart, centered on Sherwood, appeared on the screen. Three gold icons with text labels flashed—Sherwood, Antonius and Mínglàng. A scattering of green icons appeared, followed by a much smaller scattering of red icons. Each had a date and a ship name attached, in text slightly too small for Grace to read.

"The green icons are reports of our ships," he noted. "The red are the locations and times of the attacks on Mínglàng ships as provided by Hand Montgomery's people. The details of the analysis are on the chip, but the short version is that yes, our ships could have carried out every one of those attacks."

Grace felt as if someone had punched her in the gut. She'd suspected and feared that she'd been betrayed, but his words were confirmation she'd hoped to never hear.

"Any particular ships?" the Commodore commanding the Sherwood Interstellar Patrol ground out, her heart cold and her voice flat.

"There is no attack that couldn't have been carried out by at least two different ships," Accord said flatly. "Worse, no one ship could have launched all of the attacks. Sadly, Commodore, the only thing I can tell with certainty is that the *Maid Marian* and *Robin Hood* weren't involved, as neither of those ships has left the system."

That was *far* worse than she'd feared. Potentially three of her five ships were compromised? Compromised so completely that both their crews and computers were lying to her and their comrades.

"It can't be this bad," she whispered.

"Unfortunately, the *best* case I see is that only one of our ships has gone rogue," Accord said bluntly. "A significant enough portion of the attacks were not witnessed that some of them could be carried out by someone else. That... fails Occam's Razor, ma'am. It requires additional assumptions I can't justify with the evidence."

"So at least two, and possibly three, of my ship's crews are waging a private war," Grace said flatly. "I need to *know* Inspector. Get me names. I'll start measuring the rope, but I need names."

"I'll get them for you," Javier Accord promised. "And I'll swing on their feet when you hang them."

Their moment of fierce agreement was interrupted by her PC chiming for her attention. With a touch, she opened a communications channel.

"McLaughlin here."

"Ma'am, we have a jump flare in the inner system," her XO reported. "The *Duke of Magnificence* is back."

"My lord, I have Mage-Commander Renzetti on the com for you," Lieutenant Carver told Damien. "FN Twenty One Eighty Seven arrived early this morning. There'll be about a two second com lag."

"Thank you, Lieutenant. Please connect the Mage-Commander," Damien told the young officer. He flipped the channel up onto the wall-screen on the observation window and turned his chair to face the image that appeared of the courier ship captain.

"Mage-Commander Renzetti, it's good to see you made it back earlier than expected," he greeted the other man. "What did you learn?"

"My lord Hand," Renzetti greeted him, bowing slightly as his message and Damien's crossed each other in space. The Mage-Commander, an experienced spacer, then waited to see Damien's own greeting.

"Nova Industries was very cooperative," he explained once the time lag caught up. "Given the scale of Governor Wong's order, I suspect they were expecting someone from the Navy to ask questions sooner or later."

Damien nodded, trying not to audibly growl or sigh. He'd hoped he'd judged the situation wrong. Mínglìàng was starting to look more and more buried down in the muck of the whole affair.

"How big an order are we talking here?" he asked, and waited the four seconds for his response.

"Big," Renzetti replied with a sigh. "More than doubling his hulls and vastly increasing his tonnage. Mínglìàng put a *lot* of money down, my lord. Enough that TCNI diverted nearly completed units ear-marked for other customers and is paying out penalty clauses to deliver the MSF's ships first.

"If the timeline they gave me is correct, the first batch of two cruisers and eight destroyers should have arrived in Mínglìàng two days ago. That's almost thirty million tons of warships, Lord Montgomery. The second batch is due in three months and is the same size."

"That will completely change the balance of power in this sector," Damien concluded aloud. Technically, TCNI had no obligation to report sales of ships so long as they were to a planetary government. When *this* story made it back to the Mage-King and the Council that might just change.

"I checked our records of what we observed of Mínglìàng media while we were in orbit," Renzetti continued. "I don't think any of us were looking for it, but there was a hard push going on to recruit experienced spacers to the MSF."

"Send us whatever details they gave you," Damien ordered. It wouldn't be much—the Runic Transceiver Arrays only transmitted the voice of the speaking Mage. Recordings, modems, none of that was picked up—only the voice of the Mage. The general conclusion had been that the RTA wasn't actually transmitting *sound* so much as the Mage's intent to speak. The details Renzetti would have would be those related by a Mage on the other end.

"Of course, my lord. If I may ask," he said hesitantly, "what happens now?"

"We'll have to wait on those details," Damien said quietly. "But there is no way I'm not headed to Mínglìàng again next."

Damien rested his head against the glass of the observation window, watching his home world slowly grow as the *Duke* approached. A thousand questions and scenarios ran through his head, but the answers, if there were any, refused to resolve themselves.

He *knew* that ships from both Mínglìàng and Sherwood had attacked and killed civilian and military spacers from the other system. What he *wasn't* at all sure of was that the government of either system was involved in the attacks—he was reasonably sure that Grace and her grandfather weren't, but Governor Wong didn't strike him as the type either.

By now, Lieutenant Mac Duibhshíthe had made his report and Damien's ex-girlfriend was being confronted with an act of war against her star system. Grace would take it to the Governor—she had no choice, that was her job.

The Sherwood Interstellar Patrol wasn't designed to wage an interstellar war, but Damien had no doubts that Grace could manage it—and then would run into Mínglìàng's dramatically expanded fleet. Even if she was warned about those new ships, a battle between the Patrol and the Mínglìàng Security Flotilla would turn into a disaster of mutual destruction.

If Governor McLaughlin didn't at least consider a counter-force mission to reduce or destroy the Flotilla, he wasn't doing his job. From the data Damien had in hand, he couldn't even blame his home system for wanting to do so.

There was no way Hand Damien Montgomery could permit Sherwood to launch that mission. It would be the first step to open warfare between Sherwood and Mínglìàng—and in so doing, potentially lay the foundation for the utter collapse of the Protectorate.

If he stopped them, he would be unquestionably laying the interests of Mars and the Protectorate over those of his home world. He would also be keeping the peace, and if he managed to stop this war that seemed to inch closer with every day that passed, he would save thousands—*tens* of thousands—of lives.

That he would also likely destroy any chance of rekindling his relationship with Grace was such a tiny thing to stack up against that goal. If he was prepared to lay down his life in the service of Mars and peace, why would that even count?

But it did. It just wasn't enough to change what he had to do.

With a sigh, Damien touched a command to open a channel to the bridge.

"Lieutenant Carver," he greeted the on-duty com officer. "I need you to pass my regards to Governor and Commodore McLaughlin and inform them that they *will* meet me aboard the *Duke of Magnificence* as soon as we reach orbit.

"If they argue, remind them of Article Seventeen of the Charter," Damien said grimly. "Thank you, Lieutenant."

He looked back to the planet growing in front of him, trying to ignore the sinking feeling in his gut. He'd just ordered his ex-girlfriend and the Governor of his home planet to meet him, and accompanied the order with an outright threat.

Article Seventeen of the Charter of the Protectorate obligated Damien to assist Sherwood's government in protecting its citizens.

It was also the Article that gave him the authority to relieve a Governor.

CHAPTER 24

DAMIEN DIDN'T KNOW the eldest McLaughlin well enough to judge the Governor's mood by his body language, though the sheer control being exerted in his movements and gestures as he entered Damien's office gave him hints. Grace McLaughlin, on the other hand, he had once known very well indeed.

She was furious. She stalked into his office, ignoring him completely to look out the window at the planet below. Even her apparent anger at him didn't seem to immunize her from the view from the massive observation window that made up one wall of his office.

"Governor, Commodore," he said quietly. "Please sit."

They were alone in his office. Combined, the two McLaughlins could probably muster enough magical power to overcome his defenses and kill him, at least if they took him by surprise, but direct physical threats were not the problem.

"It seems we are at your disposal," Grace grounded out and Damien did his best to disguise his wince as the two McLaughlins sat.

"I presume you have reviewed whatever report Lieutenant Mac Duibhshíthe provided on the *Mistletoe Solstice* incident," he said in as calm a voice as he could manage.

"I have," Governor McLaughlin replied. "I see no options available to me but one. As a great man once said, I hate war as only a soldier who has lived it can, but the massacre of my citizens and the destruction of their ships *must* be answered."

"We can have two more Phase Two frigates available in forty-eight hours," Grace interjected. "The *Friar Tuck* and *Little John* should have returned by then, with the *Alan-a-dale* only a few hours behind. A counter-force mission to neutralize the MSF's jump-capable fleet is the cleanest option, and we should be able to avoid unnecessary civilian casualties."

"Civilian casualties like those on the twenty-plus Mínglìàng freighters that shared the *Mistletoe Solstice*'s fate, Commodore?" Damien asked gently. The degree of thought and planning already in place worried him. "Freighters that, so far as the evidence I have goes, were destroyed by Sherwood ships?

"You come to me prepared to launch a war, and yet so far as I can tell, you've already been fighting one."

Both of them were silent for a long moment, and Grace sighed.

"We are investigating," she told him. "It appears we have a rogue faction in our ranks, I won't pretend otherwise."

"But what Mínglìàng has done is an act of war, my lord Hand," the Governor interjected. "We *cannot* let it pass."

"You speak of acts of war as if Sherwood was a sovereign state, your Excellency," Damien pointed out. "It is not. It never has been. Sherwood is a member system of the Protectorate, bound by the Articles of the Charter and the Compact. You have the right to raise militia to police your system, not to use that militia to wage war against another system."

"My people are being *massacred!*" McLaughlin snapped. "I will *not* sit by, not when the tool to save them is to hand!"

"Governor," Damien said very, very quietly, forcing McLaughlin to lean forward to hear him, "let me be clear. This is not your jurisdiction. This was a ship attacked in interstellar space. The investigation was carried out by the Martian Navy. You have no authority to launch the campaign—not least, while *your* captains are killing *their* citizens, you have no *moral* authority to act."

"You *dare* lecture me about moral authority?" the Governor bellowed, rising to his feet. "If we are not sovereign, we traded it for *protection*—if that protection is lacking, I must act—by whatever means I have, including war!"

"I will not permit you to go to war," Damien said flatly. "It will not happen."

"Who do you think you are?" the older man demanded. He loomed over Damien now, *quivering* with his anger. The Mage-Governor of Sherwood was not used to being defied, and he *certainly* was not used to being ordered.

The Hand was set on a chain that was surprisingly easy to release, and it slammed down onto Damien's desk with a resounding thud. The gold icon of a clenched fist glinted in the light reflecting through the window off of Sherwood and through the massive window.

"I am the Hand of the Mage-King of Mars," Hand Damien Montgomery told him. He did not rise, but he met Miles James McLaughlin's eyes levelly. "Do not mistake the Hand for the boy you knew. Justice for the *Mistletoe Solstice*'s crew is *my* duty. I am no more certain Governor Wong is to blame for their deaths than I am certain that you are to blame for the death of the *Dreamer*'s crew. If I allow you credit for the possibility of rogue factions, should I ignore that possibility at Mínglìàng?"

"And if I refuse to be dictated to?"

"Then I will relieve you," Damien said flatly. "And if your Vice-Governor is determined to start a war as well, I will relieve him. I believe Sherwood's line of succession is what, forty-five people long? I'm sure one of them is, if nothing else, completely lacking in spine."

For a long moment, the Hand met the Governor's gaze and he could *feel* the tension cracking in the room.

Then Grace laughed, and the tension snapped like a broken wire.

"I don't think you would need to go far down that list, my lord Hand," she told the two men. "Governor—*Grandfather*—let's at least hear what Damien has to say."

The McLaughlin relaxed by inches, slowly retreating back from the standoff that had been almost fatal to his career, and nodded slowly.

"Very well, my lord Hand," he allowed. "If this is, as you say, your jurisdiction, what do you plan to do about the deaths of my people?"

"I plan to stop the deaths of *everyone's* people," Damien told him. "Right now, I currently suspect we may be facing rogue factions on both sides—factions that may be actively working together to start a war. There's always someone who hasn't fought one who thinks they can profit," he observed coldly.

"I am suspending the Patrol's license to operate outside Sherwood," he continued. He glanced at Grace and recognized the signs of her swallowing her anger and continued quickly: "I will also *immediately* proceed to Míngl, where I will suspend the Flotilla's license to operate outside Mínglàng.

"My courier will proceed to Antonius, where he will deliver my order to stop *all* ships leaving that system," Damien finished. "Captain Arrow aboard the *Dreams of Liberty* will enforce that order."

He met Grace's eyes. "All of this is a temporary measure to protect both your and Mínglàng's spacers until the Navy forces I have requested arrive. Admiral Medici will be en route within a few days, and here in a little more than two weeks. The *Protectorate* will assume responsibility for the security of both Antonius and all shipments to and from the system.

"Once Martian forces have secured Antonius and the convoys in and out, we are going to tear into the computers of both your ships and the Flotilla's and get to the bottom of this. I *will* find the guilty, but first we need to stop the dying—and going to war, Governor, is not going to do that."

Now he held Governor McLaughlin's gaze, hoping, *praying*, that the Governor understood. He didn't really want to relieve the ridiculously popular leader. He'd do it if he had to, but he would truly never be able to come home again if he did.

"Very well, Lord Montgomery," McLaughlin finally replied with a long sigh. "I will give you... time. Do not expect my patience to be infinite." He sighed again. "But you are not wrong, and your plan strikes me as the best chance for making sure the truly guilty are punished."

"Thank you, Governor," Damien told him. "I will return your faith with faith—necessity means I must depart for Mínglàng immediately and my courier ship must head for Antonius almost as quickly. I must trust you to retain your ships in Sherwood. Of course," he pointed out,

"FN Twenty One Eighty Seven will be returning here once they've been to Antonius, and they can reach us at Míngliàng *very* quickly."

"We will obey your orders, my lord," Grace promised, and something in how she used the title told him their reawakened sparks were very, very, cold now. "We will give you time."

Grace fumed the entire way back to the shuttle, following her grandfather and keeping her eyes level to keep any of the spacers surrounding her from realizing her mood. She had no doubt that Montgomery's people liked and respected him as much as hers did her, and *her* people would have made sure she learned if someone she'd been meeting with had stomped off the ship.

Finally back on the Patrol shuttle, with just her and the Governor in the back of it, she let loose a massive sigh.

"That went just about as badly as it could possibly have gone, didn't it?" she said to her grandfather.

"I think... I think not," he replied softly. "And that was thanks to you. I was about ready to call his bluff on being willing to relieve me... and in hindsight, he was not bluffing."

"I never expected Damien Montgomery to be that much of a hard-ass," Grace admitted. "He was always so... diffident? Shy?"

"Unless I am very mistaken, your boyfriend still is," he replied. "But he is also *very* certain of his authority. And he is also right."

"He hasn't been my boyfriend in five years," the head of Sherwood's naval militia objected. "And he's right? You think there's a rogue faction in Míngliàng?"

"In honesty? No," the Governor admitted. "But, if we expect the Hand to give *us* the credit of believing such a faction exists, we have no choice but accept that possibility in our enemies—and allow the Hand to try and find those truly responsible.

"As for boyfriend, my dear, you are my granddaughter, I've known you your entire life, and I am not *blind*," he finished sharply. "You are pissed at him right now for calling us on the carpet. Eventually it will matter more that he was right to do so—*especially* if he keeps us from having to go to war."

Grace shook her head at her grandfather and considered for a long moment.

"So we go into lockdown and obey his orders?" she asked finally.

"If we were going to fight, we'd want to recall everyone anyway," he pointed out reasonably. "So pulling all of your ships back to Sherwood costs us nothing. He said nothing about not accelerating the deployment of the Phase Two ships."

"So we proceed as planned, but hold off on actually moving ships anywhere?" Grace asked slowly.

"If Montgomery succeeds, nobody else dies, and that's a win in any book," Governor McLaughlin replied. "In that case, we spent a bit of money getting two ships online that we didn't need. Hardly a disaster.

"But if Montgomery fails, we will need to act to protect our people, and I'd rather you had to do that with nine frigates than with seven."

CHAPTER 25

THE *DUKE OF MAGNIFICENCE* appeared in the Mínglìàng System to a hornet's nest of activity. Jakab released the simulacrum and eyed the data codes rapidly propagating across the screens surrounding him. There were a *lot* more ships in orbit of the colony than there had been when they left.

"Talk to me, Commander," he told Rhine. "What am I looking at?"

"*Some* of those are freighters," his tactical officer said dryly. "Give me a moment."

More data codes attached themselves to the icons, and despite Commander Rhine's reassuring pronouncement, a disturbing number of them were definitely *warship* codes.

"All right," Rhine said. Data codes continued to appear as his team and the *Duke*'s computer continued to analyze the signatures around them. "So, I have the TCNI delivery *here*." A gold circle flashed on the screen around a cluster of ships. "That's eight destroyers, two cruisers, four passenger ships to bring the Nova Industries transit crews home, and a cool dozen freighters full of munitions and spare parts.

"The destroyers, here," eight of the icons flashed orange, "are in high parking orbits and nobody is really paying attention to them. The *cruisers*, unfortunately, are a different story."

The two icons flashed with bright red highlights, and more details flowed onto the screen.

"The cruisers are TCNI *Phoenix*-class ships," Rhine noted. "Nine and a half million tons, sixty missiles launchers and thirty ten-gigawatt lasers. We've got heavier guns, armor and electronic warfare, but her defensive laser suite is on par with ours. They are *nasty* pieces of work."

"And, Commander?" Kole asked.

"And those two ships are being *swarmed* with Mínglià ng Security Flotilla personnel, heavy lift, and work shuttles," Rhine replied. "Can't say for sure without going over their records, but I'd say they're less than sixteen hours from at least preliminary operational status."

"They're rushing," the Mage-Captain said.

"They're rushing *hard*," Rhine confirmed. "And, well," he highlighted a set of fourteen icons in a protective hemisphere above the cruisers, "I think I see why."

Kole looked at the icons, each marking an active MSF *Lancer*-class destroyer.

"I'm missing something, Commander," he said dryly.

"According to what the MSF gave us, they usually only keep half their ships at home," Rhine noted. "If they've got fourteen here, they recalled everybody."

"And they're wondering where ships fifteen and sixteen are," Kole said grimly. "If everybody's here... they know somebody didn't come home. Do you think they guessed what happened?"

"That's above my pay grade," the tactical officer said bluntly. "Either way, in less than twenty-four hours, the MSF is going to command enough firepower to make the *Navy* blink, let alone the Patrol."

Mage-Captain Kole Jakab considered the situation for a moment, looking at the fourteen ships already starting to maneuver towards him. No matter what they thought was going on, intercepting an unknown warship was always a good idea—good practice for the crews if nothing else—but this could go very downhill, very fast.

"Commander Rhine," he said crisply, "take the *Duke* to battle stations. Lieutenant Rain," he turned to the junior officer holding down coms, "please inform Hand Montgomery of the status of those cruisers and request that he contact the bridge as soon as possible."

As the shaven-headed young officer grabbed her microphone and started to bring up the intercom, the lights outside the bridge began to strobe, and the warbling tones of the alarm echoed in from the corridor.

Damien wasn't sure how long he'd been asleep when the battle stations alarm woke him up. He'd meant to be awake when they arrived in Míngliàng, but dreams of laughing madmen with buttons that killed millions had blurred with visions of floating in deep space without protection, making it difficult to sleep.

Even as the intercom chimed for his attention, he still took a moment to breathe deeply, controlling his rapidly beating heart. In reality, he'd stopped General James Montoya from detonating his bombs, and the rogue General had died for his attempt to blow up Ardennes's cities. That didn't stop Damien's subconscious from blowing them up in his dreams two or three times a week.

The floating in deep space without protection was new, but it was hardly a shock.

His heartbeat finally slowed to something more tolerable, he accepted the intercom request as voice only.

"Montgomery here."

"My lord, it's Lieutenant Rain from the bridge," a voice told him. "We've arrived in Míngliàng, but it appears that TCNI's shipment beat us here."

"Understood. What's our situation?" Damien asked crisply, rummaging through his closet to assemble a new black suit.

Rain summarized the status of the Security Flotilla, the new ships, and the rapidly mobilizing cruisers while he dressed. When she finished, he clasped the leather collar holding his Mage medallion around his neck and smiled grimly down at his wrist computer and its communicator.

"I'll be in my office in two minutes, Lieutenant," he told her. "What's our time delay for coms?"

"A little over six seconds, sir."

"All right. Send a stand down order to the MSF under my authorization," Damien ordered. "If you can locate Admiral Phan as well, I would appreciate it. I'll have a message for her and the Governor as soon as I have a chance to look at the data myself."

"Yes, my lord!"

"Thank you, Lieutenant," he told her, smiling against his fatigue at the young woman's nervous enthusiasm for dealing with him.

Stepping into his office, Damien tapped a series of half-unconscious commands on his wrist computer, connecting it to his console and the ship's systems, and bringing up the tactical plot across his massive window wallscreen.

Lieutenant Rain's summary had been succinct and complete. He was quickly able to identify the active warships of the MSF, the two cruisers in full mobilization mode, and the swarm of freighters from Tau Ceti Nova Industries.

The fourteen destroyers maneuvering on an intercept course for the *Duke* were probably the most worrying. The last time the *Duke of Magnificence* had run into MSF ships, they'd been forced to destroy them. To see them maneuvering so aggressively suggested huge problems.

A note from the bridge flashed onto his screen, noting that Lieutenant Rain had identified Phan's flagship and was ready to transmit to Phan and the Governor.

Facing the almost concealed dot where a camera had been embedded in his window, Damien hit the button to start recording.

"Admiral Phan, Governor Wong," he greeted them. "By now your ships should have already received the stand down order from my people. Let me reiterate it: stand your ships down and return them to orbit of Míngliàng. Given the events of the last few days, an aggressive approach by the Míngliàng Security Flotilla will result in my being forced to order Mage-Captain Jakab to defend his ship with all necessary force."

Firing the message off into the ether, Damien waited, watching the plot for a change in profile on the part of the MSF ships.

It happened before they could have received his message, all fourteen ships simultaneously flipped end for end and started accelerating back towards their initial positions. Apparently he hadn't needed to be *quite* so harsh, but better to overreact verbally than actually have to open fire.

Finally, a minute or so after they would have received his message, Phan's reply arrived.

Her image appeared on the wallscreen, replacing the tactical plot with a translucent image of Admiral Phan, her space-black skin blending with the void behind her and the bridge of her flagship bustling around her.

"Lord Montgomery," she greeted him stiffly. "I apologize for the hastiness of our reaction. Two of our destroyers are several days overdue and we are very much on edge. We were preparing for a search when we received your order to restrict our operations to three light years." She paused.

"We still need to search for our missing ships, my lord. I'm glad you're here—we are going to need an exception to allow a small task force to follow our patrol's path."

Damien sighed. There went any hope that the two ships that had jumped them *hadn't* been Míngliàng Security Flotilla ships. It was still, he supposed, possible that they'd been attacking civilian shipping without Wong or Phan's knowledge, but that theory ran up against the fact that the *Wil Scarlet* had been jumped by a full *squadron* of destroyers—half the MSF's original strength.

"Admiral, Governor, I'm afraid I know what happened to your destroyers," he said quietly into the camera. "I have answers to some of your questions, I suspect. I don't think you'll like them, and I have many questions for you. Questions whose answers I had better like," he told them grimly.

"These are all matters best discussed in person, not over even the most encrypted link. The *Duke of Magnificence* will be in orbit in a little over two hours. I will need you both to meet me aboard as soon as we make orbit."

He paused the recording, considering for a long moment if he should include more information, or make the order clearer, then sighed. Both

Phan and Wong were intelligent people or they wouldn't hold the roles they did. They'd understand.

He hit send and went looking for coffee. It was going to be a long day.

The Admiral's and Governor's shuttles arrived within a minute of each other. Damien stood at the side of the *Duke's* shuttle bay with an honor guard of dress uniformed Marines as the two spacecraft settled carefully down in the spaces cleared for them.

Invisible from inside the bay were the two Secret Service snipers Amiri had hidden in a control booth and the squad of Marines in exosuit battle armor waiting down one of the access corridors. Damien hadn't even bothered to object when his bodyguard and Mage-Captain Jakab had informed him of the security measures—after all, the only attack on the *Duke* had been launched by Míngl;iàng ships.

Governor Wong exited his shuttle first, accompanied by his husband and two dark-suited bodyguards. Admiral Phan was only moments behind, accompanied by Commodore Metharom and two men who wore junior insignia on their black and blue MSF uniforms but radiated bodyguard.

The two Mínglíàng parties combined and crossed to where Damien was waiting, Governor Wong Lee taking a slight lead and offering his hand to the Hand.

"Lord Montgomery," he said crisply. "It is good to see you."

Damien shook his hand, then Admiral Phan's in turn. He nodded to Wong Ken and Metharom genteelly before returning this attention to the Governor.

"Your Excellency," he returned the greeting. "I'm not so sure you're going to be so glad to see me once we've spoken. If you and Admiral Phan can join me in my office, Mage-Captain Jakab will see to the Minister and the Commodore's needs."

Wong looked unsurprisingly taken aback, but slowly nodded.

"Of course, Lord Montgomery," he agreed.

Damien led the way towards his office in silence. Both Phan and Wong were significantly taller than he was, but they were both noticeably struggling to keep up as he stalked through the corridors of the starship.

Finally reaching his destination, he crossed the office to stand at the massive observation window, looking out at the planet below—and the clearly visible lights of the Mínglìàng Security Flotilla's two brand new cruisers and their swarm of attendant support craft.

"Wow," he heard Wong breathe behind him as the Governor got a glance at the massive space Damien had coopted for his relatively spartan office. The two Mínglìàng officials walked up behind him, both staring out the window.

"That is quite the view you have, my lord," Wong continued after a long moment. "Makes me want to move my office into orbit."

"Ken would never forgive you," Phan told him. "He *hates* space."

"That is neither here nor there," the Governor admitted, stepping up to stand beside Damien and look down at his planet. "You told us, Lord Montgomery, that you knew what had happened to our two missing ships. You also," he continued darkly, "said we wouldn't like the answers."

"Indeed," Damien replied. "En route to Sherwood, we intercepted a pirate attack on a Sherwood registry freighter. She was attacked and killed, and then the pirates attacked the *Duke of Magnificence*. Both ships were destroyed."

"Wait, you can't mean..." Phan trailed off.

Damien tapped a command on his wrist computer, and the wall-screen overlaid on the massive window lit up with the tactical recording of the attack, and the sensor details on the two destroyers.

"Both pirates were *Lancer*-class destroyers from Tau Ceti Nova Industries Batch Twenty-Four-Fifty-D," he told her calmly. "A batch that the Mínglìàng Security Flotilla purchased all eight units of. Two of your ships, Admiral, attacked a Royal Martian Navy vessel carrying a Hand of the Mage-King of Mars.

"Do you understand?" he asked softly, "why the presence of multiple *cruisers* in Míngliàng orbit now makes me very concerned?"

"MyLlord, I swear to you on all that is holy, if ships of mine were engaged in piracy *I did not know*," Phan pleaded desperately.

"I accept that as a possibility," Damien told her. "Nonetheless, I have no choice but to restrict the operations of the MSF to the Míngliàng System."

The Admiral swallowed, glancing at the Governor for support, then back to him.

"I understand, but our ships... our people..."

"The Sherwood Patrol is also under the same order," he told her. "I have also ordered all ships currently in the Antonius System to remain there and suspended shipping from Sherwood. The same applies here. There will be no shipping to or from the Antonius System until the Royal Martian Navy is present in sufficient force to provide security."

"And how long will that be?" Wong demanded. "That is a massive portion of our industry, one of the life bloods of this system's economy!"

"No more than two, perhaps three, weeks," Damien replied. "I have already requested reinforcements from several sectors. Admiral Medici should be arriving with ships from Nia Kriti inside three weeks, and more ships will follow."

"We have the forces to maintain our own security," Phan pointed out.

"Yes," Damien conceded. "But the evidence I have to hand, Admiral, is that both the Patrol and the Flotilla have been *aggravating* factors in this situation. You *will* suspend all operations. My people will also require full sensor logs from all of your ships, and any backups from the two missing vessels."

"For what?" she demanded.

"To see what truths or lies may be concealed within them," he said bluntly. "Admiral, the Patrol lost a *frigate* four weeks ago, to an attack by ships that matched the emissions signature of Flotilla destroyers. I have evidence of a rogue faction inside the *Patrol's* ranks that they are trying to root out on their end. Currently, I have no evidence except your word that the attacks on Sherwood's shipping weren't authorized by you."

"Attacks?" Wong interjected. "More than just the two you've told us about?"

"Attacks, Governor," Damien confirmed. "More, in fact, than you've reported to me on your shipping—including the death of one of Governor McLaughlin's youngest nephews. Both of your systems have seen your civilian jump-ships—especially those heading to and from Antonius—come under attack by what appears to be the other system's militia.

"So we are restricting your militias to their home systems," he continued flatly. "The Protectorate has already assumed responsibility for security at Antonius. *Dreams of Liberty* will protect your people until Admiral Medici arrives."

He turned to face Wong and Phan, both of whom looked more shocked than anything else.

"I intend to stop the dying and the violence," he finished. "Keeping everyone *happy* isn't on my agenda."

CHAPTER 26

"MY TEAM is still going over the data the MSF provided, but one of our initial conclusions was huge enough that I felt it necessary to call this meeting," Commander Rhine said briskly, gesturing around at the small collection of officers and aides once again gathered in the *Duke's* conference room.

"What did you find, Commander?" Damien asked.

"On the left, my lord, you'll see the full spectrum diagrams for the eight ships Míngliàng purchased from Batch Twenty-Four-Fifty-D," Rhine pointed out. Images of eight destroyers, with a wide variety of colors and notations, appeared on one third of the screen. Damien could read *parts* of the diagram, but not all of it—but he could tell that all eight were quite similar.

"In the center, is the general emission profiles for that batch as provided by TCNI to the Navy," the tactical officer continued. A single diagram of a destroyer appeared, still with a wide variety of colors and notations, now with ranges and shading.

Damien could read them well enough to tell that all eight of the MSF ships fit in the ranges and shading given. That was the purpose of the profile the shipbuilder gave the Protectorate government, after all.

"As you can see, there is no question that these eight ships are the entire batch that TCNI built," Rhine noted. "They all fit the pattern TCNI recorded, and all of them have the hull numbers and other identifiers to match back to TCNI's records."

"I'm sorry, Commander," Damien said softly, "but we know all this already. What's your point?"

"My point is these," the Navy man replied, and the last third of the screen lit up with two more spectrum diagrams. "These are the spectrum diagrams of the two ships that attacked us. As the *Duke* was directly engaged with them, we have everything *our* sensors could pull, which is much better than even the regional militias would be able to assemble."

"So you've identified the ships?" Amiri asked, leaning in and studying the diagrams. Damien wasn't sure his bodyguard could read them, but he could... and what he was seeing was strange.

"No," Rhine told her. "We ran the analysis six separate times. I can say, with a roughly ninety-four percent certainty, that these two ships are part of Batch Twenty-Four-Fifty-D. I can, however, also say—with just over *ninety-nine* percent certainty—that these two ships are *not* any of the vessels from that Batch owned by the Míngliàng Security Flotilla."

Damien glanced from one set of diagrams to the next, and then the next. He trusted Rhine's analysis, and he could even see it himself if he looked. The two ships fit the Batch profile, but didn't match any of the ships *in* that Batch.

"How is that even possible?" he asked.

"It would actually be relatively easy, if not quick," Amiri said slowly, his bodyguard leaning back and studying the screen. "Back when I was a Hunter, we had to deal with ships changing their emissions signatures— any yard can do it. Matching a specific ship would be almost impossible, but getting into a profile like the one TCNI gives us for each batch? That would be straightforward enough."

She pursed her lips in thought and looked over at Damien. "Time-consuming, though. You're manually retuning every engine, every antennae."

"But any yard could do it," Damien repeated. "Son of a *bitch*."

"If the ships *we* killed weren't Míngliàng's, what happened to their ships?" Jakab asked.

"*Someone* knew we'd destroyed them," the Hand said flatly. "So they hunted down a pair of MSF ships on patrol that would match the

Batch number, and blew them to hell to make *everyone* think the MSF attacked us."

"That's assigning our theoretical enemy near-omniscience, my lord," Jakab noted. "If there was a third ship, we'd have seen them jump in with the others."

"Or our enemy could have spies in Sherwood, which I think is more likely." Damien returned. "Every time I turn around, the arrows keep pointing back to Sherwood."

"I can't see them blowing up one of their own frigates," Christoffsen pointed out. "Not to mention, we have a *damn* good idea how many destroyers came anywhere near Sherwood. Even if Sherwood could do the modification, we *know* what happened to their destroyers: they gave them to the Navy to scrap. Their budgets are transparent even for a Protectorate world —we'd *know* if Sherwood had a spare squadron of destroyers floating around somewhere."

"If they have a rogue, I could see that rogue destroying another ship to get closer to the war they seem to be trying to start," Damien growled. "I just don't see what they plan to gain out of it. A war between Sherwood and Mínglìàng doesn't benefit anyone, but it could easily tear the entire Protectorate apart!"

"Maybe that's what they're after," Christoffsen murmured. "The Protectorate has enemies, and the shared ownership of Antonius creates one hell of a pressure point. Push hard enough..."

"That's *insane*," Rhine objected. "Without the Protectorate, the Guild falls apart—and our entire *civilization* goes with it."

"Insane or not, that's what could easily happen if we don't find out just what the hell is going on in the background here," Damien reminded his people. "Rhine—keep digging. Match the data we have from the MSF against *everything* Sherwood gave us. If some of those attacks are MSF ships, I want to know. If *all* of them are launched by ships *pretending* to be MSF, we at least know Mínglìàng isn't the source of the problem."

The Commander was opening his mouth to reply when both his and Mage-Captain Jakab's wrist computers lit up with an emergency alert. Both of them read it and went very, very pale.

"What is it?" Damien demanded.

"A ship just jumped in from Antonius," Jakab said slowly. "They're transmitting an emergency beacon with a Navy code addendum."

The addendum meant a Navy ship had given the ship a message to deliver to any Royal Martian Navy vessels they encountered. It was used for emergency transmissions only and usually had a simple header for ease of prioritization.

"What code, Captain?!"

"It's a Code Omega, sir," Jakab finished, his voice shaky. "The *Dreams of Liberty* has been destroyed."

The captain of the jump freighter *Rains at Sunset* looked like he hadn't slept for a week. He was a young, dark-haired man with a Mage medallion at his throat and visible bags under his eyes.

Damien recognized the signs of a Jump Mage who'd pushed himself far too hard, probably hitting six hour jumps repeatedly. His captain aboard the *Blue Jay* had physically sat him down and stopped him when he'd tried that, but this man *was* the Captain. He hoped the man's XO had a spine of titanium.

"Captain, this is Hand Damien Montgomery aboard the RMN cruiser *Duke of Magnificence*," he greeted the other man. "We received the Code Omega in your beacon, do you have an update for me?"

Damien settled down to wait for a response. The ship was still thirty light seconds out, several days travel for a civilian ship like the *Rains at Sunset*. A minute passed, and he could tell the moment his transmission arrived, as the *Rains*'s captain suddenly straightened and tried to fix his unruly hair.

"My Lord Montgomery!" he half-gasped. "I am Captain Erik Vang. I am so glad we found you—Captain Arrow ordered us to find you, 'no matter what,' he said. You had to know what happened."

Vang swallowed, shaking his head as if to clear cobwebs.

"He died saving us, my lord," he continued. "None of the ships that made it out would have without Captain Arrow. He did everything he could to stop what happened."

That spiel seemed to exhaust Vang, and he glanced aside checking something over.

"I'm sending you the data package he gave us, as well as our sensor logs," he almost whispered. "There are other ships on their way. I don't know if they're safe."

Damien leaned forward, focusing on the other man's eyes though he knew it would be half a minute before the other man heard what he was saying.

"What *happened*, Captain Vang?" he demanded. "I'll review the data, but we know *nothing*."

A minute ticked by, and Vang nodded slowly.

"The Central Processing Facility was attacked," he replied. "A warship—I *think* a Sherwood frigate, but I know Captain Arrow's download has more data—jumped in and attacked. The *Dreams of Liberty* tried to save the station, but failed."

Vang shivered.

"She covered us all the way out to safe jump distance, my lord," he said. "None of us could have evaded that warship—but Captain Arrow took out every missile they fired straight at us. He forced them to focus their fire on him. He got eleven ships out, Hand Montgomery. Fifteen hundred people."

But he'd done it by making his attacker take the time to kill him. Arrow might have hoped to bring the frigate in range of his amplifier, but the Code Omega meant he'd failed.

It meant Damien Montgomery had sent Captain John Arrow to his death and the death of his entire crew—and the *twenty-five thousand* civilians on the Mínigliàng Antonius Central Processing Facility had died with them.

"Thank you, Captain Vang," he said levelly. "We will review the data package from Captain Arrow. If you can provide us all the information on the other ships that escaped, I will see what I can do to guarantee *their* safety as well."

"He died for us, my lord," Vang stated, his transmission passing Damien's in the space between them. "I'll never forget that. They *died* to save us."

The channel closed, and Damien felt a heavy hand fall on his shoulder. He looked up, finally reregistering the bridge of the *Duke* around him, and Mage-Captain Jakab standing behind him.

"You did what seemed best, Damien," Jakab murmured in his ear. "And John Arrow did his duty. What use is the Mage-King's Protectorate if we do not protect people?"

The image of Captain John Arrow filled the conference screen and Damien had no eyes for his subordinates gathered around him as he looked at the man he'd unknowingly sent into an impossible battle.

Arrow stood on the bridge of the *Dreams of Liberty*, his executive officer behind him hanging onto the ship's silver simulacrum. The bridge seemed calm and unshaken, but the flashing red alerts on the screens around the captain gave the lie to that calm.

"My Lord Montgomery," Arrow began. "I hope this message reaches you before the situation grows further out of control. I am forwarding it to all of the freighters currently fleeing the Antonius System, one of them should reach you in time.

"I have failed to protect the Míngliàng space station in this system, but I believe I have succeeded in guarding the freighters out to their jump points. Unfortunately, my vessel has taken critical damage and we are being actively pursued.

"Once this transmission is complete, I intend to close to amplifier range and attempt to destroy the enemy. I am attaching full sensor records from the moment they arrived until completion of this transmission, and hope that the freighters themselves can provide however this story ends."

Captain Arrow, one of the few non-Mages to ever command a starship of the Royal Martian Navy, winced as a new series of alarms lit up on one of the screens surrounding him, but focused back on the camera.

"The most important piece of information in the attached data is this: the attacking vessel is running a lot of ECM, but it's not enough to defeat our scanners. We have identified our attackers as the *Alan-a-dale*. Captain Wayne of the Sherwood Patrol is guilty of mass murder."

"She's maneuvering to clear her lasers!" a voice on the recording shouted, and the screen cut suddenly to black.

"That was the end of the recording," Rhine reported. "Captain Arrow did successfully transmit his full sensor logs."

"Show me," Damien ordered. "We'll need to share all of this with Governor Wong and the MSF, so we may as well know exactly what happened."

A moment later, the screen faded into a recording of the *Dreams's* bridge and a duplicate of the destroyer's standard tactical plot. In the center was the green triangle of the *Dreams of Liberty*. At the far edge were a scattering of small icons representing the closest sets of the in-system extractor ships that fuelled Antonius's value to Mínglìàng and Sherwood.

Close by in astronomical terms at a mere five light seconds was the impressive bulk of the Mínglìàng Antonius Central Processing Facility. It was made up of prefabricated sections carried to Antonius by freighter and did first and second stage refining on the ore and metals collected by the asteroid mining ships scattered through the belt.

A small city in space, the facility was the heart of Mínglìàng's presence in the system—and at almost *exactly* the opposite position in the system from the large asteroid Sherwood used to base its own presence. A dozen freighters were scattered along a chain from the nearest 'flat spot' in space they could jump in and out of to the station itself.

"Captain Arrow was making his first port visit at the Mínglìàng station after arriving in the system," Rhine noted. "The timing was almost accidental. I don't think Captain Wayne expected to find the *Dreams of Liberty* that close to the station."

It was theoretically possible to jump in and out of far higher gravitational levels than most civilian ships would ever risk. It was hard on the Mage, but a strong Mage would be fine if they got the usual eight hours of rest and an industrial dose of aspirin.

Captain Wayne clearly knew the trick, as the *Alan-a-dale* burst into existence on the far side of the space station from the *Dreams of Liberty* and the collection of freighters.

"Hail that ship!" Captain Arrow barked. "Demand an explanation for their presence—and take us to battle stations."

Much of the sound from the bridge recording had been muted. Damien couldn't hear the alarms, but he could see the strobing lights and the rush of Arrow's people to reach their stations.

"No response to our hail, sir," one of the junior officers replied. "I've got a bunch of ECM on the screens, but she's definitely a *Hunter*-class frigate."

"What is Sherwood playing at?" Arrow demanded. "They know they're not supposed to be here. Record for transm..."

"They've opened fire!"

The entire bridge was frozen, and Damien could only imagine the shock running through them as the *Alan-a-dale*, having closed to within barely a million kilometers of the station, launched missiles and opened fire with her battle lasers.

The Central Processing Facility was at its core a giant smelter. It was designed to contain immense heat and force... inside itself. Six-gigawatt lasers slammed into the armored containment vessel where the most intense work was done and ripped it open, scattering super-heated molten metal across the entire structure. More lasers slammed into habitation modules, docking sections, and the handful of pitiful missile defense stations the Facility had.

The station was already dead, coming apart at the seams, when the missiles arrived two minutes later. Sixty one-gigaton warheads flew to clearly pre-programmed positions and detonated, a searing blast of anti-matter fire that annihilated any chance for survivors.

"Identify that ship," Arrow ordered, his voice unnervingly calm. "Vector us to intercept her."

"Sir, I have to point that she out-masses us six to one," his XO replied, but the tactical plot showed that the woman was obeying as she spoke.

"Look at her vector, Christine," the captain told her, in that same calm voice. "She's going after the freighters. They don't have the acceleration to escape her. Your objection is noted, but we're going after her anyway."

"Wouldn't plan on anything else," she confirmed. "Bringing up the missile launchers and setting them for counter-missile mode. RFLAM turrets live and cycling. Charging the main beams and linking them into the anti-missile targeting software."

Arrow leaned back in his chair. "Take us in," he ordered.

The tactical display showed the important details now. The *Alan-a-dale* was pulling ten gravities, chasing after freighters that now pushed their own engines to three gravities—the highest any of them could safely go.

The *Dreams of Liberty* was pulling fifteen gravities, cutting the angle and charging between the two sets of ships.

"Bogey is firing," the XO reported. "Sixty missiles, looks like they're targeting the closest six freighters with ten each."

"Show the bastard why that won't play," Arrow ordered.

"Missiles on the way, lasers tracking."

The *Dreams of Liberty*'s Rapid Fire Laser Anti Missile turrets were lighter than those used by Martian cruisers, but she had almost forty of them. Twenty four missiles blasted into space, and laser beams followed as the destroyer pushed hard to cut off the frigate's salvo.

Defensive countermeasures on missiles were mostly designed to stop defensive fire coming from directly ahead. The frigate's missiles died in their dozens, and the follow-up salvo suffered the same fate. The *Dreams*'s missiles were faster and smarter, each of them easily intercepting and destroying a Sherwood missile. Those the missiles missed, the lasers swept up.

Four times, the frigate fired on the freighters she was pursuing, and four times Captain Arrow's ship ripped the missiles to shreds. The frigate wasn't *enough* faster than the freighters to bring most of them into energy range—if she needed to kill them all, she needed missiles.

Clearly, Captain Wayne agreed—and the fifth salvo fired at the *Dreams of Liberty*.

"Handle the amplifier, Christine," Arrow ordered. "I'll track lasers and missiles."

A second salvo blasted into space, and the frigate turned, adjusting her vector to bring her closer to the *Dreams*. If she took out the destroyer fast enough, she could still take down all of the freighters before they could escape.

"Sir, I've got them," the same junior officer as before shouted. "We know that ship—it's the *Alan-a-dale*."

Damien couldn't see Arrow's face in the recording, but he could see the captain shaking his head.

"Why?" he demanded uselessly. "Michael and I went for beers a week ago. Why the hell would he do this?"

Further conversation was cut off as the first salvo entered their engagement range, and Arrow focused on defending his ship. Now that the missiles were aimed at them, they were far harder targets. Only half of his missiles claimed a victim, leaving the rest for lasers and the amplifier.

The Mage-Commander's magic ripped through space, followed and surrounded by lasers. Missiles died by their dozens, and then they were clear, the entire first salvo destroyed.

"Give me a channel," Arrow ordered. "Captain Wayne," he snapped as soon as he had it, "you are firing on a Protectorate warship, and there is no way in *hell* I'm not getting a message out about this. Stand the *hell* down, and you might save your whole *system* from suffering for this."

The missile salvo closing in was the only answer. This time, the head-on intercepts fared even worse, and over fifty missiles blasted into the inner range. Dozens died to magic and missile defense lasers... but not all of them.

"Zee-plus evasion *now*," Arrow ordered, clearly realizing they weren't going to stop them all.

Emergency thrusters spun the ship ninety degrees, its massive engines laboring to blast it along a course at ninety degrees to its previous. It was almost enough.

One missile blasted past, missing by half a dozen kilometers and easy prey for the lasers once it had passed the destroyer.

The last missile was far enough back to adjust its course to match the *Dreams of Liberty*'s course change. It barreled directly in at the destroyer—only to be stopped by the XO's amplified magic... eighty meters from the hull.

Even on the recording, Damien could see the million ton mass of the destroyer *lurch* as the blast wave washed over them. Emergency alerts flared across the surrounding screens, forming a familiar pattern Damien recognized from the Captain's initial message.

"We need to send a message," Arrow told his crew, his voice still, *somehow,* calm. "Forward all of our sensor logs to *all* of the freighters. Tell them it *has* to reach Hand Montgomery—*no matter what!* I'll need to record a message to accompany the logs."

The captain looked around at his crew and nodded once, firmly. "We'll send it under Code Omega," he told them.

The recording froze.

"While Captain Arrow was recording his message to us, the *Alan-a-dale* was closing with the *Dreams of Liberty*," Rhine noted. "The *Alan-a-dale* engaged her from the maximum effective range of her own lasers, significantly outside the effective range of the *Dreams*'s laser weaponry or amplifier. Sensor records from the *Rains at Sunset* confirm that the *Dreams of Liberty* was badly damaged in the exchange that followed his transmission, and was destroyed less than five minutes after Arrow sent this message.

"By that point in time, the *Alan-a-dale* was undamaged, but out of range to successfully engage any of the eleven freighters fleeing the system with missiles or lasers. All of them made it to Antonius-Mingliàng Jump One. So far as Captain Vang is aware, the *Alan-a-dale* did not follow them."

Damien looked at the screen, now frozen on the tactical plot of the *Alan-a-dale*'s approach.

"How is that even *possible?*" he demanded. "We know where the *Alan-a-dale* was, and where she was going..." he paused, and looked over at Amiri. "Julia, would we have enough information for you to confirm where she jumped?"

Before Julia Amiri had joined the Secret Service, she'd been a bounty hunter—a terrifyingly good one. One of the reasons for that had been that she'd learned a skillset few outside the Hunters ever even knew existed—the ability to judge where a ship had jumped by the energy signature.

He'd seen it work, but she'd never managed to teach anyone else. Personally, Damien suspected that the Trackers possessed their own unique Gift, related to but distinct from that of regular Mages—and quite likely more related to his own Rune Wright abilities.

"We had the full sensor suite online investigating the *Mistletoe Solstice*," she said slowly. "We should. Damn it, Damien—I should have thought of that then."

"We weren't being paranoid enough," Damien said grimly. "Confirm it for me, Julia. If that *was* the *Alan-a-dale*—and I have no reason to doubt Captain Arrow—then Governor Wong will demand Captain Wayne's head as the price of peace.

"And I do not have the slightest issue with giving it to him."

CHAPTER 27

SPECIAL AGENT Julia Amiri sighed as she shooed the last of the crew out of the room. The tactical department techs in the *Duke of Magnificence*'s secondary sensor control room wanted to be *helpful*, but for something like this she really needed privacy.

The room wasn't big, just large enough for four techs to run a back-up set of consoles if something happened to the Combat Information Center. Its main value for her, right now, was that it had full access to the sensor logs, and a full set of surrounding screens.

She brought up the moment that the *Alan-a-dale* had jumped, and studied it for a long moment in the standard tactical plot sensor over-lay. There wasn't actually much of an energy signature when a ship disappeared. To most scanners, the ship was there one moment and gone the next.

With a keypress on one of the consoles, Julia split apart the layers. Thermal. Visible light. High wavelength radiation. Low wavelength radiation. Seventeen different bands of electromagnetic radiation all told.

Then gravity measurements. The notoriously unreliable 'thaumatur-gic signature' scanners. Tachyon and neutron scanners.

Twenty-five layers, each overlaid and separate, and Julia smiled. It had been *years* since she'd really dug into Tracking a starship. She'd tried to train people when she'd joined the service, but only a handful of her students ever really *got* what she was after.

Montgomery had come closer than many, but he'd lacked the time to study then. A year's effort had produced a grand total of *three* Trackers for the Protectorate, and she'd begged Alaura Stealey, the Hand who'd brought her in from the cold, for a field placement.

Some of those had involved Tracking, but then she and Montgomery had ended up on Ardennes, and she'd realized the Mage-King's most magically powerful Hand needed *somebody* to watch his back.

But now, she hunted the patterns. No single layer revealed anything. A first glance, in fact, showed nothing. Carefully, her tongue between her teeth, Amiri set out reorganizing the layers, hunting the patterns she knew were there.

It wasn't a fast process. But when it was done, she would *know* if it truly was Captain Wayne who'd murdered the miners at Antonius.

"Governor, I owe you my apologies as well as my condolences," Damien told Governor Wong quietly. "I honestly did not believe that *anyone* would be willing to attack a Protectorate warship—or to commit an atrocity of this scale. We failed your people."

"The crime was Sherwood's," Wong said flatly from the wallscreen in Damien's office. "I have ordered Admiral Phan to complete a full mobilization of the Míngliàng Security Flotilla. The Patrol has become a clear and present threat, and I *will* deal with it."

"This is no longer your jurisdiction," the Hand continued, his voice still quiet. "The *Protectorate* assumed responsibility for Antonius's safety. We now have responsibility for its justice as well."

"Twenty-five *thousand* of my people were murdered, Lord Montgomery—an atrocity, as you say. An act of *war* I will *not* allow to pass."

"You speak of acts of war as if you are a sovereign nation, Governor," Damien replied, remembering saying the same words to Governor McLaughlin with a chill of déjà vu. "You have no authority to wage war using the MSF, Governor. You *have* the right to ask for Protectorate assistance, and we are already in motion."

"If you were going to save us, then my people would not be dead," Wong snapped. "Your intervention has only weakened us. Only cost lives. I question your true loyalties, Montgomery!"

If they had been in the same room instead of speaking over the screen, the anger that flashed through Damien could easily have had... dangerous consequences. As it was, he was glad his hands weren't visible in the image being sent to Wong, as fire encased them and incinerated his gloves as he breathed deeply to control himself.

"Three hundred and fourteen Martian Navy personnel *died* to protect your station and your ships," he said coldly. "Had your three destroyers been there, the result would have been no different—there would only have been *more* deaths. I will *not* permit you to start this war, Governor. I will relieve you first."

"And if I refuse to be relieved?" Wong demanded. "If I refuse to bow tamely to the child of my enemy that the Mage-King has sent me? What will you do *then*, 'Lord' Montgomery?"

"You would leave me a choice between executing you or expelling Mínglìàng from the Protectorate," Damien told him. "Most likely, I think I would neutralize the MSF as non-lethally as possible. Expending those resources, however, could easily prevent me from seeking justice for your people!"

"You wouldn't dare!"

"I speak for Mars," Damien thundered, raising his voice for the first time and watching the Governor flinch backwards. "I am the Hand of the Mage-King, and I will do *whatever* I must to stop this war. I speak for Mars," he repeated. "*Will you listen?*"

Governor Wong met his glare for a moment of silence.

"Then speak," Wong ordered.

"I have grounds to believe that at least one Captain in the Sherwood Patrol has gone rogue," Damien explained. "The *Duke*'s tactical department have confirmed, with the data from the *Dreams of Liberty*, that every time your people have a confirmed frigate encounter they can identify, it was the *Alan-a-dale*. I believe Captain Wayne, as the acting second in command of the Patrol, attempted to murder Commodore

McLaughlin—with the intent of using her murder, along with the attacks by apparent Mínglìang vessels, to trigger a war between your systems."

"Wait, *apparent* Mínglìang vessels?" the Governor interjected. He appeared to be at least partially playing for time.

"We've reviewed the scan data we have," the Hand told him. "Comparing it to your actual ships and the data you gave us, the attacks on Sherwood shipping appear to have been carried out by someone with ships that have been heavily modified to appear as MSF vessels to even relatively close inspection. They faked up uniforms and armor for a boarding operation I'm now convinced we were *intended* to find footage of.

"Governor, *someone* is *trying* to start a war between you and Sherwood. The identification of the *Alan-a-dale* is the first solid lead we have—and we *know* Captain Wayne killed your people.

"Give me *time*," he begged. "Give me time, and I will bring Captain Wayne to justice for the crew of the Processing Facility. I will find his sponsors, and whoever is tarring *your* world's name. If Michael Wayne is guilty, he will pay for his crimes."

"And in what world do you think he is not guilty?" Wong demanded.

"I don't," Damien admitted. "But I am the Hand of the Mage-King, I cannot leap to conclusions without evidence. Given that I now *know* someone is using disguised ships, I cannot convict without more data."

"I understand *your* concern," the Governor finally admitted. "But my people need to see action. *My dead* deserve justice."

"I will bring them justice," Damien promised. "All of the dead, Governor—Sherwood's. Mínglìang's. The Navy's. I *will* see justice done—starting with Captain Michael Wayne."

He shook his head, glancing at his computer screen. "If you *must* be seen to do something, Governor," he noted, "there are still freighters scattered from here to Antonius whose safety is in question. I will *partially* release the operational restriction on the MSF to allow you to collect those ships safely.

"But if you take your ships to Sherwood, Governor, one way or another, the Míngliàng Security Flotilla will cease to exist," Damien promised. "Do you understand me?"

"You have seventy-two hours," Wong finally conceded. "If you have not brought me Michael Wayne, or conclusive evidence of his innocence and someone *else's* guilt, by then, I will do what I feel is necessary."

A text-only message flashed up on his screen—from Amiri.

The Alan-a-dale *jumped to Antonius. Wayne did it.*

"What?" Wong asked, as Damien stared at his Tracker's message.

"I just received that 'more data' I mentioned," he said quietly. "We will be leaving for Sherwood momentarily, Governor. I think we can give you both justice and satisfaction."

Damien entered the *Duke's* bridge to find it a scene of chaos. Officers were rushing around the normally calm room, passing datapads and electronic messages back and forth in a flurry of activity.

Jakab spotted him after a moment, and dodged past an Ensign half-running towards Commander Rhine with a patient smile.

"Apologies for the atmosphere, my lord," he told Damien. "We were expecting to be in orbit for several days, but given the news out of Antonius I ordered us moved to full combat readiness. We are fueled and ready to deploy anywhere you want us, sir."

The Mage-Captain's competence—and foresight—reassured the Hand, who glanced around at the chaos and noted the familiar patterns of a ship preparing to clear orbit. A civilian ship would have fewer personnel, but the chaos and patterns would be much the same.

"Well done, Captain," Damien finally said. "We'll need to be under way as soon as physically possible. How long?"

"One hour to jump distance," Jakab replied instantly. "Where are we headed?"

"Sherwood, Mage-Captain," the Hand told him. "We need to arrest Captain Wayne, and he should have been recalled by now."

"Understood, sir," the *Duke's* commander agreed. "I'm assuming we'll be entering the system at battle stations, then? Just in case."

"Yes," Damien confirmed. "We'll go in fully armed and watching for trouble. I don't expect to have to destroy the *Alan-a-dale*, not when she's surrounded by the rest of the Patrol, but it may be necessary."

"Unless the rest of the Patrol tries to protect her, sir, she is no match for the *Duke*," Jakab said confidently.

"I trust Commodore McLaughlin," the Hand told him. "If Wayne tries to fight, the rest of the Patrol will be with us." He paused, considering for a moment as he studied the simulacrum at the center of the bridge. "Include me on the jump rotation, Captain," he ordered finally. "I have a bad feeling about this, and I want to be in Sherwood *now*."

CHAPTER 28

GRACE MCLAUGHLIN'S office aboard the *Robin Hood* was just large enough to get a good solid pace going. Twelve steps one way, twelve steps the other, looking at the tactical plot one way and out the skylight into space the other.

She was angry with Damien. Angry with Mínglià ng. Angry with *whoever* the traitor in her own ranks was. None of these were particularly actionable angers, which left the commanding officer of the Sherwood Interstellar Patrol pacing her office impotently.

A status report on her desk informed her that the *Nottingham* and the *Lionheart* had completed their abbreviated work-ups. Both frigates were due to rendezvous with the rest of the patrol in orbit in under an hour, bringing her available force up to six frigates.

The last she'd heard from the Defender Yards was that she'd have the *Loxley* and the *Newstead Abbey* online in six hours. Neither would be fully crewed or even, honestly, fully *functional*. But they'd have missile launchers, lasers, ammunition and—thankfully!—Jump Mages.

Finding those had been a *pain,* and she wasn't sure the head of the Jump Mage program at the University of Sherwood City's Thaumaturgy department was ever going to speak to her again. She'd scooped his best professor and three un-graduated students to man *warships*.

Guilty as she felt about that, the situation had her worried enough that she'd done it anyway. Sherwood had less than eleven thousand Mages in two billion people. While a normal ratio for a MidWorld, and higher than many Fringe Worlds, it was still fewer than a Core World. The Royal Martian Navy had access to the Sol System with its million-plus Mages. She had whatever she could scrape out of a University classroom.

But, unless her math was wrong, Montgomery's courier ship should have been back hours ago. The *Alan-a-dale* was also overdue, though that could easily have been the civilian courier ship she'd hired to deliver the recall notice missing a connection and having to chase the frigate through a few jumps.

FN-2187's absence worried her. The courier had been supposed to short-stop shipping from Antonius, though that wouldn't start showing up as an impact for a day or so yet given how much slower freighters were than a Navy courier.

Even with delivering Montgomery's orders to both colonies, the courier should still have returned twelve hours ago. That kind of schedule slip she might expect from a civilian freighter but, again, not for a Navy courier.

The thought that she and her Patrol *needed* a Navy babysitter was why she was angry. Intellectually, she knew that Montgomery sitting on the Míngl---iàng Security Flotilla with a *battlecruiser* but sending a *courier* to watch her Patrol was about as much trust as the Hand could extend.

That didn't stop her feeling that a man she'd once loved and was still very much *interested* in had told her he couldn't *afford* to trust her. She could understand why, but it still hurt.

Grace stopped at the skylight, staring out into space at Sherwood Orbital. The *Robin Hood* was far enough away she couldn't see the damage where someone had tried to kill her and Montgomery. Even she could see how all of the evidence pointed back to Sherwood. All the answers led home.

Accord had promised her an update that evening, as it was still a little over twelve hours away. She was tempted to call and demand to know what lead he'd found worth following.

She turned and paced back to the tactical plot, studying the positions of her ships. Six ships. Thirty-six million tons of warship—twice what

Míngliàng had. The new warship order she'd been warned about would hugely increase the MSF's strength, but once she had all nine of her ships together—assuming the *Alan-a-dale* was just late—she'd still have the edge.

An icon flared on the tactical plot. A jump flare!

"Bridge, this is McLaughlin," she said crisply. "Identify that ship."

"Working on it, ma'am," Lieutenant Jason Anderson, the officer currently on watch replied. "We're receiving a transmission—it's the *Alan-a-dale*."

Grace sighed. At least she was down to only *one* overdue ship now, but she'd hoped it would be FN-2187. The missing courier was *really* starting to worry her.

"Tell Captain Wayne to get his ship into orbit ASAP," she ordered. "He's to refuel and be prepared for immediate deployment."

"Yes, ma'am," Anderson replied. "I have a note in their message that they need missile resupply—they had completed live fire exercises while they were out."

"He did what?" Grace said flatly while searching her memory. She had to have ordered him not to do that. Given the suspicions already laid against the Patrol, missing missiles were the *last* thing she needed... but she hadn't actually ordered him not to carry out any exercises. She'd just assumed Wayne wasn't an *idiot*.

"They conducted a live fire exercise," Anderson repeated. From his tone, he'd heard enough of the rumors to guess why his Commodore was irritated, and didn't want any of it to spill on him.

Grace sighed again.

"I will discuss that with Captain Wayne later," she conceded. "Please organize a refueling ship and a collier, Lieutenant." She paused, a moment of pure paranoia striking her. "And Jason," she said very, very quietly, "I want you to personally verify how many missiles they transfer."

"Ma'am?"

"Live fire exercises are a single salvo, Lieutenant," she reminded him. "I want you to confirm for me that the collier only loads one salvo. If Wayne fired more than that, I need to know."

She *heard* him swallow.

"Yes, ma'am," he responded levelly. "I presume we don't want Captain Wayne to know about this."

"No," she confirmed. "If all is aboveboard, it won't matter. If it isn't..."

"I understand, Commodore."

Grace eventually joined Commander Arrington on the bridge for his portion of the watch. She was too agitated to rest or do paperwork, though she hoped she was concealing that from her crew. Days like today were when she felt her relative youth and lack of experience hardest.

Michael Wayne's utter unperturbedness had been much of what had attracted her to the man when they'd been, theoretically, equals. A decade-and-a-half in civilian shipping had given the *Alan-a-dale*'s captain an astonishing ability to take *everything* in stride.

In a little over five hours, he'd managed to rendezvous with both the tanker and ammunition collier she'd sent out, fully restock his vessel for deployment, and join the squadron she was assembling in high orbit.

With seven heavily-armed ships, she was starting to feel more confident in her ability to handle whatever the galaxy decided to throw at her—confident enough that she was considering sending a ship to go looking for the missing Navy courier. FN-2187's continued absence was making her nervous.

"Still no sign of Montgomery's courier?" she asked aloud.

"Negative, ma'am," Lieutenant Anderson told her. "I just finished remote interrogating the *Teabiscuit*'s inventory system, Commodore," the pale, skinny, far too young officer continued.

Arrington looked confused, but she motioned him to wait.

"And, Lieutenant?" she asked.

"Everything looks correct," Anderson admitted. "Their inventory system shows that they shifted over sixty missiles without warheads. That's exactly what we'd expect from one live fire test."

"Thank you, Lieutenant," she told him. Paranoid as she was feeling, it was good to have at least some confirmation that Wayne wasn't outright lying to her. Probably.

"Ma'am! Jump flare!" Lieutenant Amber, the other officer on duty, announced. "On the line for Antonius, looking for an IFF beacon now."

The redheaded young woman was normally rosy-cheeked enough to attract teasing from her coworkers, but was suddenly as pale as Anderson was.

"Ma'am... it's the *Royal Learner,* one of our Antonius freighters—but her beacon is carrying a Navy Code Omega!"

"We can't access the data package the *Royal Learner* received from FN-2187," Grace told her grandfather. "We know it was a Code Omega, but we're relying on the *Learner's* sensor logs for what we've learned of the courier's fate."

"You're procrastinating, Grace," her Governor said calmly. "What is it you don't want to tell me?"

She swallowed, trying to organize the chaotic mess of thoughts and emotions ripping through in the twenty minutes since the *Royal Learner* had dumped their sensor logs to the *Robin Hood.*

"Approximately twenty-eight hours ago, less than thirty minutes after FN-2187 arrived and issued the hold shipping order, eight destroyers emerged from jump within attack distance of the Greenwood Outpost," she said mechanically. "They destroyed FN-2187 and a number of freighters within moments of emergence. *Royal Learner* had been on her way out of the system and was turning back on Commander Renzetti's orders.

"His final order was for them to reverse course and come here as fast as they could, delivering his Code Omega," she continued. "From *Royal Learner's* sensors, Mage-Commander Renzetti *attempted* to use his ship's missile defenses to cover the colony. He failed.

"The *Learner's* data is sufficient for us to confirm no less than four one gigaton antimatter strikes on the surface colony."

GLYNN STEWART

Greenwood had been built onto the surface of the largest asteroid in
Antonius, using the asteroid's gravity to anchor the big refineries needed
for their purposes while keeping them a safe distance from the primary
residential sectors. Like most such colonies with major industrial pres-
ences, the 'company town' had expanded dramatically, and Greenwood
had been home to some forty thousand people.

A surface colony, even one of domes and tunnels, was always a bit
easier to expand than a space station. That was why Sherwood had used
the asteroid as the base for their operations—and now that ease had
killed tens of thousands of people.

"We have no choice but to conclude the colony is a total loss," she
concluded, her voice still wooden as she tried not to cry. She'd had *friends*
on Greenwood. People she would now never see again.

"We cannot confirm the identity of the attackers as the *Learner* only
had civilian grade scanners," she said quietly, "but I am forced to conclude that it was almost certainly Mínglìàng forces."

Her grandfather was silent for a long time. Somehow, seconds had
seemed to age the already old Governor years, and he stared half-blankly
at the camera for almost a full minute before coughing to clear his throat
and meeting her gaze.

"What do we *do*?" he asked. Sad and desperate as he sounded, Grace
knew he wasn't a grandfather asking his granddaughter how to deal
with a tragedy—but a planetary Governor asking his senior military
commander how to respond to an atrocity of previously-unimaginable
scope.

"What we must," she replied, and if her voice was flat with rage, it
was no longer mechanical. "I have nine jump-capable warships of the
Patrol," she told him. "I intend to take them all to Antonius. There, we
will engage in search and rescue operations to make certain that all of
our surviving people are safe.

"If any of the attackers remain in Antonius," she continued, "we
will engage and destroy them. Since the MSF isn't supposed to be in
Antonius, *any* of their vessels will qualify as legitimate targets."

Calmly, levelly, she met her Governor's eyes.

"I then intend to take those nine ships on a counter-force operation into Mínglìàng," she said flatly. "I will give the MSF one opportunity to evacuate their ships, and then I will destroy every jump-capable warship they possess."

"You heard Montgomery's orders as well as I did," her Governor pointed out. "The Patrol is not permitted to leave Sherwood. The Martian Navy was responsible for the protection of Antonius."

"Montgomery underestimated our enemy," she replied. "I will leave *justice* to the Hand—but I must—*we* must—act to protect our people."

It wasn't Montgomery's fault. Despite everything, *that* was surprisingly clear to her. It wasn't his fault—but she could also no longer trust him to fix everything. No longer trust the *Protectorate* to fix everything.

Her grandfather looked positively *ancient*. Every bit of the energy and iron will that sustained him against his age seemed to have fled him, and she knew, knew in her very bones, that this would be the straw that finally took him out of office.

"You," he coughed, clearing his throat before he continued. "Your proposed operation is authorized," he said thickly. "Do what you must."

CHAPTER 29

"YOU ASKED to see me, my lord?" Professor Christoffsen asked as he entered Damien's office.

"I did," Damien confirmed. "Have a seat. Coffee?"

"Certainly."

Damien poured a second cup for the ex-Governor and slid it across to him. He waited patiently for the other man to take his first appreciative sip and smiled. He liked good coffee, and watching other people enjoy the blends he picked was a small, but real, pleasure.

Such pleasures were rare right now. Jumping the *Duke of Magnificence* had been surprisingly relaxing. It drained him less than it drained the other Jump Mages, but it was still an exhausting experience—but a familiar one, one he could control.

"Most people with your authority have someone else pour coffee, you know," Christoffsen noted as he leaned back and studied Damien. "I find it interesting that you do it yourself."

"Why would I not?" he asked. "If nothing else, Professor, it's one less person I need to get a security clearance for."

"Touché, my lord," Christoffsen laughed. "What did you need from me?"

"Perspective," Damien admitted. "You know why you were asked to help me, right? I know His Majesty called in a pretty significant favor to get you on my staff."

"Not as big as you might think," the older man told him. "Early retirement was boring me out of my skull. But... Desmond said that the runes you could use as a Rune Wright made you the most powerful Mage he'd ever trained, but you were also one of the youngest to ever carry a Hand. He wanted you to have someone with more gray in their hair to back you up. And someone with more experience in the down and dirty of politics."

"I am not the largest fan of politics," Damien agreed. "The final resolution on Ardennes worked out for everyone, but all I needed to do was keep things together until the interim Governor arrived. Now..." he shrugged.

"Now I'm about to arrest and probably execute a senior captain from one star system for crimes committed against another," Damien concluded. "We have come to the very edge of a bloody civil war because of Wayne and whoever his sponsors are. The tensions around Antonius are dangerous, and even proving Wayne was at the heart of so much of it will not ease that tension.

"I have to do *something* to keep things from getting worse, but I'm not seeing the solution."

"That's because you don't have enough information," Christoffsen noted. "You literally can't, you're not intimately involved in this mess the way the people at the heart of it are. All we can do as an outside force is end the bloodshed and get people talking."

"Lock Wong and McLaughlin in a room for a week and see what they come up with?"

"Effectively, yes," his aide replied. "I found that often my job as Governor was just to get the right people actually *talking* to each other instead of feuding from different boardrooms. It's a lot harder to assume the worst of your opponents when they're looking you in the eye and telling you what their exact problem is!"

"But hardly impossible," Damien said dryly. "I've seen *that* often enough."

"No, it's not—but if the Governors are honest, honorable men, actually getting them to *talk* to each other will help," Christoffsen said. "Half of the problem is that the two systems are sharing jurisdiction over Antonius... but nobody ever sorted out what that *meant*, so they basically had two separate colonies competing with each other."

Damien sighed and took a sip of his own coffee. It made sense, but if it was really that simple, why hadn't it happened already?

"Governors don't leave their systems," the ex-Governor sitting across from his answered his unspoken question. "They don't. There isn't really a reasoning for that beyond tradition and the fact the Mage-King never leaves Mars."

"There are reasons for that," Damien replied. He didn't say anything more—the existence of the Solar Simulacrum and the Olympus Mons Amplifier, tools that made the Mage-King almost omnipotent within the Sol System, was so classified he wasn't sure *he* was supposed to know.

"And there really isn't for Governors," Christoffsen said. "So if a Hand tells them to get off their asses and meet, they will. And that might just give us the beginning of an answer to this mess."

"Thanks," Damien told him quietly. "We'll see, I guess, but I needed a plan for once we've stopped the continuing meltdown that this whole sector has turned into."

"Once we've stopped?" his aide asked. "We're pretty much at 'Arrest Wayne and deliver his head on a platter' to achieve peace from what I can tell."

"With the way everything has gone since we got here, Professor, what makes you think it's going to be that easy?"

Damien made the final jump into Sherwood himself. While the training and experience of the *Duke of Magnificence*'s four Jump Mages exceeded his now, jumping *deep* into a gravity well was more a question of sheer power than anything else. Mage-Captain Jakab and his people were strong Mages—the Navy only recruited above the average—but they didn't have the Runes of Power a Rune Wright could carve into their own flesh.

The twelve-million-ton battlecruiser erupted into high orbit, less than forty thousand kilometers away from the Defender Yards, with active sensors singing across every wavelength with enough power to temporarily blind most civilian or militia receptors.

The Hand quickly stepped aside to let Mage-Captain Jakab reclaim the simulacrum at the heart of the bridge. At this range, it was the *Duke*'s most powerful weapon, and better in the hands of the experienced and less drained Mage-Captain rather than Damien.

"What the *hell*?"

Commander Rhine's curse echoed through the silently efficient bridge, and Damien faced the tactical officer instantly.

"Sir, my lord," he said slowly, "the Patrol is *gone*."

Rhine's team processed all of the data before it hit the main displays, so he'd seen it before anyone else had. As the main screen populated, even Damien saw it. The icons and data codes materializing on the screens that walled, floored, and roofed the bridge were almost all for civilian ships. There were a handful of small craft and in-system corvettes, but the frigates of the Patrol were missing from the scopes.

"Look at Defender Yards, too," Rhine told Damien and Jakab, highlighting the shipyard structure orbiting beneath them. "Only two of the slips have hulls in them—they must have rapid-mobilized the other two without even doing flight trials."

Damien did the math. That meant they'd pulled together nine frigates—over *fifty* million tons of warships—and taken them... somewhere. What had Grace *done*?

"Where's FN Twenty One Eighty Seven?" he asked. "Commander Renzetti should have told us about this."

"We're scanning for her," Rhine reported. "The corvettes are all standing down, I'm reading drive shut-downs and they're all requesting instructions."

The icons for the sublight ships left behind to secure the system flashed with new icons as the Patrol ships in the system desperately tried to avoid having to fight the Navy cruiser.

"Sirs..." Lieutenant Rain said slowly. "One of the freighters—her beacon is flashing a Navy Code Omega. I'm downloading the data packet now... but I think it's definitely Twenty One Eighty Seven's."

"If the Patrol killed Renzetti, *every* ship here would be flashing his Code Omega," Jakab said aloud, glancing back at Damien. "Twenty One Eighty Seven died somewhere else."

"Antonius," Damien realized. "They were destroyed at Antonius—and something happened to Greenwood." He turned to Rain. "Get me Governor McLaughlin," he ordered. "Now."

Damien stepped into the breakout conference room attached to Jakab's office to have at least *some* privacy for the meeting, and by the time he reached the room the McLaughlin was already on the screen. He'd expected the Governor to look angry, defiant... anything but utterly exhausted.

"I presume you can guess where the Patrol has gone," the McLaughlin said slowly. "Have you even bothered to find out why?"

"Jakab's people are still decrypting Mage-Commander's Renzetti's Omega data package," Damien admitted, "but I assume that Greenwood has been attacked and destroyed, along with courier FN Twenty One Eighty Seven and any civilian ships they could catch. I'll even go so far as to presume that the attackers appeared to be Mínglià̀ng Security Flotilla destroyers."

McLaughlin looked taken aback. "How did you...?"

"Fifty-five hours ago, the Sherwood Patrol frigate *Alan-a-dale*—and yes, Governor, the identification is confirmed—attacked and destroyed the Mínglià̀ng Central Processing Facility in Antonius, killing nearly thirty thousand civilians and destroying the Royal Martian Navy warship *Dreams of Liberty*," Damien told him flatly.

"For the entirety of that fifty-five-hour period, I know exactly where every single ship of the MSF was," he continued. "I also, however, have confirmed that there are at *least* eight destroyers out there modified to *appear* to be MSF ships even to RMN scanners. Given that these ships exist, and Captain Wayne's actions already show our true enemy to have no compunction about civilian casualties, this is exactly what I was afraid of."

"But... you reviewed all of our ships' sensor logs yourself," Governor McLaughlin objected. "There is no way the *Alan-a-dale* was involved in the attacks!"

"We reviewed the MSF's logs," Damien said gently. "Every case where we could identify the ship, it was Captain Wayne's vessel. He betrayed you and the Protectorate, Governor. *Someone* is trying to start a war between you and Mínglìàng—and so far as I can tell, the MSF is completely innocent. Your Patrol... is not."

If the Governor had looked exhausted before, now he looked on the verge of a heart attack. Damien wasn't sure if he should be continuing the conversation—or calling a doctor to the Governor's office.

Before either of them could say more, though, there was a commotion on the Governor's end. Someone bodily collided with a door loudly enough that Damien could hear it, followed by shouting.

"I *need* to speak with the Governor. It is *critical*."

The door behind McLaughlin crashed open, a suited bodyguard flying through it to crash on the floor. In the opening, looking somewhat sheepish, stood a gaunt older man in a plain black suit in a defensive pose.

"I apologize, sir," he said crisply, straightening and entering McLaughlin's office as if invited, "but I *needed* to speak with you—I know who tried to murder Commodore McLaughlin and the Hand, and the potential consequences are terrifying."

Then, and *only* then, did the man realize who was on the screen. He looked at Damien on the wall and swallowed hard.

"Carry on, Inspector, is it?" Damien instructed softly. "I think I need to hear this."

"Sorry about that, James," the Governor told his bodyguard. "It'll be fine."

The rumpled and embarrassed-looking bodyguard bowed his way out of the office, re-closing the door behind him.

"Hand Damien Montgomery, meet Inspector Javier Accord," the McLaughlin introduced them dryly. "He was investigating the attempt on my granddaughter's life and our suspicions that one of our Captains had gone rogue—suspicions you are telling me are confirmed."

"I'm presuming Captain Wayne planted the device?" Damien asked. "I have solid evidence that he is your rogue."

"Yes," Accord said slowly, clearly processing data. "But the *who* may be less important than the 'how', my lord. Wayne didn't do it directly, obviously. I checked every Patrol ship and every ship registered to a Patrol officer in the first day."

"Then how did you find him?" McLaughlin asked.

"I was working from one end, and I had a financial analyst on my team working from the other," Accord told them. "The analyst found it first, but he didn't see the consequences. You see, via about seventy different shell corporations, Wayne has almost one hundred percent ownership of Teatime Replenishment."

McLaughlin inhaled sharply, while Damien looked at the Inspector patiently, hoping for an answer that would justify his time.

"Teatime Replenishment is contracted to run over *half* of the Patrol's missile and fuel colliers, Lord Hand," Accord explained after a moment. "The shuttle that I believe placed the explosives for the assassination attempt was destroyed in an accident six days later with all hands, but TR ships were intimately involved in supplying the Patrol for the latest operation."

"My God," Damien murmured as the implications sunk in. There were a *lot* of things you could do to a missile if you had unlimited access to it before it was delivered. If Wayne's people had supplied the missiles on all of the Patrol's ships...

"Your Excellency," he said formally to the Governor, "we have a third party in play here—one Wayne clearly works for. They're trying to drag you into a war—don't let them. Let me help you."

"Grace was headed to Antonius to rescue everyone she could," McLaughlin admitted. "But then she was going on a counter-force operation against the MSF. If no one intercepts her... I ordered her to start that very war, Damien," he whispered. "My God, what have we done?"

"What someone spent a lot of time and blood to make you think was the right thing," Damien said grimly. "When did she leave, Miles?" he demanded, only half-aware he was using the Governor's first name for the first time.

"Sixteen hours ago," the Governor told him. "They're still fourteen hours away, but..."

"Governor McLaughlin, you and Accord need to deal with this Teatime Replenishment," Damien ordered. "You have my authority to intern all of their personnel and vessels until we have time to separate the guilty from the innocent.

"I will need a message from you to Grace," he continued. "Things have gone far enough that she may not be willing to listen to me."

"You'll have it," the Governor promised. "Though I suspect she'd listen to you anyway."

Damien shook his head, grimacing.

"We're nearing eighty thousand dead, Miles," he said quietly. "No more risks. Not one more dead innocent."

"I'll see all of my research forwarded to your ship," Accord told him. "You may need it."

"Do that. Then get yourself on a shuttle," Damien ordered. "We're leaving as soon as you're aboard."

CHAPTER 30

"**JUMP TO** Antonius System in five minutes. All hands to battle stations. All hands to battle stations. This is not a drill. Jump to Antonius System in five minutes."

The *Robin Hood* had only left the Sherwood System three times since her commissioning, but Grace's crew moved around and through the frigate's bridge with practiced ease. Months upon months of drilling served its purpose, and none of her crew seemed lost at all.

The trip to Sherwood-Antonius Jump Seven had been heart-wrenching. Each time the Patrol had jumped, her heart had leapt into her throat, hoping against hope that *this time* they'd find a surviving freighter. The hope that more than one lucky freighter had survived the massacre..

"All stations report closed up and fully crewed," Commander Arrington told her. Her executive officer stood next to the simulacrum as he would be making the final jump. The Patrol had based its designs on the Protectorate Navy, combining bridge and simulacrum chamber into a single central command nexus.

Unlike the Navy, of course, *her* ships lacked amplifiers for their Mages' powers. Only their lasers and missiles would protect them from the enemies that might still await them in Antonius.

"Squadron status report?" Grace ordered over the command network.

"*Alan-a-dale* at full readiness," Michael Wayne responded instantly. Despite her occasional twinges of discomfort with the man, he remained her most efficient and effective captain.

"*Friar Tuck* standing by."

"*Maid Marian* ready to jump."

"*Little John* closed up and ready to go."

"*Lionheart* is champing at the bit, ma'am."

"*Nottingham* clear to jump."

A pause, a few extra moments as the last two ships inevitably scrambled. With no time to work together and the inevitable minor failures of ships launched without trials, her last two ships were a strain on everyone's patience—especially their crews!

"*Newstead Abbey* here. We're down four battle lasers to a software glitch, but we are otherwise online."

Grace sighed, but nodded. That was better than she'd been afraid of, though she still had one ship...

"This is Captain MacDougal on the *Loxley*," her last captain chimed in. "Ma'am, our weapons are online, but our *entire* primary sensor array just fired up a blue screen of death and shut all the way down. My engineering crew is neck deep in wires and software, but they're warning me we're easily twelve to twenty-four hours before the array is back up."

MacDougal admitted all of this in a perfectly level tone that Grace *hoped* had been the same one she had used when her ship had thrown up that level of critical error.

"Understood, *Loxley*," Grace accepted aloud. "Link into the squadron net, we'll dump sensor data from the rest of the ships to you. You'll have some delay, but better that than nothing."

"That should work, ma'am," MacDougal replied after a moment's thought. "Targeting system is fully online, we just have no sensor data to feed them."

"You have two minutes," she told him. "Then we jump."

"Yes, Commodore."

Cutting the channel, she turned to her own crew. "Make the link happen," she ordered calmly. It was probably redundant, as the techs in her own sensor and communications departments had their heads together before she finished speaking.

The result impressed her. It took a little over ninety seconds for the techs across eight ships to get a link set up to feed all of their data to the ninth. Depending on the distances, the data could easily be delayed quite a bit—but that was why she had *all* of the ships linked instead of one.

"Commander Arrington," she said aloud as she leaned back in her chair, looking at the timer. "Jump on the clock, if you please."

Grace had reviewed the literature. Supervised test firings. Reduced some of Sherwood's outer system ice asteroids to vapor. She knew, intellectually, what the impact of an antimatter warhead looked like.

It was an entirely different experience to look at the overlapped craters of a multi-missile, multi-*gigaton*, strike and know that forty thousand people had been there when those missiles hit. Greenwood Outpost was simply *gone*. The big smelter sites had taken a pair of missiles each, and the main residential hub had been hit with *six*.

A dozen antimatter missiles had turned thirty years of investment, tens of thousands of homes and dozens of small and medium businesses, into a handful of craters that showed no sign of the settlement they'd destroyed.

"Any chance of survivors?" she asked.

"No, Commodore," Arrington admitted. "The entire Outpost was vaporized. Even if someone had been in transit between the town and the smelters, the transit tunnels were torn open at both ends. Even if they'd survived the shockwave and the radiation, the vehicles used only had a twenty-four hour emergency oxygen supply."

She nodded silently, surveying the destruction. Greenwood Outpost had been built on a large asteroid, a fifteen hundred kilometer diameter chunk of low value rock. The rock had enough gravity to help hold the settlement together, but not enough to make leaving or arriving noticeably more difficult.

All the images of the Outpost that she'd seen, though, had had another layer. Ships. The debris field slowly settling into a rough ring around the planetoid told the fate of Navy courier FN-2187 and the freighters that had been here when Greenwood's murderers arrived.

But the entire reason Greenwood had existed was to service and maintain the much smaller, sublight mining ships that actually did the hard work of extracting valuable ore from the systems many, many, asteroid belts.

"Do we have any of the mining ships on the sensors?" she asked. Eight of her ships were still pulsing full power active scanners. There should be dozens, at least, of the motley collection of working ships visible.

"Nothing," Arrington said slowly, looking over one of the junior officer's shoulders. "I've got nothing within about three light minutes, ma'am. Further than that..." he shrugged. "The computers will need a bit to grind through the background heat sources and identify active engines. We won't pick up anyone not actively burning their drives at that range though."

"How far away would we see them if they'd shut everything down and gone as silent as possible to hide from Greenwood's murderers?" Grace asked. Despite her mission, a large part of her brain refused to refer to the attackers as 'Míngliàng'. She still had too many doubts for that.

"About three light minutes, ma'am," Arrington told her with a small smile. It wasn't much of a smile, but it was as much as anyone could likely muster while hovering above the scene of a massacre.

"Lieutenant Amber," Grace called her com officer over. "I'm going to need a wide-band, omnidirectional transmission. Most likely, our miners are running and hiding. Those ships have no sensors to speak of, so they don't know we're here."

"Record on your command console and I can send it out immediately," the young officer responded crisply. "I'll get it ready."

Grace nodded and then brought up the recorder on her console. The camera showed her in her command chair and clearly displayed her uniform and its single crystal oak leaf rank tab.

"Antonius System miners, this is Commodore Grace McLaughlin," she introduced herself for any of them that hadn't been paying attention to news from the home system. "The Sherwood Interstellar Patrol is in-system on a rescue mission for any survivors of the attack on Greenwood. We should have the capacity to take everyone home where it's safe."

Antonius clearly wasn't safe anymore. Even if the *Friar Tuck* had still been guarding Greenwood, the results wouldn't have changed. The *Wil Scarlet*'s fate meant Grace already knew what would likely happen to any of her frigates that faced off with a third again their mass in destroyers. Only the Protectorate fleet that was supposed to be on its way could guard against that kind of attack.

Until it arrived, she needed to bring her people home. And if she had *enough* of them to bring home, she could justify postponing the counterforce strike on Mínglìàng. She knew the operation was necessary, but she couldn't avoid a nagging feeling that she was missing something, and it would be an irretrievable mistake.

Grace's ships were back in clear space they could jump from when they finally received a response—delayed over thirty minutes. In almost three days, even a sublight mining ship could go a *long* way if they had reason to.

"Commodore McLaughlin," a grizzled looking woman with short-cropped hair and a much-used lightweight space-suit said out of the bridge screens, "you have no idea how glad I am to see someone show up—*anyone* show up."

The ship behind the woman was apparently big enough to have a separate bridge, a rarity for many of the ships that clawed their living from Antonius's rocks. The bridge she was transmitting from was *tiny*, though, a cube maybe four meters across, with three working consoles crammed into it.

"I'm Captain Liddell of the *Thor's Digger*," Liddell continued. "We're a processor ship, which means we're the closest ones with a transmitter big enough to reach you. Everyone is headed for the *Tiāntǐ tíqǔ*. They were doing fuel cracking on an ice rock, which means they have oxygen supplies. Most of the mining ships only have food and air for a few weeks at best."

Grace glanced at Arrington, confused. She wasn't sure which ship the *Tiānti tíqǔ* was, but she sounded Mínglàng. If all of the miners were going there...

"With both colonies gone," Liddell noted, "no one was sure when we'd get help. I don't think anyone's more than an hour's flight away from the *Tiānti tíqǔ*, and we're a long way from you now. If you want to evac people, you're probably best meeting us there."

The older woman shook her head. "Thank Freya you made it," she whispered.

"*Thor's Digger* out."

"Both colonies gone," Grace repeated. "Arrington," she snapped, "are we picking up *anything* from the Mínglàng station?"

"The star is between us and them," her XO pointed out. "We wouldn't see anything either way, except maybe reflections."

"Check for them," she ordered. "If something has happened to the Central Processing Facility as well as Greenwood, we're going to have *damn* big problems."

"Yes, ma'am," Arrington agreed, gesturing for part of the tactical team to get on it. "And what about *Tiānti tíqǔ*?"

"Get me the Captains on a group channel," Grace told Lieutenant Amber. "We're going to have to check it out," she answered her exec. "If both colonies are gone, we might not have the lift to shift everybody, but I need to *know* before we do anything. Find out what we've got on the *Tiānti tíqǔ* in our system."

"I have the Captains for you, ma'am," Amber interjected. Grace gave the young woman a nod of thanks and flipped her command console over to the channel the Lieutenant had set up.

"Ladies, gentlemen," she said calmly. "Captain Liddell's message was in the clear so I presume you all saw it. We now have reason to be concerned for the safety of the Mínglàng Central Processing facility as well as our own people."

"Given that the MSF just murdered forty thousand civilians, I don't exactly see why we should *care*," Captain Wayne replied. "This could be a trap," he pointed out. "Captain Liddell could be under duress, luring us into an area controlled by Míngliàng to set us up for an ambush. We know nothing about this ship she mentions."

"That's not true," Arrington interjected as he entered the conversation. As Grace's XO, he ended up effectively commanding the *Robin Hood* half the time, so she included him in all-Captain conferences like this. "The *Tiāntǐ tíqǔ* is actually one of the few Míngliàng ships we do have a record of—she's an ice miner, a big beast of a sublight ship at a million tons. Greenwood bought oxygen and fuel from her because it was cheaper than importing it or even making it ourselves. If there's a ship in the system everyone would know, and that could provide enough oxygen to keep everyone alive, it would be the *Tiāntǐ tíqǔ*."

"Fair," Wayne allowed. "But she's still a Míngliàng ship—and Míngliàng ships just blew Greenwood to *hell*."

"I have no intention of going in blind or oblivious, Captain Wayne," Grace pointed out coolly.

"Our scanners confirm roughly what Liddell has said," Arrington told them. "The ships we can detect are all actively burning for a single location which agrees with our last reported location of the ice miner. We can jump in about five light seconds away." Grace saw her XO shrug out of the corner of her eye. "Ma'am, I don't think we have a choice."

"And neither do I," she said firmly, before Wayne or the other Captains could chime in. "Ladies, gentlemen, prepare for a short-range jump. I presume we can all handle a sixteen light minute jump without straining ourselves?"

If anyone was concerned, no one was going to admit it. Grace smiled grimly at her Captains.

"Then we jump in two minutes. I'll see you all at *Tiāntǐ tíqǔ*."

CHAPTER 31

POWER FLARED through Grace as she *stepped* through space, her magic running throughout the six million ton mass of the *Robin Hood* and telling it that no, it wasn't *there*, a million kilometers away from Greenwood, it was *here*—one and a half million kilometers away from the ice ball the Míngliàng ship was breaking down into fuel and oxygen.

The frigate shuddered and obeyed. An imperceptible instant later, all nine ships erupted into existence at their new location. The carefully arrayed formation they'd left Greenwood in came apart in the process, and Grace mentally sighed at the state of her fleet. Only the *Alan-a-dale*—of course!—was still in formation, one hundred and fifty kilometers off the *Robin Hood's* starboard bow.

The other seven ships were scattered across a sphere almost fifty thousand kilometers wide. Apparently, she needed to arrange more training in short-range formation jumping. Useless in most systems, but valuable in Antonius's notorious mess of a gravity well—and Antonius was one of the Patrol's main operations zones.

For now at least.

"Get me a count on those ships," she ordered, studying the screen in front of her. The big ice miner, still attached to the ice asteroid she was rapidly consuming, sat at the heart of a growing cloud of orbiting spaceships.

The *Tiāntǐ tíqǔ* was the largest of those ships, a million ton crescent-moon shape half a kilometer long. The processing ships like the

Thor's Digger were the next largest, portable refineries varying from five to eight hundred thousand tons. There were less than a dozen of them though.

Around them were literally *hundreds* of small miners, anything from a thousand to a hundred thousand tons, with crews varying from well-trained corporate crews of fifty or more to family units and single-person operations.

"I've got six hundred and forty-eight individual vessels in the cluster," Arrington reported. "Reading another hundred and sixty or so inbound, mostly smaller ships that would have been *way* out there."

The last count Grace had seen had put the number of Sherwood ships in the system at just under four hundred in total. Even assuming everyone had escaped the massacre at Greenwood, there was no way all of those ships were hers.

"How many are Míngliàng?" she asked. "And... do we have a read on Míngliàng's CPF from here?"

"We should," her XO told her. "MacClare?"

The tactical officer looked up and shook his head. He was a pale-skinned, dark-haired man who looked far too young for his current job. Who *was*, Grace knew, far too young for his job—which was why Arrington was doing almost half of it to keep the youth afloat.

"I've got a clean scan of where the station *should* be," MacClare said slowly, "but... there's nothing there."

"Raise your resolution," Grace suggested. "Look for debris."

What color MacClare *had* drained from his face as he hastened to obey her suggestion.

"Our Father who art in Heaven," he whispered. "I have a debris field." The youth swallowed, checked something on his screen, and then looked up to meet Grace's gaze with surprisingly level eyes. "The field is consistent with the destruction of the Míngliàng Antonius Central Processing Facility by high power laser fire."

"Damn," she murmured. She'd known. From the moment she'd heard Liddell's transmission, she'd *known* what had to have happened. Someone had killed *every* major colony in Antonius. The eight hundred ships in front of her represented roughly fifteen thousand people, but over *sixty* thousand were already dead.

Any intent to complete the counter-force mission died. The woman who'd come home and put on a uniform when her grandfather called because her world needed, the woman who'd taken the accursed crystal oak leaf when it was offered to her... that woman couldn't leave the survivors in front of her unprotected.

"All ships," she said calmly, reopening the Captains' channel. "We will get back into formation, and then we will proceed to establish a defensive perimeter around the *Tiāntǐ tíqǔ* and the other mining ships. Let's keep these people safe, folks. I won't settle for less."

To her surprise, no one disputed her orders, and she leaned back in her chair to study the screens. With a clear objective in front of her, one that *wouldn't* start a war, she actually started to relax.

Then MacClare snapped ramrod straight, staring at his screen in shock.

"Commodore!" he shouted. "We have jump flares!"

Commodore Grace McLaughlin froze. It was a matter of moments, long enough for her to feel a flash of embarrassment and for the details of the jump flares to filter onto the main screens surrounding her. Fifteen icons burned the bright flashing orange of unidentified ships, on the far side of the cluster of civilian ships.

"What am I looking at?" she demanded. "Who are they?"

"I've got two ten-megaton range signatures and thirteen one-megaton range," MacClare announced. "System is calling it two cruisers, thirteen destroyers... IFF codes coming in now." The youth swallowed and glanced helplessly at his superiors.

"IFFs confirm Mínglìàng Security Flotilla," Arrington finished for him. "They are maneuvering towards us."

"Pull us away," Grace ordered. "All ships, vector ninety degrees horizontal and vertical versus the ecliptic. Maximum safe acceleration."

The orange icons solidified into yellow icons marked with tonnage and scanner data as the Patrol maneuvered to pull the hundreds of civilian ships out of the potential line of fire. No matter what happened in the next few minutes, she did *not* want those survivors caught in the middle of it.

"Time to missile range?" she asked Arrington.

"They carry the same Phoenix VIIs we do," he replied. "We're *in* missile range. With the debris around the asteroid field, our hit probabilities are atrocious, but we're in range."

"We will not fire first," she ordered. "Spin up all missile defenses and prepare to protect ourselves and the civilians if necessary."

"Yes, ma'am," MacClare confirmed. Her command network quickly flashed up notifications showing the rest of her squadron was also prepared to defend themselves.

"Commodore," Arrington said softly from behind her shoulder, "they haven't even tried to communicate. They just started maneuvering to intercept as soon as they saw us. And... look at this."

Her XO highlighted details on her screen that she hadn't looked at closely. Examining them, she saw exactly what he meant. Three of the destroyers had fallen behind the rest of the Flotilla, accelerating at three gravities to the rest of the ships' ten. Even...

"Are they *venting atmosphere?*" she whispered.

"Those three look damaged," he agreed. "They've been in a fight, Commodore—and it wasn't with us. But the way they're maneuvering *towards* us... I'm not so sure they don't think it was."

"Amber, get over here," Grace ordered. When the communications officer finished scrabbling across the bridge, the Commodore smiled at her. "Lieutenant, we were given command-level protocols for confidential communication with the Flotilla at one point, weren't we?"

"Yes, ma'am," Amber replied crisply. "They require your personal key to operate, though."

"I thought so." The Commodore studied the ships in the surrounding screens. The Patrol was burning at ninety degrees to the ecliptic at ten gravities, and the forward group of Mínglìàng ships was on a clear intercept course at the same acceleration from fifteen light seconds away.

They weren't in effective battle laser range, yet, though God alone knew what the cruisers were carrying. If they were holding their missiles until they cleared the worst of the asteroid debris, they would be able to fire in... thirty minutes.

That was a lot of time to try to stop a war.

"Get me those protocols, Melissa," Grace ordered.

Lieutenant Melissa Amber saluted crisply and all-but-teleported away from Grace's command console. The Commodore met her executive officer's gaze. Arrington looked exhausted, still awake after making a full light year jump barely an hour before.

"What do we do if they don't respond, ma'am?" he whispered.

"We have them out-massed two to one," she said grimly. "I won't start this fight, Liam—but I won't betray our people by not returning fire if they do. Plus..." she trailed off. "If they came from Mínglìàng, where's Damien?"

Grace turned away from Arrington as an icon on her console informed her that Amber had forwarded her the necessary communication protocol. She tapped a series of keys on the touch screen, entering her personal key.

The system chirped to inform her the secure communications package was online. Leaning forward into the camera, she turned on the recorder and put on her best 'please don't make me kill you' smile.

"Admiral Yen Phan, this is Commodore Grace McLaughlin of the Sherwood Interstellar Patrol," she said calmly. "I don't know what you think is going on. I'm honestly not sure *I* know what's going on—but both of our colonies in Antonius are gone and tens of thousands of the civilians you and I are both sworn to defend are dead. Several of your vessels are damaged, and we have fifteen thousand civilians in need of rescue and succor."

She inhaled and bowed her head slightly.

"Admiral, I strongly recommend that we both cease maneuvering aggressively and return to neutral positions near the cluster of civilian ships—the ones praying that we rescue them instead of killing each other. I am prepared to hold the Patrol in Antonius until such time as Hand Montgomery arrives to mediate the situation."

Ending the recording, Grace considered it for a long moment, and then launched it into space. Fifteen seconds for her message to be received, fifteen seconds for any answer to get back to her. They were down to twenty-seven minutes to both sides clearing the asteroid field.

A minute passed. Another. The precious time before the two fleets were in position to fire on each other without asteroids or civilians in the way was slipping away, and Grace couldn't think of anything else she could do.

Even if she turned her battle group and accelerated directly away from Phan's ships, an action that stuck hard in her throat, she wouldn't change that timer. They couldn't leave the range of the Míngliàngs' missiles in time.

"Message incoming," Amber announced, and Grace breathed a sigh of relief.

"Forward to my console," she ordered. The delay and the continued maneuvers of the MSF were unpromising, but she had to at least hear what Admiral Phan had to say.

The pitch-black-skinned woman appeared on the screen of Grace's console, and Grace wished for a moment that she had more experience with people of the Admiral's skin coloring. Phan's expression was unreadable as she faced the camera in silence for several seconds.

"While I can guess why Montgomery trusts you," she finally spat, "I am surprised you think you can fool *me* as thoroughly as you can the Hand. The time for lies is done, Commodore. Your actions have defined you, here and on the way here."

The expression on Admiral Phan's face could charitably be called a smile. Maybe.

"I have watched too many of my spacers and civilians murdered by your oh-so-brave Patrol. No more. I offer you one chance to surrender and evacuate your vessels. Either way, I cannot permit the Patrol to continue its existence and threat to my world."

It was, Grace reflected, one thing to plan to deliver that very ultimatum—and another to have it directed *at* you. Having been the recipient of it, she realized her neat and clean plan to neutralize the MSF would never have worked—*no one* was going to obey that order.

She swallowed hard, checking the timer and glancing over at Arrington.

"Liam, is there *any* way we're misreading the odds here?" she asked.

"We have nine frigates, fifty-four million tons of warships," he replied. "Over five hundred launchers and a hundred and fifty battle lasers, even with the *Loxley* and *Newstead Abbey*'s issues. They have two cruisers and only ten fully functional destroyers—thirty million tons. The cruisers probably have much heavier battle lasers than we do, but..." he shrugged. "Not enough, ma'am. This isn't even going to be a fair fight."

Grace nodded slowly, studying the scanner data of the Mínglìàng Security Flotilla ships. She agreed with her executive officer. There was no way Phan could win the battle she seemed determined to court—and no way Grace could see to avoid it.

Twenty minutes.

She didn't have it in her to surrender—but she *sure* as hell didn't have it in her to massacre the Flotilla without at least *trying* to prevent the battle. She hit record again.

"Admiral Phan, I swear to you—on the honor of the Patrol, on the honor of *Sherwood*—that any attack carried out by Patrol vessels was launched without my knowledge or authorization. That would make it an act of treason and piracy, one I *will* punish given evidence.

"I do not wish to fight you, but neither will I tamely surrender. I have you outgunned and out-massed. You cannot win this battle—do *not* make me fight it!"

The message flickered its way across the void, and Grace raised a helpless gaze on her executive officer. After a moment, she sighed, and brought up the all-Captains channel.

"Ladies, gentlemen," she greeted them. "I am attempting to avoid engaging the Flotilla, but Admiral Phan blames us for the destruction of the Processing Facility and its civilians. We will *not* fire first, but if the Flotilla attacks us, we will defend ourselves.

"Make sure all defense systems are triple checked," she ordered. "Charge all battle laser capacitors. Load all missile launchers." She paused. "If they open fire, do not wait for authorization from the flagship to return fire. If it comes to a fight, I will *not* lose."

"They nuked Greenwood from orbit," Wayne objected. "Why the hell are we taking the first punch? These bastards murdered *forty thousand* people."

"And they think we murdered thirty thousand," Grace countered. "If we want even a chance at peace, we must offer the same benefit of the doubt we are demanding. My orders stand, Captain Wayne."

She took his silence for acquiescence and waited to hear from the rest. No one said anything more.

"Good luck," she told them.

The clock was at ten minutes. She should have heard back from Phan by now. Nothing.

"They're maneuvering to clear their lines of fire," MacClare warned her. "Even the three damaged ships will have a clear line of fire for their missiles. They don't look like they're planning on surrendering, ma'am."

"I know," she agreed aloud. "But no matter what, we cannot go on record as being the ones to fire the first shots of this war. The Protectorate will *destroy* the aggressor here."

"All systems are one hundred percent," her tactical officer replied. "We should be able to take their first punch and keep fighting."

"Sometimes, you gotta let the other bastard swing first," her exec chimed in.

Grace nodded in silence, watching the clock and the tactical plot as the time ticked away. Second by second, minute by minute, every moment of silence brought an increased certainty that this was going to end in violence.

Sixty seconds.

"Stand by all missile batteries," Arrington ordered over the PA. "Stand by all lasers. Be ready to fire on command."

"I'm sorry, Damien," Grace whispered. "I tried."

Thirty seconds until the Mínglìàng Security Flotilla cleared the aster-oids.

"Jump flare!" MacClare shouted—and Grace's attention snapped to the tactical plot.

In a perfectly timed demonstration of power, magic, and skill, the *Duke of Magnificence* burst into existence *exactly* between the two fleets.

CHAPTER 32

MAGE-LIEUTENANT Jessica Philips jumped the *Duke* with professional competence, dropping the big twelve million ton cruiser *exactly* where Mage-Captain Jakab had told her to—thirty light minutes up from the ecliptic, directly 'above' the star Antonius.

"Get me all passive scanners," Jakab ordered as the young Mage wavered.

Damien was there first, catching her as she stumbled against the exhaustion. The blonde woman might have been ten years younger than him, but she was notably taller than him. For a moment, he thought he might drop her regardless, but braced himself to hold her weight.

"Sorry, my lord," she murmured, managing to regain her balance and stand back up, her hand on his shoulder. "Thank you."

"Get yourself to bed," he ordered. Every so often, a jump could take more out of you than normal—especially if the Mage had been up for a while before making the jump. "We've all been there, Lieutenant," he continued as he noticed her looking rebellious. He could see both of the Mages close enough to overhear him nodding vigorously—which made Philips chuckle and bob her head in agreement.

Returning her smile, Damien passed her to Amiri. His bodyguard took the young woman with a nod and helped her towards the exit from the bridge.

The side drama had, thankfully, kept Damien distracted from looming over Jakab's shoulder as the sensor data came in. They'd picked their position carefully. With the two colonies in roughly equal orbits and exactly opposite each other, arriving at the wreckage of Greenwood or the CPF wouldn't let them see what was going on at the other. Coming in high above the ecliptic gave them a view of almost the entire star system.

A view, sadly, of what had been going on over half an hour ago, but better than nothing.

"The CPF site is abandoned," Rhine reported. "I have no ships anywhere near it. I'm reading nine ships near Greenwood, though—big ships. I'd say we're almost certainly looking at the Patrol."

"Where are the miners?" Damien asked. "There should be hundreds of sublight ships here."

"Still refining the smaller heat signatures... there," the *Duke*'s tactical officer pointed out. A section of the star system 'beneath' them was suddenly highlighted. "Every ship I can pick up is either centering their position on a chunk of ice here, or is on their way to that area."

"The miners might feud and bicker," Jakab said, "but they're the kind of hardy people that will band together when everything goes to hell. Combining everyone's resources could keep the survivors alive for longer than you might think."

"Wait—the Patrol just jumped," Lieutenant Carver interrupted. "Well, thirty-four minutes ago..."

"Where?" Jakab demanded. "Are they still in the system?"

"Give it a minute," Damien told him. "I suspect... there!"

Nine jump flares appeared on the screen, some distance away from the cluster of ships Rhine had identified. The sensors informed Damien that they were now accelerating towards the ships—many of which had to be from Mínglìàng.

"What are you thinking, Grace?" he murmured.

"Damien," Amiri whispered from just behind him. "I know... Alaura had a device that let her see what was going on light years away. It would be useful right now."

"The Star Mirror was destroyed with her ship," Damien noted. "A replacement is in the workshop I haven't entered since we left Panterra, about a third complete."

"Oh. Damn."

"However," Damien considered. The Star Mirror was a sufficiently complex piece of magic that only a Rune Wright could build one—and they were unique, even giving the pattern from one to a traditional Rune Scribe hadn't been enough to allow duplication. As Julia said, however, it was meant to see light years away. To reach thirty-odd light minutes...

He brought up a schematic of the *Duke of Magnificence*, looking for a sensor array he could associate with the view he was seeing on the bridge's—the *simulacrum chamber's*—walls.

"Mage-Captain, I'll need to borrow your simulacrum," he said calmly. "Commander Rhine—please focus your analysis computers on sensor array Kilo Seven Delta Four."

"Okay..." the tactical officer allowed as Jakab gestured Damien forward.

"The glimpse is only going to last a few seconds," the Hand noted as he removed his gloves, exposing the interface runes on his palms. When he'd carved the Runes of Power onto his flesh, he'd made very sure to leave those original two runes untouched. "I can't pull more without a dedicated tool."

Everyone on the bridge except Amiri was now looking at him in confusion as he laid his hands on the simulacrum. Ignoring them, he reached out with his magic into the space just in front of array K7D4. Through the simulacrum chambers repeated visuals and the magical properties of the simulacrum itself, he made sure he was touching the right area of space... then he *twisted* it.

His power flowed through the vacuum, and convinced it that it wasn't there—convinced the particles and waves he'd captured that they were *here*, thirty-three light minutes and change away.

He couldn't maintain it. It didn't drain *that* much energy, not with the *Duke's* amplifier to extend his existing strength, but the twist in space was inherently unstable without some kind of support.

"Damn," Rhine whispered. "I got three-and-a-half seconds of what looks like real-time data." There was awe in the tactical officer's voice. The abilities of Mages were generally considered to be *known*, their limits equally identified.

In truth, Damien knew most of that "knowledge" was defined more by the Compact that restricted Mages than by the actual limitations of Mages' abilities. But even so, his own abilities and strengths were far beyond what a regular Mage could do. The Hands of the Mage-King could work miracles with their single Rune of Power—and with five Runes on his own flesh, he was as far beyond them as they were beyond everyone else.

If only sheer power could solve all his problems.

"Analyzing the data," Rhine reported, his voice trailing off. "We have a *problem*. On the screens."

"Wha..."

The new image on the screens cut off Damien's question as Rhine zoomed in on the cluster of ships—and the two fleets maneuvering around them.

"The MSF should *not* be here," he snarled. "What the hell is Phan thinking?"

"I don't know," Jakab replied, "but she's already been in a fight. Assuming she brought *everyone*—and there's enough ships here to presume she did—she's short a destroyer, and these three," he tapped a set of icons, "have been hit, bad."

"The Patrol looks to be getting the civilians out of the line of fire, but the MSF is burning hard for an intercept," Rhine told them. "It's hard to be sure with less than four seconds of data, but I'd say they'll clear the asteroid cluster and will be able to fire on each other in less than two minutes." The tactical officer paused and swallowed. "Sir, I see nothing in their signatures or their maneuvering to suggest that either fleet is *not* going to fire."

"Mage-Captain, I will *not* stand by and watch the first battle of the Protectorate's civil war explode in front of my eyes," Damien snapped. "Get us between them."

"We need time to calculate the jump," Jakab replied, but he was already tapping away at his console.

"Commander Rhine, take the *Duke* to battle stations," the Hand ordered, trying to not distract the ship's Captain. "Be prepared to intercept missile fire—no matter what happens, nobody dies today unless *I* order it."

He felt as much as heard Amiri's snort from behind him, but his gaze was on the frozen image of a scene too far away—and far too close to bringing the entire Protectorate to its knees.

Lights began to flash on the bridge screens as stations already on alert went to battle stations. Extra personnel rushed to their stations. Capacitors charged, and missiles were loaded into launch tubes. Section after section on the ship flashed ready codes as the warship prepared for a battle he hoped—he *prayed* she wouldn't have to fight.

"Be ready to jump," Jakab snapped, the Mage-Captain half-leaping from his chair and lunging to the simulacrum. He took one look around the bridge, making sure no one was going to be surprised, then laid his hands on the simulacrum.

Then, in a flare of power, the *Duke of Magnificence* placed herself directly in the line of fire.

CHAPTER 33

"**RECORD FOR** omnidirectional transmission in the clear," Damien ordered. He stood straight, taking advantage of what height he had, and focused on the camera in front of the Captain's console he'd temporarily commandeered.

"Mingliàng and Sherwood forces, this is Hand Damien Montgomery. *Both* of your fleets are in violation of the orders and restrictions laid upon you to keep the peace—the peace you appear prepared to shatter."

He shook his head, hoping that his disappointment came through more than his anger.

"You *will* stand your ships down," he ordered calmly. "Discharge your capacitors. Power down your sensor arrays. I will permit you to maintain defensive systems only. Once all of your offensive systems are disarmed, you will match vectors with the *Duke of Magnificence* at your current distance and *all* ship Captains and squadron commanders will report aboard the *Duke*.

"Between you, you have enough information for us to sort this disaster out," he told them. "You can either cooperate, or be the first regional militia to ever fire on a Hand of the Mage-King of Mars. I don't think anyone here wants to find out how that story ends."

He made a 'cut' signal with his hand, then nodded for Jakab's crew to transmit it.

"What's our status?" he demanded.

"They are clear of the asteroid cluster," Rhine reported. "Both fleets have a clear line of fire on each other... no one has fired. They are holding fire."

"Let's see how they respond," Damien said quietly. "I want a directional laser link with the *Robin Hood*," he continued. "Encrypted, the highest level we share with the Patrol. Use the key 'Gentle Rains of Summer'. I need to speak to the Commodore in private—I don't even want the *Patrol* to know I'm talking to her, am I clear?"

"You can use my office again," Jakab told him. "Are you sure she'll know that key?"

"She'll know."

"Ma'am, we have an incoming laser-com from the *Duke of Magnificence*," Lieutenant Amber reported.

"Is anyone else getting it?" Grace asked, glancing around her bridge. Her crew looked mostly relieved that Montgomery's arrival had short-stopped a war. A couple still looked furious, likely the ones not extending *any* benefit of the doubt to the MSF.

"They're pinging our forward receiver with a signal that's less than six meters across at this range," Amber pointed out. "We're the only ones getting it. It's encrypted, ma'am. I ran it past our standard protocols for the Navy. We have the encryption, but they're using a non-standard key."

"Put it through to my office," Grace told her after a moment. "And people?" Her bridge staff looked at her. "*Nobody* hears about this—even on *this* ship. Am I clear?"

"Yes, ma'am."

Grace stepped into her attached office and brought up the communication channel. The point of a shared encrypted communication protocol was to reduce the true encryption key of a modern cryptographic defense, some billion or so digits long, down to a private key that was only a few dozen characters at most.

If it was a non-standard key, it would have to have been a certain minimum length, and something Damien thought she could guess. Even with the hell of the last few days, she knew what he'd have used—and she entered the name of the ship she'd left Sherwood on, the ship that had first taken the two of them apart.

The screen immediately resolved into the image of Damien sitting at a desk, watching the camera with a patient expression. A timer in the corner noted the time delay at just under eight seconds—the *Duke* was exactly halfway between the Patrol and the Flotilla four and a half million kilometers away.

"Your timing is perfect, Damien," she told him. "I tried to talk Phan down, but she thinks we attacked her... I swear to you, Damien, not only did I not order an attack, I know where all nine of my ships have been for *days*."

"Commodore McLaughlin," he said formally, his speech clearly begun before her message had reached him, "I have evidence that the commander of one of your ships was responsible for the destruction of the Mínglìàng Antonius Central Processing Facility, and the Navy destroyer *Dreams of Liberty*."

He stopped as her message reached him, but he'd already blown her away. One of her captains had destroyed the CPF? One of *her people* had killed thirty thousand innocents?

After a few seconds, clearly listening to her message, he sighed and shook his head.

"Bluntly, Grace, I now *know* your ships have been murdering people," he said quietly. "And I also know that every attack on Sherwood shipping has been non-Mínglìàng ships retrofitted to look like Phan's ships. Phan doesn't trust you. She doesn't entirely trust *me*, because I am prepared to trust you. You will need to make concessions to earn her trust—and she has the right to demand them."

Swallowing, Grace finally regained her composure and leaned forward.

"Damien, tell me who did this," she said flatly. "I do not doubt you, though I wish I could. Give me a name, and I will give Admiral Phan their head on a platter."

Seconds ticked by. Sixteen seconds after she spoke, Damien shook his head and sighed.

"It's Wayne, Grace," he told her. "The *Alan-a-dale* jumped to Antonius after they left us with the *Mistletoe Solstice*, destroyed the CPF and then engaged a Navy destroyer in a missile duel to try and destroy the jump-freighters that had been in the system.

"Worse, it appears Captain Wayne had his fingers in your logistics pipeline. I'm forwarding you a data package prepared by your Inspector Accord—he's aboard the *Duke*, so you can meet with him once you're here, but Wayne may have been in a position to modify the missiles loaded aboard the Patrol warships.

"To help protect your ships from any brilliant ideas he may have, I intend to arrest him aboard the *Duke*—but his people had to be involved, and I don't know what they'll do when we seize him. I need your people prepared to board and take control of the *Alan-a-dale*."

Grace just... stared at the monitor. Her trust in Michael Wayne had been fading, but *this* was beyond belief. Memories of, well, ogling the older man, with his perfectly fitted uniform and eternally unperturbable self-confidence, ran through her and she shivered—first in embarrassment, and then in rage.

He'd betrayed her trust. Betrayed the Patrol—betrayed *Sherwood*. Not just the Mínglìang space station in Antonius, but dozens of their ships too from what Damien had said. *Tens of thousands* of innocents dead at his hand, and he'd still smiled and flirted with her.

And *modifying* their missiles? The horrifying possibilities from that sent chills down her spine.

"I understand," she finally said. "I'll coordinate, quietly, on our end. We'll get the bastard. Tell Phan that by God and by the honor of Sherwood and the Patrol, she will have her justice."

Closing the channel with the Commodore, Damien heaved a sigh of relief. He'd been afraid that Grace would be so focused on revenge for

Greenwood's dead she wouldn't listen to him. He could understand *why* she was here, even if it was a violation of his orders and was creating *far* more problems than it could ever solve. So long as she would *listen* to him, he could probably salvage this.

Of course, stopping a war required *both* sides to listen.

"Lieutenant Amber, please get me another laser link to Admiral Phan," he ordered over the intercom. "We can use our standard protocol for the MSF here, I'm not as worried about traitors in her ranks."

"Coming right up, sir. Give us thirty seconds to have a solid two-way link—the delay will be about the same as you had with Commodore McLaughlin."

"Thank you, Lieutenant."

He waited patiently as the seal of the Royal Martian Navy rotated on his screen, and then finally resolved into the image of Admiral Yen Phan's office, the woman leveling a dark gaze on him.

"If you're going to order me around like an under-qualified minion, could you at least do me the courtesy of not interrupting me?" she snapped.

Damien smiled coldly.

"My minions can actually follow orders," he noted. "I don't recall authorizing the Flotilla to be anywhere near this far away from Mínglìàng. In fact, I believe I specifically *only* authorized you to go collect your merchant ships—yet somehow, you're here in Antonius. And you've been in a fight. I want answers, Admiral. *Before* I find myself having to defend your actions to a fleet convinced you just blew Greenwood to hell."

Lightspeed lag was hell—or at least purgatory. Fifteen seconds passed before he even saw Phan's reaction to his little rant, though at least he could *read* her reaction as her face visibly tightened and she leaned back in her chair.

"We didn't intend to come this far," she admitted slowly. "With the rogue from Sherwood and the mystery ships pretending to be us floating around, I brought everyone I could to make sure we could bring our ships home safe.

"Half of them had clustered together for mutual defense, ships with a single Mage each slowly jumping their way home," she continued. "We were ambushed within minutes of finding them—a frigate that jumped in at high speed and launched missiles at the freighters and our destroyers." She visibly clenched her fists as she looked flatly at the camera.

"We got there in time to watch three of the ships your Captain Arrow died to defend destroyed in front of our eyes," Phan said flatly. "One of my destroyers was killed as well, with three badly damaged. And my lord Hand," she paused, "it was *not* the *Alan-a-dale* that attacked us. My faith in your claim of a single rogue ship is very, very weak."

That was impossible. Damien trusted Grace—and trusted her when she said that every one of her ships had been with her for the last few days. The obvious damage on Phan's ships, though, told the truth of her tale as well.

"Bring all of your data with you, Admiral," he finally ordered. "If it was one of McLaughlin's ships, we will identify her, and you will have justice. The *Alan-a-dale*'s Captain Wayne will be surrendered to Protectorate authority upon arrival on the *Duke*. If more of their Captains have betrayed their oaths and their world, then they will be punished—I swear this to you on the honor of the Mage-King of Mars."

Hands did not lightly swear by the honor of their master. Their own honor could be forsworn, could be overridden by the Council. The Mage-King's honor, once committed, could not be taken back without breaking the Hand who swore by it.

"Someone has slaughtered nearly a hundred thousand people to start a war, Admiral Phan," he reminded her. "I will *not* permit them to succeed."

Somehow, having a clear target for all of the rage, frustration, and grief she'd been building up over the last several days put a new purpose in Grace's step as she returned to her bridge. Her people noticed—she watched them straighten, an extra ounce of steel settling in their spines as they turned to watch her walk to the center of the bridge.

"Commander Arrington," she greeted her XO pleasantly. "Has the shuttle bay been advised that I'll need a bird to take me over to the *Duke*?"

"They have," he confirmed. "Lieutenant Eisenhorn is preparing a ship now. He warns it will be a long, unpleasant trip—roughly seven hours at three gees."

"I didn't expect anything different," she accepted wryly, then looked around at her bridge crew again. All of them were too young or too old for their ranks, pulled in from college graduations or merchant crews. They'd been with her since before she'd been bumped to Commodore, though, and she knew them. She trusted them.

She'd also trusted Michael Wayne. Almost trusted him enough to fall into bed with him.

"Sergeant Gibbons," she addressed her bodyguard crisply. "Seal the bridge please."

That sent murmurs rippling through her bridge crew, but no one stopped the big Patroller from locking and sealing the bridge doors and bringing up a systems lockdown. While they still controlled the ship, no messages or crew could enter or leave the bridge until she released the seal.

"You need to know what I now know," she told the bridge crew. "But it can't leave this room, except as absolutely needed. There is treachery and betrayal at the *heart* of our Patrol, and we *must* excise it."

The handful of people on the *Robin Hood*'s bridge who hadn't already been giving her their undivided attention now focused on her. All the men and women on the bridge could hopefully tell she was deathly serious.

"I have been informed that the Protectorate has successfully identified the ship responsible for the destruction of Mínglìàng's Antonius Central Processing Facility," she continued. "They have conclusively confirmed that the *Alan-a-dale* attacked and destroyed both the station and the Royal Martian Navy destroyer *Dreams of Liberty*.

"One of our own is responsible for the death of tens of thousands of civilians as part, the Hand believes, of a campaign to drive us and Mínglìàng into open conflict. His motivation is *irrelevant* to me," Grace snarled, and the anger and betrayal in her crew's faces echoed her own.

"Hand Montgomery intends to arrest Captain Wayne for his crimes aboard the *Duke of Magnificence*," she warned them. "The intent is to avoid having Sherwood or Mínglìàng take the blame with whatever supporters he has back home. The Protectorate took over responsibility for Antonius's security. A Protectorate crew was killed along with thousands of civilians under their protection. The Protectorate will judge Michael Wayne."

Her bridge was silent for a long moment as her crew digested that.

"What about the *Alan-a-dale*?" Arrington asked finally, and Grace smiled grimly. She could have *kissed* the man for that opening.

"That is why you needed to know what I know," she replied. "I don't know how or why, but clearly, the *Alan-a-dale*'s crew has followed Captain Wayne into treason and murder. His arrest may well provoke them to... precipitous action. Action we cannot afford—if for no other reason than that we hope to find evidence of Wayne's crimes aboard his ship."

She turned to her bodyguard, meeting the big boarding team leader's gaze levelly.

"Sergeant Gibbons, I'll need you to coordinate with the other ships," she told him. "People you trust—NCOs, officers, whoever you need to speak to, but only those you can trust to keep the faith. When Wayne is arrested, you will need to board and seize the *Alan-a-dale*."

The big redheaded man considered for a long moment, and a big grin spread across his face.

"It'll need to be a surprise," he noted aloud. "I can make it happen, Commodore—but who'll watch your back on the *Duke*?"

"I'm a Mage, Sergeant," Grace pointed out. "I can watch my own back—and I suspect I'll be surrounded by Marines. I need *you* to stop Wayne's crew from firing on anyone else!"

She held her bodyguard's gaze for a long moment, until he nodded. His grin was no less wide, but there was a measure of seriousness in it now. She'd take what she could get.

"MacClare, Arrington," she turned to her XO and tactical officer. "I've been warned that a large portion of our missiles may have passed through the hands of people working for Wayne. We have to assume that our missiles have been compromised."

Both men were intimately familiar with the devastating power of the Phoenix VII missiles their ship carried, and looked physically *ill* at the thought of those one-gigaton warheads or twelve thousand gravity anti-matter rockets being compromised.

"I want you to reach out to every ship by whatever back-channels you can find," she ordered. "Senior NCOs, junior tactical officers, *missile techs* if that's who we can trust. I want to make *damned* sure that every single failsafe on the launchers and the magazines is live and fully functional."

She paused and took a deep breath as she looked around her bridge.

"If worst comes to worst, people," she told them calmly, "we need to be prepared to defend the *Duke of Magnificence* against missile fire from our own ships."

CHAPTER 34

DAMIEN WATCHED the shuttles slowly drift their way towards the *Duke of Magnificence*'s landing bay. It had been a punishing flight for the officers he'd required to make the seven-hour trip from their own ships. That had been more of his reason to demand they come to the *Duke* than he was likely to admit to anyone—after seven hours at three gravities, just about anyone was going to rethink their decisions.

The *Alan-a-dale*'s shuttle was one of the last to arrive, with only two MSF birds behind it, and he waited patiently for it. As each Captain arrived, he shook their hand and sent them on to the conference room Mage-Captain Jakab had set up for the meeting.

Commodore McLaughlin arrived moments before Admiral Phan. Exiting her shuttle and seeing McLaughlin in front of her, Admiral Phan immediately sped up, half-running to make sure that the two militia commanders arrived at the same time.

"Stay here," he ordered when they reached him. "You both need to witness this."

An entire platoon of Marines in exosuit battle armor waited in the corridors around the landing bay. Damien didn't expect Captain Wayne to show up with a boarding squad of his own, but the *Alan-a-dale*'s Captain *was* a Mage. If he decided to resist, things could get messy. Amiri had tried to keep Damien away—and finally insisted that the Hand strap on the concealed body armor he rarely wore under his suit before she'd let him be remotely near the shuttle when it landed.

The two women walked past him, studiously avoiding each other's gaze as they fell into place behind him. He was vaguely aware of Amiri inserting herself between the two officers, gently encouraging them to move up beside him.

Finally, the *Alan-a-dale*'s shuttle swept into the space opened by the bay staff rolling the Commodore's and Admiral's shuttles off to join the *Duke*'s own small fleet of parasite craft. If the pilot noticed that the shuttle behind him was suddenly pulling back into a holding pattern, there was no sign of it in his handling as he neatly dropped the twelve-meter-long spaceship onto the marked location.

Mist sprayed over the spaceship, cooling the shuttle's hull and the bay around it by converting to steam and being sucked away by ready hoses. The steam fogged around the shuttle for a moment, and then faded, allowing humans to exit the craft safely.

Captain Michael Wayne exited the ship on his own, and Damien got his first solid look at the man who'd tried to kill him. Wayne was an average-looking man with long sandy-blond hair tied back in a ponytail. He looked unbothered by seven hours under three Earth gravities, his uniform still in perfect array, and carried a somewhat imposing presence despite his middling height.

A small voice in the back of Damien's mind noted that he could understand what Grace had seen in the man. That voice came along with a twinge of jealousy that made what he had to do next dangerously sweet, and he suppressed it as hard as he could. The professional could *not* become personal.

He waited for Wayne to be well away from the shuttle and then gestured to Amiri as he stepped forward.

"Captain Michael Wayne?" he asked loudly.

"My Lord Montgomery," Wayne responded crisply, saluting. "It is a pleasure to be invited..."

Exosuited Marines started to file in. All of them were carrying combat stunguns: rapid-fire weapons loaded with SmartDarts that tailored their electric shocks to the target's weight and a quick assessment of their health.

"Captain Wayne," Damien repeated calmly, projecting his voice to be sure the man heard him, "you are under arrest for high treason against the Protectorate and mass murder via weapons of mass destruction."

Wayne froze in surprise, his gaze immediately going to his Commodore where she stood behind Damien.

"Grace, what the hell is going on here?" he demanded. "You *know* I didn't do any such thing!"

"I've seen the evidence, *Michael*," Grace snapped as she stepped up next to Damien.

"Evidence provided by them!" Wayne snapped, gesturing in a wide sweep that included both Damien and Admiral Phan behind him. "Míngliàng is trying to set us up! We should never have listened to Montgomery in the first place, he's working with them!"

"I watched the footage from the *Dreams of Liberty*, Michael," she said quietly, advancing on Wayne. "I watched Captain Arrow try to stop you—and I watched you blow thirty thousand civilians to hell. Surrender. Cooperate—help us find the bastards behind this whole mess and we might be able to give you clemency."

Something changed in Wayne's expression. Suddenly, the smile, the passion as he proclaimed his innocence vanished into a flat mask that showed no emotion at all.

"Sorry, Grace," Wayne murmured. She was only a few feet from the Captain now, and Damien realized he should *never* have let her get so close. On some level, neither he nor Grace hadn't truly believed that Wayne was a threat. Not to *her*.

"The Hand can't let this stand," he continued, and Damien *saw* the magic flare around the other man—channeling down and into his wrist. "And I won't be taken alive!"

"Grace, *down!*" Damien bellowed, his own magic flashing out as he realized that, somewhere along the way, Captain Wayne had acquired a Battle Mage's projector rune.

Carved at the base of the palm, the small rune didn't amplify a Mage's power. It 'just' increased their range—allowing a Mage standing at the center of the landing bay to send fire *slashing* across the armored Marines.

The Marines fell like toppled pins, several cut in half despite their armor, before Damien slammed a shield of power into place blocking the attack.

"Uh-uh-uh," Wayne snapped, and Damien saw he'd produced a gun he now held to Grace's head. "No clever ideas or we all find out what color the Commodore's brains are. I'd *hate* that, I really would, but I'm not going power-to-power with a Hand, either."

Damien met Grace's eyes. She'd been caught in Wayne's blast of fire and her side was a mess of half-cauterized wounds. Wayne didn't even need to shoot her—unless Damien missed his guess, if she didn't get medical attention *fast* she was going to die anyway.

"Stand down," he ordered. "Everybody back."

As the Marines pulled their wounded back, Damien slowly walked forward.

"I'll back Grace's offer," he said quietly. "You're right that I shouldn't. My mission—my oath—demand that you pay for your crimes, but if you help me bring the assholes who set you in motion down, I'll let you live."

"A lifetime in a Martian prison?" he laughed. "I've pulled enough people out of those holes that I'll never go in one. Here's *my* offer: I get back on my shuttle, we fly back to my ship, and my ship and I disappear into the fucking ether. I promise I'll get Grace medical attention and drop her somewhere she can get home from."

"That's *not* happening," Grace ground out, her eyes flickering to the gun. "You hear me Damien? You do *not* let this fuc–" she gasped as Wayne ground his free hand against her burn.

"Sorry, love, but this isn't your conversation," he said genteelly. "Instant I let you go; Montgomery here turns me to dust. Only way out of here is with you."

Grace struggled to stay upright against her injuries and Wayne's crushing grip, but she met Damien's eyes. She mouthed two words, hoarsely enough and with enough pain that if he'd known her even a little bit less he wouldn't have known what she'd said.

Trust me. Take him!

"So, my lord Hand," Wayne continued, genteelly, "what *are* you going to do?"

Damien looked the rogue Captain evenly in the eyes.

"My duty."

Wayne must have seen *something* in his gaze because he shivered backwards for a moment—just a fraction of a second.

A fraction of a second the gun wasn't pointed directly at Grace.

A fraction of a second in which one of the most powerful Mages alive struck.

Fire *burned* through Damien's Runes of Power as he twisted pure force into unstoppable lines of power. The first blade struck across Wayne's wrist, the second his neck. The Sherwood Captain literally *came apart* as blades of Damien's will sliced through his flesh.

Somehow, Wayne *still* fired. With his wrist removed from his arm and the gun starting to fall, he could only have triggered it with magic— but it was still pointed directly at Grace's head from centimeters away.

The shot echoed in the cavernous landing bay and Damien stared in horror. Wayne fell away from Grace, collapsing into pieces, and the Commodore wavered, staggering forward.

Damien was there to catch her as she fell, trying desperately *not* to touch her burns and staring at her miraculously undamaged skull.

"I *told* you to trust me," she slurred, and then passed out. Injured— *badly*—but alive.

Mage-Captain Kole Jakab was focused on watching the two fleets of warships now slowly pacing his vessel across the AntoniusSsystem, try-ing not to be too obvious about looking over Commander Rhine's shoul-der as the tactical officer used passive sensors to gain hard weapons locks on every ship around them.

The Hand's job was to try to negotiate the two forces down. Kole's job was to keep them alive if one of those forces decided to open fire.

It took him a moment to see practically *every* alarm go off in the shut-tle bay, and he snapped the feed from the bay's cameras to his console just in time to watch the Hand cut Michael Wayne into pieces.

"Men down," he snapped, opening a channel to the infirmary. "Medical to Shuttle Bay Two *now*."

"On our way."

On the screens, he watched as the *Alan-a-dale*'s shuttle started to lift off the deck. The Bay Landing Officer acted before he could even think to open a channel.

Even an unarmed shuttle could cause a vast amount of damage with its engines—especially to the squishy humans beyond the marked blast zones of the shuttle bay. The designers of the *Honorific*-class battlecruisers had been fully aware of that danger—and had provided a counter-measure.

A concealed panel on the innermost wall of the bay slid aside. A targeting array measured angles—and the coilgun fired.

The shuttle was barely a meter off the deck when the first twenty kilogram projectile slammed into it at over a hundred kilometers a second. With only the artificial gravity field from the runes beneath it to hold it in place, the shuttle lurched from the impact.

More projectiles followed, ripping gaping holes through the spacecraft and flinging the remains into space. Kole wasn't sure what the pilot had been intending, but he doubted it had been friendly—and it was now a moot point.

"Status report," he demanded. "Any actions from either fleet?"

Seconds ticked by. They were still just over seven light seconds distant from each fleet—outside the range of the *Duke of Magnificence*'s amplifier, if only barely, and a fifteen second round-trip even for light.

"I can't tell if the pilot transmitted," Rhine admitted after a moment. "Neither fleet seems to be responding to the destruction of the shuttle—it's quite possible they didn't even detect it."

"Sir, the shuttles still outside want to know what is going on," the current com officer reported. "What do I tell them?"

"The truth," Kole ordered after a moment. "Tell them Captain Wayne attacked Hand Montgomery and Commodore McLaughlin. They are ordered to land immediately. Warn them that anyone disobeying orders will be regarded as an accomplice to Captain Wayne and shot down."

Lieutenant Rain swallowed hard, but leaned forward into her microphone and started passing on his commands. The two orbiting shuttles had started to move away from the *Duke,* but rapidly obeyed and dropped back into their holding pattern. After a few seconds, the first in the previously established queue carefully started inching its way through the debris of the *Alan-a-dale's* shuttle towards the landing bay.

"That's strange," Lieutenant Carver said aloud, and Kole turned his attention back to his tactical section.

"What is it, Lieutenant?" he asked.

"Commander Rhine, can you double check this, sir?" Carver asked. Kole would have *preferred* an instant answer, but he still nodded approval at the young man. Sometimes, accuracy trumped speed.

"Captain, every ship in the Patrol just emergency jettisoned their ready magazines," Rhine said slowly. "Something triggered the launcher failsafes. Wait—what's that?"

"Assault shuttles," Carver replied immediately. "Every Patrol ship except the *Alan-a-dale* just launched assault shuttles—*at* the *Alan-a-dale.*"

"I guess we know what Montgomery talked to the Commodore about," Kole observed. "What about the..."

"*Holy shit!*"

Kole saw it before Rhine had finished swearing. The Patrol used an older version of a Navy launcher, with a ready magazine of four Phoenix VII missiles loaded with antimatter warheads. All nine ships had dumped the entirety of their ready magazines into space—a necessary failsafe ability in a system that contained enough explosive force to vaporize the entire ship.

Over two *thousand* missiles had drifted away from the Patrol frigates—and now *every one of them* had lit up their drives.

"What's the target?" he asked calmly—but he already knew the answer.

"They're coming straight at us, sir."

"Evasive maneuvers," Kole ordered instantly. "Missile defense status?"

"All systems online," Commander Rhine reported. "But we can't withstand *two thousand* missiles."

"We might not have to," Carver interrupted. "Take a look at *that*."

The Patrol's *missiles* might be out to destroy the *Duke of Magnificence*, but the *Patrol* didn't seem to be. The *Alan-a-dale* seemed frozen in space, some kind of override locking out her systems while an entire squadron of assault shuttles slammed into her hull, but the *other* eight frigates had rotated to train their weapons on their errant munitions.

Sherwood had designed their *Hunter*-class frigates uncompromisingly for a missile engagement, trading having far fewer and much less powerful lasers than the *Duke* to achieve a missile armament three quarters of the battlecruiser's despite being half its size. Their defensive lasers were lighter and smaller than the Martian warship's—but each of the *Hunters* carried just as *many* of them.

Over seven hundred and fifty lasers slashed into space. Two of the ships were definitely less than fully operational, Kole noted absently—six of the frigates were firing all of their one hundred lasers, but the last two were down nearly fifty between them.

Even firing from behind the missiles, the Patrol couldn't take them all out. *Hundreds* of missiles blew apart, vaporized by their motherships, but hundreds more continued on.

"Sir," Rain addressed him, "we're being hailed by the Flotilla ships—they're requesting permission to fire missiles in counter mode to help cover us."

"Granted," he snapped. "We need all the help we can get."

Fifteen seconds later, the Flotilla almost *vanished* on his screen, buried behind the icons of their own salvos of hundreds of missiles. The thought crossed his mind that if the Flotilla was going to betray them, *now* would be the perfect time.

Of course, every single Flotilla captain was currently aboard the *Duke*. That probably contributed to their willingness to help.

Even as he saw the Flotilla's salvo launched, the *Duke* herself vibrated under his feet as Rhine launched their own missiles. Their Phoenix VIII's were faster and smarter, with an extra thirty seconds of endurance that wouldn't play in this fight.

His tactical officer spent the multi-million dollar weapons like *candy*. It took almost two minutes for the missiles to clear the range of the Patrol's defenses, and a disturbing number of them had survived.

"What are the numbers, Commander?" he asked softly.

"The Patrol nailed over a thousand of them," Rhine replied instantly. "I make it... nine hundred and twenty-six still inbound."

Kole grunted, eyeing the icons of the Míngliàng salvo. Even with the *Duke* burning towards the Flotilla at its top speed, those missiles would only intercept the Patrol's missiles a few thousand kilometers away from his ship. Even *that* wouldn't have happened if the rogue missiles had been properly launched—the extra few kilometers per second from the launchers added up over a two million kilometer flight.

"One minute to missile impact," Carver reported aloud. "Thirty seconds to first intercept. Fifty seconds to second. Fifty-five seconds to Flotilla missile intercept."

He paused. "Incoming missiles are in laser range, we are engaging."

Waving one of the junior Mages to the simulacrum, Kole leaned forward in his chair and took direct control of his battlecruiser's ECM. With hundreds of missiles in space around him, the last thing he wanted was for *any* of them to have a clue where his ship really was. Terminal mode was hard to fool, but the key was to keep the missiles from getting *into* a range where they could get hard radar locks on your hull.

Lasers flared in space again, the *Duke*'s computer helpfully drawing the invisible lines of energy on the screens surrounding him as the missiles closed. More missiles died. The *Duke*'s defensive lasers were less effective than the Patrol's had been—now they were firing against the missiles' best defenses—but they were more effective than they *should* have been.

"They're on internal programming," he noted aloud. "No assistance from even the *Alan-a-dale*, just given a target and let loose."

He smiled grimly. The Navy *knew* the programs for a Phoenix VII inside and out. The Patrol could—must—have added a few tricks, but the processor in the missile was only so good.

Feeding that information into the *Duke*'s projectors and transmitters, the cruiser's Captain began to sing an electronic siren's call, urging the missiles to go *here*.

The only important thing about that point in space was that the *Duke of Magnificence* wasn't there. Any missile that missed his ship was a sitting duck.

"Missile intercepts in five seconds," Carver announced. "Darkening screens."

All the rune-laced video screens that filled the bridge dimmed—and then *flashed* brightly as the missile swarms ran into each other. The *Duke*'s eighty missiles blew simultaneously, their one gigaton warheads trying to take as many of the incoming missiles with them as possible.

The screens stayed flash-blinded for a moment, then cleared. There were gaping holes in the missile swarm now, but hundreds of missiles still remained. Amplified magic and rapid-firing lasers cut through the swarm again and again, and ECM lured dozens of missiles off-course, but there were still too many incoming.

Kole swallowed as they kept coming, fear sinking into him. He'd been spared the worst of the Battle of Ardennes as he'd been sent to aid Hand Montgomery in securing the planet, but he remembered watching the missile swarms there. A single mistake could cost hundreds of lives... and he was out of *right* things to do but wait.

The screens dimmed and flashed again as their second missile salvo intercepted the rogue weapons. They brightened only for a second... and then went *black* as the Mínglìang Flotilla's counter-salvo arrived.

The MSF had more *ships* than the Patrol, but most of theirs were *Lancer*-class destroyers, and they'd only fired one salvo versus the four effectively contained in the attack on the *Duke*. A 'mere' four hundred missiles flashed past the *Duke of Magnificence*, merging with the big cruiser's own third salvo and detonating barely five hundred kilometers from her hull.

Nearly five hundred *gigatons* of explosive force filled space, and even from that distance the *Duke* trembled as the energy waves passed over her—but the Flotilla had spaced their missiles perfectly, and Rhine had had plenty of time to set his own missiles to fill the gaps.

A solid wall of fire shielded the *Duke* from the attack and the remaining missiles flew straight into it. The missiles' deaths added to the explosions, building into a crescendo of fire that washed over the *Duke*, shaking the warship hard enough that her crew felt it... and leaving her unharmed.

"Rhine?" Kole demanded.

"We're clear," the tactical officer said softly, his voice almost awed. "I have no missiles on the scanners. We are clear," he repeated.

Mage-Captain Kole Jakab looked at the screen, at the two fleets he'd half-expected to try to kill him, and breathed a long, hard, sigh of relief. They'd saved his ships as much as Rhine's skill had. *Something* very strange had happened with the Patrol, but without their lasers, there would have been too many missiles left for even the Flotilla's intervention to save the *Duke of Magnificence*.

"Get me Hand Montgomery," he ordered Rain. "Where we go from here... is a political decision."

CHAPTER 35

DAMIEN TRADED reassuring nods with Amiri as he reached the conference room they'd stashed the ship captains and Admiral Phan in. She'd taken his orders to make sure the captains all made it safely—and without wandering off anywhere!—better than he'd expected.

"They're getting agitated in there," she warned him. "Nobody knows anything, and they're running a lot more scared than I'd expect from a bunch of warship captains."

"They're militia, not Navy," he reminded her. "But that's why I'm here. Watch my back."

His bodyguard nodded silently and fell in behind him as he opened the door and walked into the room. Anything he'd intended to say was instantly drowned out by shouted questions, and he simply let the tumult rage over him for a moment while he considered his audience.

With one Patrol captain dead and the Commodore also serving as captain of her flagship, there were only seven Patrol captains to seventeen Flotilla captains and an Admiral. That didn't seem to be slowing his homeworld's officers down, though, as they made up for their lack of numbers with volume.

He made a small gesture and teleported about a hundred cubic centimeters of air outside the *Duke*'s hull, switching it with the vacuum there. The *bang* of air rushing into the newly-created vacuum echoed louder than a gunshot, cutting the tumult like a sword.

"Enough," Damien said softly once he had everyone's attention. He walked forward, into the center of the circular, amphitheater-esque conference room. "If you have any questions once I'm done, I will take time to answer them, but for now you are all going to sit down, shut up, and listen to me."

One of the Míngliàng captains started to shout something—Damien didn't bother to let him finish the first word before *slamming* the man down into his seat with invisible bands of force. The captain, likely a Mage himself, looked stunned—and was silent.

"Sit," Damien invited, gesturing to the chairs around the room. "For any of you with a terminal lack of situational awareness, I am Damien Montgomery, Hand of the Mage-King of Mars."

He focused on the Sherwood contingent first.

"I will start by laying the inevitable rumors and speculation born of the last couple of hours to rest. Commodore Grace McLaughlin is alive. She is badly injured, and undergoing care in the *Duke of Magnificence*'s infirmary.

"She was *injured* by Captain Michael Wayne of the Patrol frigate *Alan-a-dale*. Captain Wayne is dead," Damien said flatly. "He attacked Royal Martian Marines and killed three of them in his attempt to escape arrest and I neutralized the threat he represented."

The tumult exploded again, too many shouted questions, demands, and accusations for Damien to even begin to follow. He raised his hand to create another vacuum—but the room was suddenly silent, everyone staring at him.

"In the aftermath of Captain Wayne's death," Damien told them quietly, "someone aboard the *Alan-a-dale* activated a program concealed in the Patrol's missiles that attempted to remote-fire them. While the Patrol frigates' failsafes protected them from damage, they allowed that program to launch over two thousand missiles at this ship."

The last remnants of the tumult died away, and everyone in the room was focused on him.

"Thanks to the quick and brave responses of the crews of *all* of your ships," he continued, "we are clearly still alive. Look around you, ladies and gentlemen. Had the ships from only *one* of your fleets acted, we would all be dead. But when faced with a common threat, your crews stood together and helped save you all.

"I *suggest* you take inspiration from their actions," Damien told them. "I have ordered *all* of our ships to converge on the *Alan-a-dale*. Loyal Patrol troops have boarded the vessel, but my understanding is that fighting continues."

He wondered silently if any of the men and women around him had any idea of just what that meant. The Patrol troopers had boarded the *Alan-a-dale* a full hour ago now. A second wave of assault shuttles—carrying troops their officers trusted now that Wayne's ship was in clear mutiny—had crossed over twenty minutes ago.

Memories of the *Mistletoe Solstice* and the *Blue Jay* and the aftermath of boarding actions on both ships sent a shiver down his spine. He'd only ever seen the *aftermath* of the kind of carnage the Patrol's boarding teams were fighting through—and it would still be over an hour before his Marines could reinforce them.

"Since the immediate threat is resolved," he finally said, "I can now actually explain why I called you all aboard the *Duke*—though the fate of Captain Wayne and his ship should tell you all most of the story..."

CHAPTER 36

THE ASSAULT shuttles blasted clear of the *Duke of Magnificence*'s shuttle bays at an acceleration that slammed Julia into the supports holding her down. The exosuit battle armor she wore helped compensate against acceleration, but even the Royal Martian Navy didn't bother with gravity runes on shuttlecraft.

Her screen informed her that the Marine next to her was Corporal Williams, the young Marine who she suspected Mage-Lieutenant Nguyen had assigned to bodyguard the Hand's bodyguard—*probably* without a hint of intentional irony.

"What's our ETA?" she asked on a channel that included Nguyen, Williams, and the pilot.

"Five minutes," the pilot replied. "And no, we're not dropping under ten gees at any point, so I *really* suggest all of you tin cans stay strapped down until the assault shuttle is at rest and the seatbelt light off."

With a grin, Julia linked her exosuit's internal screen to the shuttle sensors and studied the area around them. The Patrol warships *other* than the *Alan-a-dale* now formed a loose sphere around the rogue warship, with at least one of them between the frigate and the *Duke of Magnificence* at all times. If Wayne's crew managed to regain control of their weapons, the Patrol appeared determined that they would not be able to harm anyone except their fellow Patrollers.

The *Duke* herself was slowly decelerating to a relative stop behind them, well outside the sphere of warships guarding the *Alan-a-dale*.

Behind *her*, the Mínglìàng Security Flotilla was making their own approach to join the cluster of no-longer-hostile ships.

The shuttles carrying the Patrol captains back to their ships were flying significantly less aggressively than the Marine assault shuttles, but the last word from the *Alan-a-dale* was that a number of pockets of resistance remained—and that the Patrol had taken literally *hundreds* of casualties boarding the ship.

Damien had ordered the Patrollers to pull back. They'd successfully taken the bridge, engineering, and the main computer core. The remaining traitors couldn't destroy the ship, they could only kill people trying to get at them.

There was no point losing Patrollers when the Royal Martian Marine Corps was available—and this kind of mess was the Marines' *specialty*.

"Welcome aboard the *Alan-a-dale*," a Patrol officer clad in an armored space-suit greeted them as they boarded. The complete lack of atmosphere aboard the frigate meant she was using a short-range radio. "I'm Commander Ishbel McTaggart off the *Maid Marian*. For my sin of being Sergeant Gibbons's high school girlfriend, I ended up being the senior officer he trusted and in charge of this clusterfuck."

The space-suit helmet shook slightly. "I am *glad* to see you," she concluded. "What do you need from me and my people?"

"Nguyen?" Julia asked.

"We're just the first wave," the Mage-Lieutenant said calmly. "Major Elise Reid is back on the other shuttles. We need target locations, Commander."

"Data packet on its way," McTaggart confirmed, tapping a command on the computer built into the suit's wrist. "They still hold the CIC and primary life support. Both of those sections have built-in fortifications to hold against boarding actions—we took the bridge and engineering in the first assault." She shook her head again.

"They're fighting to the death," she said quietly. "We've been trying to get them to surrender since we boarded, but... nobody is giving up."

"They know the rules Montgomery works under," Julia replied. "We'll give clemency to a few who cooperate, but they're all guilty of mass murder. The Charter doesn't *allow* the death penalty for much... but they've committed crimes where it *requires* it."

"I know." Julia heard as much as saw McTaggart's wince. "These were my brothers in arms, Agent," McTaggart admitted. "Some of them I thought were my *friends*. Where did we go so wrong?"

"That's something we're going to have to investigate," Julia admitted. "I suspect, however, that the Patrol didn't go very wrong—Wayne set out to at least create the option for himself from the beginning."

"Ma'am, I suggest that we move this conversation to the bridge," Mage-Lieutenant Nguyen interrupted. "I may be able to do something with the simulacrum to ease Major Reid's assault, and some of my people are already drooling to get into the *Alan-a-dale*'s computers."

"Of course," Commander McTaggart agreed. "Keep your eyes open— we think we have all the traitors penned up, but if there're any left they may well try to ambush us."

Nguyen, clad in a two-meter-tall suit of armor, tapped the battle rifle to his chest.

"I almost hope so, ma'am."

They reached the bridge without further incident, Nguyen's troops sweeping ahead to keep the precious handful of computer techs safe.

Julia smiled in relief at the sight of Sergeant Gibbons. She'd quite liked McLaughlin's bodyguard, and she suspected that the Commodore would have been very upset if the man had got himself killed.

He had, it was clear, got himself *shot*. He was clad in the same armored space-suit as everyone else, but a medic had set up a pressure tent over his torso and was working on cleaning out and bandaging his injuries.

"I think your boss is going to be cranky with you," she told him.

"Is she okay?" he demanded. "Heard she was injured..."

"Wayne burnt her pretty badly," Julia admitted. "But she's fine. Our doctors are working on her as we speak, but the prognosis was positive."

Gibbons nodded and seemed to relax. The medic working on him swooped in and scooped out *something* that Julia couldn't see—and she heard the Sergeant's gasp of pain. Someone had done a number on him.

"Major Reid's shuttles have breached the hull at their target points," Nguyen reported.

Further discussion was cut off by a high-powered, broadband, radio signal that overrode every channel.

"Crewmen of the *Alan-a-dale*, this is Major Elise Reid of the Royal Martian Marine Corps," a calm voice said over the signal. "You are no longer facing your fellows of the Patrol, and you have few tools at your disposal that can threaten my Marines. Resistance will change nothing. If you surrender, you'll at least have an opportunity to try to come up with something worth your lives."

Julia winced. Reminding the remaining holdouts that whether they surrendered or not they were almost certainly dead wasn't going to encourage surrenders—but then, perhaps that was the point. Now that Reid was here with exosuited Marines, *they* weren't likely to take any losses blasting out the survivors—and Marines *hated* pirates.

Shaking her head, she glanced around the *Alan-a-dale*'s bridge. Mage-Lieutenant Nguyen was checking on the simulacrum to see if there was anything he could do with it. To Julia's knowledge, Combat Mages lacked the interface runes necessary to use it fully, but there might well be something the Lieutenant knew that she didn't.

The bridge had clearly been seized before the frigate's atmosphere had been dumped. The crew had fought back, but none of them had been in space-suits. The Patrol boarding team troopers who'd stormed the room were well-trained, too. Most of the crew had gone down to center of mass shots.

Nguyen's Marines were starting to shuffle bodies to one side. They'd eventually be moved down to the morgue, though it was unlikely there would be a full crew on the *Alan-a-dale* again for a long time.

She paused as they moved one of the bodies—the man who'd been standing next to the simulacrum originally. His throat still bore the golden medallion of a Mage, and his uniform marked him as a Commander... but she *knew* that face.

"Hold up," she ordered, stepping over to the body to be sure. The wrist computer she wore under her armor interfaced with the armor itself, and its memory capacity was huge. Most people would only purge or download their wrist computer's memory three or four times in their lifetime—and she hadn't done it since well before she'd come to work for the Protectorate.

The little computer happily confirmed her recognition. There'd been a bounty on this man—one of the quasi-legal ones she and her brother had pursued, not the illegal underworld ones. Her computer spat up the details.

"Who was he?" Julia asked aloud.

Gibbons leaned on his medic, crossing over to examine.

"That was the XO," he told her. "Commander Jamieson, he came with Wayne from the merchant ship he used to run. Sherwood native, but he hadn't been home in a while."

"Jamieson might *be* his name, but he was using another one for a long time," the ex-bounty hunter replied. "Because *I* knew him as Akbar Randall—when he was wanted for piracy and murder!"

"I think we now know why Wayne's crew was willing to follow him into piracy and murder," Julia told Montgomery over the com channel. "It's because they'd done so long before he joined the Patrol."

Once Reid had finished 'reducing' the remaining holdouts, a review of the ship's personnel files against her old database of outstanding bounties—and the *Duke*'s database of known pirates—had proven illuminating.

Akbar Randall, apparently originally born as Michael Jamieson on Sherwood, was a key example. Once captain of a pirate ship for the Blue Star Syndicate, he'd been captured in the sweep that had gutted the

Syndicate after Montgomery had killed its leader. Captured, convicted, and sentenced to life at hard labor with no chance of parole.

He'd then been one of several hundred prisoners liberated from a Protectorate penal colony when *la Cosa Nostra* had broken their Capo Julian Falcone free. Randall had been confirmed involved in several kidnapping and ransom incidents after that before disappearing from the Protectorate's radar—roughly when Michael Wayne had been called back to Sherwood to take up a frigate command.

The *Alan-a-dale* had carried a crew of three hundred and fifteen. Running their faces and biometrics against the Protectorate's databases had come up with over *ninety* matches—all wanted for piracy. Many known to be *la Cosa Nostra*, others had been Blue Star Syndicate members who'd fallen off the radar with the collapse of their organization.

"It looks like Wayne was affiliated with both Blue Star and *la Cosa Nostra*," Montgomery agreed. "Given the number we can identify as pirates, I'm guessing the rest were as well." He paused. "Shouldn't the Patrol have known this?"

"A third of these people we only identified from my old bounty database," she pointed out. "Most of the rest... we're not as good at sharing Protectorate-level criminal databases with regional governments as we probably should be. For that matter, there could easily be people in Protectorate databases where that update hasn't made its way to us." She shrugged at the Hand's image. "Data travels by ship, after all."

"I don't suppose this helps us sort out what the hell they were doing with their computers?" he asked.

"Not really," she admitted. "It's helpful to know, though. The Commodore will probably appreciate realizing that Wayne was rotten before he ever set foot on a Patrol ship."

Her boss shook his head.

"It's still hitting the Patrol hard," he told her. "I don't know if they've even put words to it yet, but they're feeling betrayed and dishonored."

"Is that our problem?"

"It could end up being," he replied. "If nothing else, I *know* there's at least eight destroyers out there pretending to be Míngliàng ships. Not to mention I'm still not sure how the hell Wayne could have managed that last attack on the MSF. We ran Phan's data—the ship that attacked her wasn't *any* of the frigates here."

"We'll keep digging here," Julia promised. "Now that everything's secure, I could use my analyst people. The Marines are good, but my Secret Service people *are* better."

"I'll have Jakab send them over," Montgomery agreed. "Maybe I should come over as well. The Hand might open up some doors regular overrides won't."

"No!" Julia said flatly. He was *right*, in that the override sequences hidden in his badge of office might have some impact on the computer software. But there was no way she was going to let him aboard an only recently secured rogue ship. Who *knew* what stragglers were still hiding—or what they might do if they realized a Hand was aboard!

"It's too risky," she continued. "You may not care if you live or die, but *I'm* the one who has to tell Princess Kiera if something happens to you!"

"Low blow," he replied with a laugh. Princess Kiera Alexander, second-in-line to the throne of Mars, was currently an aggressive not-quite-fourteen—and suffered from an on-again, off-again teenage crush on the youngest of her father's Hands.

"I'll send your people over," he promised. "And—since despite what you think I do *not* have a death wish—*I* will stay here. Near the simulacrum. Watching."

Julia tried to hide a shiver. She liked Montgomery. She *trusted* Montgomery. But she'd seen him in action *without* an amplifier—the thought of what he could do *with* one scared even her.

"Agent, my lord," a voice interrupted as Reid came into the channel. "Apologies for interrupting—but we have a prisoner!"

CHAPTER 37

THE PATROL had followed the Martian Navy's design standard of providing a complete secondary life support system and set of airlocks for the main medical bay aboard their warships. Even as breaches had opened vast portions of the ship to space and the crew had vented other sections to delay the boarders, the medical bay had remained intact and protected.

When the Marines had swept the medbay before dragging the prisoner and their wounded in, however, it had been empty. Julia knew they were still comparing the crew list with the dead, so it would be a while before anyone could say what had happened to the ship's doctor and medical staff.

She waited outside the secure treatment room as the Marine medics finished their rough treatment of the prisoner's wounds. Out of over three hundred crew, *one* had been taken alive, and he'd lost a leg and passed out from blood loss. The armored space-suit he'd been wearing had tourniqueted the limb to keep him alive, saving him from the vacuum that had claimed most of the other wounded in the vicious fight to take the *Alan-a-dale.*

Julia glanced up as Major Reid joined her, the Marine CO still in the exosuit armor that the Special Agent, normally taller than Reid, had shed for a hopefully somewhat less intimidating pressure suit.

"Is the ship secure?" Julia asked.

"As much as it can be at this point," Reid replied after removing her helmet. "The Patrol is restoring atmosphere in the sections that can still hold it and my people are sweeping for stragglers. I wouldn't want *Montgomery* aboard just yet," she finished dryly.

"And our friend?" the Agent asked, gesturing towards the cell-like room every military medical bay had.

"I think *his* friends thought he was dead," the Marine replied grimly. "We're going to have go over everyone's helmet footage, but I think I saw at least one incident of them putting their own wounded down. It wasn't just that they were all facing Mass Murder via Weapons of Mass Destruction charges, Agent. They really didn't want us taking prisoners."

Julia shook her head.

"That makes no *sense*," she complained. "Even with pirates, at least some will usually surrender."

Reid sighed. "I'm going to flip you a video," she said quietly. "One of my people forwarded it to me and it's disturbing as hell."

An icon popped up on Julia's wrist comp and she hit accept, starting playback. The PC promptly threw up a holographic screen she could watch on, showing the image of the *Alan-a-dale*'s primary life support plant.

Most of the defenders were dead, but a trio of them were in cover behind a big carbon dioxide scrubber. They returned fire at the Marines, but Julia could tell they didn't have weapons capable of penetrating exosuit armor.

A Marine bullet punched *through* the scrubber and slammed into the gut of the center pirate. It was hard to tell from the camera Julia had, but it looked like a non-lethal hit—at least with decent medical attention. Crippling in combat though, and dangerous in the not-quite-vacuum in the life support chamber.

The wounded pirate seemed to pause and take stock of the situation, then, without warning, shot his two companions in the back of the head. As they collapsed, he started spasming, his body jerking in unexpected ways as he collapsed violently to the floor.

"That was the ship's chief engineer," Reid said quietly. "He was on your bounty list—was identified as part of the crew of a Blue Star gun-runner, but never crossed the Protectorate's radar."

"What the *hell* happened to him?"

"Suicide implant," the Marine CO replied. "At a guess, all of Wayne's officers had them. I'm guessing they were the stick to a carrot of a giant pile of money to keep everyone on board with the mass murder plan."

"Damn." Julia shook her head again. "They must have figured there was *somebody* in-system with a remote trigger, too."

"And pirates being pirates, figured they'd take everyone else aboard down with them if they couldn't get out," Reid agreed. "Fucking self-centered nihilists."

The medic finally stepped out of the cell, stripping off his working gloves and looking up at both his armored commander and the towering Special Agent.

"He'll live," he said shortly. "I've got some stimulants running into his IV now, he'll be awake in a few minutes."

"Do we know who he is yet?" Julia asked.

"Petty Officer Christopher Truman," the medic answered. "Computer tech specialist, assigned to the Combat Information Center Bravo Shift."

Julia smiled. A computer tech? Petty Officer Truman had serious potential.

"Where am I?"

Christopher Truman's voice was nasal, annoyingly high-pitched, and foggy from the drugs.

"You are in the medical bay of the *Alan-a-dale*," Julia told him, calmly watching him from a chair several feet away from his bed. "As you may guess from your restraints, this ship is now in the possession of the Royal Martian Marine Corps, and you are under arrest. You are facing a laundry list of charges, but you and I both know only one matters: Mass Murder via Weapon of Mass Destruction."

Truman carefully sat up, gently testing the limits of the cuffs that chained him to the bed, and then looking down at his missing leg with a sick expression.

"Well, shit," he said bluntly. "And you are?"

"Special Agent Julia Amiri of the Protectorate Secret Service," she introduced herself. "And, much as it sickens me, I am also your only chance of living more than the week it would take us to get back to Sherwood and collect appropriate witnesses to the Hand sentencing and executing you."

Truman sighed and shifted in the bed, leaning his back against the wall and regarding her levelly. He didn't seem nearly nervous enough for his position.

"Well, from the rumors I heard aboard ship, I'm guessing you didn't take a single officer alive," he observed nasally. "Given the, ah, circumstances of most of the fight, I'm guessing you don't have many of us left at all. That you're here at all, Agent, tells me clemency is on the table."

"But not necessary," Julia pointed out. "We can and will tear this ship apart, hack open the encryption and find Captain Wayne's secrets. Your help would only make it easier."

"While I'll admit that my fellow crewmates aren't the most competent people around," Truman noted, "I suspect they managed to hit the flashing red icons that would dump and hash the entire system's memory. You can probably get something out of it, eventually, but you have a time limit, Agent."

Julia tried not to react to that tidbit, but she must have twitched as Truman broke out into a wide grin.

"A freebie, then, Agent," he told her. "Wayne reported to someone else—I honestly don't know who—who has a small fleet of other ships."

"And you can just happen to tell us where these ships are?"

"Maybe," the computer tech told her. "But I think that's worth a lot more than life in jail instead of a bullet, don't you? Every warship in two systems is here. Some might see that as opportunity."

That was a concern that had crossed Julia's mind, but they'd been watching for jump flares. So far as everyone aboard the *Duke* or any of the militia ships could tell, no one had left the Antonius System. With no Runic Transceiver Array in-system, only a ship could have carried the news.

Truman shook his head.

"You're thinking they can't know," he told her. "But I warn you—they know. However clever you think you are, whatever tricks are up the Hand's sleeve, your enemy knows where you are. Always."

"That would be impossible," she noted. He was talking about an RTA somehow concealed on a ship—when an RTA couldn't fit on a ship in the first place!

"I don't disagree," Truman pointed out. "But tell me it doesn't match what you've seen? I watched our missions, our timelines. They made no sense if the news we were acting on traveled by ship. Hell, Agent, if nothing else—how were we in the right place to meet the Commodore's courier without raising suspicion? We knew where they'd be, and that they'd been sent... and no, I don't know how," he admitted.

"Assuming I believe your time limit, Petty Officer, what exactly do you *want*?" Julia demanded.

"I want a ride the *hell* away from either of the systems that got tied up in this mess, a clean record, and ten million Martian dollars," Truman replied instantly.

Julia laughed in his face. It would be hard enough to justify letting a member of the *Alan-a-dale*'s crew *live*, let alone letting him *go*.

"You really think the help you can give us is worth that?" she demanded.

"Depends," he admitted. "Do you really think the people who blew away Greenwood and the Processing Facility will blink at bombing a world full of people to finish the job?"

That stopped her cold. She hadn't even considered that as a possibility. They had things mostly under control... but would even the presence of the real Míngliàng ships here stop a war if the fake ones attacked Sherwood itself?

The bud in her ear buzzed.

"I've been listening," Montgomery told her quietly. "Put me on."

She started to scrabble for her sub-vocal microphone to communicate, and then she heard the Tone settle into his voice—the tone of a Hand who had made up their mind.

"Put me on, Julia," he ordered.

She sighed and opened a channel on her PC.

A holographic image of Damien Montgomery appeared in the middle of the room, his gaze focusing on Truman.

"Petty Officer Christopher Truman," he said very calmly, "I am Hand Damien Montgomery. You paint a dire picture, Mister Truman, but I am not entirely convinced. Why should I believe you?"

Truman swallowed, his eyes flickering from Julia to the hologram of Montgomery.

"I don't want to die," he finally whispered. "But these people... I don't know who they are. I don't know where they're from. But they are without conscience. Without even a pirate's honor."

The hologram looked over at Julia. She glanced down at the camera on her wrist computer that was sending the image of the room back to Montgomery and nodded slightly. Truman was *scared*. Whoever Wayne's employers had been, they had scared someone who'd worked for Mikhail Azure witless.

"I have a compromise to suggest, Mister Truman," Montgomery said finally. "I will reduce your sentence to ten years in the Carnery Penitentiary. If you are not familiar with it, Carnery is a medium security facility used to house non-violent offenders. It is not luxurious, but it is more comfortable than any prison you'd normally go to."

Carnery was on Mars, Julia knew. It was often used for exactly this kind of deal—to the point where she wondered how many of its prisoners actually *were* the sort of white-collar criminals the prison had theoretically been built to hold.

"If your information pans out and you serve your sentence, you will leave Carnery with four million Martian dollars," the Hand continued.

"And if my information doesn't pan out, or I run?" Truman asked.

"Then I will execute you with my own hands," Montgomery told him. Julia shivered. The Hand didn't lower his voice or anything. He simply threatened the pirate in the same tone he'd offered to pay him a fortune.

She'd now worked for two, and Hands *still* terrified her.

The impact on Truman was gratifying. For the first time since he'd fully awoken, he didn't seem at ease or certain of himself. He swallowed, hard, and nodded.

"All right," he agreed, then turned to Julia. "I'm assuming you've got computer techs aboard, starting to tear into the old girl's systems? You'll want to put me in touch with them—the *Alan-a-dale* has two complete computer networks, and if they cross-wire them accidentally they could lose what's left on the real one..."

CHAPTER 38

WITH A FULL-BODY CAST wrapped around her torso, Grace McLaughlin looked far too vulnerable to Damien's eyes as he looked through the window of her infirmary room.

All things considered, today was a huge victory, pulling two systems back from the brink of outright war via the intervention of a Hand. The cost, though... Three Marines dead and ten wounded in Wayne's surprise attack. Two dozen more wounded, though thankfully no more fatalities, securing the *Alan-a-dale*. Over *two hundred* Patrol boarders dead, not to mention the over three hundred crew members from the *Alan-a-dale* themselves. They had apparently been traitors to a man, but they were still Patrol personnel who hadn't lived out the day.

"How is she doing?" he quietly asked the ship's doctor as the woman came around.

"Non-life-threatening," she replied crisply. "The wounds are all cleaned and bandaged under the cast. So long as she doesn't move too much, she should recover with minimal scarring and no mobility loss."

"Can she have visitors?"

The doctor sighed, half-glared at him, and shrugged. "You've made it this far," she admitted. "I'm kicking you out if she starts seeming strained."

Damien bowed his head slightly.

"I wouldn't dream of anything else, doctor. Thank you."

Despite her grouchiness, the doctor closed the door behind Damien as he entered the treatment room. The woman could still watch him through the window in the door, and had access to all of the equipment measuring McLaughlin's health, but the tiny amount of privacy was appreciated.

"Hey you," he said aloud.

She blinked a few times, then slowly opened her eyes.

"Hey yourself," Grace replied. "I feel like I was kicked by a mule. A burning, angry, mule that I used to be attracted to. Who was on fire."

"You remember everything?" Damien asked carefully.

"I do. What did I miss after passing out?"

"I've ordered all ships to converge on the *Alan-a-dale*," he told her. "The MSF is about twenty minutes away and once we're all in the same place, I'm calling a meeting of the captains. We've secured Wayne's ship, but..."

"I'm injured, not useless," she snapped. "How bad?"

"They fought to the death, Grace," Damien admitted. "We took *one* prisoner. Just one." He sighed. "And the last count I had from your people was two hundred and six fatalities in the boarding teams."

"My God," Grace whispered. "We only had four ten-man boarding teams per ship, and the new ships..."

Commander McTaggart had filled him in. There had only *been* two hundred and eighty trained boarders aboard the eight Patrol ships. The Patrol's Marines equivalent had just been *gutted.*

"Sergeant Gibbons survived," he told her. "He may have served us all better than he expected, too."

"What do you mean?"

"The last survivor is cooperating in exchange for a reduced sentence and a pile of money once it's over," Damien replied. "The *Alan-a-dale* had *two* complete computer networks—black boxes, scanner processors, everything. The system you had access to was living in a fantasy world constructed by the frigate's *real* computers."

"That... explains a lot."

"Apparently, on their very first out of system patrol, Wayne wandered over to a yard he knew in Amber that doesn't ask questions and had it installed," he explained. "The only thing you saw of his actions after that was what he *wanted* you to see."

"How did he even know about a yard like that?" she asked bitterly.

"We're not entirely sure what name Wayne was using while he was away from home," Damien told her gently, "but we've identified a *lot* of his crew that used to use other names—names under which they were known to the Protectorate as pirates and murderers and those sorts of scum. I think..." he sighed, "I *know*, now, that Wayne was a pirate before he came home. He must have been *ecstatic* when he got the request to come take up command of a Patrol frigate."

Grace looked sick in a way that wasn't explained by her injuries.

"And to think I used to idolize the bastard," she snarled. "Now I want to kill him again *myself*. You got all this from his computers?"

"No, so far we're mostly running on what our survivor has told us," Damien admitted. "It looks like Wayne's people managed to wipe almost the entirety of both computer systems—but that brings us back to Gibbons. He led an assault on the bridge as part of the first boarding wave. Killed the XO, which helped keep magic out of the fight until my Marines arrived, but also kept them from wiping the jump calculation computer."

Most Jump Mages kept a computer, entirely separate from the main network, on which they loaded the complex software they used to help them run jump calculations. A Mage had to visualize the jump *perfectly*, and the tools used to do so often varied from Mage to Mage.

"We now know the last two hundred or so *real* jumps that the *Alan-a-dale* took," he told her. "Our prisoners says there was a rendezvous point that Wayne had with the people behind this, and there is one fixed point in deep space he kept going back to."

"You have to find them!" Grace told him. "They destroyed Greenwood, killed our people, we have to..."

"I intend to take the Patrol, the Flotilla, and the *Duke of Magnificence* to that rendezvous point," he confirmed. "I'm meeting with the Captains in half an hour."

"I need to be there," she said. "The prospect of revenge on Greenwood's killers is probably enough, but if you're commandeering my *entire fleet*, I need to tell my people I'm on board."

Damien glanced back at the door. "I'm not sure your doctor is going to be okay with that."

"Stubborn as you are, my dear Damien, you shouldn't underestimate my ability to be convincing!"

For the second time in twenty-four hours, Damien entered the *Duke of Magnificence*'s amphitheater-like main conference chamber. This time, instead of Amiri walking behind him, a nurse from the battlecruiser's medical department pushed Grace McLaughlin in a wheelchair on his left, and Admiral Yen Phan walked on his right.

Mage-Captain Jakab waited by the center podium with its holographic display tank, and the seven remaining Patrol captains—plus Commander Liam Arrington, now Acting Captain of the *Robin Hood* out of pure necessity—faced their fifteen Flotilla counterparts across the pit.

"Ladies, gentlemen," Damien greeted them. "Let's begin with the most pertinent information: we have now fully secured the *Alan-a-dale*. Based off even a cursory review of the, ah, *oddities* to her computer network, I don't think anyone would be comfortable taking her into combat, but we can be sure no more surprises are coming from that direction."

The Patrol officers looked embarrassed, which Damien personally considered unfair. If they hadn't started shooting up their own missiles from behind, *far* more would have made it to the *Duke*. No other method had been—or could have been!—as effective.

"For those wondering just what led the crew of a Patrol frigate to the crimes we have now associated with them, the answer is, sadly, far simpler than we feared," he continued. "The crew of the *Alan-a-dale* was drawn from the pirate vessel that Michael Wayne secretly commanded before returning to Sherwood. We have reason to believe he was affiliated, at different points, with both the Blue Star Syndicate and *la Cosa Nostra*.

"Offered command of one of Sherwood's new frigates, he saw an opportunity he couldn't pass up. It *also* appears that he had outside help," Damien told them all grimly. "Our prisoner spoke of an unknown number of warships in the hands of Wayne's sponsors. Based on the attack on Greenwood, and the attack on the *Wil Scarlet*, we assume that these sponsors are in possession of at least eight destroyers retrofitted to appear to be Míngliàng units."

He smiled, looking slowly around and meeting each captain's gaze levelly. None of them looked nervous, and from the determined expressions on their faces, *all* of them had guessed what came next.

"Since I cannot be certain that those eight destroyers are the *only* forces available to these sponsors, I am officially commandeering all available warships of both the Sherwood Interstellar Patrol and the Míngliàng Security Flotilla for counter-piracy operations under my authority as Hand of the Mage-King of Mars, and placing you all under the command of Mage-Captain Jakab here."

The room was silent. Damien waited a good ten seconds for anyone to raise a comment and then tapped a command. A map of the local region of space, with Míngliàng, Sherwood, and Antonius highlighted, appeared in the holo-tank.

"Captain Wayne got up to a lot of things that he didn't tell his superiors about," he told the captains grimly. "But, again and again, he returned to a specific point in space. Our prisoner tells me he was making physical rendezvous with his sponsors, often to off-load stolen cargo. That point was here."

A new dot, about two light years away from Antonius but still equidistant from Míngliàng and Sherwood, appeared on the map.

"The exact location varies a bit," he continued, "but since we have a number of the jump calculations used to get there, we have derived the exact references used by Captain Wayne to make the rendezvous. We can be there in two jumps."

The fact that they needed to be there as soon as possible, because their prisoner believed said sponsors had a form of communication that current magical research said was *impossible*, was something he would keep to himself. They'd found no *evidence* of a miniaturized Runic Transceiver Array, but there were definitely places aboard the *Alan-a-dale* where *something* had been destroyed as part of the computer purge.

"Captain Liu," he said briskly. That worthy, the commander of one of Phan's damaged destroyers, sat up straight and looked attentive.

"We have enough firepower on hand that I think we won't need the damaged ships like yours in the hunt," he told the Captain gently. "But I need a ship to stay here, and one to go to both of the home systems carrying messages from me.

"I want you to take your ship to Sherwood. You'll be flying a Code Lambda and carrying messages under my personal seal, so you *should* be safe."

Code Lambda meant a ship had been commandeered by either the Navy or a Hand for courier duty, and was to be treated as an ambassadorial vessel.

"Captain Văn," Damien turned to another of Phan's commanders. "I want you to return to Mínglìang. You'll also be under Code Lambda and honestly, the message is identical.

"Lastly, Captain Phan," he turned to the commander of the last damaged destroyer. Even without the family name, the tall black woman was *obviously* related to her Admiral—though too old to be Phan's daughter. "I want you to remain here as a touchstone for everyone who should be *coming* here over the next few days—Admiral Medici should arrive at the same time as the Governors and I intend to leave Inspector Accord and Doctor Christoffsen here to meet them."

"The Governors are coming here, my lord?" the younger Phan asked.

"I am ordering them to," Damien confirmed. "With everything that has gone down, I think I need Governor Wong and Governor McLaughlin to sit in the same room as I explain exactly *how* they were almost fooled into going to war—so I can make *damn* sure they don't fall for it again!"

Damien gestured Christoffsen and Accord to seats in his office. The massive window of his office gave them a surprisingly clear view of the large chunk of ice that the *Tiāntǐ tíqǔ* was mining. The mining ship itself was invisible except as a tiny glint of metal on the side of the ice—as, for that matter, was the Míngliàng Security Flotilla cruiser barely a thousand kilometers away.

"Gentlemen, thank you for being willing to be thrown from ship to ship at a few minute's notice," he told them. "Your shuttle to the *Chimera* will be departing in fifteen minutes—and the fleet will be leaving Antonius less than five minute after that."

"Are we really in that much of a rush?" Christoffsen asked. "It seems unlikely that Wayne's sponsors would be moving that quickly."

"Unfortunately, everything I have seen suggests that our mysterious enemy has some form of communication we have not accounted for," Damien told them. "Our prisoner confirmed this, though he has no more information than we do on what it was. The Secret Service agents on the *Alan-a-dale* are specifically looking for anything that could duplicate an RTA's effect, but," he shrugged. "I have no idea how they could miniaturize that rune structure enough to fit in on a starship, let alone *hide* it on a starship."

"But you think they know where we all are," the Professor said slowly. "I think I understand the rush, then."

"Right now, Míngliàng and Sherwood are very vulnerable," the Hand told them. "Míngliàng at least has a squadron of corvettes, but Sherwood has no such defenses. I intend to cut off these bastards before they can launch such an attack, but that leaves an entire aspect of this mess untouched.

"Hence summoning the Governors," he concluded. "I need to sit them down in the same room and get them to *talk* to each other. I need you two to convince them to do so when they get here."

"That's a tall order," Accord admitted. "I *think* the McLaughlin will be willing to talk at this point, but..."

"Christoffsen will speak as my representative," Damien noted. "Through my authority, he will stand as a Voice of Mars. I *hope* they will listen."

"I will try not to disappoint you, my lord," the old ex-Governor replied. "But I must confess, that this situation is far worse than anything that arose during my own time as Governor."

"I think we're past the risk of outright war," the Hand said. "My concern now is dealing with the underlying tension. There was a conflict here to prod at, or it would never have got this bad. Put most simply, Antonius needs a new governing structure. One more useful than 'these two systems share ownership.'"

"Ah," Christoffsen said calmly. "If that is *all* you need me to arrange, I believe I can manage that." The older man paused and shook his head slowly.

"But realize that if *you* fail and Sherwood is attacked, I'm not sure there is anything I will be able to do to hold things together."

"I know," Damien told the two men. "But at this point, everything is down to timing—all I can do is hope that we intercept them before they attack Sherwood."

CHAPTER 39

SHIP AFTER SHIP emerged from their jump flares, and Damien didn't even need to look at Mage-Captain Jakab to know things weren't going quite as the Navy officer had expected. When he'd issued the jump order in Antonius, the two militia fleets had been assembled around the *Duke* in a relatively tight formation. They'd all received the jump order at once.

They'd arrived at the deep space target point in... a less organized state.

The ships had trickled in over thirty seconds, and any semblance of the neat formation they'd left Antonius in was long gone. The two cruisers had only been a thousand kilometers away from the *Duke* when they jumped, but now one was two thousand kilometers away—and the other was over a *hundred* thousand kilometers off.

"I see the militias have not been practicing formation jumps," Jakab observed. His XO saluted crisply before retreating from the bridge to allow Mage-Lieutenant Philips to take his place. The *Duke*'s fourth Jump Mage was aboard the *Robin Hood*, making up for the absence of Commodore McLaughlin.

"It doesn't help us," Damien agreed. "Does it change anything?"

"No," the *Duke*'s CO said flatly. "We don't have time to drill their Mages. Are you sure about this rapid cycle, my lord?"

Normally, jumps were cycled evenly—every eight hours for every Mage. If you had two Mages aboard, the way all of the Patrol and Flotilla ships did, that meant you jumped every four hours. Since more than eight hours had passed since any of the warships had arrived in the

Antonius System and they were only making two jumps, Damien had ordered the jumps to take place only ten minutes apart.

"Unless we wait *eight* hours, the militia ships still wouldn't be able to jump away from the rendezvous point any sooner after arriving," he pointed out. "But the longer we take to arrive, the more likely it is that they'll act on whatever intelligence they're getting. If they've already moved, delaying the jump won't help. But if they haven't..."

The Hand shrugged.

"Besides, Kole, would four hours of instruction via radio change anything?"

"No," the Mage-Captain repeated with a sigh. "We will coordinate. The fleet will be ready to jump on your schedule, my lord. Are you intending to remain on the bridge?"

"I can neither be as aware of the situation or as available to you, Captain, anywhere else," Damien noted. "You are in command, Kole, but I am responsible for everything and everyone here."

"The *Duke* has an entire flag bridge, Damien," Jakab pointed out. "A fully functioning secondary command center, designed to allow a senior officer to oversee everything going on *without* physically hanging over my shoulder."

Damien chuckled.

"I hear your point, Kole," he admitted. "But I have a staff of exactly twelve, most of whom are Secret Service agents. I didn't expect to end up in a fleet action, so I didn't borrow the staff needed to run a flag bridge from the Navy. In hindsight, that was an oversight—one I will rectify.

"But until I have," he told the Mage-Captain, "I'll be keeping your observer seat warm."

"As you wish, my lord," Jakab said with a gracious nod. "But if you'll excuse me, I must coordinate our next jump."

The jump to Wayne's rendezvous point went surprisingly more smoothly than the first. The ships still filtered in over thirty seconds, but they returned to something resembling the formation they'd left Antonius in.

The two Mínglìàng Security Flotilla cruisers flanked the *Duke of Magnificence*, neither exactly at the thousand kilometer mark, but both at least within ten thousand kilometers. The eight Patrol frigates were scattered around, but they had come out of their jumps in a rough protective wall in front of the cruisers. The destroyers were actually the most organized, with all ten of the million ton ships appearing within a few hundred kilometers of their positions in the layered sphere missile defense formation Mage-Captain Kole Jakab had shown them.

"Wide sensor sweeps," Kole ordered as the last ships appeared around him. "All ships, full active sensors. If there's anyone out there, they know we're here—let's make sure we know *they're* here."

Passive receptors across all twenty-one ships were already sucking in petabytes of data that the computers churned through analysis of. Here in deep space, light years away from anything, even a dormant ship should stick out like a sore thumb.

"We've got something," Carver announced. "Multiple heat signatures, distance thirty light seconds, sixty degrees by one-seventy-five. Pulling data from the rest of the fleet to triangulate."

That put the unknowns above and behind the *Duke of Magnificence* on her current vector and orientation—and, like most Protectorate ships, almost her entire arsenal pointed forwards.

"Orders to the fleet," Kole snapped. "Re-orient all ships along that vector, prepare to engage the enemy!" He turned his gaze to his tactical department. "Get me an ID, people," he ordered.

"I've got nineteen signatures," Carver reported. "Multiple mass ranges—all of them just lit up their engines. Six are headed away from us, thirteen are headed *right* at us."

"The six are reading at over ten million tons apiece," Rhine added, reviewing his staff's data. "Acceleration is slow, I'm only showing three gravities. They're freighters —big container ships, no question about it."

"The lead unit headed for us is a frigate," the junior officer continued as his boss finished. "The rest are destroyers." He paused. "I can't say for sure on the rest, but the lead matches the profile of the *Wil Scarlet*."

"She was *destroyed*," Kole objected.

"According to Michael Wayne," Montgomery said quietly from the observer seat. "I hadn't considered that—she's the ship that attacked Phan when she was rescuing her freighters. She's a surprise, but the numbers are in our favor, I believe?"

"No change to the plan," Kole agreed as he watched his fleet slowly reorient around him. "Only question is: do we fire first, sir?"

"Give me a wide-channel transmission," the Hand ordered. "We'll give them one chance. And Captain?"

"Yes?"

"If they fire *before* I'm done talking, you are authorized to blow them to hell."

A tiny light flicked on, informing Damien that his observer console was recording for transmission.

"Unidentified vessels," he said harshly, "this is Damien Montgomery, Hand of the Mage-King of Mars. This area has been identified as a pirate rendezvous point. You will cease acceleration and prepare to be boarded for inspection, as per Article Twenty-Seven of the Protectorate Charter.

"Failure to heave to will be regarded as conspiracy with the individuals responsible for the destruction of Greenwood and the Mínglìàng Antonius Central Processing Facility—and the deaths of seventy thousand Protectorate civilians."

Subtle it wasn't, but Damien wasn't actually *expecting* these people to surrender. If nothing else, the *Duke*'s CIC team was attempting to match the energy signatures of the destroyers to those responsible for the attack on Greenwood—and the attack on the *Wil Scarlet*. That ship appeared to have been captured intact, which left the Hand wondering about its crew. Had Captain Vlahovic followed Wayne into treason? Or had the *Wil Scarlet* been given an entirely new crew—and Vlahovic's people murdered?

Damien didn't know. He probably never would, now.

"That's strange," Carver said quietly. Damien's observer console was closer to the junior tactical officer's station than the Captain's chair was. He wasn't sure anyone else had heard the youth speak.

"What's strange?" Damien asked, his voice equally soft.

"I'm not sure," the youth replied. "Commander Rhine, Lord Montgomery, if you want to take a look."

Carver flipped an image to Damien's console and zoomed in on the six freighters, currently accelerating away from the Protectorate ships. They were all identical, the Hand noted. That removed the possibility of them being prizes taken in the campaign—those six ships were here for a reason.

"It's like they're ejecting something," Carver told them. "See? The engine of the furthest ship keeps being eclipsed, and I'm picking up faint heat signatures. Too big to be cargo, not sure what they could be."

A chill ran through Damien. His old ship had repeatedly used 'ejecting cargo' as cover for tricks that had helped keep the *Blue Jay* alive—but had killed a *lot* of those pursuing her.

"Any idea of the size?" he asked.

"Hard to say... thirty, forty meters across?"

That rang a bell too. "Do we have radar data on them?" he asked. "Might not have shown up as they're cold and small, but we might have it anyway."

"No response to your message, sir," Jakab noted. "What do we do?"

"Got them!" Rhine interrupted. "Strange things... look like half an egg, but they're familiar..."

Damien looked at the profile they'd pulled out. Forty meters long, twenty meters across. Each ship had been dropping them in pairs, and they looked *very* familiar.

"Son of a *bitch*," he swore. "Captain—they're deploying *gunships*."

"What? That's... impossible."

"Legatus hired the freighter I served on to deliver gunships between systems," Damien told him urgently. "That three megaton ship carried eight gunships, and the crews could access their ships from the main hull. We didn't spend a lot of effort optimizing them... but those ships are *four times the size* of my old ship. They could be carrying over *two hundred* gunships between them."

"My god," Carver breathed. "If they're anything like the Legatan ships, that's easily another two thousand launchers."

"They haven't launched them all yet," Damien noted. "Mage-Captain—you have to destroy those freighters."

"What! If there's any prisoners, any survivors..."

"Then they're aboard those ships," Damien said grimly. There was no choice. No third option. If those freighters deployed that many gunships, the fleet he'd pulled together would die. "We don't have a choice, Captain. I am *ordering* you to target those freighters with long-range laser fire.

"Take them out, Kole. There's no *time*."

"Commander Rhine, charge the main battle lasers," Jakab said slowly, holding Damien's gaze as if begging him to change his mind. Damien simply nodded.

Jakab swallowed hard, then returned Damien's nod.

"Target the gunship carriers and take them out before they finish deploying," the Mage-Captain said in a rush. "Dispersion Pattern Lambda-Four. Fire on all targets."

The *Duke of Magnificence* carried hundreds of thousands of tons of layered composite armor, including upper layers of both ablative and reflective armor designed to defeat heavy battle lasers equivalent to her own twelve-gigawatt main battery.

Even the militia ships around her were armored enough and maneuverable enough that a shot at over nine million kilometers would be a waste of energy. If the beam somehow managed to connect, the beam dispersion at thirty light seconds would be enough for their armor to shrug aside the heaviest of lasers.

Whoever had converted the freighters to gunship carriers hadn't added armor. They were maneuvering, but at barely a third of the speed of a true warship with gravity runes to protect its crew—and limited in their options by the need to deploy the gunships they were carrying inside their keels.

They never even saw death coming.

Three twelve-gigawatt beams of coherent light targeted each ship. Targeted as carefully as they could be, and then unleashed in the wide, sweeping, cuts of a Lambda—long-range—targeting program. Each ship was hit by at least one beam, most by two.

When the light made it back to the *Duke of Magnificence* it showed the utter destruction of all six ships. Fuel stores, engines, munitions... it was impossible to be sure, but all six ships vanished inside the first few seconds of sustained laser fire.

Then the parasite ships they'd deployed lit up their engines, rotating to join the traditional warships and charge at their motherships' killers.

"Cease laser fire," Kole ordered his people, trying not to guess how many people had still been aboard the freighters when they'd gone up. All six appeared to have been acting as gunship carriers, so there *probably* hadn't been prisoners aboard. Probably. "All vessels are to target the warships and prepare to fire."

He turned to Montgomery.

"My lord, should we summon them to surrender again?"

Before the Hand could reply, a muffled curse from the tactical section rapidly devolved into prayer.

"Our father, who art in Heaven, hallowed be Thy name, Thy will be done..."

Kole stared at the screen, understanding instantly why Carver had starting asking the divine for protection.

The carriers might be gone, but seventy-six gunships had apparently launched before he took out the motherships. They had brought up their engines and were charging at his fleet—and firing as they came.

Their fire was clearly the signal the main force had been waiting on, and the frigate and destroyers opened fire as well.

In a matter of moments, space was filled with missiles—almost thirteen *hundred* weapons his computers identified as Phoenix VII missiles.

"All vessels," Kole said calmly. "Focus your fire on the *Wil Scarlet*, and fire when ready."

CHAPTER 40

"STEP OUR MISSILES down to match the Phoenix VIIs' accelera-tion," the Mage-Captain continued.

It took Damien a moment to understand the reasoning—the *Duke*'s missiles were bigger and faster than the ones the militias were using. While they were superior weapons, they weren't superior *enough* to make up for arriving on their own, as opposed to arriving with the other eight hundred-plus missiles.

A few moments after Jakab's orders, nine hundred and twenty mis-siles were in space at twelve thousand gravities. Gentle nudging from the warships' computers adjusted the accelerations, tiny blips that brought all of them into line as a single giant salvo.

The strangers' missiles had a thirty second advantage on the Protectorate salvo, and one of Rhine's people had thrown up an 'Estimated Impact' timer on the surrounding screens. Six minutes and counting, with the missiles still effectively nine million kilometers away and accelerating.

"They're maneuvering to throw off any more long-range laser shots," Rhine noted. "I think we spooked them."

"I'll take small benefits," Jakab replied. "As for big ones... best guess on the capacity of those carriers?"

"These are *Orion*-class Legatan gunships, I think," the tactical officer replied. "An older model, the last Legatus built before switching to home-built fusion missiles with enough endurance to match the Phoenix's range. The LSDF has completely phased them out—and only *built* three hundred of them."

"And?"

"And if someone managed to pick them all up when they scrapped them, they could have fit all three hundred on those six ships," Rhine said quietly. "They have no gravity, less than two days endurance, and are a cheap-as-dirt method of putting twelve launchers into space to defend a planet. No one has ever tried to move them around as an offensive weapon that I know of though."

Damien shrugged as the Captain looked at him. "We were transporting them to set up defenses in another system," he explained. "We *could*, theoretically, have launched them like that, but it would have been an... interesting procedure."

The big cruiser shivered around them as a second salvo launched into space, a minute after the last. The enemy vessels seemed to have the same older launcher as the Flotilla and Patrol—if nothing else, the *Wil Scarlet* had been a Patrol ship. Their second salvo had launched thirty seconds ago.

Two timers and distances appeared on the screen, counting down the time and range.

"MSF destroyers have assumed the new formation," Rhine reported. "Everyone is now aligned, enemy first salvo is at roughly eight million kilometers and four and a half minutes to impact."

"My lord," Jakab said quietly to Damien. "I've seen you in action, but never with an amplifier." He paused. "How *much* further than I can you reach?"

The Hand glanced at the screen, the now three salvos of over a thousand missiles reaching out. With only one amplifier in the fleet, the laser turrets every ship carried would bear the biggest burden of missile defense, but even an extra light second of use of the amplifier could make a huge difference.

"We've experimented," he admitted. He'd killed Mikhail Azure, when that crime lord had tried to capture his ship, by being able to use the amplifier well beyond the range Azure had expected. "Far enough that the lightspeed lag is a real issue. Effective..." he shrugged. "Ten to twelve light seconds."

Jakab blinked, then gestured towards the simulacrum.

"That's a million kilometers more than anyone else on this ship, my lord. If you would be so kind as to see what you can do to keep us alive, I'd appreciate it," he said dryly.

The Hand nodded and quickly stepped up to the raised dais, stripping off his elbow-length black leather gloves as he did. Hands tried to keep the exact strength of their augmented magical abilities under wraps—and since his own were even *more* augmented, he had strict instructions only to use his full power when truly necessary.

If he wasn't sure that his extra power would be *enough*, then it was probably necessary.

The silver polymer inlay on Damien's palms slotted perfectly into the two blank spaces left for them on the semi-liquid silver model of the *Duke of Magnificence*. The simulacrum shivered under his fingers—and the entire ship shivered around him as a third salvo of missiles blasted into space.

Linked into the amplifier, Damien *became* the ship. The screens that surrounded him in every direction became his eyes, his senses, even as his magic reached out into the space around the mighty vessel. A few sparks, generated in an empty part of the void, tested his 'muscles' as he prepared for the incoming fire.

Seconds ticked by, and the pirates launched a fourth salvo—but this one was only from the destroyers and frigate. The gunships held their fire, the tiny ships likely out of missiles.

A fourth salvo followed from the Protectorate fleet, more and more missiles launching into space every minute from each side.

Damien couldn't truly *see* the timers anymore, but he was *aware* of the distance and speed of the missiles in a way that no computer display could ever enable. The first salvo was four million kilometers away, moving at over thirty thousand kilometers a second and everything he saw was over ten seconds delayed. By the time the light reached the sensors he was 'seeing' through, the missiles had moved another light second and more.

Precision was impossible. Attacking a starship at this range was *far* easier than stopping missiles, though at least his magic was *not* limited by the speed of light. If he judged where the missiles were correctly, he only need to know where they were... *now*.

Power flashed through space. At closer ranges, plasma balls and beams of pure energy could be effective, but they required either precision or massive scale to have a chance of stopping missiles at this range.

Instead, Damien conjured ball lightning. For all of his power, electric charges strong enough to lash out across hundreds of kilometers were a drain, and he could only produce one 'ball' at a time.

Each point source of electricity was placed closer and closer to the *Duke* and its guardian militia ships, tens of thousands of kilometers apart as the missiles traveled at a blistering pace.

He'd dropped six of the lightning balls into space by the time the light from the first reached the *Duke*, allowing him to refine his targeting. He'd been close—close enough that he heard a couple of choked off gasps around him in the bridge as the first blast took out a dozen missiles.

The results of his second and third blasts showed that he'd misestimated the missiles' speed. When the light of the sixth charge reached them, it had only taken out two missiles—but the seventh was better, sixteen missiles detonating as electricity arced into them across the vacuum and overloaded systems.

"When they hit six light seconds, leave them for the lasers," Jakab murmured in his ear. "We'll need you to hit each wave in sequence."

Damien was only loosely connected to his body at this point, but he managed to nod. The Mage-Captain, thankfully, seemed aware that the Hand had *never* actually played the missile defense role in reality.

After dropping the eighth electromagnetic charge, fifty seconds after the first missiles had entered his range, he turned his attention to the second salvo. Some of those missiles were running into the remnants of the charges, but he started dropping new charges again. This time, he had even *less* time to work.

And every missile he stopped was one that couldn't hit the ships around him—the ships that, among others, contained him, his staff and friends, and Commodore Grace McLaughlin.

Mage-Captain Jakab had never seen anything like what the Hand was doing with his ship's amplifier. An area effect weapon in *space*? The ball lightning seemed to be restricted to a thousand or so kilometers, but even *that* should have been impossible—from both a physics and a thaumaturgics perspective.

The first wave reached the outer limits of the fleet's laser range less eighty missiles from when it started. The Mínglìàng Flotilla destroyers had edged towards the enemy, extending the defensive range of the fleet by a hundred thousand kilometers, and opened fire first.

Ten ships unleashed seven hundred lasers, cutting and slashing through space. Seconds later, the Patrol added their own seven hundred and fifty—followed by the three cruisers with another hundred apiece.

The first salvo flew into the teeth of over *seventeen hundred* laser turrets. Even traveling at well over ten percent of lightspeed, the missiles still had to withstand that fire for over thirty seconds.

The last missiles died ten seconds and half a million kilometers from the *Duke*—only four hundred thousand kilometers from the destroyers strung out in front—and leaving the defenders with less than ten seconds to retarget their weapons on the second salvo.

Montgomery was improving, Kole realized. He'd blasted over a hundred and fifty missiles away with even fewer opportunities to drop his strange ball lightning mines.

That still left eleven hundred missiles hitting the laser defense perimeter, with an added delay to get the weapons on target, and some of the lasers in their secondary cool-down cycles. ECM arrays sang deadly songs, luring missiles onto fixed courses that made them easy prey, and the lasers reaped a vicious harvest.

They couldn't stop them all. Six snuck through—six of over twelve hundred. Blinded by jamming and in terminal acquisition mode, they picked up the destroyers in front of them and lunged for the kill.

Fire lit up the void, and two of the Míngliàng Security Flotilla's ships died. A third stumbled in space, venting atmosphere and debris as she slowed, over half her engines gone.

"Order the *Manticore* to fall back," Kole snapped. "Get her behind the cruisers, fast!"

"We *got* the bastard!" Rhine crowed over him, pointing at the screen.

Without checking the historical footage, Kole couldn't tell how many missiles had struck the *Wil Scarlet*, but the ex-Patrol frigate was now an expanding ball of fire. Other missiles, having lost their primary target, slammed into gunships and destroyers.

Everything the Mage-Captain saw was thirty seconds old, when his own first salvo had savaged the enemy—and *savaged* was the right word. The *Wil Scarlet* was the biggest victim, but three of the destroyers and five of the gunships followed her. The strangers had a *lot* of firepower, but no experience working as a team—even the Patrol and Flotilla ships worked better together, at least with their own comrades.

"Third salvo inbound," Carver reported. "Eleven hundred and four birds hitting the perimeter... now."

The time lag meant Kole saw the results of his own strikes at the same time as the incoming missiles hit his own ships. Even if they wiped the entire enemy fleet from the universe, he'd still be facing the six salvos currently in space, though after this one there were only three hundred and fifty missiles.

The Hand seemed to have reached the same conclusion. The strange and devastating electrical mines followed the missiles in this time, detonating more missiles as the lasers began to take their own harvest.

Short three ships, Kole realized it wasn't going to be enough. A chill settled into his heart as he saw the last full salvo from the enemy charge forward like a juggernaut come to claim his people's lives.

Eighty missiles broke through everything they threw at them. Some had lost their original targets and went for the easiest prey—the destroyers in the front line. Four more Mingliàng ships vanished in balls of antimatter fire.

Fifty charged forward, and the Patrol met them head on. More missiles died to point blank laser fire—but missiles struck home as well. The *Loxley* would never get her defenses fully online, missiles ripping through the gap in her lasers and ripping the brand new ship to shreds.

The *Friar Tuck* and *Lionheart* joined her in death, and the *Maid Marian* fell out of formation venting debris and atmosphere—and *still* a dozen missiles blasted directly for the *Duke of Magnificence*.

An arcing web of pure *power* appeared from nowhere, the Hand unleashing everything he had at a terrifyingly short range—and the *Duke's* viewscreens blanked as multiple gigaton range explosions triggered right in front of them...

Then the entire ship rang like a bell, its multi-megaton mass *lurching* as a gigaton hammer slammed into her hull. The lights flickered, the screens dimmed—and came back up.

"Damage report!" Kole ordered. "How bad were we hit?"

"One missile, Bravo broadside," Carver snapped. "We lost most of the Bravo launchers, but we're still intact."

"We hit them—tell me we hit them," the Mage-Captain demanded.

"On screen," Rhine replied, and Kole turned his gaze back to the tactical plot.

Over a dozen more gunships were gone, along with three more destroyers. Over half the enemy starships were gone and almost a quarter of the sublight gunships. With all of the full-strength salvos gone, Kole breathed a sigh of relief—now he *knew* how this was going to end.

"Sir, one of the destroyers has jumped!" Carver announced.

"So it begins," Kole said grimly. He'd seen this in the records of engagement with pirates—once it was a lost fight, if they *could* jump, they would.

"Son of a..." a new explosion lit up the screen—at least twenty seconds before their missiles would have arrived.

"Sir... unless I'm misreading this, another destroyer just *tried* to jump—and blew the hell up," Rhine reported.

Kole blinked. *That* was unexpected.

"We're being hailed!" Rain reported. "Throwing it up on the screen."

A panicked looking man in a pseudo-military uniform with *far* too much gold braid appeared.

"We surrender!" he snapped. "We'll disable our missiles—we just don't want to..."

The transmission cut off, and as Kole looked to the screen to see why, all he saw was explosions.

"What the *fuck?*"

"They all just self-destructed," Rhine said slowly. "Someone blew remote charges in *every* one of their ships."

Shaking himself to clear his thoughts, and sparing a single glance for Montgomery, still locked to the Simulacrum, Kole looked at the incoming missile salvos.

"Pull all ships back and spread us apart to clear our lines of fire," he ordered. "We've lost enough good people today, and these birds are running stupid now. Let's take them down."

CHAPTER 41

SEARCH AND RESCUE took almost two whole days. They swept for survivors from the pirate fleet, but given the fate of the *Alan-a-dale*'s crew, Damien was hardly surprised when they didn't find anyone. Just a lot of debris, vaporized wreckage, and bodies.

Whoever Wayne's sponsors had been, their secrets had died with their minions.

Far too many of the people who'd followed Damien to this unremarkable corner of the void had died with them. Six destroyers gone and two damaged had left the Mínglüàng Security flotilla with over a thousand dead, and the Patrol's three lost and one damaged Frigate had left them with similar casualties.

Thirty five of Mage-Captain Jakab's people had also died when the missile had shattered the cruiser's entire Bravo broadside. Morgues throughout the little fleet were full to overflowing, and many of the medical bays were packed with wounded from the damaged vessels.

But at this point, everyone who was going to be coming home—alive or dead—was loaded aboard the remaining ships. Damien watched the ships—once enemies, now fire-forged brothers gathering around the wounded—from the window of his office.

"All ships report ready for jump, Lord Montgomery," Jakab informed him over the intercom. "We'll be in Antonius in an hour."

"Make it happen, Mage-Captain," Damien told him. "This place is far too cold and lonely for my tastes now."

He felt as much as saw the big battlecruiser jump, rendering the carefully ordered lights he'd watched from his window were now scattered and disorganized.

Shaking his head, he returned to his computer. He didn't expect reviewing the data from the battle to give him any great leaps of insight, but there was always the chance there was something he'd missed.

When they finally made the second jump back to Antonius, the system was *far* busier than when they'd left. Both Governors appeared to have arrived, and they'd brought friends—the fastest transports they could scrounge up from the looks of it.

Damien waited patiently while the crew sorted through everything, watching as the two fleets gently went their separate ways, each falling into neat formation around the collection of freighters their government had brought.

Despite the split, their formations showed some of the change. Neither Phan's nor McLaughlin's formation was set up to cover a potential attack from the other. All the ships were looking to attacks from the outside, making certain that the civilians would be safe.

Bristling sheepdogs, still not *entirely* sure of each other—but both far more concerned about the wolves outside the pasture.

Given the price of getting them there, it was good to see. Damien still had concerns about what was going to happen in this sector—not to mention concerns about how it had *got* this bad—but he could at least be sure the *navies* involved had some respect for each other.

"My lord," Lieutenant Rain appeared on the intercom screen. "It appears Governors Wong and McLaughlin are aboard the *Tiāntǐ tíqǔ*. They have requested to meet with you and have requested that Admiral Phan and Commodore McLaughlin be included as well as Doctor Christoffsen."

"The ice miner has gravity?"

"And apparently conference facilities, sir," the shaven-headed communications officer confirmed. "My understanding is that the gravity runes are only in limited areas, but the ship is designed to function as a base for system-wide operations."

Damien considered. If the two Governors were issuing joint requests, then they'd already closed much of the distance he needed them to work through. It was time for concessions—especially when they were easy concessions.

"Inform the Governors I will meet them aboard the *Tiāntǐ tíqǔ*," he told the Lieutenant. "I need to see these ice miner conference facilities myself."

The *Tiāntǐ tíqǔ* was a massive metal crescent, with the ends of the crescent wrapped around a chunk of the ice asteroid it was rapidly turning into fuel, water, and oxygen. The conference rooms were placed at the very top of the crescent, with a set of windows looking out over the harsh but beautiful landscape of the ice.

Everyone was waiting for Damien by the time he entered the room and stopped, in awe of the view.

"Impressive, isn't it?" Governor McLaughlin said. "Puts all of mankind's achievements in perspective—eighty light years from Earth, we stand in a ship that will take that landscape out there and turn it into fuel. Mind-boggling."

"Agreed," Damien murmured. He stepped up to the long conference table in the middle of the room, gesturing for Amiri to take a seat. The owners of the *Tiāntǐ tíqǔ*—the *Celestial Miner*, so far as he could tell—had spared no expense for this space. He wondered what it was *actually* normally used for.

"You wanted to meet with me," he noted, glancing around the table. Christoffsen sat at one end of the table, looking disturbingly pleased with himself. Each Governor had an aide—his husband, in Wong Ken's case—and their military commander sitting with them. It was a small crowd for a room that could clearly handle many more.

"We wanted to apologize," Wong Ken said simply. "The situation should never have degraded to the point it did. Without your intervention, we might well be at war."

"You lost a lot of people from my intervention," Damien replied softly.

"While I would rather my people lived," Phan interrupted, "I think they would all have rather died with honor, facing our true enemy, than fighting those who should have been our friends. *You* gave them that—and stopped *more* of our people dying in a pointless war."

"The assistance of both your fleets was necessary," the Hand told them. "Your commanders did you credit, Governors—not least in knowing when it was time to make decisions of their own instead of follow their original orders."

He did, after all, *know* what orders Grace had gone to Antonius with.

"Doctor Christoffsen here," McLaughlin gestured to the ex-Governor, "helped us see at least part of the underlying issue. We were granted shared ownership of Antonius, but we didn't function with anything of the sort. Instead, we ran two *separate* administrations for a single system. Friction was inevitable—and our enemies abused that."

"We will sort out the details over the next few days," Wong told Damien. "We both brought enough staff for this negotiation to continue. We would invite you to remain with us while we negotiate—it would be our preference and our privilege to have the Hand who saved us as the Protectorate witness on the final document."

It seemed Christoffsen had been doing some day-saving of his own since Damien had left him behind. He couldn't have had more than six hours with the Governors. The Hand met his political aide's gaze and inclined his head. He was *impressed*—and also somewhat terrified. The ex-Governor was, in his own field, even scarier than Damien had thought.

"It would be my privilege," he told them. "I may need to send the *Duke of Magnificence* to Tau Ceti in any case, but the reinforcements I called for should be here in a few days. We will need to sweep the region to make sure no more of these mystery ships remain."

"Do we have any idea who they were?" Wong asked.

"Suspicions only, Governor," Damien replied. "The number of candidates who could *build* that fleet is small, but the gunships, for example, were all sold as scrap years ago. The destroyers could easily have come from similar sources and been modified in any one of four dozen yards. The missiles would have been harder to find, but..." he shrugged. "I suspect they fell out the back of a freighter delivering them to an honest system government. Without intact weapons to study that lead takes us nowhere as well."

"Can you share your suspicions, my lord Hand?" Phan asked.

Damien shook his head.

"This is not a case where I can lay accusations or even cast suspicion without evidence, Admiral," he said quietly. "Either a criminal organization of a scale I do not believe still exists is in play, or my accusation must inevitably fall on a system government. And the Charter limits what I may say about such governments without proof."

"It's Legatus, isn't it?"

Damien turned in the hallway back to his shuttle. Grace McLaughlin drove the powered chair the doctors were insisting on up to him, nodding to Amiri.

"I can't say," he told her gently.

"Please," she replied. "A moment, Julia?" she asked the bodyguard.

Amiri shook her head, then checked a door next to them and held it open for them.

"Meeting room," she told them. "Gravity runes even. I can guarantee you ten minutes without question, though I'm not sure that's enough even if she *wasn't* in a cast."

Damien flushed as his bodyguard gave him a wicked grin and closed the door behind him, whistling jauntily.

"You look like you need to talk to *someone*," Grace told him.

Sighing, the Hand took one of the seats in the small meeting room and looked back at her.

"I have no proof," he told her. "But..."

"But?"

"I *know* Ardennes was a Legatan operation," he admitted. "Panterra... the terrorists had a lot of gear from a lot of places, but all of their modern stuff? Legatan. Those gunships? Yeah, they scrapped them—but even the LSDF should have told us if one buyer picked up *three hundred* sub-light warships."

He shrugged. "Legatus could have built the destroyers easily—hell, they could have *custom-built* them to match the MSF's specs. But... I can't accuse a Core World system government of sponsoring terrorism. Not without a *lot* of proof, and evidence of some kind of *motive*."

"Could they be pushing to get the Compact lifted from their worlds?" she asked. "I didn't think Legatus *liked* the Protectorate."

"They don't," Damien agreed. "But we're the only game in town—we'd happily let Legatus declare independence and write their own rules, to be honest. But if we did, the Mage Guild would pull out of the system entirely. They'd be completely cut off from interstellar shipping, and no one has found any way except magic to travel faster than light."

"I do *not* want your job," she said prayerfully. "Mine is enough of a headache."

"I'm still impressed," he told her. "Your grandfather didn't just pick you for the role for family ties. You're doing a good job."

"But it keeps me tied to Sherwood," Grace said. "And... it's not like you'll be coming back, is it?"

"Probably not," he admitted. "Mars is my home now. There's reasons I can't even talk about for that, but it's true nonetheless."

"Couldn't get you to stay, huh?" she asked, but her tone told him she already knew the answer. "Not even for me?"

"I decided... a long time ago that the galaxy had to be more important than just me," Damien said very quietly. "If I can help—if I can serve—I have to."

"If you hadn't been here, we'd have gone to war," Grace replied. "So yeah, you can help. You can serve."

"Another Hand would have come."

"We wouldn't have trusted another Hand as far," she told him. "Only you, Damien. That would be why your boss sent you. I know you have to go. I don't have to like it."

"You could come with me," he offered. He knew the answer as well as she had when she asked him to stay.

"Took a job, swore an oath," she answered with a sad smile. "Hate this cast, too," she admitted. "I'd be asking for a ride back to your ship without it."

He laughed, and for the first time in years, reached out to touch her arm. She covered his fingers with hers and pulled him down.

When the kiss ended, she smiled, and his heart spun in very familiar circles.

"I will admit," she said huskily, "that I suggested to my grandfather the negotiations shouldn't end until the cast is off. Just so we all know."

EPILOGUE

THE BRIDGE of the pirate destroyer *Blood Savage* was very quiet. The dead aren't generally very talkative.

The Ship's Mage leaned his head against the simulacrum, obviously trying not to look too closely at the body of the ship's nominal captain. The old pirate had recognized the gas before it had taken effect and tried to resist.

The ship's new—and always true—commander knelt by the body, cleaning blood off the blades sticking out of his forearms. He knew the Mage was terrified of him—had been even before he'd ordered the pirate scum that made up most of the *Savage*'s crew gassed and then gutted the stubborn captain.

"We have a call on the Link," the only other living person on the bridge announced. With the scum dead, there were only a dozen living souls left on the ship. Enough to get it somewhere, but not enough to fight. But the commander didn't want a fight now.

"Put it on," he ordered, rising from his crouch and dropping into the captain's chair. There was a little bit of blood on it, he noted absently. They'd have to clean it up.

A slim, shaven-headed older man in a gray business suit appeared. The background could have been the office of any one of ten billion mid-level managers anywhere in the Protectorate.

"Report, Agent," the man snapped.

"The operation was a failure," the Agent said calmly. "Hand Montgomery intervened. I attempted to complete the mission regardless, but he pulled the Flotilla and Patrol together and engaged our little fleet. I was forced to activate the Clean Sweep Protocol and disengage."

"The agents with Wong and McLaughlin have already reported," the man in the image told him calmly. "This is an expensive disaster, Agent. Destroyers. Gunships. Perhaps worse, we have reason to believe Montgomery is getting suspicious."

"How did he even *find* us?" the man on the *Blood Savage*'s bridge demanded. "We were in deep space, no one had the location."

"He took the *Alan-a-dale* intact," the older man told him. "Even took a prisoner. Thankfully, it appears the Link was destroyed before it could be found."

"Damn," the Agent breathed. "Clean Sweep took out any Link they could have found here," he noted. "That technology is safe."

"Thanks to the prisoner, and your pawns' lack of caution in the Link's use, he suspects its existence."

"Then we remove him," the Agent replied. "It has been done before."

"A Hand falls, another rises," his superior replied. "It attracts attention. Almost as much as destroying entire colonies—an action, may I remind you, Agent, which was *not* within your permitted scope. Massacres will *not* help us if they even *hint* at our involvement."

"The only proof Montgomery has is of murderous pirate scum. We picked them carefully," the Agent reminded his superior. "Clean Sweep was no great loss to humanity."

"No. But it drew attention to the fact that someone has something to hide. They'll be looking for us now."

"Let them," the Agent replied. "They will find only dead ends and the *dead*."

The other man shook his head.

"You have crossed too many lines this time," he warned his agent. "Your team is being recalled. I have other agents in place to watch the aftermath—an aftermath, I may note, that appears to be likely to make this sector *more* stable. The exact *opposite* of your mission.

"Bring your team home," he repeated. "We will review your actions in detail once you're here."

The Agent bowed and gestured peremptorily for the Mage to start setting up the jump sequence.

"It will be as you command... Vice-Director Ricket."

ABOUT THE AUTHOR

GLYNN STEWART is the author of Starship's Mage, a bestselling science fiction and fantasy series where faster-than-light travel is possible–but only because of magic. His other works include science fiction series Duchy of Terra, Castle Federation and Vigilante, as well as the urban fantasy series ONSET and Changeling Blood.

Writing managed to liberate Glynn from a bleak future as an accountant. With his personality and hope for a high-tech future intact, he lives in Kitchener, Ontario with his partner, their cats, and an unstoppable writing habit.

OTHER BOOKS
BY GLYNN STEWART

For release announcements join the
mailing list or visit **GlynnStewart.com**

STARSHIP'S MAGE
Starship's Mage
Hand of Mars
Voice of Mars
Alien Arcana
Judgment of Mars
UnArcana Stars
Sword of Mars
Mountain of Mars
The Service of Mars
A Darker Magic
Mage-Commander (upcoming)

Starship's Mage: Red Falcon
Interstellar Mage
Mage-Provocateur
Agents of Mars

Pulsar Race: A Starship's Mage Universe Novella

DUCHY OF TERRA
The Terran Privateer
Duchess of Terra
Terra and Imperium
Darkness Beyond
Shield of Terra
Imperium Defiant
Relics of Eternity
Shadows of the Fall
Eyes of Tomorrow

SCATTERED STARS
Scattered Stars: Conviction
Conviction
Deception
Equilibrium
Fortitude (upcoming)

PEACEKEEPERS OF SOL
Raven's Peace
The Peacekeeper Initiative
Raven's Course
Drifter's Folly (upcoming)

EXILE
Exile
Refuge
Crusade
Ashen Stars: An Exile Novella

CASTLE FEDERATION
Space Carrier Avalon
Stellar Fox
Battle Group Avalon
Q-Ship Chameleon
Rimward Stars
Operation Medusa
A Question of Faith: A Castle Federation Novella

SCIENCE FICTION STAND ALONE NOVELLA
Excalibur Lost

VIGILANTE
(WITH TERRY MIXON)
Heart of Vengeance
Oath of Vengeance

**Bound By Stars: A Vigilante Series
(With Terry Mixon)**
Bound By Law
Bound by Honor
Bound by Blood

TEER AND KARD
Wardtown
Blood Ward

CHANGELING BLOOD
Changeling's Fealty
Hunter's Oath
Noble's Honor
Fae, Flames & Fedoras: A Changeling Blood Novella

ONSET
ONSET: To Serve and Protect
ONSET: My Enemy's Enemy
ONSET: Blood of the Innocent
ONSET: Stay of Execution
Murder by Magic: An ONSET Novella

FANTASY STAND ALONE NOVELS
Children of Prophecy
City in the Sky

Made in the USA
Las Vegas, NV
05 January 2023

65034746R00204